Said No One Ever

STEPHANIE EDING

sourcebooks
casablanca

Published by Sourcebooks Casablanca, an imprint of Sourcebooks
P.O. Box 4410, Naperville, Illinois 60567-4410
(630) 961-3900
sourcebooks.com

Printed and bound in the United States of America.
VP 10 9 8 7 6 5 4 3 2 1

To Mom and Dad. Thank you for being nothing like the parents I write about. I love you both.

– 1 –

THE TINY HOUSE IN the center of Montana made for the weirdest hideout ever. The drooling bulldog that came with it didn't make the scenario any less ridiculous.

Ellie used her hip to force the dorm-sized fridge to close on the stack of off-brand iced coffee cans and convenience foods. Consuming nothing but caffeine and high sodium microwavable meals for the next three weeks wouldn't be the healthiest choice she'd made in her adult life, but it was a small price to pay to avoid the shit show going on back home. Price being important, considering how she'd sunk every last penny she had into this romantic getaway for one.

Now to figure out how to entertain her new and unexpected roommate.

"All right, Hilda, I think I've got just the souvenir to distract you long enough so I can finish unpacking." Ellie grinned when she said the name out loud. A welcome note on the kitchen counter had introduced the resident canine and implied that she might be a bit of a nuisance to the guests of Perry Farm. "You've gotta like playing ball, right?"

Ellie reached into her purse for the Bilexin stress ball she'd gotten in the most recent "perks pack" from a local pharmaceutical company. Something like that might not last long in the jowls of an old English bulldog, but it could occupy the beast long enough for Ellie to empty her carry-on.

Maybe.

Stepping down the tiny-house steps, Ellie turned toward the soybean field and chucked the foam ball with all her might. It didn't get far, but it also didn't matter because Hilda's attention was directed elsewhere. The dog sank on her hip and stared off toward the road.

"Go get the ball, Hilda."

Although it was only late afternoon, the fatigue of dealing with airlines and travel hassles had run its course. Ellie had hoped for a quick nap before she popped her earplugs in and got to work transcribing a lecture on autoimmune disorders. She'd been lucky enough to snag that rare assignment before any of the other struggling freelancers and should probably get it done in a timely manner.

"Hilda? Go get the ball before some tractor runs it over."

Still, the dog focused her attention toward the front of the property, only now her brindle-speckled ears had perked up, her meaty brow furrowing.

The isolated farm had maintained a quiet peacefulness up to that point, with not much more than some baying animals in the barn or rustling beans in the field to tickle the senses. But the longer Ellie stood there with her bulldog companion, the more some other noise cut through the tranquility like a butcher knife.

It couldn't be sirens. Not out this far.

Ellie strained to see into the distance, one hand to her forehead to shield her eyes from the setting sun. She patted Hilda on the head. The touch didn't even come close to breaking the dog's laser focus.

Just over the budding fields and wooden fences came the flashing red and white lights of an ambulance. The siren's roar grew deafeningly loud now as the emergency crew sped up the property's long lane toward the main farmhouse and slammed on the brakes.

Ellie stood frozen, trying to process this unforeseen development after having only arrived an hour ago.

Hilda, however, took immediate action and darted toward the

commotion. Ellie lunged for the dog but could do nothing to keep her out of the emergency crew's way. Technically, since this wasn't her house, she shouldn't have to control the pets or assume any level of responsibility here anyway.

Then again, what role *did* an unsuspecting bystander renting Airbnb property play in a thing like this?

The team pulled a bright yellow stretcher from the truck and disappeared. It only took a few minutes for the crew to return to their vehicle, the yellow stretcher now loaded with someone strapped on top. Ellie couldn't take it anymore. With a growl, she ran toward the ambulance, kicking up dirt and stone along the way.

"Excuse me," she wheezed when she reached the EMT closing up the back of the truck. "Is everything okay?"

"Are you family?" The bearded man in the Choteau Fire Department T-shirt rounded the large vehicle on his way to the driver's seat.

Ellie gasped after the sprint across the property. Running was her least favorite exercise. "No, I'm staying in the rental property here, but I—"

"If Mrs. Perry's family arrives, please let them know we've taken her to the medical center." With that, he hopped into the driver's seat and shut the door.

The sirens whirred again, and a golden dust storm chased the ambulance down the driveway. Ellie wiped the sweat from her brow as she stood in the aftermath.

What in all God's green earth was she supposed to do now? After all, the driver had personally selected Ellie to deliver the news of her host, Mrs. Perry's accident...illness? No idea.

This already unrelaxing vacation had now taken on another level of responsibility. She'd really hoped to leave all that crap in Ohio.

Hilda emerged from the bushes near the front steps, her head tilted while she watched her owner vanish down the drive. Mrs. Perry could have been her special person, her sole caretaker. Someone had to come for her. They wouldn't let the family dog, or whatever other creatures who lived on the farm, starve while their human stayed at the hospital.

The wind whistling across the fields made the world seem so vast. Behind her was the large wooden farmhouse, standing amongst the trees. An old fence wrapped around part of the property, marking off a large compartmentalized section of field for animals. Towering red barns and outbuildings surrounded the house. Flower gardens, fountains, and a round gazebo filled in the empty spaces between structures.

Hilda trotted over to Ellie's feet and plopped down, shifting her legs out to the side. Her tongue unraveled from her mouth once more. Ellie tried to force down the anxiety tightening her lungs.

If all hell insisted on breaking loose, she'd focus on the dog first. A place to start, if nothing else. Ellie reached down and patted her canine buddy on the head, then marched her panic-stricken ass up to the front porch of the main house. She tried the doorknob, while Hilda waited expectantly at her side.

Ellie busied herself by examining the plethora of art decorating the porch. She'd seen no one put paintings and sayings on the *outside* of their home before. Even the doormat offered an inspirational quote: *Take the leap or get out of the way.*

Nice. Either this house was booby-trapped, or Mrs. Perry was a motivational guru who lured travelers to her homestead for a spiritual awakening.

After five minutes of intermittent knocking, no one had come to Ellie's rescue. Time to give up and move on to the next phase of this nonexistent plan.

One "Marilyn Perry" had left her phone number on the welcome note back at the tiny house, but assuming Marilyn was the one taken by EMS, it wouldn't do any good to call that number.

Hilda's silky ears perked again, and the dog shot off toward the tiny house, well ahead of her guest. She curved around the dark teal-colored home, just slightly smaller than a shipping container but larger than a garden shed, and vanished into the bean field. A moment later, she reappeared with the Bilexin ball clenched in her teeth.

At least someone was making the best of the situation.

A shrill ring sounded in Ellie's back pocket, startling Ellie into almost tripping up the first step into her vacation home. One look at her screen turned the ambulance visit into a minor inconvenience compared to the oncoming disaster that was surely about to take place.

"Hi, Mom." Ellie pushed the door open a little more aggressively than necessary as she entered.

"So, you really up and went to Montana. I figured you'd come to your senses before you actually got on an airplane." Her mother's greetings had gotten less friendly over the past few weeks. "And why are you breathing so loud?"

Ellie shook her head and slumped onto the dining stool. "I was power walking. And yes, I *up and went* to Montana as *planned*."

"Planned before you lost your job," her mother said.

Ellie hardly had the energy to argue right now, what with chaos and confusion descending on her at every turn here. "My job is being phased out eventually because they sold the company. It's not lost yet." She still cringed repeating the words she'd gotten in an email from her company a couple weeks prior. "I'm still able to get some work."

Not enough to keep her from living off her credit card. Not enough to pay the rent hike on her upcoming lease renewal. Not enough to keep her from frantically job-hunting every chance she got.

Yet here she was. On a vacation. Like an idiot.

Hilda, having made herself at home on the small couch, watched Ellie with great anticipation. Who wanted to be the one to break it to the mutt that Ellie could barely take care of herself these days, let alone keep a pet alive?

"Can I call you back later? Now isn't a great time."

Her mother quieted long enough for Ellie to assume she'd made a deeply offended face at her cell phone. "Not the best time? How much could you possibly have on your agenda moments after arriving to a remote location far away from everyone and everything you know?"

Why oh why did she even answer the phone?

"I'm trying to figure something out." Dropping this bomb might distract her mother from the job thing, if nothing else. "The owner of this place just left in an ambulance. I'm waiting for her family to show up so I can let them know where the paramedics took her."

Even though 1,700 miles separated the two women, Ellie felt certain she didn't need the phone to hear her mother's overdramatic gasp.

"Taken in an ambulance? What happened? You just got there!"

"And none of this is my fault." Weird she felt she needed to clarify that. "But I don't actually know any other details than that. When I figure it out, I'll be sure to share."

This farm crisis really had terrible timing. Ellie had hoped to make this trip a time to focus on job- and apartment-hunting, get away from the noise back home, and figure out some kind of a plan for this next phase of her life.

Newly single women also needed time away to regroup after breaking up with their successful optometrist boyfriends because God knows everyone and their aunt has an opinion about *that* little life change.

"Good grief, Eleanor. I cannot, for the life of me, figure out why you're doing this. You've got enough to do here at home, let alone deal with something like this. You're not honestly going to stay for the full three weeks, are you?"

"That's what I booked the place for." Ellie sighed. A better defense didn't exist, so why bother trying?

"Even though we all could really use your help right now? Your father and I are up to our ears trying to renovate Mom's house, and you've got more time than anybody else to tear down wallpaper." Her mother growled, like the growing list of grievances with her daughter had awoken her inner monster. "And what about Averie? She *really* needs you. You were supposed to start working for her after the weekend, and now she's up the creek looking for help with the kids."

Ellie wasn't going to get out of this conversation without mention of her sister's pressing need for a nanny to her three spoiled children—a position Ellie had to fill upon returning to Columbus if she couldn't find work elsewhere. She loved her niece and nephews, but there was something to be said about small doses.

She just had to take this phone call. Another rockin' decision in the life of Ellie Reed.

A few feet away on the makeshift couch, Hilda chomped on her Bilexin ball, oblivious to any form of stress or obligation. Lucky dog.

"Don't you choke on that," Ellie said when Hilda rolled onto her back.

"Excuse me?" her mother asked.

"No, not you. It's the dog that lives here." Her only friend in the world at the moment.

That was a bonus in this situation. Pets didn't judge or condemn. They hung around and wanted an occasional pat on the head or game of fetch. Worst-case scenario: Ellie shared her breakfast burritos and bed with a bulldog. She wasn't getting any of the wine coolers though.

Speaking of which, it was five o'clock somewhere. Not *here*, but close enough on Ohio's time.

"You're looking after a dog now too?"

Ellie didn't think you could actually hear eye-rolling, but oh, she'd heard it.

"I guess so." She rifled through her mini fridge and plucked out the nearest wine cooler. "Anyway, I'll let you know when I get more info on the ambulance thing, but I'm going to let you go for now."

"Fine," her mother said. "You know, I may not agree with you taking this trip, but at least promise me you'll be safe while you're there. Don't go getting into any trouble."

If only someone would tell *trouble* to leave *her* alone. "Sure thing. I think the most dangerous thing up here is a moose or something. Maybe a mountain lion. I don't know, but I'll be safe."

Like she really needed to put *that* thought in her mother's head on top of everything else.

"Oh, that's real nice, Ellie. Just call again *soon*." With that, she hung up.

The implications surrounding that last word set Ellie on edge. More on edge?

Maybe after Mrs. Perry's family heard the news of her "situation" and did whatever they needed to do around the farm, Ellie could get back on track. Or maybe this new hiccup meant Ellie had to pack up and leave already. And she was anything but ready to face her life back home.

Ellie drummed on the table and contemplated the hot mess that had become her daily existence. She'd never get a restful night's slumber if she didn't figure out some kind of plan for moving forward, especially if drama wanted to sock her in the jaw from every angle. Priority one had to be the care and management of the bulldog in her living room—er, well, the *only* room.

And perhaps whatever other creatures lived in the barn. Almost as if on cue, something *hee-hawed* over the whistling wind outside. A horse? Donkey? What did she know?

She could always assess the animal situation ahead of time. It'd give her some peace of mind that she could do something for her laid-up host. Make her feel like she made a difference somewhere. At this hour, the animals had likely already been fed anyway.

She swirled the pink liquid around in her bottle and gulped down the last drops.

Yep. The weirdest vacation in history was about to get a lot weirder. Instead of spending this time digging herself out of her messy situation with the help of cheap fruity beverages, she now had to wait for some heroic member of the Perry family to come save her from a whole new fiasco.

And if no one showed up by morning, Ellie would have to moonlight as a farmhand.

- 2 -

ELLIE KARATE-CHOPPED THE AIR when a piercing screech woke her from a deep slumber. She shot upright so quickly her forehead nearly cracked the low-hanging ceiling beam. Beside her, Hilda sat with a tilted head and wide eyes.

"What the heck?" Ellie muttered.

Hilda barked again, some strange, shrieking sound Ellie had never heard come out of a dog. New life flowed through her, and the creature leapt up and charged toward the steep ladder.

Ellie lunged to catch hold of her. "No! Be caref—"

The *thump, thump, aarf, splat* that cut her off proved that Hilda had, in fact, not been careful at all. Ellie scrambled to the edge of the bed and peered over the side, fully expecting to find the dog in a crumpled heap in the dining room/living room/kitchen. Instead, Hilda sat at the front door, her legs splayed out to the side, tongue flapping in a nonexistent breeze.

A rush of relief washed over Ellie—until the pain set in. "Holy crap. Ow." She held a finger up for Hilda to wait a minute before going out, like the dog totally would understand the gesture. The restless night's sleep due to constantly waking up to see if anyone had shown up for the animals had taken its toll. "I don't think I'm cut out for farming, Hilda. Just *living* on a farm hurts me."

Ellie kicked her legs over the loft's edge and slowly descended the steps. The backs of her thighs burned from the amount of times she'd gone up and down it during the night.

"They don't make coffee strong enough for this." Ellie pressed her hands into her lower back and leaned until she heard the desired crack. After farm chores, a shower, and a breakfast burrito, she could go complete her transcription assignment and collect the fifty dollars a lecture of that length would pay.

What a depressing existence.

While she'd packed plenty of tank tops, shorts, and flip-flops to comfortably sit around an Airbnb tiny house, she'd somehow forgotten to pack overalls and rubber boots for Act I of this production. Her best option was to face the music and surrender her Keds to the farm muck and pray they survived the washing machine at the trip's finale.

Ellie opened the door for Hilda. The dog charged like a racehorse reacting to a starter pistol, missed the steps entirely, then did a tailspin and ran back into the house. She tripped over the edge of the sofa midleap but somehow snatched her Bilexin ball before crashing to the floor. Just like that, she returned to her feet and rocketed off toward the barns.

Whatever this dog was on, Ellie needed a strong dose of it. The darned thing had more energy in her nubby tail than Ellie could have collected in a lifetime. At least she slept well during the night, even if the snoring made the bed shake a little. Ellie couldn't bring herself to just let the dog fend for herself against the Montana bears and wolves—or whatever.

The dirt and stone path between the tiny house and barnyard amplified the heat from the early morning sun. Ellie somehow doubted these outbuildings would provide any respite by way of air-conditioning.

With one last hopeful glance toward the main house, Ellie unhinged the latch and slid the aging barn door open. Where she'd expected herds of cattle or an army of horses, only a few creatures met her gaze. Well, "stared in complete confusion" explained it better.

"Um, hello." Ellie held up her hands to show she came in peace. "I'm going to feed you if I can find your food. I'm not scary, I promise. But I also have no idea what I'm doing, so…"

The sliding door creaked when Hilda barreled into the barn, having abandoned her ball in favor of helping her new human companion. Her presence could either make things better in the barn or far, far worse. Time would tell.

Ellie took a quick census of the population: one donkey, two sheep, and an undetermined amount of chickens coming and going through the fence at the barn's rear. She'd start with the biggest.

"Hi, donkey. My experience with your type includes watching both *Winnie the Pooh* and *Shrek* in my childhood, which leaves a big gap in what to expect from you." She slowly approached his pen while doing a quick Google search for what to feed the dear boy. "Okay, so…straw, hay, silage. What the hell is silage?"

Before falling down some internet search rabbit hole, Ellie took herself on a quick barn tour. A teetering stack of some kind of field grass caught her eye, the remnants of which already sat in the bottom of the donkey's trough. Bingo!

"Here you go, bud. Hopefully this is a good amount, and you neither starve nor yack it back up like my parents' binge-eating cat." When the donkey trotted forward and eagerly snatched up his breakfast, Ellie gave him a gentle pat on the snout.

Did she need to clean out his pen? The thought made her cringe. Surely someone would show up before she had to resort to *that*.

At the back of the barn, a gate separated the stall from a larger fenced-in pasture she could *presumably* let him out in for the day. He could poop to his heart's delight with minimal cleanup efforts on her part.

Next, she moved onto the wide-eyed sheep. The pair of them stood so still, Ellie wasn't quite sure if they were even real. It wasn't until she opened their pen that they began bleating and crashing into one another in some random sheep freak-out. Getting anything done for the two of them might prove a little tricky, unless she felt like being bowled over by two oversized cotton balls.

"Whoa, guys! Calm down!" Ellie backed out of the pen slowly, but not before Hilda darted inside and gleefully joined the sheep in their ritual.

That made sense.

Ellie followed the same strategy she'd used with the donkey, Edgar—he needed a name and that was about all she could come up with—and dropped some of the hay stuff into their trough. Sheep ate grass too, right?

They'd benefit from some pasture time with Edgar too.

To her delight, Ellie found a tub with an actual chicken feed label. The birds stopped their coming-and-going the moment Ellie unscrewed the large lid, flapping and clucking their way toward their provider. Before they could peck her to death, she began scattering chicken feed like Cinderella did in the Disney classic. Because that's about the only time she'd ever seen it done.

Thank God there weren't any cows to milk. The poor moos would have exploded if left to Ellie's capabilities. She only knew how to get milk out of gallon jugs, not udders.

That was it. Being a farmer wasn't too hard. All she had to do was unlock the back gate to let everyone out into the pasture, and she'd be done with farm chores for the day—hopefully.

She glanced at the clock on her phone: 9:35 a.m. If she'd been a real farm person, she'd have gotten up before the sun to do all this. Her tardiness, however, clearly hadn't affected the animals on a survival level. It'd have been quite embarrassing to call Mrs. Perry and confess to inadvertently murdering all her critters.

Ah, Mrs. Perry. Ellie really should try to speak with her host and find out if she did everything right.

Another hurried internet search on her way to unhinge the back gate gave her the phone number for the area medical center, and she mentally ran down a list of questions for Marilyn on the off chance the woman could take calls. Her condition remained a mystery. But after almost twenty-four hours alone on the ranch with none of Marilyn's family making an appearance, Ellie needed a more sustainable plan than guesswork and Google.

"Med Center. How may I direct your call?"

Ellie nearly dropped the phone when a human voice answered, rather than the automated options she got at medical facilities back home. "Hi. Um, my name is Eleanor Reed, and I'm calling to speak with Marilyn Perry. They took her by ambulance yesterday, but I'm not sure what department they have her in."

"Of course, Ms. Reed. Let me look that up for you. One second." The cheery woman on the other end tapped away on her computer for several long minutes. "Looks like they transported her to the nursing home for rehabilitation. I can forward your call there, if you'd like."

Choteau-ians were super helpful. "That would be amazing. Thank you."

Ellie headed out of the barn to hear a little better against the cacophony of animal sounds surrounding her. Almost immediately, another bright, chipper voice let her know that Mrs. Marilyn Perry had arrived safely and would be "ready for visitors in rehab room 34." Not even a hello or who's calling. Ellie tried to interrupt, but the joyous woman insisted Marilyn would love some company since "No one has visited her after her accident. Not even her children or grandchildren. *At all.*"

Okay, so a bit of a guilt trip there, but not something she should take personally as a total stranger to Marilyn. She *would*. Totally. But she *shouldn't*. Grandmas were kind of her weakness, thanks to the close relationship she had with her own grandmother, Val. If Grandma Val had gotten injured and taken away, Ellie would have chased the ambulance all the way into Choteau on foot to be with her if needed.

And it wasn't like Ellie's work time had already been pushed off in favor of caring for her new furry friends; she might as well swing over to the local nursing home and make another acquaintance, awkward as it may be. Not like she had any other assignments waiting for her after the one she'd already claimed.

Urgh.

Ellie's finger hovered over the Uber app. This was happening. She was going to summon a car she couldn't afford to take her to a nursing home where she'd meet with a total stranger and ask about farm animal care. Just the kind of vacation every girl dreams of.

Said no one ever.

- 3 -

THE AIDE WAVED AN arm for Ellie to follow her down the long corridor. Ellie tripped on her un-farmer-like flip-flop when she stepped around the countertop and into a hallway painted in a blinding shade of lemon. Her stomach whirled with nerves.

Down the hall, flower boxes with fake purple and red petunias flanked each resident's door, complete with a small white awning overtop to make the units look like individual cottages. A nameplate and number labeled each room.

When her Grandma Val had moved into a nursing home in the year before her death, it wasn't anywhere near this cheery. The drab brown walls of that institution were hardly more festive than a morgue.

Such a contrast stung Ellie's insides. Despite the depressing setting, Ellie would give anything to be walking into *that* nursing home to see Val again. Her grandmother would have imparted so much wisdom into Ellie's life, offering words of encouragement and hope. Though Grandma Val, like everyone else, would have been sorely disappointed in Ellie for breaking up with her flawless boyfriend Sean. She never got to find out what an epic failure Ellie really was.

The aide stopped in front of room 34. No name plaque decorated the door yet, the resident inside too new to the facility to have received her specialty plate.

"Ms. Marilyn, you have a visitor," the nurse cooed.

"Who the hell came to visit me?" The gravelly voice sounded

more shocked than angry. Still, Ellie asked herself for the hundredth time why she put herself through this.

She clutched the assortment of wildflowers she'd picked from around the edge of the Perry's field and nodded her thanks to the aide.

Sitting in a reclining chair near the window, with a cup of steaming liquid in one hand and a copy of *Better Homes and Gardens* in the other, was Marilyn. She wore a short-sleeved button-up top with a red bird pattern. Her gray hair flowed past her shoulders and framed her mismatched earrings: one large brown gemstone and one long red feather. Her piercing blue eyes focused on her company.

"Huh. I do not know you." Marilyn closed her magazine and laid it across her lap, where a peach-colored cast wrapped her leg. "Social worker?"

Ellie forced a smile and stepped farther into the room. "No, ma'am. I'm Ellie Reed." She held the flowers outstretched, pretending she wasn't the most socially inept human on earth. "I'm staying at your Airbnb rental and wanted to make sure you were okay. I saw the ambulance yesterday and—"

"Merciful…" Marilyn drew her hand to her heart. She smiled sympathetically when she took the flowers from her guest. "Ellie, I am so sorry, honey. I had every intention of greeting you on your arrival and making you breakfast today. *Ack.* I was so excited about your visit, and then that damn dog saw a damn rabbit and took out my damn legs. Right out from under me and down I went. Shattered my kneecap is what they tell me." She accompanied her words with wild hand gestures that added a bit of comic relief.

So Hilda was the culprit in all of this. Ellie had been housing a menace.

Marilyn leaned as far forward as her propped leg allowed. "I didn't know you'd already arrived when all that happened. I tried to tell them I had a guest coming, but they wouldn't do anything about it. You know, when you get older, people assume your mind is gone and everything you say is gibberish. Damn shame."

"Yeah, that kinda sucks." Ellie didn't know how else to respond to such a deep social justice issue right off the bat. "But please don't worry about it. I tried to see if anyone else lived with you and didn't know if I should call you or—"

"No use. I dropped my phone in the garden somewhere when they loaded me up. That's all I can figure. And it's only me at the house." Marilyn stuffed the flower stems into the small glass of ice water on her portable table. "Husband died a few years back."

"Oh, I'm sorry."

Marilyn winked. "Don't be."

"Okay…" Ellie crossed her arms over her chest. At some point, she'd begun swaying where she stood. Probably a subconscious reaction to a resident down the hall blaring Post Malone. Not the music she'd expected to hear in a nursing home. This generation was supposed to be obsessed with Lawrence Welk and his bubble-blowing. At least, that's who Grandma Val loved most. She even had his picture up on the wall with all their family photos.

"Have a seat, honey. You don't have to stand there." Marilyn waved to the bed, the only other seating option. "I would have much nicer chairs for you to sit in at home, but here we are. Tell me about yourself, so we're not strangers."

Ellie nearly missed the edge of the bed when she sat down. "Well, I'm not sure where to start."

"You can start by telling me what sort of brave young thing like yourself travels solo for an almost monthlong trip out west." Marilyn's eyes lit up as if completely intrigued by the prospect. "I couldn't hardly wait to ask you that when you made the reservation. Thought it might have been a mistake at first."

"No mistake." Ellie breathed an embarrassed laugh. While hearing Mrs. Perry lay it out like that certainly sounded like an

Eat, Pray, Love scenario, the reality was significantly less charming. "Actually, I originally meant it to be a working holiday, since I'm a freelance medical transcriptionist. Then I found out they're cutting a bunch of their freelance workers because a bigger company bought them out, so that's fun. Now, I'm kind of using the trip to decompress and figure out a new plan, I guess."

She came to check on Mrs. Perry and get tips on animal care, not present a web of unfortunate events that had overtaken her life lately. At least she'd kept it to herself that the next step in her journey involved turning over her certified medical transcriptionist credentials in favor of diapers, drool, and the deafeningly loud screams of her niece and nephews destroying everything in their path like little tornadoes.

Ellie cleared her throat. "But hey, I wanted to make sure it's all right that I'm still staying here. If I need to end my trip, I can—"

"Nonsense." Marilyn reached for her cup of coffee and took a long swig. Her feather earring brushed over her wrinkled hand that had no less than eight rings stacked up her finger. "You stay right where you are. I was so eager to host you, but then *this* happened. Hilda hasn't been bugging you too much, has she?"

Ellie grinned. "She's been at my side since I arrived."

"Oh, that dumb beast." Marilyn shook her head and wrapped her fingers tighter around her mug. "My daughters have been telling me to get rid of her for years. They say she's a hazard to my health. They're right, obviously. That dog is pure adrenaline. But damn it all if I don't love the stupid thing like she was one of my children. And speaking of children, no one has come out there to the farm yet?" Her gray eyebrows shot up when a new thought popped into her brain. "Did anyone come take care of my animals? I gave the hospital nurses some of the neighbors' phone numbers and left voicemails with my girls, but nobody's keeping me in the loop. Just moving me all around and telling me to relax."

Oof. Poor Marilyn. The woman had an entire farm to manage on her own and couldn't even wrangle the help she needed.

"No one's been out there." Ellie scooted to the edge of the bed and touched the armrest on Marilyn's chair. "I took some liberties and fed everyone this morning. Though, I don't know if I did it right, which is why I wanted to come here and get some instruction. I mean, I'm from Columbus, Ohio, and the most animal care I've done involved house cats, but—"

"Child. Well, doesn't that just bind the cheese?"

Ellie stilled while trying to figure out the appropriate response to such a strange question. "Which part? Er, what?"

Marilyn continued, "I can't believe you just jumped right in like that. Thank you, sincerely. You are a treasure. I assumed Savannah would have taken care of *something* if the neighbors didn't show. Savannah's my eldest daughter. I never intended for you to have to do anything like this, Ellie. I'm so embarrassed." She covered her face with her free hand. "I will demand use of the phone and call everyone again after you leave. A couple of them will receive a few choice words I do not wish your delicate ears to hear."

More cheese-binding words? "Honestly, Mrs. Perry, it's really fine. I don't mind doing it, as long as I'm doing it right. I like animals. Hilda even stayed the night with me. I hope that was okay. I don't know if she's allowed in the tiny house."

"God love you. You are going to regret letting her cozy up to you. She'll expect such treatment every time now, and I'm telling you, that dog can pass gas like you would not believe. It'll burn the corneas straight out of your head. And call me Marilyn. Mrs. Perry sounds like an old lady name."

Ellie laughed. Marilyn spoke so quickly Ellie had a hard time keeping up, but the woman had spunk. Maybe a trip to the nursing home was exactly what this wacky vacation needed. "Thanks. I'll keep at the business end of Hilda then. And Marilyn it is."

"And you're getting a refund on this stay if you're working and not getting the homemade breakfasts I'd planned. I started this Airbnb for fun so I could meet interesting people. Thought it'd bring some liveliness out to my little corner of Choteau, but so far, you're the only one who's booked it."

A full refund? The money Ellie had sunk into this trip would easily pay for her first month's rent in a new apartment. This meant Ellie could practically have her cake and eat it too. Life just didn't let her do that sort of thing ever. Life *never* let her do that.

Marilyn continued, "My daughters know nothing about me starting this rental, so we have to keep it our little secret. They'd have a conniption if they found out I was taking on a business venture at eighty-two." Marilyn patted Ellie's bare knee. "Here. Hand me that pad of paper and pen on the nightstand. I'll write down the animals' routine. Just watch out for the sheep. They're notoriously dumb animals anyway, but those two are a few sprinkles short of a sundae. Ordered them online. Did you know you could do that? You'll have to try it."

Ellie bit her lip to keep from losing it at the idea of mail-order sheep. This lady was awesome. So awesome that accepting such a generous offer to refund the entire three-week stay would likely cripple her with guilt, no matter how much she needed that right now.

"You really don't have to refund the trip. It's just nice to be away and out of the city for a bit." That part was true. Being alone in a totally different life was like a breath of fresh air—even if it was a little dusty and smelled like manure.

Marilyn scribbled away on her notepad. "This is happening, Ellie. You're not paying for this stay." She ripped the sheet off the pad and handed it to her guest. "That should be all they need. Don't overdo it though. I don't want to put you out. They're happy if someone shows up, feeds them, lets them roam around, and sings a song every now and again. I should have written that down."

"I think I can remember." Ellie drew the paper up to hide her face. Her Disney princess attempt at animal care may have been more on point than she'd originally thought. "Is there anything else you need me to take care of?"

"Oh, no. The neighbor down the road rents my fields, so you don't have to fire up the tractor or anything. I doubt you'll see any of them at all. When one of my daughters comes, I'll have them bring me clothes. They gave me a few things here, so it's not urgent. Plus, I like these bird patterns. As long as my animals are in good hands, then I'm content to sit tight and heal." She reached for her coffee again. "Did you pack a pair of boots?"

Ellie followed Marilyn's gaze down to her plum-painted toenails sticking out of her flip-flops. "Uh, no."

"Mine are on the porch. You look to be about my size, so just grab those." She tapped her nose like she had a knack for guessing strangers' shoe sizes. "I won't be needing them. Sounds like they're keeping me locked up here for a few weeks for therapy, which I do not need, but they don't care. So long as they don't go calling Reverend Kaehr in to read me my last rites, I suppose therapy ain't the worst thing."

Ellie nodded. A woman of Marilyn's age could definitely benefit from physical therapy in her recovery plan, especially if the injury required a future surgery.

"Oh, you know what? I actually do have something you can help me with." Marilyn grabbed her notepad again and started writing something else down. "You don't mind coming back here again later this week, do you?"

How was she supposed to answer something like that? A half hour drive separated the nursing home and farm. Ubers weren't cheap, and Ellie grew poorer by the day.

But how could she say no to an injured woman in a nursing home recliner looking at her with such big, hopeful eyes? "I can make that work, sure."

Marilyn clapped her hands together. "Oh, you're a doll and a true lifesaver, Ellie. Really. I don't need much, but if you could do a quick walk through the garden to find my phone and hang on to it so it doesn't get ruined, I'd love ya for it. And on your way out of here, have a nurse bring me some of those pain pills. Tell her I want the good ones. The most illegal thing she's got."

Ellie laughed. "Okay. I think I can handle that. Anything else?"

"Can't think of anything. You relax and enjoy the solitude of the farm. It'll be a great place for you to clear your head."

Now *that* sounded more like it.

– 4 –

ELLIE WATCHED THE PICTURESQUE countryside fly past her window and breathed deeply to wash away the chaos of the last twenty-four hours. At least she finally got to see the town, having bypassed it completely when the Uber drove her to the tiny house from Great Falls International Airport. Choteau was charming, rich with history and archeological finds, which was displayed in the form of random dinosaur statues advertising a small local museum—delightful quirks she might have otherwise missed if she hadn't gone after Marilyn.

For now, she could get back on track having visited her host and gotten proper instruction for moving forward with the animals.

A buzz in her pocket reminded her she had awaiting text messages. Might as well face whatever her life back home dealt this time.

For starters, her sister, Averie, had taken time out of her busy day saving lives as a nurse practitioner to rub salt in the wound:

> Averie: Heard you had some excitement yesterday. Still don't know why you didn't cancel this trip given your circumstances. Bet you wish you did now, huh?

Ellie couldn't click off the message fast enough. Not that she was any more enthused about reading the texts from her mother:

> Mom: Call me and give me an update on the host lady.

Mom: Ellie? Are you all right? Why aren't you answering your
     phone?
Mom: You really should have taken someone with you if you had
     to sow your wild oats like this. So many bad things could
     happen to you. CALL ME!

The last thing Ellie felt like doing was calling her mother, especially with the Uber driver within earshot. Though it'd for sure provide the poor chap with plenty of entertainment at her expense.

Instead, Ellie typed out a response: Can't call now. Everything is fine. I met with Marilyn, and I'm going to help with the farm animals while she's laid up.

Typing out the words gave her a hint of empowerment. While her planned escape from life had spiraled out of control rather quickly, she still did something of worth—much more than she'd done back home, anyway.

Her mother's answer came quickly:

Mom: THANK GOD YOU'RE OK! How in the world are you
     qualified to take care of farm animals? You quit walking
     Aunt Millie's dog because it scared you…

Well, that wasn't a fair comparison. Aunt Millie's dog was a demon Chihuahua that routinely drew blood. This donkey and friends are tamer.

Mom: 🙍 Surely someone else is more equipped for this task.
     Maybe you can just ask for a refund and come home. No
     need to traumatize the animals just because you're going
     through some weird millennial-life crisis.

Ellie's hand fell into her lap, and she let the screen go black. Every which direction, Ellie received a vote of no confidence these days. She probably deserved that. It's not like she was getting gold stars in any aspect of her life right now.

Grandma Val had been about the only person who thought Ellie did all right for herself, even if she didn't meet the high successes of her sister. How she missed that woman. Everyone needed an unconditional cheerleader to get through the rough patches.

Once Ellie arrived back on the farm, which should be any minute now, she'd grab some coffee, park her butt in that cute little gazebo near the main house, and finish her assignment. She still had plenty of time left in the day to browse Indeed for more jobs and search apartment listings before the animals needed their evening meal. Ellie had more thorough instruction on that aspect now—and she could *totally* handle it without jeopardizing any lives.

The driver slowed to turn down another back country road. Not many animals filled the past few fields, various crops taking over most of the area closer to Perry Farm. Although the adorable donkey randomly standing amongst the sprouting wheat seemed to be enjoying himself all alone in this particular field. Ellie pressed against the window to get a better look before the car picked up speed again.

But this donkey wasn't alone.

A short distance away, a brindle and white bulldog danced through the wheat in hot pursuit of a butterfly—a bulldog that looked entirely too familiar.

"Stop the car!" Ellie stomped her foot on the floor mat as if she could control the brakes herself.

The startled driver obliged with a slight jerk to the wheel. "What's wrong?"

"I think those animals belong to the farm I'm staying at." Ellie rolled down the window and leaned out to inspect her surroundings. "How much farther until we get there?"

He checked his phone. "It's about a mile down this road. See the silos?"

She saw them all right. *All the way* down the road.

How had Edgar gotten out? The back pen was fenced all the way around, unless there was some gate open somewhere. Why hadn't she thought to check that?

Ellie groaned. "You can let me out here."

"Are you sure?" he asked.

"Unfortunately, yes."

Ellie swung her purse over her shoulder and stepped slowly into the hot afternoon sun. She braced for impact when Hilda recognized her new friend and abandoned the butterfly. Suddenly, letting the Uber driver go seemed like a really bad idea.

"What are you two doing out here?" Ellie brushed Hilda's muddy paws from her thighs. "Are you trying to get me in trouble? I literally just told your owner I'd take care of you, and you run off like this?"

This was a story she'd definitely not be sharing with her family. She didn't need to give them any more proof of her shortcomings.

Ellie trudged her way into the field—whether Marilyn's property or someone else's, she didn't know. It only mattered that she got the pair back home safely before anyone found out.

"Come on, Edgar." Waving did nothing for the donkey. They didn't follow commands like dogs. Well, like *trained* dogs. Hilda only grew more excited with each wave of Ellie's arm.

Since Edgar didn't appear frightened by Ellie's presence, she approached and tried to gently lead him toward the farm.

Still nothing.

Sweat beaded on her brow, mud caking between her toes when her flip-flops sunk deeper into the field. What if she couldn't get them back before the sun went down?

A million scenarios ran through Ellie's head. It wasn't like she could leave the two creatures out here to fend for themselves unprotected. Then again, *she* couldn't stay out there unprotected either. She'd be a sitting duck for wildlife.

Ellie groaned again and circled around the stubborn donkey. That nickname they'd earned themselves made so much sense now. Pushing from behind wouldn't work. One hoof to the chest and Ellie'd find herself wrapped in a cast next to Marilyn in the rehab unit at the nursing home.

"You're going to have to work with me, Edgar. Hilda, make yourself useful." The dog had rediscovered the butterfly by the road, floating from one flowering weed to the next. She yipped joyfully and leapt alongside it. Had Hilda followed the donkey away from the farm or was her appearance out here a completely separate incident?

Ellie placed both hands on Edgar's shoulder and pushed. He took a few steps, mostly to catch his balance, then readjusted himself into the same stance. With an irritated bray, he glanced over his shoulder. If a donkey held the ability to roll his eyes, that's exactly what he'd done.

Hopeless. Most of the day had been eaten up by animals, visitation, and now animals again. Ellie didn't even know where to begin in fixing this current mess either.

If this wasn't the most jacked-up metaphor for how things had gone recently...

Hilda's barking grew more intense—like a warning.

Ellie peeked over Edgar to see a huge black pickup coming down the road. Hilda's bark mixed with intermittent growls when the truck slowed and came to a stop in front of them. Hitched to the back was a trailer suited for hauling large farm animals. Something Ellie found herself in great need of.

A man hopped down from the driver's side. He wore dark denim jeans and a black polo shirt. His onyx hair matched his outfit, offset only by the piercing green eyes that locked on his target. He seemed completely unconcerned with Hilda's ruckus, walking straight past her and into the field.

"Hi there," Ellie called out, inching her way around the donkey, still unsure if she wanted to fully present herself to this total stranger while far, far away from civilization.

"You having a bit of trouble out here?" the man asked when he approached. From up close, he was even more attractive, his pearly white teeth catching the sun's light like in some toothpaste commercial. "That's Marilyn Perry's dog, if I'm not mistaken. And I'm guessing her donkey got out again?"

He ran a calloused hand over Edgar's neck. The donkey snorted and took a step back, nearly knocking Ellie over with the speed of his movement.

"He does this a lot?" Information Ellie should have gotten up front. Nothing in her welcome note—nor the written instructions Marilyn had given her at the nursing home—had indicated this would be an ongoing concern.

The man laughed and extended a hand for Ellie to shake. "I'm Blake Robinson. I live down the road there. My family tends Marilyn's fields, so we find this guy out here often. I'm not sure I've ever seen you around before though."

"Ellie Reed." Relief washed over her. Marilyn had mentioned this man's family offhandedly. That meant he wasn't that much of a stranger. "I'm staying at the tiny house on Marilyn's property for a few weeks. I told her I'd take care of the animals while she's—"

"Ah, while she's laid up. I heard about her little fall yesterday."

Hilda had quieted down now but stayed by Blake's truck, watching the interaction with great interest from beside the road.

"Yeah, I said I'd help as much as I could, but I don't totally know what I'm doing." Ellie threw her hands up. Nothing like a meet-cute going down while she was covered in sweat and mud. "Any suggestions on how to get a really stubborn donkey and an equally stubborn bulldog to walk a mile down the road?"

Blake laughed. "I'll do you one better. How about we load you all up in the truck, and I drive you back myself?"

A much nicer prospect than shoving the half-ton beast the entire way. "That would be amazing. Seriously, thank you."

"My pleasure." Blake urged Edgar toward his trailer with the skill of someone who'd done this infinitely more times than Ellie had.

Hilda growled again at the prospect of her donkey friend getting pushed around, but allowed Ellie to guide her toward the passenger side and hoist her up into the cab.

In no time, everyone was loaded, and Blake resumed his place in the driver's seat.

Ellie leaned closer to the air-conditioning vent and prayed the sweat hadn't made her mascara run or her hair stick to the side of her face. The air didn't help her cool down any though, with Hilda insisting on sitting so close Ellie thought they might actually fuse.

"I really appreciate this. If you hadn't come along, I don't know what I'd have done. I was getting kind of panicky, to tell you the truth."

"It's no trouble." The rough terrain of Marilyn's drive grew more pronounced in the jacked-up truck. "Marilyn planning to stay at the nursing home very long?"

"She said it might be a few weeks because they want her to do therapy, but she's hopeful it won't take that long." Ellie swallowed hard. The heat parched her. That, and she couldn't quite remember the last time she'd had a casual conversation with an attractive man she wasn't in a relationship with. Ellie was single now—after six years with the same guy. This, like all of Montana, was new territory for her.

Blake put the truck in park, and Ellie opened the door to release Hilda, who shot off toward the barn and out of sight. Ellie had only just swung her leg out before Blake appeared and offered her a hand down. A hand bare of any wedding band.

"I'll give you my phone number. That way, if you need me, I can be here in a matter of minutes." He flashed that glistening smile again. "Keep me updated on Marilyn's well-being too, if you can. We've always loved this farm and want to make sure it gets the care it needs—guests included."

The added wink at the end of his words made Ellie flush, unless that was another side effect of the summer heat. Panic set in all over again. Had she forgotten how to flirt? Was *he* flirting? She'd definitely forgotten how to recognize the difference between flirtation and general politeness. Those two things could be *so flippin' similar.*

"Yes, I'll do that. And thank you again." Ellie started making her way toward the rear of the trailer, but Blake held out a hand to stop her. "I'll get him back where he belongs. Don't worry about it."

"Oh, thank you." That meant seeking relief in the air-conditioned tiny house a little sooner. "I'll be seeing you then."

He nodded and disappeared around the trailer to march Edgar back to his pen.

Despite all the craziness dumped on her since arriving on the farm, Ellie now had an ally—someone to answer her questions, chase livestock, and possibly further distract her from her life derailment…

Just what she needed.

– 5 –

SHEEP ONE AND SHEEP Two bleated simultaneously with what could only be mutton mockery. Ellie rolled onto her butt to examine her scraped up knees and mud-covered palms. Thank goodness she'd packed all those bandages from the Wound-erful Seminar's gift basket.

If she tripped over Hilda one more time, she might reconsider letting the dog hog three-quarters of the bed at night. For a medium-sized canine, Hilda was dense. Like boulder-dense. Her constant desire to do whatever Ellie did made feeding the farm animals almost impossible. But, after some determination and a can of iced Starbucks coffee, Ellie finally finished her new morning chores, plus an inspection of the exterior fencing for donkey escape holes.

Hilda's meaty head barreled into her side over and over as Ellie tried to stand, the dog eager to play whatever fun game Ellie had initiated by getting down on the floor at eye level. The chickens ran amuck in the sheep pen, and Edgar stood stoically, ignoring the entire circus going on around him. Ellie gave him the stink eye often for the trouble he'd put her through yesterday.

"You pull that crap again, and you're going to time-out, buster." She wagged a finger at him, but he didn't care. Next time she left the premises, she'd tuck him safely away in the barn.

Ellie followed the rest of Marilyn's feeding instructions to the letter, even using a pitchfork to scoop poo from the pens and into the pile Marilyn had indicated outside the barn door. Aside from neglecting to sing for the animals, since it was too early for that kind of nonsense, she had to assume she'd crushed this new farmtastic endeavor.

As far as tackling other chores, Ellie and Hilda walked the dirt path up to the mailbox—a ten-mile journey from the feel of it—and gathered the mail to take to Marilyn at their next visit. She often looked both ways up and down the road in case a certain black truck came around again. Hopefully, Blake Robinson was the type of guy that called first before appearing unannounced because she did not want him popping by when she looked like *this*. Though, it might be an improvement from the day before.

Now that everyone depending on Ellie for survival had been cared for, she had to get something accomplished in her own realm. For once, she actually looked forward to sitting down to work and job hunt, if for no other reason than the sitting part.

Before work, however, she needed to take care of a few things: shower to scrub away the farm dirt and eat whatever was fastest. Oh, and try desperately not to fall asleep. She'd had a hard enough time sleeping back home with everything falling apart. This new lifestyle, however, kicked her butt. Now, she just didn't have the *time* to sleep.

The wind whipped the red dirt across her mud-stained legs as she battled her way toward her tiny house. Ellie retrieved her phone from her pocket to check any recent messages.

Same old, same old. All from Mom.

Mom: Did you find someone else to take care of the animals?
Mom: I was just thinking: Of all the places, why did you choose a
    small town in Montana away from people? Aren't you alone
    enough working from home all day?
Mom: Did Averie text you? She won an award for excellence in
    nursing! They surprised her at the Miami conference. I'm
    sure she'll send you the picture. A nurse magazine is going

to do a story on her. This will probably make her schedule even busier, so she's going to be extra busy and need your help even more now.

Of course Averie had won an award. At only thirty-four years old, she was one of the most successful people Ellie knew. It all came easy for her too. She was everything her parents wanted in a child: was happily married to her high school sweetheart (another stupidly successful individual), had already paid off all her student loan debt (like, how?), had insurance (with a low deductible and everything), and somehow made time to birth three wildly active children.

And then there was Ellie, nursing school dropout, unattached, medical transcriptionist on the brink of unemployment, working from an apartment that she'd have to move out of in less than six weeks, so very and painfully broke.

She glanced at the last line of the text again, more energy being siphoned from her body with the implications. *Need your help even more now* didn't bode well. Averie would probably want her to cook and clean in addition to caring for the kids on a more-than-full-time schedule.

Ellie's gut churned when she considered the possibility that Averie would ask her to move in and be on call 24/7. That was the one aspect of her life the family hadn't tried to butt their noses into. Ellie had full control of her apartment search and future living situation. She made sure to keep that out of all conversations to avoid opening the door to unsolicited advice.

Her fingers reluctantly typed a response: Love that for her.

After a quick shower and a microwavable dinner, Ellie pulled out the retractable dining table and situated her stool close enough that she could still use her foot pedal comfortably. She popped her headphones in, opened her assignment, and got to work.

Plaque buildup in the arteries due to high blood pressure, diabetes, smoking, and an increased intake of saturated fats can lead to atheroscle-rosis, a condition that...

The table vibrated, and Ellie tapped her foot to the pedal to pause the lecture.

Mom flashed across her phone screen.

"I'll congratulate Averie later, Mom. Promise. I'm working right now and—"

"Oh, that's not why I'm calling, but yes, you need to get to that because it's a big deal." Medical professionals received awards, plaques, magazine articles, and extra acronyms around their names. Transcriptionists got bookstore gift cards at Christmastime and a virtual pat-on-the-back in place of severance pay.

Ellie pushed her computer away so she wouldn't accidentally type anything when she slumped forward on the table. "So, what's up then?"

"You're never going to believe what just happened." Her mother sounded breathless, as if she'd raced to the phone with whatever gossip she'd recently gathered. "I went in to get the frames replaced on my prescription sunglasses, and I ran into Sean in the lobby."

The air sucked out of the room like a vacuum. Oh, this was much worse than discussing Averie's successes. "Mother, he *works* there. You couldn't get your glasses fixed somewhere else now?"

"I have been a patient of Dr. Haverman's since you were in diapers. I have to go through the hassle of transferring my files just because you broke up with his associate?" She scoffed.

Ellie wanted to scoff right back but resisted. "I'm just saying..."

"*Anyway*, Sean looks pretty rough, Ellie. Have you spoken to him lately? Maybe that would help."

The knife in Ellie's chest twisted a little deeper.

She flattened the side of her face on the tabletop, the phone barely propped to her cheek. "I haven't talked to him since the breakup and don't really plan to either. I should get back to work, can we—"

"What about Chloe? Have you talked to her?" The rapid-fire questions left no room for Ellie to answer. "I asked Sean how she was, but he only gave me one-word answers. It was so uncomfortable."

Most people would have taken that as a hint.

"I haven't spoken with Chloe, no. She's not real happy that I broke up with her brother." Ellie's entire body grew heavier. Even if her mom hung up now, the prospect of getting back to work on something that took so much focus didn't seem possible.

Her mother clicked her tongue. "Well, none of us are. Have you tried apologizing?"

She seriously had to stop answering these phone calls. "I don't want to talk about this."

"Well, we liked him, Ellie. Sean was a great guy with a great job and a great family. Forgive us if we're still trying to figure out why you dumped him out of nowhere." Her mother took in a long breath. "I'm sorry. I didn't mean for it to come out like that. We're just concerned about some of your life choices lately. We just want to help you get things back on track. Seeing Sean looking so upset really drove things home that your decisions are affecting other people, Ellie."

For real? They were having this conversation?

Thank God her mother hadn't witnessed the actual breakup, if she wanted to comment on how badly Ellie hurt people. Sean had never looked at her like that before. It was a miracle she had the strength to end it at all. Though, it wasn't quite a decision that came out of nowhere like insinuated. In fact, everyone getting mad at her, including his very sweet family, factored into why Ellie stuck around as long as she did.

From somewhere outside, Hilda barked and yipped. Ellie tried to let the sound ground her in her new surroundings, remind her she'd gotten far away from all that mess. For the next few weeks, if nothing else. Her family needed to let her have this.

"I really don't want to talk about it right now," Ellie said.

Her mother sighed. "Fine. I won't make you, but I just hope you're taking this time away to really think about things and get your head together if you insist on staying."

This conversation would never end. "I'm trying."

Deciding to end things with Sean was the absolute hardest thing she'd ever done. The repercussions of that choice continued in waves. But she didn't regret it, and she wouldn't rescind her decision. She also had so much more to worry about right now than that particular aspect of her life.

Hilda's yipping grew shriller as she got closer to the tiny house. Out of the corner of her eye, Ellie caught a whirl of brown and white zipping by.

"I'm always here if you want to talk things out." Or talk Ellie *into* things.

"Thanks, but I'm okay for now. I just need some space to—"

Hilda zipped past the front window again, shutting down Ellie's train of thought. The dog shrieked at some new and alarming octave. It didn't take long for Ellie to see why.

Hot on her nubby tail, a large rooster zoomed after the dog, fiery orange wings spread, beak extended like an arrow ready to cut clean through her target if she caught up.

"Mom, I gotta go!" The stool toppled out from under Ellie when she stood and rushed to the door.

"What's wrong?" her mother echoed the panic on the other end of the phone.

Ellie searched the room for any sort of weapon to use against the attack bird, but came up short. "There's a massive rooster chasing Hilda. I didn't even know Marilyn had a rooster! I—I gotta go."

Dropping the phone to the couch, Ellie snatched up one of the decorative couch pillows to use as a shield and charged out the front door in her bare feet.

"Hilda!"

The distressed canine rounded the barn, taloned monster in hot pursuit. Ellie cursed at her choice of armament. A bird that size would tear her sunflower pillow to shreds within seconds.

"Come on!" Ellie waved for the dog to follow her to the door. Even with a head start, she wasn't sure if she could outrun such a speedy foe, especially with the stray stones digging into her skin. Hilda had only managed to keep a few feet between them during the chase and certainly wouldn't hold out much longer either.

Adrenaline surged through Ellie's veins. This had to be one of those conditions leading to atherosclerosis. If she lived through this to complete the assignment, she'd be sure to leave it as feedback for future talks.

Ellie raced up the small set of stairs to the tiny house and fumbled with the doorknob. Hilda closed the gap between them, drawing the beast ever nearer. Darting inside, Ellie dropped the pillow and spun around to make sure Hilda still followed.

Scenarios raced through her head about what might happen if she had to leap out the door and tackle the rooster. She knew very little about the animal—only that they'd descended from T. rexes or something like that and could peck the hell out of you.

She did not want to find out what that felt like. "Run, Hilda!"

The dog summoned her strength and picked up the pace, shooting over the steps and crashing into the doorframe on her way through. Ellie rammed her shoulder into the door and shoved it closed, flipping the deadbolt on her way down when she sunk to the floor.

Hilda's loud panting mixed with Ellie's gasps as the two of them stared at each other from across the room. Outside, the rooster crowed its defeat. As long as the wretched thing couldn't peck through the window, they might be safe for the night.

"What part of hell did that thing come from?" She hated the thought that she'd wandered about the farm the past couple of days without knowing a feathered assassin could have been watching and waiting for the right time to strike.

She'd be sure to check in with Marilyn soon about ways to tame the fiend. If that failed, she might have to call Blake Robinson back to save her once more. Though admittedly, that would come with some level of embarrassment, given the *type* of threat. The damsel in distress bit worked, but there were lines she didn't want to cross.

"You'll be safe in here tonight, Hilda."

The dog crashed to the floor and rested its head on the sunflower pillow Ellie had flung upon reentering the home.

"For now, I'd say we could both use a drink. I know I'm making mine a strong one."

– 6 –

Farm life was not for the faint of heart—or those with an affinity for sleeping in. The devil rooster belted out his alarming song well before the sun rose. No amount of pillows over her head could block him out. Violent threat or not, the barn animals still depended on Ellie for their morning meals.

Armed with a broom from the house and a nervous bulldog, then the addition of a rake she found leaning against a fence, Ellie cared for Edgar, the sheep, and the chicken traitors who had failed to mention their rooster leader.

Every *cock-a-doodle-doo* sent chills down her spine, but more disturbingly yet, throughout the full hour she spent in the barn, Ellie never once saw the stupid cock. It had become a phantom, a master of mind games.

The entire morning was a wash as she and her doggy sidekick hunted the premises. With any luck, she'd trap the rooster in the unused pen in the barn. It best suited a large animal, like a horse, but hopefully it kept an unruly rooster contained as well. The other chickens might enjoy the free-range lifestyle, but Ellie had to draw the line somewhere.

By lunch time, exhaustion battled with paranoia, leading Ellie and Hilda to give up the quest and move on. She still needed to finish that piece on atherosclerosis before she surpassed the time limit. The company didn't need an excuse to cut her loose early, especially since they'd already cut so much of the available workflow for freelancers in preparation for the change in management.

At least she had a preliminary plan for the day: she'd ignore communication attempts from blood relatives, call Marilyn to schedule their next visit so she could drop off the mail and her phone, and then focus exclusively on being productive for *herself*. Several job openings had popped up in her email, courtesy of the many online job search sites she'd perused, so she'd have to flip through those. Though the chances of any of them being legit, and not some company hoping to take advantage of the work-from-home crowd, was slim to none.

The moment Ellie stepped foot inside her small air-conditioned oasis, she yanked her sticky shirt over her head and threw it toward the ladder stairs. Her sweaty skin instantly chilled, a welcome refreshment. She needed to add laundry to her to-do list already. Fortunately, the darling tiny house came equipped with an equally darling washer/dryer combo that might actually fit into Ellie's pocket.

But first: a shower. The warm water provided a welcome contrast to the frosty air. Soapy bubbles tumbled from her hair as she hummed to herself under the showerhead. Even through the water's roar at her ear, she still heard Hilda barking her strange turkey-like squawk somewhere in the house.

Had Godzilla Rooster reappeared, taunting her from outside the window? Then again, it took little for the dog to throw a hissy fit. There could be a spider on the ceiling. Her ball could have rolled under the couch. A beanstalk could have gently swayed in the breeze. A grain of—

The bathroom door smacked the wall, and a large hand yanked the shower curtain to the side. Ellie screamed, dropping into the corner. On instinct, she grabbed the bottom of the drape to shield her naked body. The shampoo and conditioner bottles crashed to the floor beside her, and she realized she'd shut her eyes in anticipation of whatever came next.

"Who are you, and what are you doing here?" a deep voice growled.

Ellie opened her eyes and adjusted the shower curtain to further protect her modesty. Her words were hardly more than a pure shriek when she finally responded to the intruder. "Get out!"

"This is *my* house. Why are *you* in it?" The man didn't budge, but he kept his gaze averted, which confused her even more. He just stood there, one fist balled and the other clutching a glass vase from the dining room table he might have meant to club her with, all while staring determinately at the wall over her head.

He didn't dress like a murderer either: gray, preppy shorts and a plaid button-up shirt rolled to the elbow. Vicious killer or not, he still posed a risk a few feet away with nothing but a half-torn shower curtain separating him from her nakedness.

Hilda peeked her head into the room, tongue dangling out the side of her mouth, thrilled that her new friends got along so splendidly. She'd been more protective when Blake saved them in the field the day before, and she'd have seen him around all the time. But this intruder barging in unannounced didn't faze her at all. She had to be the world's worst guard dog.

Ellie scanned her immediate surroundings, but found nothing to throw at this dude. "I rented this place from Marilyn Perry through Airbnb. You're breaking and entering, and—"

"*What?*" The stranger took a big step back and slapped his open palm to his forehead.

Not exactly the reaction she'd expected.

She pulled the curtain higher under her chin. "Get out of here!"

The man shook his head and reached for the doorknob. "Put your clothes on and come out here."

With that, he slammed the door behind him.

Who was this guy? And did he say this was *his* house? Marilyn definitely would have mentioned something like that.

Ellie released her pent-up breath, shoulders dropping, heart still pounding like it might spring right out of her chest. She swore she'd locked the front door when she came back from feeding the animals. This guy had to have busted through the window or something. And now he wanted her to get dressed and meet him in the other room?

With shaking fingers, she flipped the lock on the bathroom door, snatched up her clothes, and got dressed as quickly as possible.

This bloke was crazy if he thought she'd casually join him out there for a chat or whatever he wanted from her. She could survive in the bathroom for several days without food. Probably.

The man rapped on the door instead of breaking in again. "Hurry up."

"Get out," she answered for the third time.

"Like I said, this is *my* house. Just come here." He sighed heavily on the other side and tapped his fingers on the wood frame. "I'm not here to murder you or anything."

"Thanks. That's super reassuring." Unless she shot him with body wash or tied him up with toilet paper, Ellie would have to depend entirely on the skills she learned during that kickboxing workout she tried for a week, like, a million years ago.

He groaned. "Fine. I'll go outside and wait for you *out there*." His footsteps led away from the bathroom as he muttered, "Come on, Hilda."

The front door opened and shut, leaving the hum of the air-conditioner as the only lingering sound.

So he knew Hilda. And Hilda was unshaken by him. Something sinister was definitely afoot here.

She side-eyed the bathroom door and the man somewhere out there on the other side of it.

Ellie toweled off her long hair and tied it into a messy bun at the base of her neck. The girls in movies always fought off danger with their flowing locks loose and lovely, but that so wasn't real life.

Ellie cursed under her breath and flung open the bathroom door. Hilda barked again and drew her attention to the front window.

The man bent down to pry the Bilexin ball from Hilda's jowls and chucked it toward the barn. The dog tripped over her paws on the way, but quickly retrieved her target and returned to dance around the man, ready to go again. His presence obviously made her forget all about the rooster that nearly impaled her a day before.

Dogs were excellent judges of character, right? But Hilda wasn't quite like most dogs. Much more like a hyper codependent turkey who missed vital details about her surroundings and occasionally choked when she drank water.

Since it didn't look like this dude planned to leave and had some sort of claim over the tiny home, Ellie needed some answers. Getting those answers while trying not to think how he'd seen her nude might be a whole different story. It made it worse, somehow, that he appeared to be about the same age as her and wasn't at all unfortunate looking from what she gathered during their brief, horrifying encounter.

Ellie opened the door, drawing the stranger's attention away from an excited Hilda. He said nothing at first, simply watched her descend the steps and slowly approach. Now that she had clothes on and her heart had resumed a somewhat steady beat, she took a better look at him.

His light brown hair whipped across his forehead in the Montana breeze. He shoved his hands into his pockets and shifted on his slide sandals, dark blue eyes squinting to see her in the bright sun. Her guess was right: he had to be about her age, maybe a little older. Occupation: unknown.

He still said nothing. The way he stared made her tug at the hem of her shirt. She'd put *all* her clothes on, right?

"Should we try this again?" he finally asked.

"Probably a good idea." Ellie folded her arms across her chest and planted her feet firmly in the dirt to keep from getting knocked on her butt when Hilda rubbed against her knee. "You start."

He raised a thick eyebrow. "Fine. Warren Oliver. This is my grandmother's farm, and I built this tiny house so I'd have a place to stay when I come to visit. Now your turn. Because I am dying to know why I can't find Gram at the house, but her truck is still here. Why is Hilda playing with a ball advertising some drug company? And, most intriguingly, why was there a naked woman in *my* shower?"

Her cheeks blazed under the heat of his comments. "Most people shower naked, Mr. Oliver, so if you could never bring that up again, I'd appreciate it."

"Fair enough." He threw his hands up and nudged Hilda away from licking his heels. "So who are you then, and what are you talking about with this Airbnb nonsense?"

This day could not get more awkward. "Well, I'm Ellie Reed. The tiny house is listed as a vacation rental on Airbnb's website. I booked it a couple weeks ago to get away, and now I'm stuck here on the strangest vacation of my life, feeding farm animals, dog-sitting, and getting barged in on by strange men while I wait for your grandmother to get better."

"Get better? What's wrong with her? Where is she?" Warren took a step closer. His face turned from an expression of accusation to genuine concern. It softened Ellie's insides a little. But *only* a little.

"Are you being serious right now? Marilyn said someone from her family would come and bring her clothes and stuff to the nursing home. But you're looking at me like this is brand new information..."

Family would *definitely* know about this.

"Nursing home? No one told me anything about that. I come here every few months to check up on Gram and work on the projects she has for me and always stay for a while during the summer. I told her I was coming this week to patch the barn siding." He scratched his head and raised his chin to the sky. "My family's wonderful communication style strikes again. But a nursing home? Holy shit. Like, what happened?"

A *dysfunctional* family made sense. "She's okay. She fell and hurt her leg. She'll just have to stay at the rehab unit until they release her. Not a permanent thing, I don't think. I visited her a couple days ago, but when I asked if I needed to know anything else about the farm, your visit didn't come up."

Warren's expression morphed again, but this time, Ellie couldn't read it. He kicked at the stones on his way toward his white pickup truck, then leaned against it and stared at the ground. "This is unbelievably confusing. You know that? You're supposedly an Airbnb guest, but you also visit my grandmother in the nursing home and, what, take care of the farm now?"

"Yup." Ellie shrugged because that summed it up accurately, no matter how ridiculous it sounded.

"And you've been here how long?" he asked.

She examined the sky to calculate. "Couple days."

"Seems fishy."

The truth didn't always have to make sense. "Well, it is what it is."

Parenthetical dimples encased his grin, a welcome change from the scowl that painted his face before. "Well, then. I guess I should thank you for interrupting your hipster vacation to help my grandma. Right?"

"Whoa, dude. I'm not a hipster. Just because I work from home, drink wine for breakfast, and enjoy tiny houses does not mean..." Her nose scrunched, and she nodded. "Yeah, I hear it now."

"Sorry to be the bearer of bad news." He licked his lips and swatted a bug off his arm. "And, um, sorry about bursting in on you in the shower."

Ellie offered a slight head tilt, finding nothing to say in response.

"I suppose I'll stay at the big house then, since you're here. Going to call the nursing home and figure out what Gram was thinking, starting a bed and breakfast on a whim. And I'll be taking care of the animals, so you don't have to do that. For the record, she's not supposed to have *them* either. We've told her countless times they're dangerous for her to be around at this age, but does she listen?"

Hilda brushed Ellie's leg, and they shared a look that could only mean they'd keep their little secret about Hilda causing Marilyn's fall between the two of them.

"Actually, I'm fine with caring for the animals. Marilyn already gave me all the instructions for it." Putting the task in more capable hands would ease her physical stress considerably, but it would take away her free stay. She couldn't afford to turn down an offer like that at the moment. "I'll let you deal with the rooster though."

Warren frowned. "I didn't know Gram had a rooster."

"Apparently, she does. And he is horrible." Ellie glanced down at Hilda again, as if the dog could back up the claim.

Warren pushed his hair from his face and clicked his tongue. "I'll keep an eye out for him and make a note to remind Gram again that she's not even supposed to have the animals she does, let alone bringing on aggressive newbies." He rolled his eyes. "Um, I guess just enjoy your stay or whatever we're supposed to say to our guests because this is all totally normal and not at all jacked up. I'm going to call Gram and pick a fight."

"Yeah, good luck with that." Ellie had only recently met Marilyn, but she had a strong feeling Warren would need all the luck he could get if he meant to take on such a woman.

WITH SO MANY SURPRISES popping up around the farm, Ellie opted for a workspace with a 360-degree view of her surroundings. Montana seemed to be raining men—some heroic rescuers, some accusatory buttheads, some attack roosters.

When entering the dark wood gazebo near the main house, Ellie placed her canned coffee and computer on the glass patio tabletop and tried not to think about the new hipster level she'd reached in her life, thanks to Warren's accusation. It was fine, really, but did it have to be so obvious? Somehow, simply adapting to a life of being her former boyfriend's hermit-y sidekick had changed her identity even more than she'd imagined. The unemployed, couch-surfing phase up next might make it so much worse.

Ellie opened her laptop and plugged in her pedal and headphones. Time to learn more about those heart valves, while simultaneously keeping watch for Intruder Warren and Godzilla Rooster. If either caused her issue today, she might have to call Blake in to be a buffer.

The thought of him coming over gave her goose bumps. That very rom-com-like scenario wasn't one that often played out in her life. She really had no idea how to navigate it. She met Sean because her mother thought he was cute when he first started working in their healthcare center. She then practically forced them together at the Christmas party over a bowl of punch and Chex mix.

Superduper romantic.

Ellie exhaled the daydreams of both past and present.

Patients experiencing symptoms of atherosclerosis may be subject to tests that include computerized tomography, Doppler sonography, radionuclide angiography, and cardiac catheterization, in which a catheter passes through the coronary arteries in conjunction with an injected dye to determine blockages and abnormalities.

Ellie cringed. She could type up symptoms all day and spell lengthy medical jargon better than anyone she knew, but the descriptions of procedures, no matter how minor, always made her queasy.

Just one more reminder of why she'd only survived a single semester in nursing school and would forever remain a disappointment to her family—well, one of many reasons. Still, that pretty much knocked all medical professions off the table for future consideration, though she had a promising application in as a receptionist at a dental office. It'd be even more promising if they'd actually schedule her for an interview.

Job-hunting had to be the most stressful task on earth.

Or was it apartment-hunting? Every place seemed to be raising their rates, which did nothing to help the single, low-income crowd. All of her friends had settled down and either married or moved away, so pairing up with a roommate she actually knew wasn't very likely.

Either way, the calendar counted down the days until she had to figure it out. Might be the quickest six weeks of her life.

"Focus." She readjusted her headphones and forced her attention on the assignment.

Notable differences in blood pressure comparison between the ankle and arm can also indicate obstructions to blood flow.

Across the drive, Warren backed his truck up to the barn and began unloading tools, beams, and all kinds of other unidentifiable objects. He'd changed from his preppy-boy attire into a sleeveless blue T-shirt and raggedy jeans. He wore his baseball cap backward, sunglasses shading his eyes.

If the heart muscle does not receive adequate blood flow…

Ellie's phone lit up beside her with a call from an unknown Montana number. Her own heart valves worked a little harder at the thought of Blake calling. But she had his number saved in her phone. There was only one other person in the state who knew how to reach her.

"My God, Ellie, I'm so sorry about Warren," a panicked Marilyn cried.

Ellie pursed her lips to keep from laughing out loud at the amusing greeting. "Hi, Marilyn."

"I called my daughter when I first got here, but she didn't mention Warren coming, and I didn't figure she'd *send* him because between you and the neighbors, everything would be taken care of." She paused to take a quick breath. "I thought Warren was coming in July, but I got the damn J-months wrong on my calendar. I told that boy—I told him if he mentions one word of my Airbnb to his mother, I will wring his neck."

That'd be a sight worth sticking around for.

Marilyn didn't give Ellie a chance to respond. "Warren's a good boy, Ellie. He helps me out more'n anybody else in my family, but he can be wound so tight. If he gives you any sass, you let me know right away. He said he'd take care of everything on the farm while I'm tied up here, but he's already out there fixing the siding on my barn. He's liable to work himself to death if he tries to do all that himself. I told him not to come visit me this morning. I need more time to strategize what to say to him about all this. I've got some explaining to do, you know, and I'll be damned if I tell the whole truth."

Ellie laughed again. Her new goal in life was to grow up to be like Marilyn. "Well, I told him I'd still help with the animals since you and I'd already discussed it. I really am happy to help however you need, but I'm not sure if he's going to let me." How much of their morning interaction had Warren told his grandmother? "I feel bad I'm staying in his house though. He—"

"You don't worry a thing about that. There're plenty of bedrooms made up in my house. You stay right there. He might have built the little home, but he put it on *my* property."

Ellie waited for more, but Marilyn went quiet now.

"Well, um…" Ellie pushed some things around on her makeshift desk to have something to do. "I'll keep on doing what I'm doing then."

"And don't forget threatening to wring his neck. It's always worked on him, even when he was a kid, and—oh, you know what? Just let me talk to him again." Marilyn made a lip-smacking sound and waited.

Waited for what? For Ellie to go get Warren? The woman had to know it'd be easier to call him on his own cell phone. This wasn't 1995.

"Uh, you want me to go get him and put him on the phone?" Ellie asked.

"Yes, I'll wait."

Ellie calculated the space between the gazebo and the barn. It'd take her several minutes to walk that distance. Well, seconds if the trek involved being chased by a rooster. Then, there was the added time it'd take to find Warren when she got there. "I think you should try to call him on his phone. I don't really know where he—"

"I've already got you on the phone. Plus, I wouldn't be surprised if he just ignores me after our earlier phone conversation. Hardly any of them answer me these days."

Ouch. Ellie placed a hand over her heart at the twinge of sadness that came across in the older woman's words. As much as she didn't want to hunt down Warren, or look him in the eye at all, she also couldn't say no to Marilyn. She'd never been able to deny Grandma Val of anything—and vice versa. Ellie would have moved heaven and earth to grant her grandmother's wishes if she'd been at the other end of this call.

"Yeah, okay. I'll go see if he's out at the barn. Just one sec."

"God love ya," Marilyn replied.

Ellie lowered the phone in her hand and stepped from the shady gazebo into the blazing sun. As expected, the walk to the barn took forever, especially since she paused often to check her surroundings. Sweat beaded on her forehead. She readjusted the jean shorts that clung to her thighs and lifted the front of her tank top to ensure no cleavage peeked out. Warren didn't need another show.

She rounded the corner of the barn and found Warren bent over a pile of fresh siding, his circular saw roaring as it cut through the piece he needed. Getting his attention without causing him to saw off a limb might prove tricky.

Ellie loudly cleared her throat, but that did nothing.

"Warren?" she called out. No acknowledgment. Poor Marilyn had to listen to their noise through the phone, but then again, she'd asked for this. Ellie forced her voice up a notch. "Warren!"

He startled and took a step back, pulling his safety headphones from his ears as he turned to regard her. When he realized who stood before him, he reached down to power off the circular saw. "You scared the shit out of me."

"So, we're even now?" She wanted to add something about him being more clothed than when *he* scared *her*, but her embarrassment levels wouldn't allow it—not to mention Marilyn could still hear everything.

"Ha-ha. What do you need?"

"Your grandmother is on the phone and would like to talk to you." She held up her cell for him to take.

"On your phone? Why didn't she call me?" He peeled off his gloves and approached rather apprehensively.

Ellie shrugged and gestured to the phone to show Marilyn was still listening on the other end.

With a grumble, he grabbed it out of Ellie's hand. "Yes, Gram?"

The next uncomfortable conundrum unfolded: Should she stay and get her phone back or leave him some privacy and go do her job? So far, this entire week had been one strange instance after another.

She needed a vacation.

"Yeah, but I told her she didn't have to take care of the animals since I'm—" Warren paced back and forth in the space between Ellie and his workstation. "I get that, but—" Marilyn didn't want to hear his arguments. They spoke only that morning, but she'd come up with an entirely new lecture for him in a couple hours' time. "Now, that's just weird. Airbnbs don't do that. It's a bed-and-breakfast thing, and I can't even cook. Gram, this is—"

Warren pulled off his sunglasses and wiped his fist across his brow. Ellie backed away, really wishing she'd left him with her phone and dodged all this. She still could run…

The second he caught sight of her movement though, he held up a finger to keep her in place. Fine. She'd just stand there for no reason at all and try not to watch him rant. But on the back side of the farm, there was hardly anything to look at besides the barn wall and a bean field. That left nothing for her to do other than observe random details in her surroundings: the chips in the siding that required replacement, a beetle sitting on a stray dandelion, the flecks of sawdust coating Warren's biceps.

She swallowed hard and drew her attention to the sky, searching for something that *actually* mattered.

"I'm not some middle school bully, Gram. I'll be nice to her. I—" Warren's shoulders sank, and he pressed his back to the barn for support. "Yes, I promise I'll be a gentleman or whatever, even though this is all shady as—" He stared at the ground while Marilyn talked some more. "No, as per our earlier conversation, you told me to come after your euchre tournament this afternoon. Why do I have to wait till—" His eyes met Ellie's then. "Fine. I'll ask her, but I'm not forcing it. She's on vacation, after all."

Ask her what? Ellie's stomach did a little flip.

"Yep, here she is." Warren held the phone out to Ellie. "You're up again, slugger."

This phone conversation might never end. They'd stand here behind the barn, volleying until the sun set or Marilyn left for this supposed euchre tournament, whichever came first.

"Hello?" With any luck, Marilyn had hung up, and Ellie could get on with her weird day.

Marilyn hadn't ended the call. "Ellie, if he doesn't keep his promise to be nice to you or make you a proper breakfast, tell me immediately. He's bringing you for a visit tomorrow because I need to talk to you again. In person."

Ellie turned her back on Warren so he couldn't see the face she made. "Tomorrow?" The first visit had gone better than she'd expected, but this time, Warren would drive her. And vacations didn't involve this sort of thing. At this rate, she'd never finish her assignment, nor fill out another application, and she'd be one step closer to having to set up a tent in her parents' backyard for a place to live.

She tried to summon the courage to decline the visit, but Marilyn's quiet urgency stopped her in her tracks. "I want to see you face-to-face because I have one more favor to ask of you, and Warren can't know anything about this."

– 8 –

THE CRUNCH OF HER scoop in the chicken feed tub called the birds to the barn within seconds. A frenzy of flapping wings, excited clucks, and pecking beaks made Ellie throw the food and take a step back. There had to be a more effective way to do this.

So far, the rooster hadn't shown up for breakfast. In fact, Ellie hadn't heard his wake-up call that morning either, even though she'd gotten up well before the sun to tend to her chores, lest Warren beat her to it.

Hilda, too, appeared relaxed and unconcerned about the usual threat, as she rubbed her back along a bale of hay to satisfy an itch. While Ellie wouldn't want to tell Marilyn she'd lost an animal, she had a hard time feeling sad about the bird experiencing any level of misfortune.

Opening the back gate to let Edgar and his sheep buddies out into the pasture concluded her new morning routine. If any barn residents ran off this time, she could always send Warren to retrieve them. He owed her that much after the shower incident.

After getting all cleaned up—without Warren's company this time—Ellie sat at the tiny fold-down table and stared out the window toward the main house. Hilda snored on the sofa, exhausted from all the "hard work" she'd done so early in the morning. The prospect of a nap sounded much more enticing than wading through the plethora of help-wanted postings while she waited for Warren to take her to the nursing home—especially since sleep had mostly evaded her the night before.

Ellie's phone pinged, and the nerves kicked up another level.

> **Blake Robinson-Neighbor:** Hey Ellie. It's Blake Robinson from down the road. Just wondered if you're getting along okay and if you'd be around this afternoon. Maybe I can pop in for a visit.

Oh boy.

Ellie tapped her fingernail on the tabletop and tried to formulate a reply. She mentally reviewed her schedule and how long it might take to get back from Choteau. Though, if today went like every other day here, it didn't really matter what she had planned. Somehow, it'd end up going in a totally different direction.

> **Ellie:** Hi Blake! I'm about to go visit Marilyn, but I'll let you know when I'm headed back.

Should she mention Warren's arrival? On one hand, it seemed rude to invite a guest to someone else's property. On the other, Blake was Marilyn's neighbor offering help during a difficult time, and Marilyn had stated that her neighbors might stop in to assist. Warren would—or should—understand that.

Also, who gave a rat's ass what he thought?

> **Blake Robinson-Neighbor:** Perfect. Looking forward to it.

Gravel kicked up in the driveway, causing Hilda to wake up and yip toward the front door. The phone nearly slipped from her hand. If it weren't for that first weird and horrible encounter in her bathroom, Warren wouldn't make her so flipping nervous. Now, she had to ride in a truck with him for thirty minutes each way to and from the nursing home. She just had to focus on the money saved by not having to hire an Uber. It might be the only thing to get her through it.

Outside, Warren put the truck in park and hopped out. Ellie grabbed her purse on the way through the door and released the excited pup to greet their visitor—then stopped short on the first step when she caught sight of him.

Warren leaned against his truck. He'd reverted to his preppier wardrobe of black shorts and a gray V-neck shirt. In his right hand, he held a travel mug; in his left, a paper plate with two slices of toast.

"I've been instructed to make you breakfast on pain of death. Unfortunately, toast is your best option, unless you like old people food. I could have brought you plain oatmeal, Fig Newtons, or yogurt that makes you poop." He wiggled the travel mug slightly to entice her forward. "And I made the coffee the way I like it, since I don't know how you take it. Cream and sugar. Though, it's heavy whipping cream because Gram thinks regular cream is just milk sold at a higher price. She tells me this often."

Ellie descended the step and offered a knowing smile. "You really didn't have to make me anything. It's not like I expected breakfast to come with this stay."

"See, I tried to tell her that wasn't a thing, but if you don't take this, she'll murder me when we get there." Warren extended his offering until Ellie took it. "And I'm still weirded out with this, by the way. She's acting all flustered and telling me not to come visit until I have you with me? It makes no sense."

Ellie shrugged to readjust her purse on her shoulder, tucked the travel mug into the crook of her elbow, and reached for the door handle, while Warren hurried around to the driver's side. "None of this is what I expected when I booked this trip either, trust me."

Though, admittedly, Marilyn's situation provided a worthy distraction, which was something she had hoped to get on this trip.

Warren's brow rose as he buckled his seatbelt and kicked the truck into drive. "Regardless, I feel it's only fair to warn you that if you're here for any reason other than you say you are, and you hurt my gram, there will be hell to pay."

"Wow. Thanks for the heads up."

"I'm just saying. Scams are getting more creative these days." He didn't take his eyes off the road.

Ellie swirled the coffee around in her travel cup. Had he poisoned it or something? A paranoid stranger would totally do something like that. "This is not a scam, dude. You accepted my story yesterday, but question it today?"

"Your *story*?" He raised an eyebrow and took up his mug from the cup holder.

"Nonfiction. My word choice doesn't mean I made it up." She rearranged the seatbelt across her chest. "I thought we were starting over after the whole break-in thing yesterday. And you're going to present yourself as being this unlikeable?"

Warren reached forward to lower the radio volume, though it did nothing because the radio wasn't even on. "The elderly are easy prey for these types of scams, as I'm sure you're aware."

"Still doesn't mean *I'm* conning her," Ellie offered.

"But it *could*. That's all I'm saying."

Aaaaand that was enough of that.

Thank goodness Marilyn had already offered a refund on the stay, because dealing with a jackass like Warren certainly necessitated some kind of compensation.

Ellie's phone buzzed with yet another call from her mom. Impeccably timed as usual. She silenced the ring and stuffed the phone into her purse. Warren's gaze flickered from the road to her in the passenger seat. The oaf likely assumed she sent information to her accomplices on how to destroy this poor old lady and take down the meddling grandson in the process.

She and Warren said nothing else for the rest of the thirty-four-minute drive into Choteau.

At a stop sign, Warren turned right, and the scenery grew unfamiliar. She remembered exactly which adorable dinosaurs she'd seen, and these were not it.

"Weren't you supposed to go left there?" The Uber driver had gone left and gotten her where she needed to go the last time.

"We're stopping at the hardware store first. I need some things for the barn."

Go figure. He hadn't even bothered to ask if an extra stop was okay. Guys had a reputation for spending ridiculous amounts of time in hardware stores too. Marilyn would end up waiting forever and get even fussier over things, leaving Ellie caught in the middle once more. Her hand gripped tighter on the armrest.

Warren parked and started to get out, but didn't say a word to Ellie.

"Am I supposed to come with you?" she asked.

"I'm not leaving my truck running with a stranger sitting in it, so that might be best if you don't want to cook." He flashed a sarcastic thumbs-up, which bumped Ellie's rage a notch.

Marilyn had seemed so nice and accepting when Ellie met her. How had this jerkface come from that same family line? There must have been a real hiccup in generations.

A bell chimed when Warren opened the heavy door that nearly hit Ellie in the butt before she could get all the way through. The scent of grass seed and popcorn enveloped her. At least this store offered customer appreciation snacks for awkward patrons who didn't care to eat burnt toast in uncomfortable truck cabs.

"Warren Oliver. I haven't seen you in months. How have you been?" A man in yellow suspenders rounded the red counter and stretched out a hand for Warren to shake. He had a pencil tucked behind his ear and a folded sheet of paper in his front shirt pocket.

"Hey, Barry. Good to see you." Warren's voice portrayed someone else—someone *nice*. A total lie, obviously. "I'm here to fix up that barn siding. The winter winds weren't kind to that east wall."

Barry scanned the area behind Warren. "No Hilda today?"

Warren's half-smirk grew. "You know Hilda can't behave in public."

Ellie tried to imagine Hilda riding in a car with Warren for that half-hour trip, her dripping tongue hanging out the window. Undoubtedly, the dog would have bulldozed every display in the store and leapt directly into the popcorn machine for a treat.

Hardware Store Barry nodded his understanding. "I'm so sorry to hear about Marilyn's fall, by the way. Oh, I bet that frustrates her to be laid up like she is."

News traveled fast in Choteau. A town this size probably only printed local news about injuries, county fairs, or who grew the largest produce. Columbus news reported a lot of traffic deaths, breaking medical research, road construction delays, and crime. Bit of a difference.

"She won't want to stay in that nursing home long. I'm sure of that." Instead of heading off to find whatever tool he needed, Warren rested against the counter like it was a bar and not a retail establishment. Perhaps Barry served beer with his popcorn.

"And who is this young lady with you?" Barry nudged Warren with his elbow on his way past to shake Ellie's hand.

She reached forward to awkwardly greet the man. "I'm Ellie."

"She's cute, Warren. I approve," Barry said.

Ellie's heart picked up pace. She tried to object, but nothing came out.

"Whoa. Wait. No." Warren pressed away from the counter and stiffened, raising his hands like Barry had taken a swing instead of merely making an implication. "Not even a little bit like that. Ellie is staying on Gram's property as an *Airbnb guest*." He used finger quotes to further emphasize the ridiculousness of it.

"Airbnb? Like those little personal property hotels?" Barry waited for Warren's confirmation. "Marilyn's doing?" Another nod from Warren. "Do her girls know about that?"

Ellie inched forward, awaiting whatever tea this guy meant to spill. If ever there was a time for popcorn, it was now.

"They do not." Warren took an interest in a caulking set near the register. "Gram's been keeping this little endeavor a big secret, *if* that's all that's happening here."

Ellie growled and crossed her arms over her chest. Not this crap again.

But Warren continued, "Because, Ms. Reed, it'd be easier to deal with if it weren't an Airbnb situation. I'd actually prefer you being a con artist messing with Gram over Gram about to start an epic round of family drama."

Barry laughed. He knew way more about the Oliver/Perry family than Ellie did. And, at this point, Ellie preferred to keep it that way.

"Sorry to disappoint you, but it is what it is," she said.

"Well, for your sakes, let's hope dear Savannah and Janey don't pay a surprise visit." Barry tried not to make it obvious, but Ellie didn't miss the way he offhandedly gestured toward her—almost like she was a dead woman walking.

Ellie was an innocent vacationer in all this. None of the blame could fall on her when/if Marilyn's daughters came to town. Though, if they were anything like Warren personality-wise, Ellie should head back to the farm and pack her bags now because she had no desire to be around Warren on steroids.

"Amen, brother." Warren headed off into the aisles to hunt down his supplies, leaving Ellie standing in the store's front, wondering what fresh hell the rest of this trip could manifest.

– 9 –

"Seriously? Are we ever going to get to the nursing home, or can I call this in as a kidnapping?" Another wrong turn had Ellie contemplating crawling through the window to escape. The way this guy kept her in the dark with their plans and still continued to issue her a judging eye proved absolutely maddening.

"I have no interest in kidnapping you. Trust me." Warren eased into the parking lot of a tiny oak shack with a sign that read Daily Brew. "But if we don't bring Gram her favorite beverage from her favorite coffee shop, I'm pretty sure she'll just send us right back out to get it."

Whether or not that was true, fresh coffee didn't sound half bad.

Plus, she'd often swung through Winans for coffee and chocolates when she spent the day with Grandma Val. Specialty coffees and grandmas went together like peanut butter and jelly.

"If we're doing this, then I'm getting a *good* cup of coffee." She reached into her purse and foraged her wallet. A few dollar bills and a handful of change should cover her order. It'd better, since she didn't have much more than that.

Plucking the money from her hands, Warren sighed as if she'd horribly inconvenienced him.

Good.

"Hi. Can I help— Hey, Warren! I didn't realize it was time for your visit already." A middle-aged woman with tight black curls and plum lipstick rested her hand on her hip as she stood hunched in the drive-thru window.

Everybody knew everybody. By the end of her stay, they might know Ellie's life story too. Hell, they might even try to get her back together with Sean, like her family and friends back home. That'd just be great.

"Hey, Babs. How's it going? I'm on a mission for Gram this morning."

"Oh, then I bet you need a marshmallow steamer." The giddy woman clapped her hands together and signaled for her coworker to get on making that. "When I heard about her fall, I felt terrible. This one's on the house. You tell her Babs needs her feeling better ASAP."

Ellie grinned in the passenger seat. Maybe it wasn't all bad that everybody knew everyone and their business. It filled her with the warm fuzzies of a cheesy Hallmark movie. Well, until Warren opened his stupid mouth again.

"That's very sweet of you, Babs. I'm sure Gram will greatly appreciate it. I'm also gonna need something for this stranger I found wandering around the farm."

"Oh my gosh." Ellie turned her attention to the friendly barista. "Can I get a latte, please?"

Babs just laughed. "What flavor can I get you, sweetie?"

"Caramel, if you have it." Ellie's polite tone ended with a scowl toward Warren.

It was too bad she lived on the other side of the country. A small-town coffee shop like this would be an amazing employer, and Babs seemed like the ideal boss.

While Ellie desperately wanted to keep working from home, available remote jobs were few and far between. Most required special licensing, certification, or a ridiculous amount of experience. She had no choice but to apply for positions in a physical office with a real boss watching over her shoulder or micromanaging her every task. Oh, how she dreaded that transition.

Still, it beat that boss being Averie. Her sister had always had one over her in every aspect of life. Averie now controlling her schedule and paycheck made her want to vomit. She had to find another option and fast.

"You two have a great day, and take care of that grandmother of yours," Babs said to Warren and waved a farewell.

Ellie held her breath again when they came to the main intersection in town, but relaxed her shoulders when Warren turned in the proper direction.

She swung her purse over her shoulder and cradled the piping hot latte in her hands as she climbed down from the truck. The temps had to be in the mid-eighties already, warranting a cold drink. But this caramel treat was one of the best drinks she'd ever had in her life. The brew managed a level of flawlessness the big chain joints back home couldn't even hope to achieve.

Inside, Warren stopped at the nurse's station to inquire about Marilyn's room number, but Ellie breezed past him. She knew the room number, unlike Marilyn's *actual* family.

He dropped his conversation with the nurse midsentence and hurried to catch up to Ellie.

"You know where you're going?" he asked.

"I told you. I've been here before." She scowled over her shoulder. "You know, as part of my scheme to take your grandmother for all she's got, I came to visit her while she was laid up in the rehab unit like a proper con artist would."

With an eye roll, she rounded the corridor and knocked on Marilyn's open door. Their arrival kept Warren from any comeback. Thank the Lord.

When the older woman's voice beckoned them inside, Warren brushed past Ellie, his fierce blue eyes staring her down as he went.

"Get over here." Marilyn waved for her grandson and took hold of his arm, tugged him down to her level, and kissed him on the cheek, both hands sandwiching his face. "You look good, kid. You finally shaved. I like it."

"Too hot for a beard." He stuffed his hands into his pockets and crossed one foot over the other as he leaned on the wall beside Marilyn's chair. "You look good too, for being captive in a nursing home. Brought you something."

"Oh, heavenly marshmallowy goodness! Warren, you magnificent angel." She took a long whiff and closed her eyes. "I've asked for one of these countless times since I arrived, but they look at me like I'm in a loony bin and not rehab center. Why would they not run our errands to help us recover faster?"

Warren shook his head. "Well, you can thank Babs for this one. She says to feel better soon."

"Warren, I love that woman. She is a saint, and the next time you see her, you give her a hug for me. I don't care if you have to climb out of the truck and through that window. You do it. And that daughter of hers is a treasure too. You can hug Tori for me too while you're at it. I'm sure she'll be out to see you soon."

He scratched the back of his head. "I'm not so sure about—"

"Do it, Warren." Her multi-ringed finger could have stabbed through his chest if she'd applied the proper pressure. "That girl does so much for my animals when you're away. You just gotta hug her for it."

"Sure, Gram. Whatever. Now, are you ready to tell me what happened to you this week?"

The older woman didn't miss a beat.

"Tripped over a shovel in the garden." Marilyn swiveled away from Warren and winked in Ellie's direction. "Come have a seat on the bed so we can talk, Ellie. Warren, I appreciate this beverage with my every breath, but my business today is with this young woman. You gotta leave."

"I just got here." His shoulders sank.

Marilyn reached out and squeezed his hand. "And I love you for it, darlin'. You can come back in a little while. We've plenty of time for chatting over the next month, and I'll need to discuss this barn repair plan in greater detail before you go pulling some fancy renovation like on TV."

Warren huffed and stared hard at Ellie again. She averted her gaze, tired of his accusing expression. Today, Marilyn could clear everything up, the mysterious secret would come out, and Ellie could get back to the farm and start getting her Ohio life together instead of treading water in this Montana life.

Ellie reached into her purse and handed Marilyn a small plastic shopping bag containing mail and her cell phone from the garden. "Found it next to the daisies. Doesn't appear to have any damage from being outside."

"Oh, thank you. This will make communication so much easier. The nurses weren't happy about me asking for the phone all the time," Marilyn said.

"You had her phone?" Warren's face scrunched.

Ellie plopped down on the bed and drew her knees up into her. "She asked me to find it for her, so I did."

He gave her that same stupid look that made her want to deck him. "Did you do anything to—"

"Warren Michael, I will talk with you in a little bit." Marilyn's stern tone made Ellie straighten. She seemed like one of those people who didn't get mad very often, but you wanted to do whatever you had to do to keep her happy.

"Don't you have some other errands you can run? Surely, we didn't hit them *all* this morning," Ellie suggested.

"As a matter of fact, I do have more places to go. I'll grab some groceries and come back for you, *Ellie*," he said.

"Thanks. I'd appreciate that." She picked at her fingernails in her lap and waited for him to leave already.

When his footsteps had cleared the room, Marilyn reclined in her chair. Her cool composure returned, and she smiled. "Oh, he likes you."

Ellie groaned, but her cheeks burned anyway. "He most definitely does not. He thinks I'm a con artist here to steal your family fortune or some such garbage, which I would appreciate you clearing up with him. He started in on it this morning, like he was up all night Googling 'is the girl living in my tiny house here to steal our souls' or something."

Why was she rambling? Letting him get to her like this was letting him win. And he should *not* win, because he was wrong.

Marilyn shook her head. "That sounds like my grandson. Don't worry. I'll have a talk with him. You're my first and last Airbnb guest, so don't bother leaving me a bad review based on his poor behavior."

"Yes, ma'am." Ellie laughed, a welcome release after the tense car ride over.

"You should know, Ellie, my daughters still don't know about the Airbnb. After Warren blabs about this, which he will, the rest of the family is sure to flock to the farm to make things right. The boy has always had my best interests in mind, even if he's a turd about it. Poor thing's caught between his mother and me more often than not. Either way he goes, one of us will whoop his ass red." Marilyn picked up her paper cup and took a sip. "I sure do love that boy. And you will too, with some time."

Huh? Ellie's heart sped up again. Perhaps that was just some odd old people saying—like the weird "cheese" thing she said at their first meeting. But to imply Ellie would end up enjoying Warren's company or *liking* him… Yeah, no.

And if Marilyn meant to imply that Ellie would eventually *love* love him. That'd be—well, that'd be as effed up as the rest of this trip had been. Of all the supposedly eligible bachelors presented to her since arriving, she'd date the rooster before she'd go for Warren Oliver.

"I'm sure he's very nice when he's not questioning someone's integrity." Ellie resumed picking at the skin next to her thumbnail. "Also, Warren and Hardware Store Barry were also talking about how if your daughters got wind of the Airbnb, there'd be big trouble. What kind of trouble are we talking about?"

"Isn't Barry fantastic? One of the best of fellows. Anyway, you let me deal with my daughters. I told Savannah not to come, so we're safe there. She's a busy woman. And Janey only comes at Christmas." Marilyn's words lacked the confidence Ellie desired. The way she instantly checked her phone also proved a bit alarming. Like the very mention of her daughters might summon a phone call or something. "How are my animals? Any problems?"

Ellie nearly choked on her sip. "Well, that's a loaded question. They're all alive and fine. I had to chase Edgar and Hilda down the road, but your neighbor helped me get him back home."

"Edgar?" Marilyn cocked her head.

"Oh, sorry. The donkey. I didn't know his name, so that's what I've been calling him."

She laughed. "That's cute. I'm going to keep that in mind for next time. It's actually Sheriff Humphrey—Sheriff for short. He's in charge 'round these parts. That's why I gave him such a name. Kind of a stinker though, isn't he? I should have warned you he occasionally remembers he can lift the latch on that back gate. Doesn't happen all the time, but when it does, it's loads of fun. Glad my neighbor came to your aid. They're good people down there."

"Yes, I was glad he came when he did. I didn't know how else I'd get Ed—Sheriff back home otherwise."

"Apples." Marilyn clicked her tongue and tapped her index finger to her temple. "That muckinfuzz will do anything for an apple. I've led him home many a times that way."

Ellie would have to make sure she kept some fruit in stock or found Marilyn's current stash. Then again, Blake was prepared to come to help whenever necessary, and loading Sheriff up in the trailer struck her as a much easier solution than walking all over the county with an apple in hand.

She shifted in her seat when she thought about the prospect of Blake visiting again that afternoon. It wouldn't allow for much work time. But what else was new? His presence would offset Warren's and give her much more pleasurable company…and a chance to get to know him a little better.

"Apples, okay. Good to know." Ellie cleared her throat. "Any tips on calming your attack rooster?"

Marilyn's brow furrowed when she regarded her company. "I don't believe I have a rooster."

Warren had sounded equally surprised when Ellie brought up the demon bird. "Well, there's definitely a rooster on the farm—blue and orange coloring, stands taller than all the chickens, big red comb on top of his head, beak like a dagger."

"Sounds like a rooster, all right." Marilyn laughed. "Sometimes those blamed things show up uninvited. If the neighbors pop by again, have them take him. They'll figure out where he belongs. My hens don't need a man. They know those bad-boy types are nothin' but trouble."

"Preach," Ellie said.

It was impossible to spend any amount of time with Marilyn and not love the woman a little more. As much as Ellie hadn't wanted to take this trip with Warren, it definitely beat rewording one more cover letter for a job that would likely never even acknowledge receiving her resume in the first place.

Ellie took another long drink of her latte. The air-conditioning had already cooled the drink significantly since their arrival. "Well, since we got that taken care of and Warren's not here to butt in, I have to admit, I'm very curious about this favor you need from me. What do you—?"

"Oh, that boy. You know, he's a lot like my late husband in some ways: suspicious, hardworking, stubborn. So, so stubborn. But Warren's much more amiable than Sam was." Marilyn's eyebrows rose as she took another sip.

Her late husband must have been a beast. Still, an odd thing to say about one's lifelong mate. Not to mention, a drastic change in subject. "Okay…?"

Marilyn sighed. "It's tough to explain. It's almost like… Well, have you ever loved someone, only to realize that you never *liked* them?"

"More like the opposite, maybe." In fact, her most recent relationship with Sean fit that bill.

"Liked someone without love?" Marilyn asked.

Ellie bit at her nail now. "Sort of. My last boyfriend—a guy I broke up with shortly before coming on this trip, actually—was one of the nicest men on the planet. He'd give the shirt off his back to anyone in need. We were together for several years, but I just…I felt nothing. And I hate saying that because he was so *good*, and it makes me feel like the worst person ever for ending it."

There she went rambling again. What was it about Marilyn that made Ellie spill her guts? She hadn't said as much to anyone, really. It's not like she could have told Chloe any of this about her brother. Her parents didn't get it. She and her sister definitely didn't speak to each other on this sort of level.

It felt good to confess as much out loud—that she did feel guilty for ending things with Sean. Regret? No. But the guilt had burrowed in deep. He would have moved heaven and earth to help her now in her work and housing peril. For the hundredth time, he'd have invited her to move in with him, save herself the cost of renting. He'd have rearranged the entire optometry office to create a position for her there if she just said the word.

But she couldn't let him do that. She could never give herself up to him in that way, not when her own heart had friend-zoned him, no matter how many wonderful qualities he had.

Marilyn hummed to herself. "You're braver than I was, then."

Brave? No one had ever called her *that*. Cowardice kept her in the relationship to begin with.

Ellie regarded her older companion as she watched out the window, caught up in some memory. The implication itself caught Ellie a bit off guard too. This couldn't be what Marilyn wanted to talk about: that Marilyn's marriage wasn't all sunshine and rainbows.

Without facing her company, Marilyn continued, "I'm sorry again that your vacation isn't what you thought it would be. I can promise you I didn't mean for any of this to happen. I'm still refunding your entire cost, by the way. Took me forever to even post on that Airbnb site in the first place, and we both know damn well I couldn't ask for help."

"It's okay, really." Ellie didn't know what else to say.

"It's not okay. I'm sure you're ready to hightail it out of here and be done with us. I wouldn't blame you for that. And I feel terrible asking you to come again today, but since I've been through the mill this week"—she patted her knee brace—"I wanted to see if you'd help me with something else before the rest of the family investigates me. And they absolutely will, I assure you."

Ellie sat quietly on the bed. All of this screamed of some emotional trap. Marilyn certainly pulled on Ellie's heartstrings. Grandmas did that to her. But if she said yes, it could lead to any number of random things that might suck Ellie deeper into this new world and further away from the work she was *supposed* to be doing.

"It might depend on what it is." Ellie tested that bravery thing. "I don't mean to be disrespectful. Honestly, I don't. But it's kind of sounding like it might be a sensitive family issue, and I'm not sure I'm the person to help, especially if we're already going to be in trouble for the Airbnb fiasco. Plus, with Warren throwing his tantrums about me now, it makes everything—" She groaned. "What I'm trying to say is, he's here now, seems eager to help you, and he's family."

"You're right. My family should be the ones taking care of this." Marilyn sat forward in her chair. "But they're not. When the girls come, they want to tell me I can't do things. That I should be in a home like this rehab unit. They've already sent me a million brochures for places in Spokane and insist on moving me soon. They're probably thrilled this happened, truth be told. Moves their plot along."

"Don't say that. No one wants their family member to get hurt like this." Ellie didn't know the people directly, but they couldn't be *that* heartless.

Marilyn frowned. "No, they don't want me injured. But having me out there by myself on that big farm makes them feel responsible for me. They can't really be free to live their lives as long as I'm here doing my own thing. Doesn't matter how many times I tell them I'm fine. They want the farm out of their hands and me planted safely under the care of somebody else. It's no fun when someone thinks they know what's best for you and expects you to follow along without a fuss."

No, it really wasn't.

Marilyn brushed her wrinkled finger across the nursing home patch on her lap blanket. "I don't mean to dump this all on you or guilt you into helping me. I'm trying to tell it like it is. And really, Ellie, I'm okay with giving up the farm and living here, but I want to do it on *my* terms and in *my* time. I don't want anyone telling me what to do like I'm not capable of making my own decisions."

"That makes sense." Too much sense.

Marilyn glanced around her room and smiled. "To be honest, this place hasn't been nearly as bad as I expected it to be. The steak is a little chewy, bingo goes slow enough to put you to sleep, and they keep denying my request to get my baths from Connor down in food services." She flicked her feather earring flirtatiously. "But there are plenty of people to talk to here, and that's what I miss the most while living on my own. Even with the animals, I get lonely out there sometimes."

Ellie's eyes misted. "Is that why you tried to open an Airbnb?"

"You know what they say about the best-laid plans." She nestled into her chair and sighed. "But the reason I asked you here is because I've got a good many irons in the fire there at the farm, and I could use some help. Woman to woman, I'd rather Warren stayed out of this, if you're catching what I'm throwing."

Ellie chuckled. She had no idea what Marilyn was *throwing*. "What do you need me to do?"

Somehow, in the course of their 20-minute visit, Ellie'd gone from apprehensive to fully invested in whatever Marilyn's next mission required of her. Marilyn could ask for a kidney, and Elle would pop one out for her. The older woman needed a friend. Ellie just so happened to find herself in need of the same thing.

It didn't hurt that part of proposition involved leaving Warren high and dry either...

Marilyn's gray-blue eyes lit with excitement. "Thank you, Ellie. I appreciate you more than I could say. God will have a special place in heaven for you for helping an old woman out." She took hold of Ellie's hand, giving it a squeeze. "I'll make sure you have full access to the house, and my truck is yours for the driving. But it's very important you don't tell Warren what you're doing. He wouldn't understand it all, and I'm not ready to explain it to him. In time, he'll know. For now, I'm going to make you a list."

"All right..." Instant regret.

The older woman held tighter to her guest. "First, and most importantly, I'm going to need you to bring me the liver from my freezer."

– 10 –

It took all of sixteen whole driving minutes before Warren changed his mind about the country music station, shut it off, and shifted to rest his arm on the center console. "That was the second strangest morning of my life, you know that? Yesterday being the first. Gram wants you to have access to the house for some reason. She's giving you her car keys so you can come visit her without me. And she insists that I have to treat you like a queen or suffer the consequences, even though I'm her grandson and you're a complete stranger."

"If any of it made any sense to *me*, I'd love to enlighten you." Ellie crossed one leg over the other and tugged at the seatbelt hell-bent on strangling her.

"And all that time you spent in there alone with her while I went to the store, you didn't *convince* her to make these decisions for you?"

She spun toward him. "Dude, what is your life like that you're this suspicious of me? Are you a lawyer? CIA? What? Marilyn fell and none of your family came to be with her, so I went. That is the connection I have to your grandmother. Got it?"

Warren rubbed his face and focused on the road, which kept that intense stare off her for the time being. Something about those piercing eyes set her on edge. In fact, *everything* about him made her nervous.

"Then do you mind telling me what she wanted to talk to you about in private? Like, what mysterious business did she have with someone she's never met before this week that her flesh and blood couldn't be in the room for?" he asked.

Actually, Ellie very much minded telling him about it. Marilyn had asked her to keep this operation a secret. Though, Ellie hadn't fully reviewed the list Marilyn gave her. She definitely didn't want to do that where Warren could see.

Marilyn said she'd explain it all to him eventually. Until then, Ellie had to keep her promise to a desperate woman and tackle the first request: gathering frozen liver, apparently. It might be something she could keep from Warren—just hopefully not something she had to keep from the police as well…

"She wanted to make sure I was comfortable in the tiny house and apologize for the way things went down." A sly smile crossed her lips. "Oh, and she wanted me to remind you that you were raised better than this."

He rolled his eyes. "So you got her on speed dial then? Just in case I act up?"

Ellie shrugged and watched the mountains meet the prairie in the distance. This guy was impossible to get along with. If Marilyn had been upfront with her family and kept them in the loop, Ellie wouldn't even have to deal with Warren at all. She could go about her own tasks, he could do his work around the farm, and they wouldn't have to speak to each other at all.

"Look." Warren's hand nearly brushed her leg when he gestured. "Priority one is getting this Airbnb listing down and figuring out if there's anyone else signed up to come out here. I'm sure you've got plans of your own or whatever, but if you could help me with that, I'd appreciate it."

Assisting Warren would push back her visit with Blake a little longer, but surely, he'd understand. Hell, Blake would know the family way better than Ellie did and by way, what a massive, demanding pain in the ass Warren was.

His hand still dangled onto her side, finger inches from touching her knee. Ellie shifted to keep out of reach. "Great segue from accusing me to requesting my assistance. Really. Very well done."

"Would it help if I said *please*?" His sarcastic tone made him seem juvenile, immature, and other bad adjectives. "I know nothing about that site, and you obviously found Gram's listing. I'll take a night off your bill or whatever it is hotels do for guests they need favors from."

Ellie couldn't be certain, but she thought she caught a hint of blush color his cheeks. She had to face the window again so he didn't see her evil smirk. Marilyn must not have passed along the information that she planned to waive the entire stay.

"Fine. I'll help you take it down, then I have to tend to my own work. Y'all are killing my schedule with your 'favors.'" Now, *she* blushed a little. They had to stop using that oddly suggestive word.

"Deal." Warren turned down another country road, and the terrain grew bumpier. "After we get home, unload these groceries, and kill my grandmother's entrepreneurial spirit, you can be free to go back to whatever boring computer job you have. I won't bother you anymore."

"Wow. Dreams really do come true," Ellie said.

Ellie sat a case of Pepsi on the counter and instinctively put the deli meat in the refrigerator like she knew exactly where it went. Warren squeezed past her to place a few beers in the vegetable drawer, forcing Ellie against the wall to avoid touching him.

"Want one?" he asked.

"Nope." She inched along the wall to move freely again.

He grabbed one for himself and nodded for her to follow him. "Then come on."

Warren pulled the rolling chair out from the secretary's desk and motioned for Ellie to have a seat in front of an old laptop. She slumped into the chair and opened Marilyn's computer. Either Warren didn't know how to use a computer, or he was one of those d-bags who enjoyed bossing people around. Either way, Ellie didn't feel like arguing anymore. A few clicks on Airbnb's website, and Marilyn would be off the hook with her family. That had to be one task listed on the sheet in her pocket.

Ellie navigated the login page. Luckily, Marilyn's username and password had been saved to the site, so Ellie didn't have to rely on Warren's help for that or call Marilyn to get it. Warren occupied himself with flipping through Marilyn's calendar.

"Well, according to this," he said, "I'm not expected to arrive here until July 15, even though we agreed on June 15 multiple times. Other than that, there aren't any more names listed, unless she forgot to write them down or mixed up those dates too." He flipped the datebook shut and dropped it onto the desktop with a smack. "You really came on this trip all by yourself? Or are there more of you hanging around here somewhere?"

Ellie clenched her jaw and focused on removing the property from the listings.

She just *had* to search for secluded locations out in the middle of nowhere…

"If you won't talk to me, I guess I'll go put the rest of these drinks in the barn fridge. I'll let you know if I find any of your friends." Warren returned to the dining room, grabbed a case of beer, and headed out the front door without another word.

It was high school study hall all over again, where Mrs. Patterson walked the aisles for the full hour, inspecting everyone's desk and scolding them if they did anything but homework or studying.

And now the crotchety observer had gone off to the barn, leaving her totally alone in the house. It was too bad she couldn't get a job delisting Airbnb rentals and completing to-do lists for the elderly because her resume was soon to be flooded with experience.

Ellie slumped in her chair and pulled out her phone to dictate a message to Blake.

> Ellie: Hey, I'm going to have to take a raincheck on this after-noon. Marilyn's grandson showed up, and he's making everything difficult.

Warren's appearance certainly put a damper on things. On one hand, it kept her from getting to know Blake better—which could be a good or bad thing, depending on how she looked at it. Ellie had very little interest in a rebound relationship, especially after the amount of courage it took to get single again. However, if an attractive neighbor wanted to pop by and hang out for a few hours here and there, it wouldn't be the worst thing. A little tryst could also provide some escape from her sucky life.

> Blake Robinson-Neighbor: You must mean Warren. And that sounds about right. We'll find another time when he's gone then.

Ah, finally. Someone who got it.

Ellie swiveled the chair to examine the room. An assortment of "stuff" cluttered the space, with even more décor covering the walls. It made her think of those hidden pictures puzzles from the *Highlights* magazines she loved as a kid.

Might as well find out what sort of tasks Marilyn had planned out for her while she had a minute away from Warren's prying eyes.

She pulled the list out of her pocket and squinted to read the tiny writing. Marilyn had arranged one of the weirdest scavenger hunt chore lists Ellie had seen in her adult life.

ELLie's To-Do List—NOT FOR WARREN'S EYES!

1. LIVER!!!

2. Bring me the gold locket from the hidden drawer in my jewelry box (downstairs bedroom).

3. Make sure the creeping Charlie doesn't kill my zinnias.

4. Get me my pocketbook, checkbook, and laptop from the desk.

5. Pack a bag of my clothing from the bedroom drawers. The bird patterns have run their course. (Skip the undies. We don't need to get that close, dear.)

6. Find the TOP SECRET envelope hidden in the living room.

7. If a Shannon Tipton shows up at the farm, chase her off. Use whatever you have to: pitchfork, donkey dung, violent threats. Dealer's choice.

8. Eat the cheese in the fridge before it goes bad.

9. Bring me the trinket box from the bookshelf.

10. Don't butcher any chickens yet.

Ellie's eyes went wide. Marilyn had given her a lot to process… and something to snack on. Some requests made sense, some dripped with mystery. Others were downright terrifying.

While she couldn't justify throwing some poor animal's (she hoped) organ into a cooler until right before she left to visit Marilyn again, the laptop, purse—er, pocketbook— and checkbook were in sight. Might as well gather some of those things and get started crossing items off the agenda.

Ellie slipped the paper back into her pocket and gathered

everything in her arms. It took a minute to seek out the bedroom around the corner from the living room. She sat the computer and purse on the bedspread while she hunted down a suitcase or anything that might hold all the accumulated items. Hanging in the closet, she found a black duffel bag, possibly from the 1800s from the looks of it.

That only left the clothes and the locket, which had to be important since it got its own line on the to-do list.

Ellie began rifling through the lone jewelry box on the dresser and the excess of mismatched costume jewelry. Finally, a small notch on the side of the box revealed the hidden drawer with a discolored envelope tucked inside. In her outstretched hand, she dumped the contents, revealing a faded locket, the latch broken in a way that left the oval necklace open like a book.

The old black-and-white photo before her made Ellie grin. A young man in shorts much shorter than she'd ever seen anyone her age wear held a laughing woman draped over his shoulder. He beamed. Maybe because he adored her; maybe because his hand was on her butt. Maybe both.

Ellie leaned into the sunlight coming in through the window to get a better look at the image. The woman had the same smile as Marilyn. Her eyes crinkled the same way too, when she laughed. Behind the couple, a white picket fence ran in front of a dark barn. That had to be here, on *this* farm.

The trinket seemed a strange thing to keep hidden away, unless the gold chain held enough worth Marilyn feared thieves might take it. Regardless, the older woman might enjoy the image of her and her husband during happier, simpler times to get her through the waiting process of nursing home life.

"What are you doing?" Warren stood in the entrance between the two rooms.

Ellie stumbled to her feet, the tattered envelope slipping to the floor beside her. The long necklace chain dangled through her fingers, and she instinctively clasped it to her chest.

"I leave you for five minutes, and you start snooping around and collecting Gram's jewelry?" He set his beer can on the nightstand and approached the bed where Ellie had placed Marilyn's other belongings beside the open duffle bag. "Please tell me again how you're not here to rob my grandmother."

"That's not what I'm doing at all." Ellie's back dug into the dresser. Every truth sounded so ridiculous she couldn't bring herself to confess it.

"I'm waiting for whatever new excuse you've got, but if you can't come up with something *really good*, you're out of here. I'm so done with this." Warren retrieved his phone from his pocket and swiped across the screen.

Ellie pinched her eyes shut. She'd have to beg Marilyn's forgiveness later, but she sure as hell wasn't going to jail over some stupid misunderstanding. Whatever secret Marilyn had, it couldn't have pertained to simple personal belongings.

"Marilyn asked me to bring her the stuff from her desk and some clothes from her bedroom," she blurted. "She gave me a list."

"She needs all her jewelry too? For all those black-tie events at the nursing home?" He kept his phone outstretched in his palm like a threat.

She might as well pack her bags and start contemplating conversation topics to discuss with her cellmate. "Actually, yes, jewelry. Well, a locket. Take it if you want it. It's all yours." Ellie held the necklace out for him. "I'm done with all this too. I'm sick of you accusing me for simply trying to help her. It's just a picture of her and your grandfather. Not as mysterious and pressing as she made it seem."

Warren snatched the necklace out of her hand and stepped back to inspect the antique. His brow furrowed when he squinted to get a better look at the tiny image. "Huh."

An odd response to a family relic. But it didn't matter. Ellie was ready to get the hell out of there if his wide shoulders weren't block-ing the exit, because she certainly wasn't going to touch him and *make* him move.

"It might be," he added.

"Might be what?" She cursed herself for inquiring, rather than ignoring him and leaping out the window.

"It might be mysterious. She asked for this specifically?" He spun the necklace's image around for Ellie to see again.

She growled. "Yes!"

"Because that is *not* my grandfather."

- 11 -

"DAMN IT, WOMAN. ANSWER the phone." Warren clicked End on his call again. "I'll try the nursing home's number."

Ellie sank into her chair. "That's great. You keep trying, buddy. Can I leave now?"

"No. You sit until I have answers." He held out a finger to keep her in place and dialed another number. "Yeah, hi. Can I speak to Marilyn Perry in 34, please?"

A small yellow bird shot out of the cuckoo clock on the wall and did a lunch hour dance.

Warren hadn't exactly held her there with any force, but she was pretty sure if she left, he'd just follow her until he got the answers he desired. Besides, she wanted some answers too. Leaving would be like turning off a soap opera right before the heroine came back from her honeymoon and found her previously dead ex-husband in bed with her sister. Grandma Val never would have approved of abandoning a storyline during a scene like *that*.

In honor of her late grandmother, she'd wait until *after* Warren found out who this mystery guy was, then maybe she should consider packing up and heading home. Even though she'd have to start working with Averie immediately, she could at least start packing up her apartment in the evenings and cover more ground searching jobs and housing on foot. The stress levels might be about the same in both places...

Warren put the phone on speaker and set it down next to the

computer. He shuffled through papers on the desk, looking for answers. On the other end of the phone, a muffled voice told Marilyn she had a call.

"I didn't answer my phone for a reason, Warren," came Marilyn's gruff voice.

Warren cursed and side-eyed his phone on the desktop. "How long are you going to ignore me? I've got questions, Gram. It's kind of important."

"I'll talk to Ellie if you're going to take that tone with me, boy. Put her on."

Ellie wouldn't get out of this as easily as she thought. In the past few days, she'd become Marilyn's favorite person, even above her own family. Though Ellie kind of felt the same, come to think of it.

"Gram, she was going through your jewelry box. She found this necklace—"

"So help me, Warren Michael, if you don't leave that girl alone, I'll bust out of this nursing home and string you up in the cornfield," Marilyn scolded.

A muffled nurse on the other end of the line tried to calm her patient, but Marilyn hushed her.

"This is stupid, Gram. Come on." Warren picked up a random stack of papers and relocated them on the desk. "None of this is normal. You realize that, right? We don't even know this woman, yet you're giving her full access to your house and letting her go through your things? And who is this guy in the locket? What's with all the secrets between you and Ellie that I'm supposedly not privy to?"

"Simmer down, hoss." Marilyn sighed on the other end. "Let me talk to her. I'll talk to *you* later."

Warren's head fell into his hands, and he muttered a string of barely audible swears. "This is getting ridiculous. I cannot even believe this is my life right now."

"Yeah, this must be so difficult for *you*." Ellie stood, her shoulder crashing into Warren's when she passed him. "I'll just go. I'm done."

"Don't let her leave!" Marilyn shrieked on the other end of the phone.

"I'll call you later, Marilyn." Ellie shouted on her way out the door.

Warren didn't follow. Thank God. Ellie made it all the way outside without resistance, minus the jumping Hilda, who tried to knock her to the ground the second she stepped foot onto the porch. Ellie didn't even bother looking around for the rooster. This would be a bad day for him to try messing with her.

Hilda chased Ellie all the way across the drive to the tiny house, where Ellie slammed the door and flipped the lock. It probably didn't matter though. Warren had a key.

Going home early under the radar and spending some quiet time locked away in her own bedroom with Netflix, ice cream, and no human interaction might be the pity party she needed right now. That's why she wanted this spontaneous vacation in the first place.

Ellie pulled out her phone and dialed Marilyn's number. She only meant to offer a formal apology for not completing the assigned tasks and hand everything over to Warren. There was no reason to fight a battle on two fronts.

"Ellie, why do I feel like I'm always apologizing for that boy?" Marilyn asked right away.

"Because he's being an ass. No offense." She climbed the narrow stairway on her hands and knees, Hilda close behind. "I'm so sorry, but I can't do your list. I shouldn't be getting between family like this."

Marilyn paused on the other end, and Ellie braced herself for some sassy lecture. She'd end up getting death threats like Warren at this rate.

"I understand, sweetie," Marilyn whispered.

Huh? That was way too easy.

Ellie sank to the mattress. A calm, non-deadly response was the last thing she'd expected. "You do?"

Hilda flopped onto the pillow and rolled to her back. She panted with glee, her tongue swinging from one side of her mouth to the other.

"I know I put you in a strange position. If I hadn't fallen, none of this would have happened. And if I'd remembered Warren was coming in June instead of July, everything would have gone so much smoother." A deep sigh proved how those words hurt her to say. "I don't blame you for wanting to get out of here. I feel bad for ruining your trip. That was never my intention. I hope you know that."

Ellie fell to the mattress, her hand resting over her heart. "I'm so sorry you got hurt." And that her family hadn't come to help her. And that her grandson had caused extra drama. And that Ellie couldn't help the way they'd planned.

The list went on and on.

"My family was probably right about me getting too old to have animals, but who wants to admit that? I'd have sooner let them take my car than my critters." Marilyn chuckled. "I'm not as forgetful and useless as they think I am though. Did you know I canned two hundred and eight jars of fruits and vegetables last fall all on my own? I even figured out that rental website with no help. And it would have been successful too. The only hitch was getting into that damn loft to change the bedsheets. Honestly, I don't care for heights, and that wretched thing needs some railings. I blame the contractor for the terrible construction flaw."

Ellie smiled over the newest jab at Warren. "I do really like this house. In other circumstances, it would have been the perfect getaway." She slid to the floor, where she began folding clothes. "I really appreciate you opening your farm up to me."

"My pleasure, dear. Regardless of whether I'm on the website, you're welcome here anytime. Well, until my daughters take over and sell the place off. May not be the most welcoming stay after that point."

Ellie had never thought too hard on what it'd be like to get old. Slowly, your independence disappears, and you become someone else's decision. You lose your ability to make your own choices, select your own path, even live on your own property.

Was thirty-two the new eighty-two?

"Yeah, that's hard." Ellie paused her task and fell back to look out the skylight. "Tell me about your daughters."

Why did she do this to herself? The less she knew about the older woman, the easier it'd be to get away. Still, Ellie would give anything to talk to Grandma Val again, and here was another loveable grandmother craving conversation.

Marilyn laughed. "Warren's mother, Savannah, is my oldest. She's always been headstrong and a real go-getter. The second she graduated high school, she ran off to Spokane to live the big city life. She's an executive now in some computer firm, but I couldn't even tell you what it is she does there. It keeps her busy—so busy I don't see her more than once or twice a year if I'm lucky."

Ouch. No wonder Marilyn got lonely enough to rent out a space on the farm to get some human interaction.

"And your other daughter?" Ellie asked.

"Janey followed her sister to Spokane, but not because they're chummy. I'd hoped for them to be, but they've got their father's competitive spirit. Anything Savannah did, Janey could do it better. Oh, Janey and Savannah talk, but it's mostly over my welfare and what they should do with me. Janey's really pushing for me to sell the farm already and move on. There's quite a bit of equity built up here, and land is in high demand. I see their point; I'm not stupid. But I'm not ready yet either. I'm only eighty-two, and this is my home." Marilyn sighed. "I've got memories built up here, and I need to sort through those before I let the past go. I've been working on a little mission, you see."

"A mission?"

"The man in that photo you found is John Clay." Though Ellie couldn't see her, she heard Marilyn's smile loud and clear through the phone. "He was my first love."

"Oh." That explained the joyful expression on young Marilyn's face—and the discreet way Marilyn hid these sorts of trinkets around the house after being married to someone else.

Marilyn giggled. "We had grand plans of getting married after graduation and having a brood of kids here on this farm. It was his family's property, you know. But my parents and his parents hated one another—something about business deals gone wrong. Everything John and I did had to be done in secret, usually sneaking off around the property. Eventually, though, his family moved away, and we were forbidden to see one another. My late husband, Sam, bought the farm from them. That's how we met."

She paused long enough to sigh deeply, then continued. "I felt like such a traitor, but John had written to me and told me to move on—said it was better for both of us that way. It broke my heart, Ellie. But I married Sam because my parents wanted me to, and our life here on the farm was all laid out for us. Those were different times back then. You did what your family thought best above the call of your heart."

Ellie inched toward the stairs and scooted down the steps one by one, her free hand pressed to her heart. "Are you trying to find him? Is that your mission?"

Out the window, Ellie spotted Warren on his way to the barn. He'd changed into his work clothes and didn't even look toward her house as he went.

"There are many John Clays around the world, according to my searches. It's hard to peg him down after all these years." Marilyn paused before her voice grew more determined. "Before I go—whether it be my children or Death who takes me—I'd love to get a hold of him, maybe bring him back to the farm so I could show him how I've cared for it all these years in his absence. I know that sounds silly, but—"

"No. Not silly at all." Tears pricked at Ellie's eyes. The farm was a special place, and now she knew why. "Is that what the top secret envelope is on my to-do list?"

Marilyn hummed. "And the locket and trinket box. How does one explain to her grandson or daughters that she's kept letters and gifts from an old flame all these years? That I've never really stopped loving John? The envelope has what little research I've been able to accomplish."

"I see." She retrieved the list from inside her shorts pocket. "And Shannon Tipton? How does she play into this?"

Marilyn snorted. "She doesn't. That nightmare of a woman is a local realtor who has popped by the farm almost weekly for the last year, practically begging me to let her sell it. I don't want her around. When I am ready to sell, I will not be partnering with her to do it. I don't care that she's my great niece. It's not happening."

Ellie couldn't suppress her laugh. "Marilyn, I don't think I'd want you as my enemy. I am happy we had this talk though."

She could almost see the older woman's warm smile through the phone. "Any chance my sob story persuaded you not to hightail it out of state?"

Oh, Marilyn.

As much as Ellie hated interacting with the pompous grandson who was absolutely convinced she was a terrible person, this mission-of-the-heart might be just the thing to put some spark back into her life after a failed romance of her own. "I think it did. But under one condition."

"Whatever you want, kid."

"Get Warren off my back, would you?" Ellie begged.

"I will try my best," Marilyn agreed. "It's going to take some courage on my part to talk to him about this, Ellie. I need you to understand that. We have to take life by the horns, you and me. I think we both need that right now."

Those words couldn't have been any truer. With Warren calmed, the prospect of an old love interest to dig up, and her vacation back on, Ellie might be able to get things on track again.

"One more question," Ellie began. "Why did you tell me not to butcher the chickens yet?"

Marilyn paused long enough that Ellie thought she might have actually hung up, and then, "Were you getting anxious to start on that?"

"No! Oh my goodness, no!"

The older woman howled. Of course, that's why she added such a request to a simple to-do list: pure amusement.

"I don't eat my chickens, Ellie. Just their eggs. If you can't keep up with them, feel free to take the extras to Barry at the hardware. His family could eat egg salad sandwiches for days if given the chance."

Eggs. Duh. Chickens laid eggs. That was definitely a thing chickens did.

Marilyn hadn't exactly included it in her initial instruction either. Life in Columbus only required gathering eggs from the refrigerated section at the supermarket.

"Yep, I'll totally have time for that," Ellie said.

– 12 –

SYMPTOMS MAY BE DECREASED *with proper medication, surgery, or diet and lifestyle changes.*

Ellie glanced at the clock in the corner of her laptop screen. According to her calculations, it only took four days to type up a thirty-minute lecture. Perhaps that was the main reason why they wanted to eliminate the freelance employees.

She groaned. Next up, she needed to hunt down where the chickens laid their eggs because it wasn't happening in the barn.

From her window seat, Ellie watched Warren exit the main farmhouse and load some lumber into his pickup truck. This time, he *did* offer a quick glance toward the tiny house. Ellie ducked in case he had super vision and could make out details from such a distance.

He patted Hilda on the head, got in the truck, and took off. It didn't matter where he'd gone. Nothing was close by, and his absence bought her some time alone.

Ellie swiped across her phone screen to check her messages again. She'd neglected to respond to the last few from her mother and sister—more about Averie's success at the Miami conference and struggle with childcare arrangements, a guilt-trippy reminder that her niece and nephews missed her and wanted her to spend all day every day with them, and a screenshot of a sad quote Sean shared on Facebook.

Oh, and there was a fun one from her cousin Penny after six months of silence:

Penny: I heard you broke up with Sean???? 1. What is wrong with you? 2. Can I have him???

Ellie rested her cheek in her palm and watched the tranquil farm scene out the window. She tried to imagine a young Marilyn hand-in-hand with John as they snuck around the property Romeo-and-Juliet style.

What would have changed if Marilyn had gone down the path she wanted most back then rather than followed the direction set forth by her family?

Ellie browsed the assignment queue again: absolutely nothing.

She switched over to her email, but no one had responded to her most recent applications, just a few new suggestions on open positions she could apply for: police officer, radiology specialist, mechanic.

Made sense.

This day required a strong distraction.

Holding her breath, she typed out a new message:

Ellie: What do you know about gathering eggs out from under chickens possibly guarded by a killer rooster?

The response came almost immediately.

Blake Robinson-Neighbor: That's my specialty. ;) Be right over.

Though she'd been the one to make the plans, she hadn't left enough time to prepare for them. Ellie shut her computer and hurried to the bathroom to fix her hair and make sure her mascara hadn't smudged. She did not need her cosmetics making her look any more haggard than she already felt.

Ellie chugged her remaining iced coffee, straightened her fitted

T-shirt over her cargo shorts, and slipped on her Keds. She'd save Marilyn's boots for another time—one that was less date-y.

Within moments, Hilda's bark signaled a new arrival, and Ellie's heart sped up.

Blake parked his truck and greeted Ellie with a smile. "Glad to hear from you. Wasn't sure you were going to invite me out again while you were here."

Ellie closed the front door behind her. "Well, it got a little hectic here, what with Marilyn being laid up and her wretched grandson making an appearance."

"Ah, Warren. He too afraid of this rooster to help you?" Blake snickered and nodded for Ellie to come with him to the barn.

"More like I refuse to ask him for help. We don't exactly get along."

From the front porch, Hilda watched the pair walk the dusty drive. She didn't bother coming out to say hello, perhaps noticing their path to rooster territory.

"Nobody gets along with Warren Oliver. That's why he moved away all those years ago." Blake led Ellie between the barn and a shed toward what was obviously a chicken coop—one Ellie hadn't gone looking for since the chickens always met her in the barn.

"That makes sense," she said. It still didn't compute how a sweet and spunky woman like Marilyn could be related to a wet blanket like Warren.

The foul (fowl?) smell wafting from the chicken coop nearly knocked Ellie backward. This task would take a strong stomach. Adding this to her chore regimen might become the worst part of her day.

Excluding Warren interactions, obviously.

"I'd say we've got our work cut out for us, Miss Ellie. You haven't been gathering these every day?" Blake asked.

Ellie shrugged. "I was not aware that I had to. This is all new territory for me. I live in a city."

"Well, City Girl, welcome to farm country." Blake's laugh was cut off by the *cock-a-doodle-doo* of Ellie's nightmares. "You want me to take that bird with me when I go? I'm guessing he's a runaway."

"Yes, please take him. He doesn't belong to Marilyn, and he's without a doubt possessed by demons." Ellie grabbed one of the empty baskets by the coop door and tried not to gag on each breath. "You're welcome to take eggs too. I'm not going to eat any of these."

Blake started retrieving the eggs like he'd done it a million times before. Because he had. "I don't think I'd recommend you eat them after they've been sitting out here in this heat all week. We're just going to put them in the compost pile."

This guy really was a gift. Now, if he could come out to the farm *every* day…

"So, you've been keeping in touch with Marilyn? How is the old girl?" He shooed a chicken off her nest and gathered the eggs.

As much as she enjoyed having a friend to talk to, Ellie wished he'd save his questions until they returned to the fresh air. "She's doing very well. If you couldn't see her leg cast, you wouldn't know anything had happened to her."

"She's always been a spunky one. Still kind of figured this would be the type of thing that'd put her in a home for good. This farm is getting to be a lot for a woman of her age. I know there's been considerable interest in this place, and she'd be wise to make some money while the market's hot."

"I think that's how her daughters feel too. Marilyn's not quite ready to throw in the towel though." Ellie grabbed her heaping-full basket and hurried out of the coop to gulp down the fresh air. Unfortunately, this meant she'd have to continue their little "date" smelling of chicken crap and partially rotten eggs. Very sexy.

"Not even for the right price?" Blake gathered Ellie's basket in his arms and weaved between the buildings toward a large, rather smellier pile of trash and other fun excrement.

"This farm means a lot to her. I just know she said she'll sell it when she's ready." They needed a more exciting topic to discuss, but she'd forgotten how to do this. "What animals do you have at your farm?"

Blake dumped the eggs and returned the empty baskets to the coop. "Little of everything. Lot of cattle." The rooster crowed from somewhere close by. "Couple of those fellas, but they don't give us any fits."

Ellie moved nearer to Blake when the paranoia set in. "Really? Because this guy is wildly cranky."

"Might be contagious on this farm." He waggled his eyebrows. "You might want to take some precautions. Keeping clear of Warren will help."

"Oh, I already plan to do that." She giggled. Yes, giggled.

"You met his mother yet? I figured she and Janey would be out to visit, what with Marilyn's condition." A tilt of his head begged Ellie to follow him to his truck and get away from the stench of the chicken coop.

She happily obliged. "No, not yet. I guess Marilyn doesn't really want them to come because they won't be happy about the Airbnb thing. She, um, wasn't really supposed to do that. Well, and she's afraid they'll ship her off to a nursing home over in Spokane and get on with selling the farm."

Blake's hearty laugh filled the farmyard and brought some genuine joy in Warren's absence. Inviting him over in favor of work was the best decision she'd made yet.

"Think they'd do that?" He reached for a large dog cage in the truck bed and dragged it to the edge of the truck bed.

"It sure sounds like they would. I guess they've been wanting that for a while," Ellie said.

"Huh." Blake pointed toward the opposite corner of the truck bed. "Pass me that ratchet strap, would you?"

Ellie bent far enough that she went up on tiptoe to grab the neon orange straps. Blake secured the dog cage to the truck and popped open the latch, readying the cage for when he caught the bird. Presumably.

"Can I get you something to drink or—"

"Oh, no. I really can't stay all that long. I sort of abandoned my task when you texted, so I should probably get back."

She tried to hide her disappointment. It would have been nice to have someone around who knew exactly what they were doing, made good conversation, and added to the attractive scenery. *He* didn't accuse her of anything illegal or make implications. It was very refreshing.

"That's okay. Another time?" she asked.

"Absolutely." He shielded his face from the sun as he surveyed the surroundings. "How long you staying out here? Till Savannah or Janey find you?"

He smirked and leaned on the truck. It was even nice to joke without feeling like it'd backfire horribly.

"Well, we'll see. Couple more weeks if things go according to plan. If they come, who knows? I have to keep my bags packed, I guess." No part of this vacation involved Ellie "taking it easy." Her Montana life would soon catch up with the drama of her Ohio life if she wasn't careful.

Ellie spied Hilda sitting on the porch, watching and waiting. That was, until a large navy-blue SUV coming up the drive caught her attention. This time, she ran toward it like she meant to tackle it straight off the path.

Ellie sighed. "Now what?"

Blake took one quick look at the vehicle and continued on with readjusting the dog cage.

The SUV parked and a woman with a brunette ponytail exited. What if this was that Shannon Tipton, who Ellie was supposed to keep away from the farm? That was one awkward situation she really wanted to avoid. She'd have to ask if Blake minded removing a realtor along with the rooster.

The woman approached, somehow looking extra cute in blue overalls and a scrub top, complete with knee-high rubber boots. She held a small case in one hand. The other hand fished treats out of her pocket to subdue Hilda.

Realtors didn't dress, nor accessorize, in such a way. Not the ones in Columbus, anyway.

"Blake." She nodded her hello and dug into her pocket for another Hilda treat.

"Tori," he said.

Ellie glanced between the pair of them. Neither person smiled nor gave any indication their relationship went beyond knowing the other's name. But at least this wasn't the infamous Shannon.

"Ellie?" Ellie tried to break the tension.

It must have worked, because Tori offered a friendly smile and a hand to shake. "Nice to meet you, Ellie. Mom told me about Marilyn's fall and that she had a guest staying out here. I heard Warren is around too?"

She did a quick sweep of the surroundings but came up empty.

Ellie was forever trying to put the pieces together in Marilyn's absence. "He left a bit ago, but I'm guessing he'll be back soon." The pieces still weren't fitting. "I'm sorry. Who is your mom?"

"Babs from the Daily Brew. She said she met you yesterday at the drive-thru."

Ah, yes. Babs had mentioned her daughter popping over. But why?

"Tori is our resident veterinarian." Blake turned his focus from the dog crate. "If you need anything neutered, she's great at ball crushing."

"Don't you have somewhere you need to be?" Tori's voice bit like a flame, causing Ellie to take a step back. "I highly doubt you can be of much use to anyone *here*."

Blake laughed. "As a matter of fact, I've been helping Miss Reed with some farm chores, and I'm about to collect a loose rooster causing some havoc around here, so I'd—"

"Go about your business, then." Tori took Ellie by the arm and began leading her toward the barn.

"I'll text you later," Blake called after them.

Ellie managed a quick wave and shout of "thank you" before Tori had her completely out of earshot. If he hadn't already stated that his visit would be cut short, Ellie might be angrier.

"What was that all about?" she finally asked when they stepped foot into the barn.

Tori took a deep breath, unbothered by the scent of animal manure. "Sorry. Not a huge fan of Blake Robinson and have some trouble keeping my poker face intact sometimes. But anyway, I'm here to give the sheep their vaccinations and dewormer, check them out, and make sure they're good. I talked with Marilyn prior to coming out about what all they need, so you don't have to worry about it. She said she's overwhelmed you enough as it is."

Living in the city really had nothing on the busyness of Perry Farm. Stepping into Marilyn's life practically required a full-time assistant to keep everything organized.

"She's right about that. I'm not used to juggling…all this." Ellie waved her arms around. "Why aren't you a fan of Blake? He's been very nice."

Nicer than Warren. More helpful than Warren. Less accusatory than Warren.

"I'm sure he's been very helpful." Tori walked to the back gate and yelled, "Sheep sheep!"

Amazingly, moments later, both sheep trotted into the barn. Ellie hadn't even been able to get them to hold still in one place for feeding.

"But?" Ellie leaned against the gate and waited.

"But he's one of those people who does whatever he has to do to get what he wants." Tori prepared her vaccines and coaxing the sheep into place. "Not always in the most upstanding way either."

Ellie had to look away when the needles made their appearance.

She'd have ditched vet school about as quickly as she dropped out of her nursing program.

"Did you guys date or something?" Ellie asked.

"Oh, hell no." She paused and shifted on her rubber boots. "I turned him down for prom senior year. In addition to his family hiring a vet from a much bigger city instead of me, you can say we've got a bit of bad blood between us. *You* aren't dating him, are you?"

While she definitely found Blake attractive, dating him required they spend more than a few minutes together at a time.

"No, I just met him." Ellie rested her chin on her palm as she watched Tori work.

Tori paused and turned her full attention to Ellie. "And was he asking about the farm?"

"Yes. Well, enough to make civil small talk."

Tori rolled her eyes. "Blake's family farms the fields for Marilyn, and they've been trying to buy it from her for a long time, according to my mom. Does Warren know Blake's been coming around?"

The mention of his name soured the conversation even more. "No. Warren and I aren't exactly on friendly speaking terms. He got here a couple days ago, and he's been anything but hospitable."

Tori chuckled as she resumed administering dewormer down a sheep's throat. "I can see that. He's always been a cranky soul. Hard to believe he's Marilyn's relative, huh?"

"That's exactly what I've been saying." It was hard not to like Tori, despite her determination to turn Ellie against Blake.

"My mom and Marilyn used to conspire about setting us up, Warren and me." She shook her head as she put the second sheep in a professional headlock and continued on as if she divulged such information to every client.

This woman had obviously fallen into the ideal profession for her skill set. Why hadn't anything come that easily for Ellie? Nothing ever felt like the right fit.

"They tried to set you up with Warren?" Ellie asked.

"It's a small town. A girl's options are limited." Tori just smiled. "I refused to date any guys I went to high school with. Instead, I married the first man I dated in college. It was a good strategy." She winked at Ellie and packed her bag. "They're all done. I'll leave you with my card in case you have questions while you're here, or, you know, if you need someone to show you around. It's kind of nice to have some fresh blood around here."

"I appreciate that very much. Thank you." Ellie pocketed the card.

"That's my personal cell number on the card, by the way. Seriously, don't hesitate to reach out. My usual interactions are with animals and my two toddlers, so you'll have to forgive my poor social skills."

Ellie laughed. "Well, I've been working remotely for years from the comfort of my living room, so if you can forgive *mine*, it should be all good."

Hopefully the jobs she'd applied to could also forgive said social awkwardness. Her interview for the hospital records room comprised a whole lot of rambling, fidgeting, and dry mouth. No one had called to tell her she *hadn't* gotten the job yet, which seemed like a good sign. Then again, maybe they just wanted to avoid having to talk to her altogether after what they witnessed at the interview.

She'd never get a decent job at that rate.

As Tori returned to her vehicle, now the lone guest car on Perry Farm, Ellie waved goodbye and took in the rare moment of silence around her. Not even a rooster crowed.

Apparently Blake had come through on ridding them of the intruder. So for now, she'd throw the Bilexin ball for Hilda a few times to wear her out, and then park her butt at the desk and try to score another interview.

After all, that's why she was here.

– 13 –

"I HAVE TO GET into the office, but I thought I'd check in and see if your plans had changed at all. My neighbor's high schooler has been watching the kids, but volleyball camp starts soon so I need you," Averie whined.

Ellie's eyes narrowed, and she swallowed the surfacing groan. "I'm still planning to stay the whole time. And, if you recall, I told you about the trip when you asked me to start watching the kids."

"Ellie, do you have any idea how hard it is to find childcare?" Averie loved asking these types of questions that reminded Ellie of their very different life experience. "And I don't get it. If you're as broke as you say you are, how are you paying for this trip? Seems to me like the smart thing to do would be come home and start working. I told you I'd pay you better than your current job."

Averie playing the part of her wealthy savior made Ellie so queasy. "So you've said."

All she wanted was to pull herself up by the bootstraps, settle into a life she felt proud of, and show everyone in her family that she didn't need Sean. But every attempt to set things in order failed. And while she didn't have to spend nearly as much on this trip now that Marilyn had comped the stay—something she didn't intend to share with her sister—it also didn't leave much time to focus on getting things on the right track either.

"I don't get how you're qualified to play farmer either. You know nothing about big animals." Averie laughed.

Ah yes. There were those little Easter eggs of doubt Averie hid in Ellie's brain. "Well, I've managed to keep everyone alive so far."

And speaking of eggs, Ellie either needed to find some good omelet recipes on Pinterest or go visit Hardware Store Barry before her tiny refrigerator burst at the seams. While it wasn't one of her favorite foods, the eggs were free, fresh, and considerably healthier than the cheap convenience stuff she had on hand. That'd be one adult win she could take for herself at least.

"That's impressive, I guess." The shrill chime of Averie's car door signaled that she'd exited her vehicle. "Have you heard anything from Sean since you got out there?"

"I thought you had to go to work now." Not even ailing patients at the family practice could keep Averie from digging a knife into an open wound. Thank God the woman hadn't chosen a surgical specialty.

Background chatter and ringing phones filled Ellie's ear, paired with the faint sound of an oldies station—Family Health's anthem.

"I do, but you know what they say about inquiring minds," Averie said.

"Yeah, I do, but I gotta go. I'm taking Marilyn some stuff from the house." She shouldn't have divulged any details. That'd only invoke more questions.

"What kind of stuff do you have to take her?"

From the window, Ellie spotted Warren leaving the house to work on the barn siding with a bubbly Hilda at his side. Now was a great time to access the house without him breathing down her neck.

"Just some stuff. Have fun at the office. Talk to you later." Ellie hung up. She'd hear about the short goodbye in a text message later, but her mission took precedence over an interrogation.

Head high, Ellie power walked toward the main house and burst through the front door. Finding the suitcase still on the bed, she began regathering all of Marilyn's requested supplies and reviewed the to-do list.

1. LIVER!!!

2. Bring me the gold locket from the hidden drawer in my jewelry box (downstairs bedroom).

3. Make sure the creeping Charlie doesn't kill my zinnias.

4. ~~Get me my pocketbook, checkbook, and laptop to from the desk.~~

5. ~~Pack a bag of my clothing from the bedroom drawers. The bird patterns have run their course. (Skip the undies. We don't need to get that close, dear.)~~

6. Find the TOP SECRET envelope hidden in the living room.

7. If a Shannon Tipton shows up at the farm, chase her off. Use whatever you have to: pitchfork, donkey dung, violent threats. Dealer's choice.

8. Eat the cheese in the fridge before it goes bad.

9. Bring me the trinket box from the bookshelf.

10. ~~Don't butcher any chickens yet.~~

Ellie worked her way to the front room, where she found a floor-to-ceiling bookshelf and began perusing each title. Between *Love in the Time of Cholera* and *Persuasion*, she pulled out a decorative box turned on its side. A quick peek inside revealed Marilyn's treasures: newspaper clippings, ticket stubs, and a small stack of handwritten letters.

She smiled to herself as she closed the box and tucked it securely into the suitcase.

Next, Ellie hunted through the living room for the TOP SECRET envelope. She checked under the couch cushions, in the pile of papers stacked on the coffee table, and throughout the magazine and DVD mountain on the entertainment stand, but still found nothing.

She plucked her phone from her pocket and clicked Marilyn's contact info.

"Ellie," the chipper woman greeted. "Are you coming?"

"I'm packing up your stuff now, but I can't find the TOP SECRET envelope on your list. I've been searching all over the living room and—"

Marilyn swore. "You know what? I don't even know that it *is* in the living room now that you say it, but damn if I can't think of where else I'd have put it. Just forget it and grab the rest of the stuff. I'll let you know when it comes to me. Right now, they're fixing up the bed beside me, and I gotta figure out what in the blazin' they think they're doing."

"Okay. No problem." Ellie laughed. "I'll grab the liver and be on my way."

"Yay liver!" Without a goodbye, Marilyn hung up.

Just as Marilyn had directed, Ellie found a foil lump in the back of the freezer with the word LIVER scribbled across it.

"So gross." Ellie pulled it out, using only two fingers to minimize contact, and grabbed a couple of the ice packs in the freezer door. The last thing she needed was the meat thawing and bleeding all over the truck. A small lunch pail-like cooler on the kitchen counter would carry the *treat* nicely.

The only thing missing was the locket, and Ellie had a pretty good idea where that had gone. With the suitcase zipped, she grabbed the set of car keys hanging by the front door and made her way to the barn where Marilyn's small blue pickup sat near the animals' pen.

Alas, collecting the locket meant yet another interaction with that stubborn ass of a man.

"Hey, douche canoe!" Ellie placed her hand on her hip to balance out the weight of the suitcase. "Where'd you put the locket?"

Warren tossed his drill onto the workbench and approached, his eyes examining her like a detective trying to solve a case. "You leaving town?"

"Sorry to disappoint you, but I'm not. I figured it'd piss you off most if I stuck around, so that's what I'm doing." She readjusted the strap on her shoulder where the cooler cut into her collarbone. "You can have all the theories you want about me. It doesn't make them true."

"That's what Gram tried to tell me, but it's hard not to have my doubts. You know, given the very weird circumstances of your appearance out here." He stepped closer until he had to tilt his head to look down at her.

He wouldn't win this time. This was Ellie doing her part, taking this bull by the horns. It felt kind of okay. Empowering, even.

She'd never stood up to *anyone* like this before. It gave her such a rush. Why couldn't this level of confidence carry through to her interviews? "Be that as it may, I really like your grandmother, and she's asked for my help. I'm willing to put up with your garbage attitude and all this excessive family drama for her sake. For now. And I'm going back to the nursing home to bring some things to her, and that locket is on her list."

"Did she tell *you* whose picture it is?"

"What?" That time, she backed up. Not because he stood so close, but mostly because her balance waned under the bags' weight, and she did *not* want to fall forward.

His hand gestures grew more animated. "Did she tell you who that is in the picture in her locket? Because she's continuing to leave that little detail out of our conversations."

Ellie had to force away the surfacing grin at the image of Warren and Marilyn having a visit yesterday, with Warren asking a million questions and Marilyn ignoring each one.

Still, it wasn't Ellie's secret to tell. "No."

"Uh-huh. So everyone's just agreed to trust you with gathering all Gram's stuff—including valuables—and driving off with her truck. Those are her keys, right?"

"Yeah, that's exactly what the plan is. You can call the police over your ridiculous suspicions, but they'll only find me parked at the Choteau nursing home, delivering supplies to my favorite old lady in Montana. So you listen good, Warren Oliver. I've only done three illegal things in my life: speeding, downloading music off LimeWire my freshman year of college, and shoplifting—and the shoplifting thing was an accident that I went back and paid for, so really, it's only two illegal things. Ripping off grandmothers is not anywhere on my list. Got it?"

Ellie took another step back and tried to make her sharp inhale seem as casual as possible. She'd totally let him have it like those dramatic speeches people say in movies. In retrospect though, she hardly knew what she said, thanks to the adrenaline rush that accompanied it.

Like the ginormous mood killer he was, Warren smiled. He should have been pretty ticked off, really. It put a huge damper on her internal celebration.

"I like the way you say 'Choteau.' It's not even close to right," he said.

The cooler bag slipped from her arm. She caught it before it hit the ground. "You so missed my point."

"No, I got your point. That came out loud and clear. Now you can listen to my point: I get it. You're not some mastermind criminal, but you're still dealing with my grandmother, who is the most important woman in my life—don't tell my mom." He raised an eyebrow like he meant it as a genuine threat. "And it sure sounds like Gram is sucking you into yet another messed-up arrangement, and we don't need it ending in a lawsuit or something, okay? So, you're welcome to drive, milady, but you're taking me with you."

Warren unfastened the tool belt around his waist and let it drop to the ground. He brushed his dirty hands on his jeans and folded his arms across his chest, which amplified the muscles showing from his sleeveless shirt. Was this some masculine display of strength?

"You are not coming with me." The last thing she needed was

this guy sitting in the passenger seat, criticizing the way she drove like he criticized every other thing she did.

He shrugged. "I am."

"You have work to do. Give me the necklace." Ellie held her hand outstretched to receive the trinket so she could escape.

Warren pushed her hand away and started toward the car. "It's in my pocket. Now, let's go."

Ellie growled and hurried after him. "Fine. But don't even try to talk to me, because I will ignore you. Just sit there, shut up, and mind your business."

"Whatever you say, boss." Warren arrived at the blue pickup and let himself in. He kept his face forward, and indignant, as he waited for her to join.

On the driver's side, she pushed the heavy bag between them, then prepared to start the truck. To her unpleasant surprise, the wretched thing was a manual. She'd learned to drive stick in high school in her mother's Subaru, but they sold that car a decade ago. She hadn't driven one since. Hopefully, she still remembered how to do it.

"You can handle a stick, right?" Warren's condescending voice made her want to ram his side of the truck into the barn.

"I told you not to speak to me." The stick in this old truck was stubborn, but she let her anger give her strength when she shoved the beast into reverse and released the clutch. "But, yes, I can."

Oh, thank goodness that'd gone accordingly. She'd have been mortified if she'd stalled out.

Warren ran his pinched fingers across his lips to show he'd keep them zipped, then watched out the window as they pulled away from the farm. In the rearview mirror, Hilda realized she'd been left behind; she ran up the drive and slumped her meaty shoulders.

Much to Ellie's absolute shock, Warren kept his promise to be quiet. The radio played some AM oldies station, and neither of them bothered to change it. It transported Ellie to a time long ago, and she let her mind wander again to Marilyn and John's dating relationship. Everything she imagined made her smile, and she had to continually fight the look off her face before Warren inquired about it.

As they rolled into Choteau, whose very name now annoyed her since Warren had to point out she pronounced it wrong, Ellie clicked off the phone's GPS when they reached the first stop sign. It took two trips into this quaint town for Ellie to memorize the layout, but she still needed her phone's assistance to get through the countryside. Warren hadn't argued her use of that either to offer his help, which she preferred. He also hadn't said a thing when she stalled the truck at the stoplight. If he kept quiet like this for the rest of her vacation, it might be survivable, especially since she had a car to get around in now.

The pair climbed from the truck and entered the nursing home, veering right toward room 34.

A woman popped her head out of the central nursing station and waved an arm to get their attention. "Are you two here for Marilyn?"

"Yeah, I'm her grandson," Warren confirmed. "I was just here yesterday."

"Oh, you're welcome to visit her, but I wanted to warn you that they brought her a roommate about an hour ago. If you want some more privacy, you can take Marilyn out to the common room for complimentary tea and coffee."

Warren turned to Ellie with an inquisitive look.

Ellie shrugged. "I talked to her an hour ago, and she said something was going on but didn't know what."

"Yes, kind of a last-minute addition," the nurse chimed. "Belle just came over from the hospital. I'm sure they'll get along fine. Enjoy your visit."

"This oughta be interesting," Warren muttered when he continued down the hall.

Ellie kept hot on his trail, and when they finally came to a stop, the two of them peered around the corner to Marilyn's room. Inside, two women howled with laughter, which kept both Ellie and Warren cemented in the doorway.

"Oh, kids!" Marilyn waved wildly for them to enter. "Get in here and meet my new roommate. What a hoot!"

Ellie shuffled in behind Warren, and the two of them stood awkwardly at the foot of Marilyn's bed. The new roommate, Belle, clapped her good hand to her thigh. Her other hand hung from a sling around her shoulder. A deep purple bruise painted the base of her neck, which spoke of a rather serious injury. She wore a hospital gown, which wasn't strange. But her hair kept Ellie's attention even more than the injury itself. It was blue. Like electric mermaid blue. Ellie couldn't recall ever seeing a woman of Belle's age with hair such a vibrant color. Belle had to be in her eighties, at least.

Marilyn beamed with pride. "Belle, this is my grandson Warren, from Spokane. He's a contractor who builds the cutest little houses. And this is Ellie; she's a guest at my bed-and-breakfast."

"So good to meet you two." Belle's face shone with delight, as if her own family stood before her. "Are you married?"

"To each other?" Warren's voice squeaked.

"Absolutely not." Ellie reached out her left hand to shake Belle's uninjured one. "I'm not married to anyone, but especially not *him*. It's nice to meet you."

"Honestly, Belle, these two hate each other. It's an amusing story, really. I'll tell you all about it later." Marilyn had turned an unexpected roommate situation into the slumber party of the century.

Belle's eyebrows waggled. "Well, in that case, I've got a couple of single grandkids I'd be happy to set you up with."

Ellie's cheeks flushed. "We'll keep that in mind."

She glanced beside her to meet Warren's gaze. He offered the slightest nod to thank her for steering them out of a blind date, which made Ellie regret dodging the bullet for *both* of them.

"Belle just told me how she came to end up in rehab with me," Marilyn said.

"Fell off my damned roof cleaning gutters." Belle cackled and slapped her leg again.

Marilyn roared too. "Can you believe it? The two of us, in our prime, laid up here for climbing on roofs and getting tackled by a dog."

The laughter grew so loud, Ellie checked the doorway to see if any of the staff would come and force them to keep quiet.

"Tackled by a dog?" Warren's harsh voice cut through the hilarity. "You fell over Hilda? You told me it was a shovel."

"Well, shit." Marilyn stopped laughing in an instant and reached for her water bottle. She took a long sip, avoiding eye contact with her grandson. "Forgot I didn't want you to know about that."

Ellie brought her fist to her mouth to hide her smile, but not before Warren noticed it.

"You knew it was Hilda?" he asked her.

She shrugged. Marilyn hadn't been afraid to tell Ellie what happened because of family backlash, after all. "Anyway, I have your stuff, Marilyn." She set the duffel bag on the floor beside Marilyn's chair. "We won't stay long. Warren has a lot to do on the farm. I told him he didn't have to come, but he insisted, lest this bag be full of your most valuable possessions and I be on my way out of the country with them."

"Warren Michael." Marilyn placed the back of her hand to her forehead.

"Thanks for throwing me under the bus," he muttered.

Ellie curtsied, which sent Belle into a hushed fit of giggles. "And here's your liver."

She held the cooler out for Marilyn to take, which made the room fall silent now. Stranger words had never come out of Ellie's mouth.

Marilyn chuckled as she unzipped the pail and retrieved the foil lump from between the ice packs. "Bless your heart. You are the cutest, but your packaging here was unnecessary." She began unwrapping the foil bit by bit to reveal a very large wad of cash.

"Gram, what in the—"

"Depression kids," Belle said, as if that explained everything. "My mama wrote 'giblets' on our freezer cash. Nobody's gonna get into giblets."

Thank goodness Marilyn hadn't expressed to either Ellie or Warren what the package contained, or he'd never have let her leave the farm with so much of Marilyn's money.

Marilyn thumbed through some of the twenty-dollar bills. "You came to see me in a groober the first time you came, right?"

"A groober?" Ellie stepped closer to make sure she heard right.

"Yeah, like a cab," Marilyn clarified.

Belle snapped her fingers. "I know those. My grandkids are always talking about 'em. They bring fast food to your house in the big cities."

"That's Grub Hub." Warren pinched the bridge of his nose and sank against the wall. "I believe Gram is asking if you took an Uber."

Ellie had a hard time even managing a nod to confirm Marilyn's original question.

"Well, Uber, Groober, or Hub Dub, I want you to have this." Marilyn extended two twenties toward Ellie.

Grandma Val always tried to pay her for everything too. "You don't have to do that. It was my pleasure to come."

"I insist. I want to thank you for all you're doing and for bringing my things and putting up with Warren. I knew you were brave." Marilyn winked and pushed the suitcase farther behind her chair like she meant to protect it.

"Brave?" Warren's head tilted.

Belle seemed to feed off the girl-power vibe in the room. "Oh, I like a brave woman. Don't you worry, Ms. Ellie. I'll be here helping Marilyn every step of the way."

"Helping with what?" Warren threw his hands up, but all three women shifted in his direction to give him the stink eye. "What conspiracy are you all plotting anyway?"

"Give her the locket, please, Warren," Ellie instructed.

He growled when he took it out of his pocket. "Is this about the guy in the photo?"

"Boy, mind your business." Belle turned up her nose, which set Marilyn off on another fit of giggles.

"Getting a little tired of hearing that one," Warren mumbled.

In that moment, Ellie wanted to move to the nursing home too, and spend all her days with these awesome women who fueled her strength. She believed Belle really would make a wonderful accomplice to Marilyn, and clearly Marilyn had already laid out her plot in the last hour or so of them knowing each other.

"I'll leave the two of you to your devices, and we'll head back home." Ellie cringed at referencing the farm as both her and Warren's home, but maintained her power stance.

"That's it? That's all we came here for?" Warren laughed like the entire trip had been for naught, valuable work time wasted away.

While Ellie would have preferred a productive day of filling out applications in the gazebo, frustrating Warren to this extent with a quick visit to town was worth every inconvenient second.

"I told you not to come." She snickered, waved goodbye to her new friends, and walked out of the room.

– 14 –

WARREN HAD TRIED TO ask questions the entire way home, but Ellie didn't answer. She rather liked this newfound power she had over him. It had thrilled her to park Marilyn's truck by the barn, pocket the keys, and return to her tiny home without a single look in his direction.

Now, if only she could figure out how to channel this power in the rest of her life.

On the downside, however, summoning such strength drained her mentally on a level she'd never known. The new assignment that popped up in the transcribing queue had terrible timing, but it wasn't like she could pass it up when they were so few and far between these days.

…in the biliary track, connecting the pancreas, liver, and gallbladder.

Ellie paused the lecture and flipped her phone right side up. Putting it on silent and facedown to avoid distraction hadn't worked at all.

> Blake Robinson-Neighbor: Sorry about yesterday's abrupt end.
>   Maybe we can try again soon.
> Blake Robinson-Neighbor: PS the rooster belonged to a guy two
>   miles away. That's a well-traveled bird.

Ellie drew her legs up under her and gazed out the window into the darkness. How did one respond to a man she'd had a very odd morning date/hangout/whatever with, which was then interrupted by a stranger waving a red flag?

Ellie: Thanks for taking care of that. Hilda and I will both sleep
    better now. :)

She couldn't, in good conscience, rule him out based on what
Tori said. Technically, she'd known Blake longer—about fifteen
whole minutes longer. Other people telling her how to feel about a
man had kind of gotten on her nerves too.

Avoiding the drama and ignoring him altogether didn't sound
like the worst idea either. She'd had quite enough of that to satisfy
her for a while.

Ellie groaned.

This day, or night, or whatever this blur of existence was, had
done her in. She couldn't sit still anymore. But where else could she
go at 10:00 p.m. a zillion miles from civilization?

Since Hilda had gone out to do who-knew-what-sort-of-doggy-
business an hour ago, Ellie had no one else to confide in but her
other animal friends in the barn. In her normal life, a month before,
she'd have had no choice but to talk things over with Sean or call up
his sister Chloe. Both options were gone now.

She grabbed her olive-green athletic shorts from the back of the
couch—where they conveniently landed when she flung them from
the loft earlier that afternoon—and readjusted her twisted-up black
tank top around her middle. After shaking out her hair to restyle the
messy bun on top of her head, she headed out into the night, the
flashlight on her phone leading the way.

Up at the main house a side room shone with shades of blue,
which she figured meant Warren was watching TV inside and
wouldn't bother her out here. That helped calm her nerves. And
since Hilda hadn't tackled her when she stepped outside, she must
also be locked away in the main house too.

Ellie crept into the barn and found the light switch beside the
door, illuminating only the back portion of the stables where the

animals had settled in for the night. There didn't appear to be any lurking predatory birds or ax-murderers-in-hiding, so Ellie made her way across the dirt floor to greet her furry friends.

Sheriff brayed when he saw her approach, trotting to the fence for cuddles. Ellie scratched his donkey chin and traced the cross pattern on his forehead with her fingertips. His floppy ears fell back, white eyelashes fluttering shut. He really was a gorgeous creature.

"You're such a good boy, Sheriff. Thanks for not running away on me again. I appreciate it." She kissed his forehead, and he pushed against the gate for more affection. "Do you get bored out here in the country with only a few sheep friends and chickens? Or are you happy with the simplicity of your life?"

Yeah, she'd resorted to asking a donkey philosophical questions. If that didn't just sum up how things were going for her, nothing did.

"I don't know what I'm doing here, bud. This entire trip has been such a roller coaster of weird. You might be the only good part of it. Well, your owner is a pretty exceptional lady too." She swirled her hands around Sheriff's cheeks, his hooves clopping in some donkey stationary march. "I wanted to get away from my life to catch my breath. But I'm not so sure I'm doing any better here."

One sheep let out a long baa, and the other flopped over onto its back, black hooves straight up in the air. Ellie'd never seen a sheep do that before.

"I feel that, Sheep Two. I really do." She laughed and propped her foot up on the fence. Sheriff nudged her when she stopped stroking his fur. She rested her cheek on his nose. "Being an adult sucks. Cherish your animal-ness, okay? Eat your hay, make your sounds, and poop all you want. I wish it was that easy. I don't even know where the hell I'm going to live when I go back. If I have to move in with Averie and be at her beck and call all day and night, I'm going to lose my mind. At this point, I'd rather live in the stable with you and sort straw by length for pay."

He nudged her again. Ellie scratched behind his ears like he was a dog, not a donkey. "Thanks for listening to me vent, Sheriff. You seem so wise. You must be an old man, full of knowledge."

"He's three."

Ellie spun around, her back crashing into the fence and startling the donkey into a loud bray. Across the barn, Warren leaned against a large support beam, his arms folded over his chest.

"You scared the crap out of me." Ellie clutched her chest.

Warren approached the pen. "The sheep are Bo and Peep. I don't know what the chickens' names are, but I'm sure Gram has named them all."

"How long have you been standing there?" Her cheeks grew warmer the nearer he got.

"Long enough to hear you using Sheriff as your own personal therapist." He flashed a crooked smile.

"Ass!" Her thoughts bounced between shoving him like an angry kindergartner or running out of the barn in tears. Neither happened. She just stood there, then growled and covered her face with her hands.

Warren took another step forward. Between the cracks in her fingers, she saw him reach out like he might take hold of her arm, but he pulled back at the last minute.

"Hey, I'm sorry. I couldn't hear all of it from across the room." He shook his head and glanced up at the ceiling. "Something about you living in a stable and sorting straw."

"Oh my gosh…"

"But you're talking to me now."

Great. Of all people, he had to be the one who walked in on what should have definitely been an inner monologue.

"I'll just go," she said.

"Hang on a sec, will ya?" He backed away to the end of the pen until he reached the small refrigerator that hummed and rattled with age. "I came out here to see if you'd talk to me now, and I've already gotten this far. Can I get you a drink?" Warren opened the fridge. "I've got Pepsi, beer, lemon tea, and some kind of fruit juice. Can't really read the label on it, so only pick that one if you're feeling lucky."

Ellie blinked much slower than usual as she watched him. Rather than his usual ominous persona, Warren acted almost *pleasant*.

"Tea." She forgot her manners. Didn't care.

"Tea it is." He snatched a Pepsi for himself and returned to the pen, passing the beverage to Ellie and turning toward the donkey. "Come here, Sheriff. Didn't mean to scare you off."

At the sound of his voice, the donkey trotted over for more head scratches.

"Gram comes up with some interesting names, huh? There used to be a cat out here she called Sir Block of Cheese for no other reason than he was orange." Warren rested both arms on top of the gate, the curves of his biceps predominant in his cutoff T-shirt. He'd put on athletic shorts and slides, his hair sticking up in different directions, still damp from his shower.

Ellie had come to the barn to get away from her thoughts. It didn't help that one of the forerunning stresses in her brain happened to join her out here.

"Look. You don't have to talk to me. But if you'd listen for a second, I'd appreciate it." Warren lowered his head, shifting slightly in her direction. "I didn't mean to come out here and eavesdrop. I have this habit of terrible timing and didn't know at what point in your 'conversation' to interrupt. I promise I don't think you're crazy."

She gripped harder on the gate. "You sound super convinced."

He laughed, much louder than she expected him to. "Sheriff's a good listener. I get it."

"Right." She had a hard time imagining him venting to the barn animals. He seemed much more likely to punch walls or yell at children to get off his lawn. "You wanted to talk to me? Or was that the talk?"

"Yeah, I saw your flashlight from the window and thought it'd be a good time to make amends for Gram's sake." He rubbed at the back of his neck. "I ended up calling her when we got back today because it's really bothering me how secretive she's being with this. She gets caught up in schemes so easily. Believe me, the woman has submitted her personal information to Publisher's Clearing House every week for the last thirty-some years. She once sent money to some kid that called pretending to be me in a traffic accident. She even bought a timeshare in Florida and rented it out for six months before the police got involved and let her know she wouldn't see any of that money."

"I see," Ellie said.

"So, she's obviously very trusting of strangers." Warren nodded and bit his lip. He rubbed Sheriff's nose and shifted to face Ellie full on.

His suspicions made sense, sure. But having no way to prove her innocence had gotten so old. "Yeah, I get it, but—"

"But she really likes you."

Marilyn was the only common ground the pair of them shared. "Well, I really like her too, but aren't you here to apologize or something?"

The sheep on its back, Peep, Ellie now knew, thrashed against the wall until it got its footing and stood, knocking into Bo. The two of them trotted dizzily on until they got their balance again. Ellie had a very hard time not laughing at the sight when she needed to be serious in front of Warren. She didn't like him, after all.

"I was getting to that." He took a sip of his pop and leaned on the fence. "Gram finally cracked about the guy in the locket. She told me about how he used to own this place and how she loved him. I guess she wants to find him and catch up or something. Bit of a shock, I'll be honest. She and Gramps were married for almost sixty years, so it's weird to imagine things any other way." He let out a long breath. "And I guess she didn't want me or anyone else in the family to know about this little fling—maybe ever—but she figured she had to come clean to keep me off your back."

Ellie swirled her tea around in the bottle but kept silent.

"Gram also talked about how much it meant to her that you came to her rescue after she fell when no one else was there," he continued. "And you've somehow kept the animals alive, despite the sloppiness of your methods. So that's good."

"Sloppiness of my methods?" She scanned the dimly lit barn for proof of his claim. They were animals. They were supposed to be messy. "This is the first time I've ever done this, so—"

"I know. I'm not here to criticize."

"You're doing a bang-up job of resisting." This was the worst apology she'd ever heard.

He shrugged. "What I'm trying to say is that, while I'm taking Gram's vote of confidence with a grain of salt, I thoroughly stalked your social media profiles. Unlike a legit hustler, you're very easy to track, and no professional scammer would post the shit you do."

Ellie's cheeks grew warm. "I like funny cat videos."

"Yeah, I noticed."

Despite relenting on his claim that she was a con artist, Warren still hadn't actually apologized. But prying genuine remorse out of a guy like this would only exhaust her further. She'd have better luck teaching Sherriff the alphabet.

"So, does this mean you're going to stop being a butthead?" she finally asked.

"It means I'm going to try to see past reason and, yes, be a little more civil." He lifted his pop can up for her to clink.

She stared at the outstretched can for a moment before lifting her bottle. Civil was a start. "Yeah, okay. Whatever."

– 15 –

THE SCENT OF CHICKEN poo had permanently embedded itself in her skin.

Four rounds of body wash and two rounds of shampoo hadn't made it go away. The itty-bitty washing machine ran another cycle, but Ellie could still smell it on her clothes too.

Warren's offhanded comment about her sloppy care of the farm animals still stank worse. Shoveling out the chicken coop was her first defense against that claim. She'd even gotten up over an hour early to tackle the task after a particularly rough night's sleep. Now, somehow, she had to focus on her actual work.

...of the millions suffering from cirrhosis, hepatitis, fnufccccctyjwei2ur—

Ellie sprang upright when her phone chimed at full volume beside her, saving her from smashing her head on the keyboard as she drifted off to sleep.

She paused the lecture and snatched up the phone without noting who had called. "Hello?"

"Why haven't you been checking in?" her mother snapped.

"Mom?" Ellie rubbed a hand over her face and reached for her cold coffee. She'd have to start that entire assignment over to make sure she hadn't nodded off more than once. "I'm on vacation."

And what a lovely and relaxing trip it had been so far.

"So? We'd still like to know you're not dead. You could post pictures on Facebook at the very least," her mom said.

"I'm not doing a whole lot of sightseeing." Among other things, every Facebook post she'd done in the last month led to either a direct message or comment asking about her ex. Those freaking cat videos were about all she could get away with.

Her mother sighed. "You have to be doing *something*."

"Yeah, work." Work attending to Marilyn's to-do list. Work taking care of the farm animals. Work throwing a ball for a hyper bulldog. Work dodging Warren around the barn.

The past nine days included very little *actual* work or finding solutions to her many woes.

"You know what I'm going to say, so I'm not even going to say it."

"Uh-huh." Of course Ellie knew. Like she needed any more reminders that she shouldn't have taken the trip in the first place.

Her mother cleared her throat. "Anyway, I'm not calling to start a fight with you, so I'll get on with it. I actually have a proposition for you."

Well, no good could come from that.

"A proposition?"

"We've collectively solved all your problems while you were away. Isn't that nice of us?" She laughed.

Ellie missed the humor in it. "Okay?"

"So, Averie has you covered on the job front. She and I were talking about how you could just move in to her house so you didn't even have to commute to watch the kids, but we figured that, at your age, you should have a place of your own."

Because thirty-two was that determining age. The time in a woman's life where she shouldn't have to be cared for by her family, and yet here they were.

"Yup," Ellie said.

"I ran it by your father, and we've both agreed to let you move into Grandma Val's house for the time being." The enthusiasm in her mother's voice made it sound like she offered an all-inclusive cruise or something.

Ellie sat up straighter. She'd always loved Grandma Val's house... because Grandma Val was there. Since her death, the house felt so empty, a sad reminder of the happy times they once had together there. Now, because her parents wanted to fix the place up and sell it, everything inside had been stripped away, leaving an even more depressing shell in its wake.

"I thought you were getting it ready to sell." Ellie couldn't even fake excitement at this proposition.

"We are, but we can hold off a few months. We agreed that you could live there rent-free in exchange for finishing the remodel, since you'll have more free time these days. Then you can look for a place of your own once it's ready to go on the market."

This just got better and better. "You want me to finish the remodel by myself? I don't know anything about that stuff."

"It's not hard, Ellie. It's just painting, laying tile, and sticking some backsplash on the wall. You watch those HGTV shows; it's like that." She tsked. "And it's a free place to stay. It's just what you need to get back on your feet."

Working for her sister, living in the house her parents owned. All Ellie needed was an arranged marriage and things would be *perfect*.

"That's a lot though. I don't think I'll have time—"

"You don't seem very excited about this." Her mom had called expecting this gift to be well received, to be a huge blessing. Like every other blessing they bestowed upon their youngest daughter, the screwup.

Ellie sighed. "I'm just trying to think through the logistics, and depending on what job I get and the hours—"

"What do you mean 'what job you get?' Aren't you watching Poppy, Noah, and Nash?" she interrupted. "Averie is counting on you for that. You're not looking for something else, are you?"

She should have kept her mouth shut. "It's not like I'll be their nanny forever…"

"With what she's offering to pay you, you'd be silly to look for another job. Anyone else would kill to spend their days in a nice home like that watching those sweet children. If I didn't have my own career and projects, I'd do it myself."

But Ellie didn't have a career, home, projects. Nothing. She was completely and totally available to fill in where needed for her family.

A brown and white blur whirled past the window and shot toward the front drive. The flying dust signaled yet another arrival on the farm. Ellie was pretty sure she didn't have the energy to deal with whoever it was but also wanted to hug them for saving her from this conversation. Since Warren had left for his daily grandmother visit and hardware store restock, Ellie had to play the part of Perry Farm secretary today.

"Mom, I have to let you go. Someone's here," she said.

"Who?" Her voice kicked up an octave.

Ellie slid from her chair and squinted for a better look. "I don't know."

"We aren't done talking about the house," she said.

"We'll have to table it for later." While Ellie prayed that *later* didn't come until she had a better backup plan.

Her mother hummed her reluctant agreement. "Fine. Just think about it and be safe."

The call ended as the vehicle veered away from the main house and headed toward her tiny home. Now, she recognized the truck.

Ellie tilted her head from side to side to get the kinks out of her neck, ready to walk out into the sun and figure out what Blake was up to. While the idea of spending more time with him definitely appealed to her, she couldn't help but replay Tori's words over in her head.

Blake stepped out of the truck, two paper coffee cups in hand. "I wanted to come apologize."

The second man in two days wanting to reconcile. Maybe Blake would actually get his apology out instead of dancing around it the way Warren had.

"For?" She kept one hand on the doorknob so the fatigue didn't send her toppling down the front steps.

"Our brief visit and awkward departure the other day." He held a drink out for Ellie. "I brought you a caramel breve as a peace offering."

Already better than Warren's barn refrigerator options, but Ellie couldn't let her need for caffeine cloud her senses. "Thank you."

"Warren around?" he asked. When Ellie shook her head, he gestured toward the tiny house. "Can we sit?"

Blake did whatever he had to do to get what he wanted. Okay… so, what did he want?

Ellie nodded for him to follow her to the steps, where she took a seat. "Thanks for the coffee. I need it today."

"I'm sure you're keeping busy out here."

Unlike her family, Blake said the words without a hint of sarcasm. Ellie relaxed her shoulders somewhat. "It's helped not having to worry about being impaled by a rooster beak. I get a lot more done now."

Blake laughed. "We see a lot of traveling animals in these parts. Our dog made it all the way into town once. Found him at the coffee shop, begging Babs for a treat at the drive-thru window."

"I like Babs." Ellie felt the reality of small-town living spilling out with her words. She knew people in Choteau already after just over a week of visiting. The town had a population of, what, five? Ten people total? "I take it you're not fond of her daughter though."

The mention of Tori made Blake freeze. "I should apologize for our cold greeting, too, huh? I'd imagine she gave me a *glowing* review after I left."

"She was vague." She willed the coffee to go directly into her veins.

"What'd she say?" His dark green eyes focused on Ellie.

Listening to a talk on liver functions or hearing a job pitch from her mother didn't sound so bad now.

"She just said you go after whatever you want." Ellie cleared her throat. "Not necessarily in an honorable manner, or something like that."

Rather than argue it, Blake simply took a sip of his coffee and surveyed the landscape for a long moment. Then, he nodded. "She's not wrong about me going after what I want. I don't know about being dishonorable. I'm guessing she referenced when I made that deal with the auctioneer before her uncle's estate sale?"

"That didn't come up, no…" Though now she was curious.

"Then she suspects I'm here to take down Marilyn in some mastermind scheme." He shook his head. "Because I've expressed interest in this place, she assumes the worst."

Ellie knew all too well how that felt. "But you do want to buy this place?"

"I do. We've been farming this land for a decade. It'd be easier and more cost effective to own it outright."

"That makes sense." The feud between Blake and Tori must have stemmed all the way back to their failed high school romance if they still carried this much contempt for each other over a legitimate property transaction. "Like I said though, I don't think Marilyn's ready."

He shrugged. "I understand that, but to be honest, I'm getting a little tired of waiting. I don't mean that to sound like a threat or anything, believe me. It's just that I've been working on my parents' farm my entire life. And I sure would like to branch out on my own for once instead of piggybacking off their livelihood." He went to take another sip, then thought of something else. "I failed to mention that I live in a one-bedroom house in Choteau and drive out to their farm every day. But they're getting older. I'm going to have to take over eventually, and when I do, I'd like to have a place out here of my own that's close enough to manage both properties. I want to make a name for myself and not just be Jeremy Robinson's son and farmhand."

"I get that too." Another peer living under the thumb of their family. "Have you presented your case to Marilyn yet?"

"Of course I have. Many times." His brow furrowed, gaze still watching the horizon instead of making any sort of eye contact. "She shuts me down every time. Now, with her being laid up like she is, I feel the transferring of properties could be beneficial to both parties."

It was too early in the day to interpret such intense phrasing. "Uh, yeah. I guess I don't know what to tell you then."

"It's all right. If Janey and Savannah have everything under control for Marilyn like you say they do, then I'll try and be patient." He nudged her with his elbow. "Just don't let Tori go painting a bad image of me. She's the most successful member of my graduating class and likes to remind us lowly folk of that. Most of our classmates left town after school; some of us are stuck here and have to deal with her attitude."

"You think she's a snob?" Ellie didn't quite get that impression, though they'd hardly spent enough time together to make a fair assessment.

"A little? I dunno. It'd be nice not to have to feel like I'm playing catch up at thirty-two, you know?"

All too well. Recent developments continued to set her back even farther. "I hope it works out for you one of these days."

If Marilyn had to eventually hand the farm over to someone else, she could take some comfort in knowing it went to someone who really cared about the place. That had to help.

Ellie inspected the farm from her perch on the front steps. The location was gorgeous, the land fertile—maybe. She didn't actually know that for a fact. It obviously had great potential for animals with plenty of pens. And while quirky as hell, decked out in Marilyn's signature style, the large farmhouse offered everything a person could want in a home.

Who wouldn't want to buy this property? Ellie would if she had any money at all. Geesh, that'd save her from so much grief back home too. A place like this with the accompanying land would cost more than Grandma Val's house plus Averie's new build put together.

"For the record, I don't think you're a bad guy, Blake."

"Thank you. I was worried when I left you alone with Tori the other day what she might say about me, so I'm glad I could clear some things up." He stood and offered a hand to help Ellie to her feet.

Blake then dug his keys from his pocket. Another brief, *brief* visit. At least Ellie didn't have to worry about fixing him a meal or anything when he showed up.

He flashed a big smile. "Have a good one, Ellie. I'm sure I'll see you around real soon."

Before she could thank him again for the coffee, Blake hopped into his truck and sped up the driveway. Hilda leapt from the porch to follow him.

"Hilda, don't run off again!" Ellie yelled.

The dog veered off the lane and ducked under the fence where the grass had grown knee-high. Ellie power walked to catch up. She had way too much work to do to go on a dog hunt today.

As she got closer to the side pen, Ellie slowed and forgot all about Hilda. There, in the empty, overgrown pasture, were no less than a dozen goats.

She knew she'd reached the point of exhaustion, but a herd of goats popping up out of nowhere? Had she lost her mind completely?

A glance toward the main house and barn showed that Warren still hadn't returned from Choteau, so the mystery of the goats' appearance remained. Hopefully, this wasn't like the egg situation, and the goats had been there the entire time—Ellie just hadn't noticed.

Or maybe it was a rooster situation, and they escaped from another farm. But that many goats all making their way securely into a pen?

Why couldn't any of this be easy?

– 16 –

GOATS WERE THE ABSOLUTE worst.

"Are you sure it's going to be two whole weeks?" Ellie asked in place of a greeting.

Marilyn giggled on the other end of the phone. "Yes, dear. Or until the grass is gone. Think of it this way: if the Ottos hadn't loaned us those goats, we'd have to mow."

Correction: *Ellie* would have to mow.

Ellie sighed. "Can you run down the list again? I brought them inside last night, but now what?"

"Oh, they're easy. Won't give you a lick of trouble. Just keep bringing them in at night, don't let them jump on anything important, feed them some of the grain and corn in the barn bins, make sure they have fresh water, and keep an eye on the weather. You'll want to check their pen too. You know what they say about fencing."

Ellie tapped her fingers a little harder against the post. "I do not."

"If the fence won't hold water, it won't hold goats."

In the background, an excited Belle chimed, "Boy, ain't that the truth?"

Not much work.

Goats are easy.

Not a lick of trouble.

Ellie narrowed her eyes on the miscreant flock she'd practically dragged into Bo and Peep's pen the night before. She could have called Warren for help—in hindsight, that might have preserved a bit more of her sanity—but she had little interest in admitting her struggle to him.

"All right. I'll try to keep them alive." Not only did the fate of Marilyn's animals lie in Ellie's hands, but someone else's animals had become her responsibility now too. Of all the ridiculous scenarios: a barnyard daycare run by a city girl who couldn't ask for help.

It sounded like a children's book.

"Hilda will help you. She likes bossing them around," Marilyn said. "Or you can delegate this task to Warren. I'm sure he—"

"I've got it. He's busy enough." That response was so much nicer than *I can handle this without his condescending opinion on my sloppy methods.*

"You're such a peach, Ellie. Thank you again for being the best Airbnb guest an old woman could ask for." She made a kissing sound and hung up.

Ellie sucked in a deep breath and got busy, starting with the chickens. They followed her to the grain bin and practically climbed her legs to be the first one for breakfast. She spread their feed across the dirt floor, far enough from her she could escape them to fill the troughs for the rest of the animals.

Sheriff trotted over to the fence to snag her attention before she even reached for the latch.

"Hey, buddy. You still recovering from my vent session the other night?" She glanced around the barn. If Warren had snuck in during her donkey confessions once, he could do it again.

Ellie pressed a finger to her lips to show Sheriff she meant to keep quiet this time. Not that a donkey understood the gesture.

On the other side of the gate, Warren rounded the corner, tool belt on his waist, a wooden beam over his shoulder, and what looked to be a cup of coffee in his free hand. He shifted to see around the beam on his shoulder and nodded a quick greeting when he spotted her.

Ellie clutched the barn door and offered a nod back. This attempt at starting fresh could not be more awkward.

After replenishing the animals' water, Ellie made her way back to the house to grab her laptop, a bottle of water, and some Tums to deal with the latest nausea created by the plethora of smells.

The noonday sun cooked the land. The shady gazebo by the main house made for a charming work spot, but it did nothing to keep her cool. Ellie wrapped up the rest of her assignment and spent the next forty minutes filling out the questionnaire for a position in healthcare customer service. Talking on the phone all day with angry patients would be the pits. But it beat potty training Nash and keeping Poppy from cutting her brothers' hair. Noah loved to color on walls, throw things over the stair railing, and scream at the top of his lungs—anything to get attention.

And to think, when she finished spending a long day doing that, she'd get to go "home" and tile a bathroom floor or stain woodwork because "she had the most time to do it." Her family had hardly ever taken her work-from-home job seriously all these years; they absolutely wouldn't recognize babysitting her niece and nephews as a real job either. Plus, without dear Sean to entertain her in the evenings, an old spinster like Ellie would be hard up for things to do.

Her inner rage rivaled the midday heat. If she stayed out there any longer, either her body or the laptop would overheat. She reached for her water bottle, but it'd run out a while ago. Her stomach rumbled, making for an excellent excuse to call it a day.

On the table beside the computer, her phone rang with a call from her mother, who would undoubtedly want to talk more about her recent proposition. Ignoring the call would only lead to a string of irritated texts. She might as well get it over with.

"Hi again, Mom," Ellie greeted.

"Hi again, yourself. Just sat down for some Chipotle, which got me thinking about you. Thought we should talk some more about the house since you've had some time to sleep on it."

Chipotle sounded like the medicine Ellie needed right now. Too bad there probably wasn't one short of a five-hour drive.

"I guess I don't really know what to say." Grandma Val's house was, unfortunately, her best option. Everything else she'd looked at either had no vacancies or was wildly out of her price range.

Her mom *did* know what to say, however. "Do you have something else lined up? If not, I don't see how you could afford to pass on this."

"You're right. I can't." Ellie was trapped. In less than five weeks, her lease ended, and the apartment manager expected her to be out. She'd made no concrete plans, still searching for a miracle.

"Then it's settled. You can move in when you get back, and we'll hold off on contacting the realtor."

Ellie could potentially delay her next eviction by taking her sweet time fixing the place up, but knowing how her family worked, she'd be badgered about it the entire time.

"Thanks for the opportunity." She flinched when the words came out of her mouth. Words she'd said at the past two interviews she hadn't heard back from. Her entire life had been one big rejection—a failure.

"We're happy to help until you get things sorted out for yourself. Plus, this is a mutually beneficial arrangement."

Ellie had signed over her entire life now. When her plane landed in Ohio, she no longer belonged to herself.

"And how's everything else going?" her mother asked. "Are you being safe?"

At least she could answer one of those questions truthfully.

"I'm safe. No wild animal attacks, though I had a herd of demonic-eyed goats dropped on me last night. And Warren has decided I'm not a con artist. I'm just winning all over the place."

"What?" Something crunched on the other end of the phone, definitely a deliciously salty tortilla chip Ellie couldn't share. "Who's Warren, and why did he think you were a con artist?"

Ellie placed her hand over her grumbling stomach. "He's Marilyn's grandson. I guess he comes every summer to do projects around the farm but didn't know I was staying at the Airbnb."

"Is he fighting with you? Maybe he should be taking care of the animals instead of you. I'd imagine he knows way more about it than you do." Her mother's words picked up in both speed and pitch. "Wait. You're out there in the middle of nowhere all alone with a strange man? He's not trying to stay in the same house as you, is he?"

"No, he's not. Warren is a ginormous pain in the ass, but he's not a murderer or anything. At least, I don't think so." She couldn't resist fueling her mother's panicky nature sometimes. "And I'm still taking on the animals because Marilyn said she'd comp my stay because of it."

Her mother groaned. "Serial killers don't *tell* you they're serial killers, Ellie. And you're going to take money from an old woman?"

First, it wasn't okay that Ellie paid for the trip herself. Now, she couldn't take the trip for free. "I'm not *taking* it from her. She adamantly offered."

"I don't like any of this. You shouldn't be doing someone else's chores, accepting money from strangers, or hanging around unknown men with God-knows-what intentions." The sound of foil crunching filled the void between them as her mother aggressively wadded up her burrito wrapping. "Sean would have known what to do and protected you from all this."

Ellie slumped in her chair. She'd never be free of that decision. "What does he have to do with anything?"

"If you'd stayed together, he would have come with you on this trip, and I'd know for sure that you were safe. You were together for seven years; you couldn't wait a few more weeks before you broke his heart?"

"We were together for six years," Ellie corrected. The only way this conversation could go in a worse direction was if Sean passed by in the parking lot, and her mother offered to let him join the call. Because of all the blessed coincidences, the optometrist office was in the same complex where her mother worked. Back when Ellie and Sean were together, her mother even bought Sean lunch from time to time. Hopefully that had stopped since the breakup, but you never knew with her mother. "Wouldn't that make it so much worse to take him on vacation and *then* dump him?"

"He was good for you."

Yes. Good for her. He had money and a "real job." He wanted marriage and kids and a big house in the suburbs. He even encouraged her to go back to nursing school, sure that her stomach would eventually get used to the blood and gore, and she'd be the best nurse ever.

She shivered at the thought of being so swept up in the life her family wanted for her—in being Sean's little wifey. If she'd stuck it out with him, it wouldn't have mattered if she succeeded in the medical profession or made a name for herself the way Averie did. She could piggyback off of Sean's success. How romantic.

"Uh-huh." Ellie grabbed her Visality cleaning cloth to wipe down her computer screen for something to do.

"Just keep your distance from the boy and stay vigilant."

Her mother wouldn't be happy unless she knew Ellie carried around a pair of brass knuckles and a bo staff for protection. She'd look like some backwoods Ninja Turtle.

Ellie looked toward the barn, but she couldn't see anything—or any*one*. The sound of the circular saw was the only proof anyone else was on the farm. The goats sang their goaty song in the pen behind the house. Hilda barked at a hawk sitting on the weather vane. Chickens flapped their flightless wings as they came and went at their leisure.

This place was wild. And yet, the physical exhaustion she felt here couldn't compare to the emotional exhaustion she battled on the home front.

"Warren won't hurt me. It'll be okay."

"And that's a prissy name for a creep," her mother said.

Ellie chuckled. "Agreed."

"Your father says hi, by the way. And he misses you," her mother added, derailing Ellie's train of thought.

"I miss him too." Ellie leaned back in her chair.

Her mother hummed dreamily on the other end. "Glad we got things settled on the house and could cross that off your list. I'd better finish up and get back inside but wanted to call and check in on you. Don't let Creepy Guy get too close."

Ellie's eyes focused on the barn again. "I'll do my best."

– 17 –

THERE WERE REGULAR WEEDS—AND then there was creeping Charlie, a whole fresh layer of flowering hell.

Ellie wiped the sweat from her forehead and reached for another vine. The wretched weed had curled around the zinnia's stem so many times, she could hardly tell where one plant began and the other ended. Nevertheless, the zinnias smelled nice, and mud was supposed to be good for the skin. Thank God, because she was absolutely coated in it.

Hilda snorted as she wriggled on her back against the filthy concrete slab beside Ellie, enjoying every second of the sun-soaked warmth and simultaneous back scratch. She didn't even budge when Warren rounded the corner. Ellie, however, almost toppled into the flower bed.

"Graceful," he teased. "Having fun crawling in the mud, Shakira?"

"Shut up." She wiped her forehead again, just smearing more dirt around at this point.

Warren shifted on his legs as he surveyed the garden like a supervisor Ellie had no interest in working for. "I'm heading to the lumberyard. Ran out of siding and want to replace some of the fence slats tomorrow. Getting dinner with a friend after. You need anything from town?"

The gesture almost sent her back into the flower bed. Two-days-ago Warren wouldn't have bothered seeking her out for such a question.

Ellie thought about it for a quick second. More wine would be helpful. A hot, hearty meal from some takeout joint would make a great treat after the hard day's work. Literally anything from Babs's coffee shop…

Regardless of their new attempt at getting along, which they'd hardly had the opportunity to practice, Ellie didn't want to test the waters yet. "Any chance the lumberyard is part of the hardware store or close to it?"

"Same thing. Why?" He stepped further into the garden to give Hilda's exposed belly a rub.

"There are about two million eggs in the barn refrigerator. Can you take them to Barry before there's an overflow?" She imagined the amount of egg salad his family could eat from the bounty. Enough for the entire town, if not the whole state of Montana. Yuck.

He gave Hilda another pat, and the dog shot off toward the barn. "I'll grab them on my way out."

"Thank you." Being civil was nice, even if her shoulders still tensed and her breath still hitched in his presence. "Are you going to visit Marilyn?"

"Nah. I talked to her earlier, and she has therapy, dinner, purse bingo, and a visit with Reverend Kaehr tonight." He retrieved his keys from his pocket and smiled. "The woman has a very full social life for her age."

Ellie couldn't disagree with that. Back home, especially now that Sean was out of the picture, her typical day included working in her pajamas, ordering something from Door Dash, and binging *Ghost Adventures*.

It'd all change now. She'd get up before the sun to arrive at Averie's house, spend all day trying to keep the children out of trouble, and then go home to do even more physical labor in a big, empty house that was once full of love and laughter.

Warren breathed a laugh and adjusted his sunglasses. "Gram

also wanted to know if you'd found the super-secret envelope yet. Apparently, she and Belle are following a 'hot lead' and want to double check their new research with what she already has—or something? I don't even know with them anymore."

"Shoot." That ten-item to-do list had no end in sight. As long as the creeping Charlie didn't grow back in the next couple of weeks, she could cross that item off and never have to worry about it again. "I'll get to it, eventually."

"K. Oh, and make sure to bring the goats in. It's supposed to rain tonight."

Ellie's knee dug deeper into the dirt. "I planned on it."

"Just reminding you," he said over his shoulder on his way toward the truck.

Ellie's eyes narrowed, though the way her nose scrunched hurt her newly acquired sunburn. She didn't need his reminder. So far, she'd handled all the animal dealings herself, without his help, thank you very much. Even the recent addition of those unruly goats hadn't rattled her.

Too much, anyway.

With a growl, she returned to her task of plucking weeds out of the flower bed. As time crept on, the sky grew cloudy and a cool breeze blew through the garden.

Ellie gathered up the pile of weeds in her arms and dropped them into the mulch bin Marilyn kept by the fence. She wiped her dirty hand on her shorts and pulled out her phone to check the weather app. A large, green blob made its way across the radar. Ellie had less than an hour to get everyone in the barn before the skies opened up, if the predictions were correct.

That left no time to respond to her text messages.

Averie: Which day are you coming home again? Nick is going to have to take off work to stay with the kids if you're not back on time.

Blake Robinson-Neighbor: Appreciated getting to talk to you
yesterday about the farm.

Mom: We're picking out paint for that back bedroom today. I'll
send you pics!
Mom: Did that boy start any fights with you today?
Mom: I realized Sean's birthday is this week. Now I feel bad!
Should I still send him a card? I think I should still send the
card. It's the least we can do.

Just once, Ellie wanted to look at her phone and see a text that
made her smile. One that didn't come loaded with guilt or confusion
or high expectations.

"Hilda!" Ellie shouted into the void. "Come help me with these
goats."

Marilyn had suggested Ellie use the bulldog to make herding
them easier. *How* she was supposed to use Hilda remained a mystery,
however.

Ellie rounded the house and weaved past the evergreen trees that
lined the garden. Hilda had situated herself on the tiny house steps
across the drive, clearly uninterested in being a helpful farmhand
tonight. Though when Ellie caught sight of the goats in their pen,
she realized with a great sigh of relief that she might not need the
help, anyway.

The animals of Perry Farm must have sensed the change in the
weather and all filed into the barn on their own. Ellie stepped up on
the first railing and did a head count.

"...eleven, twelve, thirteen goats. One donkey. Sheep..." She
squinted to better see the dirty cotton balls amongst the goats. "One
sheep. Where's two sheep?"

She climbed down from the rail and weaved between the animals,
praying the missing animal was simply skipped during her count.

"Are you freaking kidding me?" Bo or Peep—she couldn't tell which was which—was gone. "She'd better not have gotten through that fence…"

Ellie groaned and ran into the pasture. The wind had picked up, the weather vane rattling atop the roof, a long tree branch keeping rhythm on the siding. Clumps of animal dung dotted the pasture, making for a rather unpleasant maze as Ellie tried to dodge each landmine and keep watch for the missing sheep.

A muffled *baa* in the distance was the only thing that pulled her from her disgust. There, in the back corner of the pasture, was her lost sheep, nose pressed into the fence post, front legs stomping as if it meant to keep moving forward had the post not gotten in the way.

"What on earth are you doing?" Ellie clicked her tongue to get the sheep's attention, but it continued bumping its head into the fence. She clapped her hands and tapped the sheep's hindquarters. The startled sheep spun and shot off toward the barn like a rocket. "What even is my life right now?"

Sheep were the animal version of preschoolers. This was merely a preview of her future life with Averie's children. There wasn't enough Tylenol in the world…

Ellie returned to the barn and closed the gate behind her. That was it, she was done.

Time to relax. *Finally.*

Raindrops tickled her skin as they fell down the backs of her legs, and Ellie brushed them away—a simple gesture that shouldn't have caused panic. However, the smear of blood across her palm when she righted herself did just that.

Ellie began frantically patting herself down, searching for the wound, though she felt no pain. In the adrenaline rush of wrestling a sheep in a poopy pasture, she might not have even noticed she'd cut herself on something. But there was nothing there.

She rushed across the barn to flip on the lights and caught sight of the blood trail leading from somewhere out in the pasture to the edge of the gate and into the barn.

The bloody path led directly to the only possible suspect.

"Sheriff!" Ellie rushed to the donkey's side and dropped to her knees, where blood pooled at his hoof.

She muttered a long string of swears as she ran over all the possible options of what to do. Sheriff had been entrusted to her care, and she'd failed him. Now, even worse, she didn't know how to fix it.

Ellie stared at the gash on Sheriff's knee—or whatever that body part is called on a donkey—and willed her stomach not to empty all over the barn floor.

It was fine. This was totally fine. Absolutely *fine*.

Summoning all the knowledge of her one semester in nursing school, Ellie grabbed a rag from the cupboard to stop the bleeding with one hand and made a phone call with the other.

– 18 –

"I CANNOT THANK YOU enough for coming." Ellie let her head fall back against the gate. "You saved my life and probably Sheriff's too."

Rain beat the barn's tin rooftop. The goats and sheep had piled together in the corner but still bleated their opinions at random intervals. On the surface, everything appeared as it should. Inside, Ellie's heart still pounded.

"It's my job, and I'm happy to help." Tori brushed her hand down Sheriff's shoulder as she muttered calming affirmations. "You were right to call me. That splinter could have gotten infected if left untreated. It was in there pretty deep. You'd never have known if you hadn't caught the blood right away."

She wrapped the bandage around the donkey's leg and let him know what a good patient he was. Sheriff munched on his hay, oblivious to his brush with death.

He coped with blood and injury so much better than Ellie did. While they waited for their veterinarian hero, Sheriff had focused on food; Ellie maintained pressure on the wound and recited the side effects of the asthma medication continuously advertised on her internet homepage, thanks to all the cookies she got from her transcription work.

"Have you gotten a hold of Marilyn yet?" Tori used the wash basin to clean the dried blood from her hands.

She'd tried calling every five minutes to let her know about Sheriff's condition, but Marilyn never picked up. Her purse bingo and visitation must have meant she left her phone behind. "No. I'll keep trying. Warren should be back soon though."

Ellie knew the older woman would understand the trouble a donkey could get into and would be worried for her furry baby. Warren, however, might chalk this up to one more *sloppy* caregiving technique. She rolled her eyes.

"Oh, goody." Tori's smile dripped with sarcasm. "You got yourself sandwiched between two real gems out here, didn't you?"

"Warren and Marilyn?" Beef with Warren made sense, but who could hate Marilyn?

Tori returned to Sheriff and checked him over for additional injuries. "No. Marilyn is one of the greatest humans on earth. I mean Warren and Blake. I hope you didn't come all this way specifically to find a man because you will be sorely disappointed in the options."

This trip had been anything but a romantic excursion—the opposite, really. "Absolutely not. I just got out of a long relationship, and Blake and Warren would add to the drama already on my plate. Blake did stop by yesterday and—"

"Oh, I know. I ran into him in town this morning, and he told me he smoothed things over with you. He assumed I'd bad-mouth him after he left because that's what I do." Tori took Sheriff's face in her hands and looked him square in the eye, her voice shifting to the sweeter, higher tone she used when addressing the animals. "He's an idiot, isn't he, Sheriff? Yeah. A big, giant moron."

Ellie couldn't help but laugh. "He explained how he wanted the land to prove himself to his parents and be more independent or something." She'd leave the bits about Tori being stuck up out of it, so as not to offend the woman saving her favorite farm animal. "Does that face you're making mean you don't believe him?"

Tori held an apple in her hand to reward Sheriff. "It absolutely does, yes." She closed the distance between them and plopped down on the hay bale next to Ellie. "I know you're not from around here, so you have no way of knowing Blake or his history, but like I said, he can be a bit—I don't know—conniving? Is that the right word for it? They're the ones who always sweep in and snatch up everything at sales and then resell things for a higher price. He did that at my uncle's. They aren't known for being fair in deals they strike and have manipulated people into contracts. I just don't like them."

"But Marilyn said they help her out by farming her crops and paying her for it or something?" She didn't know how that worked.

"Probably. They do that with a lot of folks around here. It can be mutually beneficial if it's done right, but I wouldn't be surprised if Marilyn isn't getting the best deal she could get on it." Tori hopped up and headed toward the barn refrigerator. "She still keep drinks out here?"

Before Ellie could confirm, Tori had helped herself to an iced tea and grabbed a second for Ellie. She sank down once more and crossed her ankles as she leaned against the barn wall and sighed like she sat on a plush couch and not a wildly itchy cube of animal food.

Blake had painted Tori as a stuck-up success, but this woman before her was anything but the white-coat-wearing pompous type in the healthcare building Sean and her mother worked in. She'd hated going to functions with him for holidays and office parties. His colleagues always made her feel so dumb.

Or maybe she did that to herself. She'd never quite figured it out.

Regardless, it was nice to feel like she had a female friend again, even if they'd just met. It'd been too long since she and Chloe had spent the evening sipping beverages and chatting away. It was too bad that an animal had to get hurt to make it happen.

"And Warren? You didn't really explain your dislike of him." The cold iced tea did nothing to warm her in her damp clothes, but the refreshment was much needed after such a trying day.

Tori shrugged. "I don't hate him. He's just a grumpy old soul. Always has been. Even in high school, he had this cantankerous air about him. It must be a family thing, because his mom always scared me. You can be glad she's all the way out in Spokane. His grandpa was the same way too. I hated coming out here when he was alive because he gave me such grief over everything I did. I think it was a combination of me being young and him not believing in veterinary care for livestock. He'd have put them out to pasture if they so much as sneezed. Lucky for them, Marilyn wore the proverbial pants for those decisions. That's why I like her. She's so spicy."

That was it exactly: spicy. It'd been several days since their last visit, and Ellie had begun to miss the older woman and her equally fiery roommate. She'd have to get a visit in soon since they had so much to talk about.

"It makes me wonder what our relationship would have been like if she hadn't fallen and ended up in the nursing home. Would I still have gotten to know her or the animals? Would Warren and Blake leave me alone? I dunno." Ellie might have been left to her devices, staring at her work queue and hoping something popped up for her, searching for apartments outside the city limits to expand her options, filling out many more applications that would never get a response. It sounded about as relaxing as a root canal and about as productive as scooping water out of a sinking boat with a spoon.

Tori shifted to face Ellie. "I'll admit I've been wondering since I met you the other day… Why did you book a trip here? Alone. In the dead of summer. At the world's smallest house. In central Montana. Alone."

"You said that already." She laughed even harder now at the way Tori's face morphed with each additional phrase.

"Well, it perplexes me." Tori showed no signs of packing up her medical supplies and going home, which didn't bother Ellie one bit—so long as Marilyn didn't get charged by the hour.

"Well, it's a little bit complicated." How much should she tell this almost total stranger? Did it even matter if she spilled her guts?

In a couple weeks, she'd never see any of them again. Probably. "I broke up with my boyfriend of six years against literally every person in my life's advice, and they like to let me know that often. Since I'm a remote medical transcriptionist, I thought a getaway to focus on my job and clear my head would be nice, but then they dropped the bomb on us that they sold the company and will be phasing out the contract employees. Instead of canceling my trip, I still chose to get away to try and create a plan to get my life back on track, but it's not really going so well. I'm pretty much fated to go back home, move into a gutted house that I'll be responsible for repairing while I work for my super successful sister as a nanny to her hyper children. It's, uh…it's stressing me out a little."

Tori's nose scrunched as she processed the info dump. "Well, that sounds like a lot. This probably hasn't been the best place to clear your head, huh?"

"Absolutely not." Ellie might have had more luck seeking solitude in Times Square. "This is the wildest vacation of my entire life."

"Why are you moving into a gutted house?" she asked.

Ellie squeezed a little tighter on her bottle. "My apartment lease is up in a few weeks. With my job phasing out and the building raising their rates, I can't afford to stay there anymore. It's just a one-bedroom, so getting a roommate wasn't an option unless I wanted to get real cozy with a stranger. So, in true fashion, my family decided to come to my rescue and offer a free stay at my grandmother's old house if I agree to fix it up for them to sell."

"Um, speaking as a mother of two, when do they expect you to have time for that on top of nannying all day?"

"Thank you!" Ellie threw her hands up. "It has also been determined that since I am a single woman with no hobbies, this shouldn't be a problem."

"Oof. Your family sounds like a gas." Tori forced a dramatic smile.

Ellie didn't even know how much she needed to hear someone tell her she wasn't crazy for thinking the way she did. "They are. How old are your kids?"

"Mila's four, and Ruby's two. My husband, Mitch, is thirty-four and probably the biggest kid of them all." She tapped away on her phone screen as if she was responding to a message while simultaneously carrying on a totally separate conversation with Ellie. "He's having a time tonight. The girls are fighting him on bath time, and I'm needed to referee. Didn't realize how late it was. I'll check those bandages again, and then I'd better head out."

"Sorry to keep you so long," Ellie said. "I really do appreciate your help tonight."

"Not a problem at all."

Tori expertly checked her wrapping by flashlight and spoke words of comfort to her patient. Somehow, this hero balanced a husband, two very young children, and an incredibly demanding job that required house calls at all hours. She still managed to smile and take the time to offer a listening ear to a total stranger panicking in a country barn.

Ellie needed to find that balance if she planned to survive this next phase of life back home.

"You might be my new idol, Tori. I'm extremely grateful the sheep needed to be dewormed when they did so I could meet you." She really had no clue what she'd have done with Sheriff otherwise. Cried, fainted, run off into the nearest cornfield, never to be seen again?

Tori began packing her case and offered her biggest smile yet. "You have my number. Call or text for whatever. Seriously. Even if it's just to vent or if you need more advice on the prowling men of Choteau. There aren't all that many people our age around here, so it's kind of nice to make a new friend."

Friend. It sounded so wonderful. "I will definitely keep that—"

"Whoa. What happened?" Warren's elevated voice cut through the sweet moment like a serrated knife. "What's wrong with Sheriff?"

"He got his leg caught on a piece of fence post and had a large splinter in the skin," Tori explained as she stood and gathered her bag. "He'll be fine."

Warren turned to Ellie still sitting atop the hay bale, covered in dried mud up to her knees. "When did all this happen?"

"I noticed it when I brought everyone in before the storm." His hard stare made her feel as naked as she was at their first meeting.

"Ellie handled it." Tori stepped out from behind Sheriff to face Warren. "She applied pressure to stop the bleeding and called me to remove the shard. Exactly as she should have done."

Warren shifted on his legs and dug his hands into his pockets as he observed the confident veterinarian laying out the facts. "And the bill?"

"Also taken care of." Tori glanced over her shoulder and offered another friendly wink. "Keep up the good work out here, Ellie. I'll see you around."

With that, she took her case and ran off into the night to be a champion to someone else.

Dr. Tori Hill was the absolute coolest.

Warren checked Sheriff over, assessing the damage. "I guess I'm glad I got new wood for those fence posts then."

"Yeah, don't want to go through that again." She returned to the donkey's side and scratched his neck. Sheriff obviously loved all the extra attention his injury got him tonight.

"You are filthy." Amusement consumed Warren's expression now.

Ellie's cheeks warmed, and she smoothed the frizzing hair of her braid, which did nothing at all to improve its appearance. "I finished weeding and had to track down a lost sheep in the rain."

"Bo forget which way the barn was again?" He laughed like he'd been there and done that.

"One hundred percent." So, Bo was the culprit. She'd be sure to keep a special eye on that particular sheep—if she could ever distinguish it from Peep.

"You tell Gram about Sheriff's injury yet?" He retrieved his phone from his back pocket. A smirk still played on his lips when he observed the mud splattered across Ellie's shirt.

She crossed her arms to hide herself. "I tried several times but couldn't get a hold of her. I don't think she took her phone to bingo or whatever she was up to tonight."

"I'll try her again then." His grin widened as he looked her up and down in an even more obvious fashion. "You'd better get cleaned up because I'd doubt that's *all* mud if you've been out in the pasture."

Ellie cringed and backed slowly toward the exit. "Yeah…"

"Oh, and I forgot to tell you earlier, but Gram asked if I'd bring you for a visit tomorrow. Says she misses you."

The words took some of the chill out of the evening air. "I still need to find that envelope before I—"

"We'll worry about that later. I'm sure she'll be more interested in hearing about Sheriff's adventures than fretting over whatever bizarre secret life she has tucked away in that envelope." He began double-checking that everything in the barn was secure for the night. "I'll pick you up around nine."

Ellie gave a thumbs-up as she continued backing out of the barn toward the promise of a hot, soapy shower, a hearty snack, and a soft mattress.

She'd need that rest more than anything if she had to have all her morning farm chores done by nine so she could spend a wonderfully awkward half an hour trapped in a car with her "cantankerous" host.

– 19 –

ELLIE EMERGED FROM THE bathroom, tying her still-damp hair into a low bun. Out the window, she saw Warren's truck speeding across the drive. Stones flew as he hit the brakes in front of the tiny house.

It was only 8:40. He wasn't supposed to pick her up for another twenty minutes.

Warren jumped down from the truck, phone to his ear. Ellie opened the door before bothering with her shoes, his grave expression making it impossible to change the order of her actions.

Warren pressed his palm to his forehead. "They're going to kick you out for a prank?"

"What's wrong?" Ellie mouthed.

He turned his attention to Ellie now. "Apparently, either Gram or Belle faked their death this morning, and now they're in trouble with nursing home management."

Marilyn's high-pitched cackle rang through the phone. She then added something else Ellie couldn't quite make out from her position a few feet away.

Warren groaned. "She wants me to put her on speaker so you can hear."

"Ellie!" Marilyn's voice boomed. "Thank you for taking care of my sweet, ornery Sheriff last night. You get your butt into Choteau so I can hug you for that one, while Warren gets me out of trouble with the staff. They told us we're too loud, and the other residents can't sleep. Bunch of old people—always trying to sleep at inappropriate times. If they'd sleep normal times, there wouldn't be any issues."

Belle howled, and Marilyn shushed her through her own giggles.

"Where are your shoes?" Warren whispered.

"You were early," she whispered back.

Marilyn kept on talking. "Warren, you need to hurry. They have been trying to get a hold of your mother, but I gave them the wrong number on all their forms. If they figure that out, I'm toast."

"You gave them the wrong number *on purpose*?" he asked.

"Yeah." She sounded as if the reason was so obvious she couldn't believe Warren hadn't put it together. "I don't want them tattling on me for every little thing—least of all summoning her here where she could find out about Ellie and the Airbnb. God help me, she doesn't need more reason to speed up my move to Spokane."

From the background, Belle chimed, "If they try to separate us, we're burning this place to the ground, Warren. We decided at breakfast."

"Calm down, ladies. Don't burn anything down until I get there. Gram, you have to use real phone numbers on your paperwork. They want those in case of emergency." Warren opened his truck door and tossed a silver package to Ellie: Pop-Tarts. Nice. She hadn't gotten a chance to eat anything either since he arrived ahead of schedule.

Marilyn hemmed and hawed. "Well, I'll give them yours. You're on your way though, right? Belle's son is coming this afternoon to make his plea. He's a lawyer, so he's got experience with this stuff."

"As soon as Ellie puts on some shoes, we're coming." He waved for her to go finish getting ready.

"Get her a coffee too, Warren. Be a gentleman, since I know you're not cooking for her like I told you to," Marilyn scolded.

"I brought her Pop-Tarts. That's already way above and beyond what an Airbnb is supposed to do." Warren ran a hand through his dirty blond hair and stared at the sky like it might hold some answers to his grandmother's particular brand of chaos.

"Five stars," Ellie shouted, then signaled to Warren that she meant to hurry inside to grab her shoes and bag.

As if the morning drive didn't already promise its share of awkward silence and interaction, now they had more Marilyn messes to clean up, which meant an even crankier Warren for company.

❦

When Ellie and Warren walked through the doors at the nursing home, no one greeted them with a smile or wave. Instead, the staff offered silent scowls.

The pair kept quiet as they moved down the corridor—almost as quiet as they'd been on the drive into town. If she could have gotten a decent signal on her phone, she could have checked the new listings on Indeed.

"I'm not happy about this," Warren mumbled when they approached room 34.

"Really? I hadn't noticed." The lack of uproarious laughter coming from the room stopped her from any further teasing and, luckily, kept Warren from issuing a biting comeback.

Inside, both women sat in their chairs, blankets pulled up to cover their mouths.

"We thought you were the manager again," Marilyn said and lowered her blanket. "We're trying to be on our best behavior so they don't split us up, but it's so hard."

Warren took a seat on Marilyn's bed, and Ellie sat on Belle's. "Gram, you can't go faking your death in a nursing home. I can't believe this is something I have to tell you. They're out there looking at us like we're aiding and abetting criminals here."

Belle reached out to squeeze Ellie's hand, still trying to muffle her giggles.

Marilyn's head whipped toward her grandson, her feather earring slapping her in the face. "I didn't pretend to be dead; Belle did. I just shrieked until the nurses came."

Warren closed his eyes, though his lips formed a silent prayer— or string of curses. It wasn't clear. Ellie debated grabbing another corner of Belle's blanket to hide her chuckles too.

"Look, Gram. I'm going to go meet with the manager and try to smooth things over. I wanted to run this by you under less ridiculous circumstances, but I'm going to ask them about bringing you back to the farm this week. We can come into town for therapy or get nurses to come out to the house or whatever they want you to have, but—"

"You're busting me out early?" Marilyn scratched at the cast over her leg.

Ellie, too, sat up a little straighter. Having Marilyn close by would make everything so much easier and provide a necessary buffer zone between her and Warren.

He nodded. "I'm going to try. Not sure how it all works. And there are some things I'll have to do around the farm to prepare, like making sure you can access everything in your wheelchair."

"Can Belle come?" Marilyn's earnest question nearly melted Ellie to the floor.

Belle slapped her knee. "I'm in. We could get into so much more trouble if the authorities aren't monitoring us."

"Warren will keep us on the straight and narrow," Marilyn volunteered.

He held up his hands. "Okay, slow down here. I'm sure Belle's family might have something to say about that, Gram. And I'm not exactly qualified for this task…"

"Nonsense," Ellie said. The image of Warren chasing the two spunky, injured women around the farm would forever bring Ellie great joy. "Warren would make a fantastic gerontologist."

"Well, he's no Connor in food services," Belle said matter-of-factly. "But he ain't too rough on the old eyes either, are you, sugar?"

Anyone in a ten-mile radius could have felt the heat coming from Warren's cheeks when he buried his face in his hands.

Belle continued. "When my son, Marv, gets here this afternoon, I'll run this by him. No worries."

"Super." Warren truly had no say in this.

Marilyn turned more serious at the mention of grown children. "You didn't call your mother and tattle on your way over, did you?"

"No, I didn't." Warren pulled his leg up onto the mattress and pressed his back to the bedframe.

Marilyn's eyes went wide. "Have you talked to her *at all* since you got to town?"

She studied her grandson, fishing for whatever information he had. Ellie, too, found herself tilted more in his direction.

Warren's face softened. "No. I thought about it after I found Ellie out there staying in your Airbnb. I thought about it *again* when I found out you were laid up in here. And then again when you were giving this stranger access to your house, vehicle, and precious memories, but I didn't."

"Why not?" Marilyn might fall from the chair if she shifted any more toward her grandson.

"Because I'm pretty sure I'd be in as much trouble as you are for all this." He placed a hand over Marilyn's forearm, his tone becoming more stern. "Now, as long as you behave and don't get yourself kicked out before I'm ready for you, we might keep all this between us and stay in her good graces."

Marilyn rested her hand on his. "We'll get our summer together back? I was afraid I might miss it all."

"My favorite time of year." He winked and gave her hand a squeeze.

Ellie's blood warmed. She couldn't take her eyes off the pair. What did their summers usually entail when Marilyn wasn't injured? How long had this been their tradition?

Someone rapped on the door and rolled a metal cart inside.

The tall young man had jet-black, shaggy curls. His eyes shone like emeralds, and his formfitting scrubs revealed his commitment to a structured workout routine. He placed a cup of coffee and a small plate of cookies at Belle's side table.

"I thought a couple of lovely ladies like yourselves could use some refreshment," he said.

"Well, aren't you as sweet as you are handsome." Belle's voice dropped low and sultry when she ran a finger across his hand.

He winked and moved to take Marilyn her portion. "That's a stunning blouse, Miss Marilyn. Really brings out your eyes."

"Wore it just for you, sugar." Marilyn growled like a cat—or some next-level cougar, really.

With another dramatic wink, the aide took his cart and exited the room.

Warren looked back and forth between the two older women. "What the—"

"I'm going to guess that's Connor from food services." Ellie laughed, receiving enthusiastic nods from the two nursing home residents.

"Isn't he a dish? Midmorning coffee is the best time of day." Marilyn slapped both hands to her thighs, cackling along with Belle.

"You have got to be kidding me," Warren said. "Remind me why I'm protecting you from Mom again?"

"Because you love me." Marilyn clapped her hands together at her heart. "You going to go talk to the manager now?"

"I thought I was, but now I'm afraid, to be real honest." He gestured toward Ellie for help.

"Don't look at me. I'm not family. This is *your* battle." She smiled. "I'm just the animal caretaker."

"And a damn good one at that," Marilyn said.

Warren hummed in opposition. "Ish."

Before Ellie could object, Marilyn swatted her grandson. "Warren, I'm getting real sick of your attitude."

Warren ducked out of hitting distance. "Well, I'm getting tired of yours too, Gram."

Down the hallway, someone cranked their music again. This time it was...Lil Wayne? That couldn't be right either. The nursing home staff had their hands full with a hallway of partiers.

Marilyn waved her grandson off and turned her attention to Ellie. "Honey, again, I'm so thankful you took such good care of Sheriff. I talked to Tori first thing this morning, and she assured me of your quick thinking. I'm glad my babies are in such expert care."

Ellie avoided all eye contact with Warren while she spoke with Marilyn. "*Expert* is a strong word. I panicked, applied my first aid knowledge, and called for the *actual* expert."

"Anybody else coming out to offer help?" She scowled over her shoulder. "Or is Grumpy Gus here scaring everyone away?"

That nickname suited him all too well. Ellie quieted her voice to keep Warren from hearing and/or teasing her. "Your neighbor has popped by a few times to offer—"

"Oh, isn't he a nice fellow?" Marilyn kept her voice hushed as well, something Ellie didn't know she was capable of. "They're always my first call when I need something, and they don't charge me for the use of their goats. That's a winner in my book."

Hm. Another mixed review on Blake and his family. Ellie needed to start keeping a tally of his rights and wrongs to finish forming her opinion on him. By the time she figured it out, it'd be time to go home.

"You find that envelope?" Belle wrestled with a newspaper in her lap, shaking out a page to scan the local obituaries. "I'm real curious what Marilyn has found so far."

"Got a real promising lead in Missoula at some horse ranch, but they don't have enough info listed for us to know if it's the right John Clay," Marilyn said.

"They had some really good-looking horses for sale though." Belle tapped a finger to her lips.

"Oh, heavens, yes," Marilyn agreed. "We looked through every one of those horses. Forgot what we were doing on that site in the first place."

Belle clicked her tongue. "So many distractions on that internet. Makes it hard to get anything done."

"They put those damn advertisements on every damn website. Sales everywhere. You kids wouldn't believe it." Marilyn pointed to her computer and addressed her grandson. "There's a lady in Billings making sweaters out of cat hair, Warren. They're cute, but don't you dare get me one of those for Christmas."

"Noted." Warren straightened his jeans and started making his way toward the door. "Just remember, Gram, if you end up finding this long-lost love of yours, there won't be anything I can do to protect you from Mom and Janey on *that* one."

"Oh, pishposh. I don't need your protection." Marilyn waved him off.

"You're going to need *someone's* protection."

Belle waved between the two of them. "One of my sons is a cop. Another's a lawyer. The computer science one will be useless to you, so we'll just forget about him."

"All true." Marilyn agreed because she'd gotten to know Belle *so well* in the past few days. "Hopefully we don't have to involve the police. How much longer are you staying with us, Ellie? I can't remember what I had on the calendar. Maybe I can still make you breakfast one of these mornings at the farm like I planned, if my strapping grandson is bringing me home soon."

"About a week and a half. I'm happy to have coffee with you and help you find your hidden envelope or whatever else you need, but you're under no obligation to cook for me." The promise of more frequent chats and giggles with Marilyn would brighten the rest of the vacation. She'd do whatever she needed to—even work alongside Warren if necessary—to bring Marilyn home.

And possibly Belle too. That would be such a cherry on top of all the glorious pandemonium.

Marilyn sat up at the mention of the Airbnb again and pointed her bony, ringed finger at Warren. "If Janey or your mom make a surprise inspection, you do whatever you have to do to hide Ellie. Don't let them get a hold of her or find out why she's there. Understood? Keep her under wraps."

What exactly did they think her daughters would do if they found Ellie out there?

"You want me to stick her in the basement?" Warren looked over at her through his fallen bangs and grinned.

She forced a threatening look his way, but inside, her stomach knotted. "I can handle myself. I'll make up a story if I have to. Or, you know, hightail it out of Montana."

"Oh, you will do no such thing. You're my guest out there, and no one is cutting your visit short." Marilyn waved off the thought. "You lie low with Warren until the coast is clear. It'll be fine."

Belle chuckled to herself, then held her hand over her mouth like she could shield Warren from hearing her next words to Ellie. "No harm in hunkering down with a handsome man, kiddo. Just enjoy it. Unless your heart is set on Connor in food services?"

"Oooh boy." As much as Ellie tried to avoid eye contact with Warren, she couldn't help it.

His face burned even redder as he tapped his palm to the doorframe. The smart thing would have been to go speak to management a long time ago, but he just had to stick around.

"You're going to have some major competition with Connor, Ellie. We won't give him up so easily." Marilyn held up her fists and mustered her most terrifying face.

Ellie surrendered. "Connor's all yours, ladies. Pretty sure he's about ten years younger than me."

"And about, what, sixty younger than y'all?" Warren made a sound in between a cough and a throat clearing. "I do not want to get a call that you're harassing food services for any other reason than *food*. Got it?"

Marilyn smiled at her accomplice across the room. "No promises."

He waved for Ellie to join him there. "We're going to go plead your case with the director and hopefully get you off the hook with your troublemaking before heading out. And don't worry, I'll steer Ellie clear of Connor in the hallway."

"Shut up." Ellie swatted at him the way Marilyn always did, hitting him square in the chest. The contact sent a shiver up her arm.

Their provocation hadn't reached a physical level yet, and she had to go and cross that line. She swallowed hard and turned to bid Marilyn and Belle goodbye, but the words caught in her throat when Warren's "retaliation" came in the form of a gentle hand resting against the small of her back to lead her out the door and around the corner.

Mom: Do you know how to install crown molding? We think the dining room could use that too.

Dr. Tori-Hero Veterinarian: How's Sheriff today? How are YOU?

Averie: Saw a girl in the office that reminded me of you. Carpal tunnel at twenty-six years old because of a computer job! Maybe it's a good thing you're switching careers.

CAREER SWITCH. THAT WAS an interesting way to phrase it.

Ellie finished putting the eggs in the barn refrigerator and popped out the back door to snap a picture of the beautiful Montana horizon. She sent the image to both her mother and sister. The scenery should be enough to distract them for a hot minute.

Her response to Tori was much friendlier and in depth: You wouldn't even know he got hurt. He's been patrolling the pasture all morning like always. And I'm calm now, so long as that doesn't happen ever again. ;) Hope bath time went smoothly! Thanks again for coming to my rescue last night.

It was nice to have an ally, especially one who understood her current situation on the farm and didn't care who she'd recently broken up with. It took the sting out of losing Chloe in the breakup a little bit. Friendship shouldn't be based on who you're dating, but that was the reality of it sometimes.

Ellie shoved her phone back into her pocket and kicked at the stones on her way across the lot, slowing when Hilda bounded from the barn and made walking much more difficult. Chickens cried as they ran to get out of the way, their wings flapping wildly. Ellie was the real target of the dog's enthusiasm.

"Easy, girl," Ellie called, and braced herself for impact.

Hilda slowed, but still leapt up, her nubby tail wagging a mile a minute. Ellie patted the dog's soft head and gently pushed her down.

"Ellie!" Warren called from the distance.

His booming voice almost made her fall over her own feet. She hadn't even seen him around the farm since they'd gotten back from the nursing home. Even now, he didn't approach. Just stood there at a distance and waited.

"What's up?" she called back.

"You want to meet me at the house in about an hour to eat some cheese?" he asked.

Wow. She never would have imagined that question to come out of his mouth. Or, well, anyone's. "Eat cheese?"

"Gram called *again,* all worried about this smoked gouda going bad. Said we need to eat it." It was, hands down, the strangest conversation ever shouted across a farmyard. "Plus, I thought we could look for that envelope."

Ah, the TOP SECRET envelope. Number six on the to-do list. If she found that *and* ate the cheese, she'd kill two weird birds with one weird stone.

Then again, doing both of those things with Warren would be… interesting.

"Sounds like a blast," she called out.

He gave a thumbs-up and whistled for Hilda to return to his side as he went back to work.

It took Ellie a second to get her bearings. Rather than thinking her an intruder ready to take Marilyn for all she had, he now planned to help her dig through the older woman's things over hors d'oeuvres.

Ellie headed to her tiny home and put away her computer. She kept a close watch on the clock as she heated up some late lunch, reapplied deodorant, and tried to stay hydrated after spending the morning in the hot gazebo. Her mascara held up acceptably against the heat, and with some coaxing, the frayed hair around her braid smoothed into place.

Another quick check of her phone proved that her mother and sister were successfully distracted by the scenic pic. Unfortunately, there still weren't any missed calls or emails from job prospects either. A lot of those listings hadn't given her a number to call and check on her applications, and the email inquiries she made went unanswered.

It was also kind of odd that she hadn't gotten any new messages from Blake recently. Not that she needed him to reach out when she was about to go to Warren's for cheese.

Or that she needed to think too hard about sharing cheese with Warren…

At exactly the one-hour mark, she trekked across the lot once again. Walking the expanse between the two houses a few times a day gave her more exercise than she'd ever gotten in Columbus. The most cardio she partook of there was when she tried to keep up with her mom at Easton mall. Not an experience for the faint of heart.

Oooh. Maybe she could get a job at that little skincare store there she loved so much. It wouldn't pay much, but their heavily scented products might be the only thing able to combat the farm smells she'd surely bring back home. That was a job perk for sure.

In the distance, Hilda ran through the animal pen, Bilexin ball in her mouth, chasing the chickens with it like she wanted them to play along. Hilda's absence from the main house must mean Warren hadn't come up yet. And since he seemingly trusted her now, she let herself in without knocking first.

But she'd been wrong about Warren's location, because the very first thing she saw when entering the kitchen was him exiting the bathroom, pulling a fresh shirt over his bare chest as he walked.

"Ope." Her eyes went wide, and she averted her gaze—mostly because she'd said *ope* out loud like a total dork and not because she'd caught him dressing.

"Could have been worse, am I right?" He'd promised her he'd seen nothing when he'd busted in on her in the shower, but maybe he'd lied.

She wanted to puke right there on the kitchen tile. A breakfast burrito might have been the worst possible idea for lunch. Nevertheless, from now on, she would knock first.

"You want crackers with this cheese?" he asked.

She tried to find her voice again. "Well, I don't want to eat a brick of cheese plain."

"Never seen someone so worked up about food going bad." He reached into the fridge and grabbed two cans of pop, picked up the cheese plate, then nodded for her to follow him into the living room. "There's at least a dozen other groceries well past their dates in the fridge, but the cheese was *not* on sale, and the deli tried *very hard* to slice it just the way she likes."

"I love her." Ellie laughed. Marilyn was exactly the kind of person Ellie wanted to be when she grew up: spicy, quirky, passionate, fun. And she left her mark everywhere she went.

The home's interior design expertly reflected that personality. Barely an inch of wall was visible. Two couches lined the perimeter, with two *very* different flower patterns that clashed rather amusingly. Ellie took a moment to peruse the family photos on the wall. One showed a little blond-haired, blue-eyed boy smiling wide as he used a toy bulldozer to push around a pile of dirt. That had to be little Warren.

"She says she's now positive the envelope is in this room, but she still can't remember where." Warren handed Ellie a drink and examined his surroundings. "Says she's hidden a lot of things around the house over the years, which will make things extra fun when she does move out for good."

"I don't envy you when that time comes." The very mention of Marilyn moving out brought Blake to mind again. He'd happily come help them search for all of Marilyn's hidden treasures if it meant getting her out the door any faster. She shook away the thought. "It took us forever to go through Grandma Val's house when she went to the nursing home. She kept some of the strangest stuff."

"Maybe it's a grandma thing," Warren said. "I have a feeling this will all fall to me when the time comes, and secret envelopes and jewelry will only scratch the surface of the weird."

That sounded right. She'd love to be a fly on the wall when he got down to that project. "You think she'll have to move out of here soon? It sounded like your mom and aunt want her to go to Spokane in the near future."

He shrugged. "They've been saying that for years, and nobody's done anything about it. I think Gram and I have both learned to just nod our heads when they get to talking like that. They're very used to being the boss—they say what they want done, then wait for someone else to do it for them."

"Sounds kind of similar to my family. Though, they're more delegators, and I might be their only employee..." She tapped her finger to her chin dramatically.

"Pretty sure they see me as their employee too. Albeit one they wish they could fire."

Hey, there was an idea.

She took a sip of the ice-cold beverage in her hand. "I gotta say, I'm a little surprised you're willing to help me find this envelope after the reservations you've had. It's nice not to be total enemies."

He shrugged and put his pop on the coffee table. "I apologized, didn't I?"

"Actually, no." Ellie crossed her arms over her chest and tried to force her most menacing face. "You said you were going to, but you skirted around that part."

His head rolled on his shoulders. "Fine. I'm sorry. I'm sorry I thought you were an evil genius. Is that better?"

The facetious tone made her want to knock him over, but her head still reeled from that passing moment of physical contact at the nursing home. It was like his fingers still lingered on the small of her back, leaving a burning impression.

Don't overthink it.

"Apology accepted, even if it's a bit pathetic." She coughed into her shoulder and mumbled under her breath, "And I guess I'm sorry about the names I've been calling you in the meantime."

Warren laughed as he sandwiched several slices of cheese between two butter crackers. "Wouldn't be the first time a woman has done that."

"That is not hard to believe." Ellie had to think fast when he threw a cracker. "Hey!"

"*Anyway*, I figure if Gram is determined to find this John Clay guy, there's no use fighting her. She's extremely stubborn, and I wouldn't win that battle if I tried."

"You make a good point," she said.

He offered a crooked smile, not too unlike the grin on his childhood photo. "Well, we'd better get started. I don't have high hopes for success. We're talking about a woman who used to hide Easter eggs so well that it took us kids hours to find them—all while she laughed maniacally from her chair."

"Also not hard to believe." Marilyn was likely the biggest kid of them all.

Ellie put her drink beside Warren's and started hunting between couch cushions.

Warren followed suit. His shoulders nearly touched hers when he began lifting pillows and feeling between the sections.

"I cannot believe she's still hiding stuff around here, even though she lives alone now. I can't believe my *grandpa* didn't know when he was alive," he said.

Even if Marilyn had put her treasures in plain sight, they had a hell of a task ahead in the anarchy that was Marilyn's home decor.

"And this doesn't bother you at all? Her hiding feelings like that for all these years?" If Grandma Val had dropped a bomb like that, Ellie might have needed professional help to sort through the shock.

Warren peered over at her. "Don't think I haven't been mulling it over constantly since the second she confessed."

"And?" Ellie drew a throw pillow to her chest as she watched him.

"Well, as for Gramps, I guess it didn't shock me a ton. My other grandparents, on my dad's side, were always super handsy. Even in their nineties, they'd make us all uncomfortable with their kissing or butt-pinching. In retrospect, maybe kind of adorable? At the time: nauseating." He examined a shattered peppermint he pulled from between the cushions and set it aside. "But Gram and Gramps Perry didn't do that stuff. They didn't even talk much, really. Gramps was a workaholic. Taught me most of what I know today: how to fish, hunt, repair a lawnmower—but he wasn't much for chatting. Gram always talked my ear off. They were so different from each other."

"That's sad." She wouldn't want to be eighty-some years old and regretting the person she'd chosen to spend her life with.

"I dunno. They took really good care of each other. It was functional, you know? Almost like a business partnership."

"Functional sounds like the opposite of romantic." Functional was how she spent the last six years of her life. "And about her wanting to find John now?"

Warren used his phone flashlight to inspect underneath the

couch but didn't find what he was looking for. "If that's what she wants, I hope it works out for her. To be honest, I'm a little curious to meet him myself now." He breathed an awkward laugh. "Mom and Janey would have a fit if they knew any of this. Well, all of Gram's actions lately would send them to an early grave. Let's count ourselves lucky that they barely take time away from the office to sleep, let alone fly to Montana to get anyone in trouble."

Ellie bit her lip. "You think once she finds John, she'll be ready to sell this place and move on?"

"Sell?" He slapped a hand to one of the couch cushions. "I'm going to check behind this couch."

"Yeah, she said your mom and aunt are pushing her to sell, but she's not quite ready. Do you think the John factor is what would make her ready?" Ellie knelt and dumped out the basket full of magazines so she could riffle through it thoroughly.

"It could be. Lord knows she's been offered a lot of money for this place, so it's definitely not a financial thing keeping her here. Don't know if it's driven more by John or more by her desire for independence at this point." Warren peered behind the couch. "There's something down there."

Ellie crawled up beside him and followed his line of vision. Near the baseboard, torn wallpaper revealed a small hole.

"I have this fear we're going to mistake a Marilyn hole for a rat hole," Ellie said.

"That's a genuine possibility. You go ahead and reach in there and let me know."

She narrowed her eyes, then realized how closely she'd positioned herself to him on the couch. "Are you looking to start another fight already?"

He lifted his hands in surrender. "Hell no. Your silent treatment game is agonizing."

Ellie shrugged. "Everybody's good at something."

Warren led the way to the other side of the sofa and crouched to the floor. He pulled back the wallpaper to reveal some crumpled drywall.

"Nothing." He pulled his hand back quickly before anything could grab hold of him. "We may be looking for a while. Let's hope it really is in this room, and we don't have to search the entire property. You sure you're not staying longer?"

She laughed. "Sorry. You have my help for about nine more days, and then you're on your own."

The cuckoo clock in the dining room chimed and brought to mind just how many more hours she might spend in this house searching for Marilyn's memories.

Possibly with Warren.

"At least you've calmed down with the accusations. I don't want to punch you or anything today." She smiled and sank back to the floor and fanned out the stack of magazines in front of her. "I guess the day is young, so I shouldn't cross that off the agenda yet."

"I'll admit, it's more pleasant not thinking you're a threat to my gram too. Frees up a lot of my time not having to keep an eye on you." He pushed the end table out of the way to search behind it.

"Creep." She laughed to herself, thinking of the way her mother referred to Warren.

"Well, if you were planning a future life of crime, maybe you'll stop and reconsider now." He shrugged and chuckled into his hand, clearly amused with himself.

A life of crime certainly sounded more exciting than working for Averie and literally watching paint dry in her new home. "I'd rather just stick to medical transcribing."

Warren crawled between the chair and end table to grab their drinks. He handed Ellie's to her and joined her on the floor. Ellie crossed her legs in front of her to get more comfortable.

"Thought you told Sheriff you were going to sort his straw for pay now." His raised eyebrows above his hand revealed his attempt at hiding his amusement.

Ellie's shoulders slumped. "I'm pretty sure all my life's most embarrassing moments have happened around you, so that's great."

"I feel so privileged."

At least she got to leave him behind in just over a week. That'd save her from having to bury him in the backyard to hide her disgrace. "You would."

"So, Miss Not-a-Con-Artist. I'll admit I've been curious since that night in the barn why you don't have a place to live and want a job sorting straw." He busied himself layering cheese and crackers into a multi-decker treat. "Because that sounds like the kind of backstory a con artist would have…"

"You would think that." They'd never find the envelope at this rate. "I'm afraid it's not nearly as exciting as all that. Since you already know enough dirt on me, I guess I shouldn't be ashamed to inform you that it gets so much worse, actually."

"Ooh," he jested. "Let's hear it."

This would be fun. "As of this moment in time, I live a very independent and professional life in my own apartment employed as a medical transcriptionist. In a few more weeks, however, I lose my lease and my job, thanks to my company changing ownership and my apartment raising their rent. It's not at all stressful."

"Indeed. Sounds very tranquil." He offered the cheese plate again. "So, then what?"

She grabbed a cracker and snapped it in half. "Lucky for me, my family is going to take complete care of everything. I'll be working as a nanny for my sister's three kids and living in my grandmother's old house that my parents now own—if I play renovation specialist and fix it up so they can sell it while I'm there."

"You don't strike me as a home contractor." He smirked.

"I am not, sir."

Warren nodded as he processed the information. "Being a nanny is a big jump from transcription."

"Not a job that was ever on my radar. I have the patience of an agitated wasp when it comes to these children—who I love, mind you." After a week with Aunt Ellie, the kids might beg their mom for a new sitter. She just really needed something else to come through. And fast.

"Aren't there other transcription jobs out there?" he asked.

She hated when people tried to help her find a job—like she wasn't trying hard enough on her own. Warren, however, seemed genuinely curious. "If there are, I can't find them. There are a ton of listings on job sites, but most of them end up being scams in some way or never respond to my inquiries. I kind of can't believe how many of these places just ghost applicants."

The cracker broke even more in her hand. She popped the rest of it in her mouth before it turned to powder and got all over the carpet.

Why was she even telling him all of this? Simple answers would have sufficed while they looked for the envelope. But *nooooooo*.

"And how does one go about becoming a medical transcription-ist? Did you go to college for that?" He made it sound so much fancier than it was.

"Technically, I went to college to be a nurse. For all of one se-mester. Then I dropped out, took certification exams, and became a CMT. Been freelance full time ever since. Like a champ."

Had her life always sounded this dull out loud?

"Why'd you drop out of nursing school?" Warren asked.

"They tried to take us to the morgue, and I blacked out. Needles make me want to vomit, and I have a zero-tolerance policy for gore. I can memorize body parts like a pro, but you try to get me to remove stitches, and I'm gonna have a straight-up panic attack."

"I guess those are important parts of nursing, huh?" He laughed. "But if I ever need body parts memorized, I'll keep you in mind."

Ellie nearly choked on a bit of cracker. "I swear that wasn't a pickup line."

"You sure? Cause it was a real winner." He flashed a thumbs-up that heightened the overwhelming sense of awkwardness filling the room.

Her phone buzzed in her pocket, but the text wasn't a response from Tori.

Blake Robinson-Neighbor: Heard updates on Marilyn?

There he was. Ellie's fingers hovered over the keys, but she couldn't form a reply. What did he expect? Ellie was just a guest on the farm. She wasn't going to text him and tell him to start packing his bags.

"Who's that?" Warren stretched like he meant to read the message in her hand.

"Nobody." She shut off the screen and slid the phone back in her pocket before he could inquire further. No need to fuel discord between all the millennials in this area. "And speaking of jobs, Mr. Tiny House Contractor…" If he was going to give her dumb nicknames, two could play at that game. "I've been meaning to tell you that your job makes you pretty hipster too."

He moaned like the suggestion wounded him deeply. "Just because *you hipsters* like my tiny houses doesn't mean I'm one of you. It simply means I get to *profit* off y'all. Besides, I like the creative factor that comes with fitting all the elements of a full-size home into a single room. It's a challenge. And I didn't even go to college, so you've got a whole semester on me, Pukey." Oh good. More great nicknames. "So does this success of yours mean you have a large construction crew working for you, then?"

"Something like that." He climbed to his feet and offered her a hand. "Enough that I can take a month off during the busiest season to spend time with my grandmother and not have to deal with the additional hipsters trying to talk me down on the price of a composting toilet."

For a second, she stared at his extended hand, wondering if this was a trick or if he meant to smack her or something. But now that they were being friendly, she might as well take advantage.

She slid her hand into his and let him pull her upward. "So, we're just two socially awkward loners, ransacking an old lady's house and denying our hipster nature?"

Warren grinned down at her. "Tale as old as time."

- 21 -

Ellie bit her thumbnail as she stared at the open email.

...appreciate your hard work all these years.

...apologize for any inconvenience.

...reach out if you need a reference.

That was it. They'd cut her loose.

A heavy tear rolled down her cheek. Even though she knew it was coming, seeing it written out in print made it so much more real.

Ellie sucked in a deep breath and shook out her hands. There would be time to lick her wounds later. In fact, that's about all she'd do when she got back home.

Visions of sobbing on the new floor grout filled her head. Children asking, "What's wrong, Aunt Ellie?" Reminders that she didn't act like this when she was with Sean.

As if leaving him was the real problem here.

Grandma Val always said to focus on what you can control. Considering how little control Ellie had in almost every area of her life right now, she would have to focus on the present instead. There was only a week left of this vacation, and she had company coming to help distract her. Thankfully.

Tori had pulled up to the barn to remove Sheriff's bandages, and Ellie wouldn't miss the chance to visit, even if Warren planned to be in attendance as well.

Ellie slipped her feet into rubber boots that went up to her knees. Her toes had plenty of wiggle room, since Marilyn's shoe size was a bit bigger. The chief obstacle was making sure she didn't trip and fall with every step. She tromped out the front door and started across the drive, ready to get out of her head for a little while.

"Hey, cowgirl!" Warren shouted when he rounded the corner of the house. "We've got more rain coming, so I'm going to help you with the animals—maybe teach you a thing or two."

"Oh, how lucky for me," she said when she met up with him halfway.

Warren propped the doors the rest of the way open. It stunk of manure and hay, which honestly wasn't the worst combination Ellie could imagine, even with her tender stomach.

"Hi, you two." Tori knelt by the penned donkey, used bandages pooling in her lap. "He's healing up nicely."

Ellie brushed her hand over the cross-pattern on Sheriff's brow, grounding herself in the feel of his soft but dirty fur. "That's great to hear."

"I got that post fixed, so it shouldn't happen again. Well, not from that particular corner." No wonder Warren had to come to the farm every summer to fix things for Marilyn and the animals. The real shocker was that he didn't have to come every month.

"Thought you'd be at the home this morning," Tori directed toward Warren. "Mom said you've been coming by like clockwork before you visit Marilyn."

Warren shrugged. "I'd planned on it, but Gram said they had some sort of field trip scheduled at the plant nursery today."

"So, instead, he's taking time away from his busy barn-fixing schedule to teach me how to be less sloppy in my animal care." Ellie flashed him a fake smile. "Aren't I blessed?"

"Oh, this is a course I'm definitely auditing." Tori massaged some ointment around Sheriff's wound.

"Great." Warren waved his hand over the donkey. "Then I'll let you two take care of him, while I clean out and refill his trough with water *and* electrolytes because the summer heat can deplete him." He picked up a canister from the shelving unit and displayed it Vanna White style. "I'm sure Dr. Hill here can put everything into medical terminology if you prefer—just don't go throwing up on any of us, Pukey."

"Quit it." Ellie raised a threatening eyebrow.

He ignored it. "Also, you gotta keep his teeth and coat clean. Looks like the farrier came not too long ago and took care of him."

"I don't know what a farrier is." Ellie's thoughts traveled to a Grim Reaper–looking creature that took souls to the underworld.

"Farriers care for equine hooves, trimming and shoeing," Tori said as if that clarified anything. "Sheriff's had a nice little pedicure recently."

Up to this point, Ellie had mostly cared for the Perry animals like one cared for a cat or a dog. This new vocabulary lesson put a more complicated spin on things.

Warren handed her a couple brushes and patted the donkey's hindquarters. "Why don't you get started brushing some of that dirt off him? Use the soft brush for his face; hard brush for everything else."

"Can do." This additional task might consume more of her time, but it beat having to scoop poop or scrub floors. There were always animal groomers hiring. She could put herself out there as a donkey specialist.

Marilyn's rubber boots made it harder to shuffle from side to side without tripping. At the feel of the first brush, Sheriff began his gleeful trotting in place.

"Easy there." Tori hopped up to put some space between her and the dancing beast. She gave him a pat and offered to take the second brush from Ellie.

Somehow, Ellie doubted many other vets finished their work and helped with farm chores. That's what made Tori better than the rest.

"Marilyn will be so happy to be reunited with her animals," Tori said. "It's got to be killing her to be away from them."

"Well, you'll be happy to know that Warren plans to bring her home soon and keep an eye on her the rest of the summer." The idea still brought a big smile to her face. Not just because Marilyn got to be in her own home for the remainder of her recovery, but because she had a grandson willing to do that for her. Perhaps he had a gooey center inside that tough exterior shell—like a Cadbury egg.

Warren glanced up from his task. "Nothing is set in stone. I haven't mentioned any of this to Mom or Aunt Janey, so don't go spreading it around. I still have to make some changes around here so it's safe for her and figure out a therapy or nursing plan or whatever."

"I can just see Marilyn in her wheelchair, sitting out here supervising and sipping her lemonade." Ellie so hoped she got a chance to witness it before she left.

Tori laughed. "You really want her watching you work? She seems like a micromanager."

"Oh, the worst kind." Warren took up his shovel. "But whatever she dishes out, I give it right back."

"Well, you'll have to dish it times two if Belle comes along. I'm pretty sure the pair of them will be like those two old hecklers from the Muppets." Ellie cracked herself up with the comparison.

"She wants to bring a friend?" Tori nearly dropped the brush to the floor. "I'd watch the hell out of that sitcom."

"You'd better believe I'm filming every second if it happens while I'm here." Whether she was productive in her actual day job or not, brushing dirt out of a donkey's fur felt like the most fruitful task she'd done in years. Sheriff nudged her with his long snout, a sweet thank you for her efforts.

Maybe being a groomer wasn't the worst idea, with a little bit of professional training. She liked animals, and it'd keep her busy enough throughout the day to pass the time. All of her searches had involved healthcare or remote work in some respect, but branching out could be fun too.

Tori paused her brushing and listened. "Is someone's phone going off?"

Ellie's back pocket vibrated again. "It's mine. I should have left it in the house."

"Aren't you going to see who it is?" She moved to hang her brush on the wall and plucked a large bale of hay from the stacks like it weighed nothing. These farm people were a boss breed.

"It's probably my family wanting to talk about something I *don't* want to talk about." She thought of the even more likely possibility of it being follow-up messages from Blake since she'd ignored his text the day before. Ellie hung her brush on the wall too, ready to change the subject before Tori thought to ask about Blake. "So, you two went to high school together?"

Warren rolled his full wheelbarrow over and situated it next to Ellie. "Yep. Go Bulldogs. Now, grab a shovel and start scooping shit in here. You can't just push it out the back door and hope for the best."

She crinkled her nose at the jab but grabbed the shovel as he'd asked. "Tell me, Tori. Was Warren this much fun in high school?"

"Oh, absolutely." She answered without hesitation. "Imagine a scrawnier version of what you see today. Typical FFA, 4H, and industrial arts club enthusiast. But I also recall you collecting your share of Pokémon cards…"

"Not in high school," Warren snapped. "That was elementary."

Hilda ran past the open barn door toward the pasture. The goats' chatter kicked up a notch at her presence, and the chickens tried their best to take flight to get out of her way.

"My bad." Tori raked hay into a pile and tossed it into a second wheelbarrow. "Warren and I had a graduating class of forty-one students, and that's actually pretty big for this area. Everybody knows everybody else. And that's why I told you the other day that I never dated any of the guys here."

"Because we're that repulsive?" Warren stopped what he was doing and sauntered closer.

"Because it'd be like dating my cousin. I know you all entirely too well, and it's a hard pass from me. Though, yeah, some of you are totally repulsive. Blake Robinson included."

Ellie could feel Tori's stare embedded in the back of her head. She tried to keep shoveling, but the new silence wasn't conducive to scooping manure.

"Why are you looking at her like that?" Warren asked and turned his attention on Ellie. "Do you know Blake?"

She couldn't avoid the question when he stood that close. "*Know* isn't the word I'd use. He came and got that stray rooster and took it back to where it belonged. Helped me with Sheriff before you got here too."

Rather than expressing gratitude, Warren's face portrayed disgust. "And what did he want in return?"

"Nothing." She couldn't bring herself to admit Blake asked about the farm. Not like Blake could do anything about buying the place without Marilyn's consent, so it didn't matter.

Warren guffawed. "He always wants something."

"I take it you're not a fan either?" That was one more check on the negative side of opinions on Blake Robinson. Though, Warren liked so few things...

"No. Do *you* like him?" He took a step closer. There might as well have been a spotlight shining down from the barn rafters onto Ellie.

Tori, too, moved in and waited. An ornery smirk played on her lips.

"I don't know him enough to make that call." Shoveling dung appealed to her so much more than this conversation. "Where do we dump the wheelbarrows when they're full?"

"Smooth subject change." Tori laughed and pulled her phone from her pocket. "Shoot. I gotta get over to Lynn Schoenle's and vaccinate some horses." She pushed the shovel handle into Warren's chest like she meant it as a threat. "Play nice. I like having her around."

"I'm glad someone does." He grabbed Tori's shovel and ducked out of the way before anyone could hit him with something else.

Tori bid her goodbye and hurried on her way, leaving Ellie alone with Warren once again.

"You gave up on being civil to me awfully fast," Ellie said.

"I have commitment issues." Warren hoisted the wheelbarrow and waved for Ellie to follow him out back to the compost pile. "And you're an easy target."

She huffed. "You know, Warren, since you're planning to bring Marilyn home, I'm thinking about staying on as a farmhand. You're only enabling my chances by teaching me the ropes." Blake had shown her the compost pile when he chucked the old eggs, but she hadn't thought to put the manure from the pens back there too.

"No. No. You have to go back to Ohio. I don't need you and every other woman in Choteau ganging up on me. It used to be really peaceful out here before you came." He dumped the barrel and spun back around. "You definitely need to bail before you start getting all romantic with the neighbor boys."

Ellie rolled her head on her shoulders to mimic her eye roll. "Romantic? In this setting? I'm scraping crap off a dirt floor, sleeping with a farty bulldog, and enjoying long, luxurious walks from my closet-house to the gazebo for a decent Wi-Fi signal. And then there's that other super romantic element where I make frequent nursing home visits to meet with a stranger, eat cheese plates nearing expiration, and—bonus—get harassed by a random contractor who used to think me a criminal." She tapped her finger to her lip. "You know, when I lay it all out like that, you're right. This is the sexiest time of my life."

With a loud thud, Warren dropped the wheelbarrow and approached his farming assistant.

"You're certainly dressed seductively enough." He gestured to her feet, then crossed his arms over his chest as he stared at her from a rather close proximity.

"I'm wearing the shoes of an eighty-two-year-old woman, which are designed to get men's attention, and it's clearly working." Ellie forced confidence into her voice, even though it grew harder to joke the longer he stared her down.

Warren's mouth twisted into a half smirk. "Would you really stay out here after all of this?"

It really had been a doozy of a trip. After graduation, Ellie's family spent a week at the beach in North Carolina. During that time, she got stung by a jellyfish, found a dead minnow in her swimsuit bottoms, and dropped out of the sky during a parasailing excursion because the boat ran out of gas. *That* was a more relaxing vacation that *this*.

"It's a nice break from the rest of my life. I'll put it that way," Ellie said.

Warren rested his arms on top of Sheriff. "Is working for your sister and parents really worse than staying here to get bossed around by a feral old lady and her grandson who thought you were a criminal?"

"I didn't say *you* had to be here if I stayed. The feral old lady is fine." Her cheeks blazed hotter, and she was pretty sure her eyebrow twitched or something as she tried to maintain eye contact.

"Uh-huh. And what about Blake Robinson?"

The accusatory way he said Blake's name sent chills up her arms. "He doesn't have to be here either."

Whether or not she'd made up her mind about Blake's character—and *despite* his good looks—Ellie didn't feel like cozying up too closely to him. After all, no part of this trip had been designated as rebound time.

Then again, no part of the trip had been designated for livestock care, scavenger hunts, elderly visitation, or proving her morality. She only meant to try and put the shattered pieces of her life back together. This was a very funny way of doing that.

"Sure." Warren shook his head. "Now, if you can make some room on that busy dance card of yours, we've got some goats to wrangle."

Case in point.

– 22 –

THE WHITE PICKUP ROUNDED another corner, forcing Ellie closer to the driver. She righted herself and clung tighter to the armrest. What exactly was the "day after" etiquette for two unattached individuals who spent the evening wrestling goats into a pen?

"Depending on how much I get done around the house over the next few days, I should be able to bring Gram home soon." Warren's voice cut through the awkward silence. Ellie was getting dangerously close to talking about the weather, or worse—responding to her sister's latest text attempt to guilt-trip her into coming home early.

"Do you need any help?" Now, why'd she go and ask a thing like that? For one, she had no skills. Her efforts would be more of a hindrance, if anything. And two, volunteering to spend quality time with Warren didn't rank all that high on her to-do list.

"I thought you said you weren't good at renovation." Warren grinned and scratched at his stubbly chin. "I'm building a ramp."

"I'm sure there's a YouTube video on it somewhere." Yes, one-on-one time with Warren would be awkward as hell, but helping prepare the home for Marilyn would be the perfect distraction to get her through the rest of the trip. It was something she could actually feel good about at least.

Warren shook his head as he veered into the nursing home parking lot. "Yeah, that's how we professionals all do it."

The sun blazed hotter than it had since Ellie arrived in Montana, casting an inferior mirage over the blacktop. Caring for the animals had caused her to work up quite a sweat earlier in the day, but building a ramp in the afternoon might make her melt away completely.

They made their way through the double sliding doors, and Warren nodded to the nurse behind the welcome desk as he usually did. This time, however, she quickly turned away from him.

Ellie tried to make eye contact too, but the nurse put in extra effort to avoid them. What pranks had Marilyn and Belle pulled this time? One of these days, they'd arrive and find both women sitting on the curb with their bags.

At room 34, Warren rapped twice on the door and entered with some apprehension. Ellie, too, slowed her pace when she realized Marilyn wasn't there. Her bed had been made to perfection, the blanket Marilyn kept on her chair folded and draped over the armrest. Even more concerning was the way Belle fidgeted with her kerchief in her lap, without the usual excited hello or teasing.

"Belle, where's Gram?" Warren took a small step toward her.

She wadded the kerchief in her palm and shook her head. "Oh, it's bad, sweetie. It's real bad."

"What's bad? What happened?" Warren sank to Belle's mattress.

Ellie sat beside him. Marilyn had been entirely healthy the day before. Surely, if something had happened to her, the nursing home would have called right away. Wouldn't they?

"Caught her by surprise. We never saw it coming. She…" Belle bit her bottom lip and shook her head as she stared at Marilyn's empty chair.

"Oh, God. Is Gram—"

"Dead?" Belle finished. Her eyes had gone wide as she clutched the armrest.

Warren's shoulders tensed. "How? When?"

Belle reached forward and slapped him on the knee. "No, she ain't dead. You didn't let me finish."

All air left Ellie's body like a deflating balloon.

"What? What is happening?" Warren ran his hands over his head like he might explode without the pressure. "You said 'dead,' and you're acting all somber and..."

When Warren trailed off and replaced coherent thoughts with a chain of swears, Belle placed a hand over her heart. "You stop being so dramatic. That woman is healthy as a horse in heat 'cept for that busted-up knee. You just went assuming things about us elderly folk. It's rude."

Warren beat his fist to his forehead and looked over at Ellie, a signal for her to take things from here before he fully erupted.

Ellie didn't fumble. "Okay, let's back up here. What happened, Belle? Where is Marilyn?"

Belle wadded her kerchief again and wiped her nose. "It's so much worse than death. So much worse."

Voices grew louder in the hallway, and Belle reached forward, digging her nails into Warren's knee. He had no time to react, as a nurse indicated they'd reached their destination, followed by another person offering a cold thanks.

Warren stiffened.

Marilyn's propped leg entered first, followed by a wide-eyed Marilyn in the wheelchair. The vibe she gave off suited Belle's panic-inducing greetings. Even the nurse pushing the chair appeared exhausted, as if she'd taken Marilyn for a morning jog around Choteau and not—well, whatever it was they did.

And then a third woman entered the room, dressed in a sleeveless black dress, with a long gold necklace. Her professionally manicured fingers readjusted the expensive-looking sunglasses on top of her flawlessly highlighted hair. She scanned the room until her gaze locked on Warren, and her lips curled up into a smile.

"Mom." He stood with more effort than it should take. "What are you doing here?"

The woman took Warren's hand, pulling him closer to give

him a quick kiss on the cheek. Behind him, Belle grimaced like she watched a horror movie.

With Marilyn's wheelchair on her side of the room, the nurse hurried away. This one also avoided eye contact with Ellie, even though they'd been friendly on every other occasion.

The air-conditioning blew much, much colder.

At the sight of Ellie sitting on Belle's bed, Marilyn turned her face to the heavens and mouthed either a prayer or curses just as Warren had done before. If they were both this much on edge, Ellie didn't stand a chance.

"And who's this?" Warren's mom looked Ellie over.

Warren cleared his throat. "Um, this is Ellie Reed. She's—"

"Warren's girlfriend," Marilyn practically yelled from across the room.

Behind Savannah, Marilyn put her hands together, begging them to play along. Whatever happened this morning at the nursing home, Marilyn didn't want to out herself as an Airbnb host on top of it.

Ellie's heart raced as she slowly turned to Warren.

"Your girlfriend?" Savannah quirked an eyebrow. "You didn't tell me you were dating someone."

Marilyn clapped her hands to pull Savannah's attention away from the young couple. "Lovely girl. She's from the Middle East. Well, of the United States, that is. Just got here. But don't you worry. She's staying in the tiny house, and he's at the farmhouse. No funny business on my watch." She laughed nervously.

Belle's gaze drifted from one person to the next, her shoulders vibrating as her jovial attitude resurfaced with the new development. She only needed a bowl of popcorn, and she'd really get to enjoy the show.

"Yeah, Ellie's my girlfriend." Warren spoke the words like he had to test them out. Then he looked to her to test her reaction as well. "Been together for…some time."

Even though she might vomit her heart out at any second, Ellie managed a shrug and extended her hand to Savannah. If they were going to throw her into these wild scenarios, she should have prepared better. "I've told Warren he needs to call his mother more often. It's nice to finally meet you, Ms. Oliver."

Savannah shook Ellie's hand and nodded to her son as if this mystery girlfriend spoke some legitimate truth. "I think I like you already."

Warren scowled at his grandmother for getting him into this mess.

"What brings you to Choteau? This isn't exactly romantic getaway material." Savannah tapped a polished nail against her hip.

The tension in the room thickened by the second. If Ellie had known Warren's mom meant to surprise them with a visit, she would have stayed at the farmhouse. She had a strong feeling Warren would have too.

"Actually, it was a terribly sweet gesture." Ellie fought to keep an awful English accent out of her voice. Something about the fancy rich woman vibes Savannah gave off made Ellie crave tea and crumpets. "For our three-month anniversary, Warren surprised me with this trip because of my affinity for donkeys."

Warren's hand flattened on his forehead, and he mouthed some more colorful swears.

So, this wasn't too bad of a pretend game. She could have some fun at Warren's expense, especially if it meant lightening the severity for Marilyn too.

"Millennials and their donkeys." Belle cackled now, and Marilyn stared at the ceiling to avoid making eye contact with anyone.

"Wow. Okay." Warren held up his hands to settle everyone. "Ellie likes animals. It's nothing—" He groaned. "Never mind. What brings *you* here, Mom? We weren't expecting your visit."

Savannah drew her phone from her dress pocket and checked

the screen. "Well, I wasn't planning to come, but I got a call from the nursing home yesterday afternoon stating you planned to take Mom home."

Oh no.

"Why did they call you about that?" Warren's question reflected the chill in the room.

"Because I'm her next of kin, power of attorney, and all that." Savannah rested a hand on her hip and shifted her weight. "Apparently, Mom listed my phone number incorrectly on her forms, but the administrator got that sorted out. She called me *and* Janey at that point, which I'm sure you can imagine how well that went over. I got such an earful about it from her. But, honestly, Warren, what were you thinking?"

"I was thinking that Gram would be happier in her own home, and since I'm going to be here for the summer, I could keep an eye on her. I'll hire a nurse to come check on her, and I'm going to put in a ramp this afternoon. She's just got a busted knee; it's not like it was a heart attack or something."

"Warren, you have a career. You have a life in Spokane. You can't give all that up at this point in your life. That farm is so much work. Mom shouldn't be dealing with any of that at her age, and you don't have the time either." Savannah turned to her mother. "I know it's not ideal, Mom, but you can't expect him to put his life on hold right now."

Ellie knew she shouldn't participate in this conversation, however much she wanted to. Even if she was Warren's girlfriend, it'd be a topic well out of her wheelhouse. Being a total stranger to the family and being this deep in their drama wouldn't go over well *at all*.

"I would never want that," Marilyn said.

"Gram." Warren's shoulders slumped when Marilyn changed sides on him.

Marilyn only shook her head. "Your mother's right, Warren. I couldn't ask you to put everything on hold for me. I really appreciate all you've done, but it's all right if I have to stay here a while longer."

"Or at one of the fine establishments we have in Spokane." Savannah's correction did nothing for morale.

"We can talk about it later," Marilyn added. She winked behind Savannah's back, but it lacked the usual spunk.

Savannah had crushed everybody's spirits in one fell swoop. Hopefully she didn't plan to stay long, and Warren and Ellie could return to helping Marilyn accomplish her goals.

"Now, since we have that all settled, why don't you two join me for lunch." Savannah checked her phone again. "I had an early flight, and I'd love to grab a bite before I head to the hotel."

"The hotel?" Warren asked.

Savannah nodded. "I'm staying at the Hilton in Great Falls tonight."

"That's an hour away." Warren raised an eyebrow at his mother, but she only waved away the comment. "You know there's plenty of room at the farm, right?"

"I'll be back to visit again tomorrow, Mom." Savannah didn't offer a hug or kiss.

Marilyn slumped in her chair. "Looking forward to it."

"Shall we?" Savannah gestured for Warren and Ellie to follow and headed out of the room.

Savannah really hadn't given them a choice on what might very well be the most uncomfortable meal of Ellie's entire life.

With a look that spoke a heartfelt apology to his grandmother, Warren sauntered toward Ellie and wrapped a heavy arm around her shoulder. "We'd better go. I'd hate to miss the chance to let my mother scrutinize my *girlfriend* in addition to killing my grandmother's hopes and dreams."

Yeah, lunch would be a total blast.

– 23 –

THANK GOD SAVANNAH RENTED a ridiculously expensive BMW with only *two* seats so they couldn't ride with her to Dinah's Café.

"If you want to come clean, you don't have to keep up with this ruse. It's my family. I can face this music alone; you can escape with your dignity." Warren pulled into the parking lot of what looked like a small log cabin with a porch full of eclectic rocking chairs. The "E" in the restaurant's name had fallen off the sign, but the number of cars proved the little dive might be a diamond in the rough.

Ellie watched Warren's mother in the car next to them as she tapped away on her phone like she didn't plan to get out. "I don't mind playing along for a little while. Your mom is intimidating as hell, but we can take this lunch and use it for our benefit. Maybe change her mind about Marilyn's living situation?"

"Good luck with that. If my mother has decided on something, there's no convincing her otherwise." He squinted in Ellie's direction. "You don't mind playing the part of the doting girlfriend?"

"I can suffer through it." Ellie gathered her purse and reached for the door handle. "Though, don't count on a lot of 'doting.'"

"Whatever. Just keep the donkey comments to a minimum, will you?"

"No promises." She was under no contractual obligation to behave. Though, she definitely had to dredge up some creativity if Savannah wanted information about her life. No way would Ellie give her the truth about her sad situation. A successful woman like Savannah would never approve of a girl like Ellie dating her son.

Did Sean's family ever think that about her too?

Savannah remained silent and statuesque as they took their seats in the bar section of the quirky little café. The walls showcased a variety of taxidermied animal heads, big screen televisions, and auto-graphed images of celebrities Ellie had never heard of. If there was a theme to this place, she hadn't figured it out yet.

When Warren ordered a beer and asked the server to keep them coming, Ellie regretted requesting sweet tea. She might end up having to drive *him* home if he coped with stress this way.

"So, how'd you two meet? Last I knew in regards to your love life, Warren, you were still getting over that cute little schoolteacher from Greenwood you almost married. I'm blanking on her name." Savannah took a sip of her red wine.

Yep. Ellie had some serious regrets regarding her nonalcoholic iced tea.

"That was two years ago, and I'd rather not discuss it." Warren shot a quick glance at Ellie to gauge her reaction, then searched the air for an answer to his mother's initial question. "Ellie needed a contractor. I did a project for her. Simple as that."

If only Marilyn had come along. The woman had such a knack for breaking the tension. If nothing else, Ellie could channel the older woman and have a solid story to report on later. How often did she get to have a fake boyfriend and alternate life?

"You make it sound so casual, Warren." Ellie reached across the table and placed her hand on his wrist. He startled under her grasp. "I'd just moved from Ohio and wanted to live in one of those tiny houses like I saw on TV. So I hired Warren to build it. But you'll never believe this: when I tried to tell him about myself, he thought I was a con artist and didn't trust me. Said I was too hipster or something."

"I told you I was sorry and have since come around to your

hipster ways, *darling*." Warren rested his free hand over Ellie's and gave it a squeeze. A "shut up with this story" squeeze, if she had to take a guess.

Ellie grinned. "And I'm so glad you did, or we wouldn't be here right now. *Together.*"

"Why did he think you were a con artist?" Savannah swirled her wine around in her glass.

Warren pulled Ellie's hand closer to him and smirked a little too sinisterly for her liking. "Because she tried to seduce me by luring me in to find her in the shower."

Ellie clenched her jaw so it didn't drop to the table. He seriously went there. And in front of his own mother too.

"I think I've heard enough of *that* story." Savannah held her empty glass out and searched the restaurant for their server.

With Savannah distracted, Ellie yanked her hand from Warren's as he waggled his eyebrows. She cleared her throat and picked up her tea for the only solace she could find.

"Then tell us more about *your* story." Warren pushed an empty bottle forward on the table and took up the next one the server had dropped off on his last pass-by. "You would have stayed in Spokane, but you came down here on a whim because I was taking Gram out of the nursing home?"

Wow. Warren didn't waste any time getting right to the point. His family lived in a totally different world than Ellie's. She preferred to push the beef with her family deep down inside where it threatened her sanity, rather than dealing with it outright.

"You do not need to get all dramatic with me. I came down here to save you," Savannah said.

"*Save* me?" He slid his chair back and placed an elbow to his knee like he couldn't wait to hear this.

Savannah rolled her eyes. "I know you love your grandmother, but you're not understanding how much work you are about to get yourself into. She's eighty-two years old. She has no business living out there on her own or requiring anyone else to live out there with her. That farm is in the middle of nowhere. It's not like you can expect to run your business the same way with the tiniest fraction of the clientele on top of caring for an elderly woman and whatever ridiculous animals she's rescued lately. She's better off at one of our nursing homes where she can get round-the-clock care and be closer to her children."

"I already planned to be out here for the next month. It's not like I'm being hugely inconvenienced. By the time I'm ready to leave, she'll be up walking and—"

"You don't know that." Savannah's wineglass remained untainted by her ruby lipstick as she held it out for a refill. That's what happens when you have a budget large enough to shop at makeup stores other than Walmart. "We need to start thinking long-term here."

"It's a short-term injury. Bringing her back to the farm with me saves money and buys us time until she's ready to move on to something else," Warren argued.

Savannah's stare grew more intense. "You're worried about the cost of the nursing home but not the cost of running the farm? It's too much of a responsibility for an old woman and too much of a financial risk to you. Summer is your busiest season. I can't fathom why you'd give up the extra income potential to come out here in the summer."

"Because I want to," he spat through gritted teeth.

"And after summer? What then?" Savannah asked.

Ellie hadn't considered how much Warren had sacrificed to help his grandmother. He mentioned having a crew cover for him, but at what cost? Obviously his priorities didn't line up with his mother's, and that spoke volumes. Ellie had to help *somehow*.

"A lot of people in this town seem to care about her. I'm sure it wouldn't be hard to find her some help." Warren wasn't wrong. Considering the local vet had assisted with cleaning out the barn for free, the coffee shop owner adored her, and the hardware man could feed his family (and a small army) on Marilyn's egg donation, she wouldn't be left high and dry.

Ellie wouldn't dare mention Blake, however—not in present company. Despite his potential character flaws, he would help if called upon. Just as he'd done for Ellie.

Savannah scoffed. "Who's going to help her? The neighbors? They only care about her land. We could sell it to them in a heartbeat, which would solve about a million problems, honestly."

"She doesn't want that." Ellie didn't have to bring Blake into it. He'd found his way to the conversation without her help.

"Look, sweetie, I'm sure you're a nice girl, but you don't know my mother well enough to make these kinds of assumptions. We're her *family*."

The chill in the air disappeared, and Ellie's blood flowed hotter. "I know her well enough to understand she's not ready to move on yet. To know she still has plans and goals and—"

"Ellie." Warren tapped the table but didn't look at her.

She wouldn't reveal the rest of their secrets, if that's what he was worried about. "Just telling it like it is, *sweetheart*."

Savannah groaned and adjusted her long necklace across her chest. "Please tell me my mother hasn't been making me out to be a villain in this."

"I don't dislike you. I don't even know you," Ellie deadpanned.

"You've spent about as much time with me as you have my mother, yet you seem to know all about *her*."

Warren pressed into the table when he tried to control his voice. "Mom, seriously."

"What? Your *girlfriend* is making inaccurate assumptions about us. I'm just trying to straighten things out." She drew her attention to the weather report scrolling across the TV behind them. "One day, your parents will reach the age when they can't properly care for themselves, and you'll have to make these decisions. Maybe your children will villainize you the way you're doing to me. Who knows?"

"I'm not trying to villainize you." Grandma Val's move to the nursing home had been so difficult on everyone, even though she needed the expert help they could give her there. Marilyn wanted to—and deserved to—maintain her independence for as long as possible. "I'm just trying to help."

Savannah's long fingernails tapped her glass. "We don't need help from an outsider, but thank you."

And there it was again. Ellie really had been a stranger to the Oliver/Perry family, and yet she went and got all kinds of involved. Despite how much she had grown to care for Marilyn over the past couple of weeks, this woman stranded at the nursing home about to lose her house and dream was *none of her business.*

Warren chugged down the rest of his second bottle. As much as Ellie wanted to walk out of the restaurant right now, she couldn't go without him.

Since Savannah focused on the TV, obviously done discussing her mother's situation with the peons across the table, and Warren had given his energy to flagging the server down for more to drink, Ellie pulled her phone out of her pocket to type a quick message to Tori. No way could she keep this all to herself right now.

Warren shifted in his chair so his shoulder bumped hers. "You gonna call a getaway car?"

"Thought about it," she whispered.

He peeked across the table at his mother, but she had engaged their server in some chitchat about what was taking their food so long—even though the wait time seemed completely average. It was the vile conversation that made the lunch date drag on forever.

Warren's head nearly rested on Ellie's shoulder when he moved even closer to avoid being overheard. "You gonna fake break up with me after meeting my mother?"

Her jaw clenched tightly when she mumbled back, "Au contraire, I'm going to spite-marry you so I can take her down from the inside."

"Solid plan." He laughed.

"What's a solid plan?" Savannah returned her attention to her son.

He pinched his eyes shut. "Nothing. Just what romantic boyfriend and girlfriend things we're going to do later."

Ellie elbowed him, but retaliating did nothing to settle the butterflies that manifested in her stomach.

Whether it was her business or not, she had to stick this out and see how the story ended. Even if it meant keeping up the ruse of being Warren's girlfriend.

For Marilyn's sake.

– 24 –

THE BLT AND FRIES did not sit well. Nothing about her lunch with Warren and his mother did.

"The deal still stands to ditch the scam and never have to face my mother again." Warren hadn't even shut the car door the entire way before he offered Ellie the newest way out.

"You're really trying to get rid of me, aren't you? I thought we had something special, Warren." Ellie fastened her belt and read-justed the seat so she could reach the pedals in Warren's truck. Across the way, Savannah pulled from the parking lot to head to the hotel almost an hour away—not back to the nursing home or out to see the farm.

Warren shook his head. "That's not it. I mean, you shouldn't have to play nice with my family based on subterfuge alone."

"*Did* I play nice? It was kind of a blur." Bits and pieces of the day came back to her. Marilyn's horrified face when she entered the room with Savannah. Warren mentioning boyfriend and girlfriend things at lunch. Savannah's attitude that made Ellie want to throw her iced tea across the table and cause a real scene.

Things had been going so well with Marilyn and the hope of bringing her back to the farm, avoiding a premature move to Spokane, and even indulging her in the search for John Clay. Everything had blown up—just like it had back home. Ellie couldn't catch a break.

"I'm with you on that. I know we've joked about Mom showing up, but I honestly didn't think it'd happen." There might not be a point to making the house accessible if Savannah had her say in things. "I can't believe she'd come here just to ensure I didn't take Gram out of the nursing home. Mom likes to have her way, but this is pretty extreme, even for her. I wonder what else is up."

Ellie rested her forearm on the steering wheel. "That's a lot of effort to give you her opinion."

The fact that Ellie's own family hadn't jumped a plane to Montana to try and talk sense into her was actually quite baffling. Though, they'd already solved all her problems in their minds. Ellie now had a job and house lined up that would save her from her perilous life crisis. The only thing missing that would make her life truly *complete* was a reunion with Sean—one they'd better not be planning in her absence.

"Mom thinks very highly of that opinion too, I assure you," Warren said.

"She's definitely worried about your business." Ellie glanced at him in the passenger seat. He looked so tired, like the few hours they'd been out of the house had worn him down more than a full day of building houses.

Warren tugged at his seatbelt. "Yeah, well, she's very career-oriented. I didn't go into computers like she did, so we always had some tension about that, especially when my cousin Miles started climbing the corporate ladder at a different tech company. I couldn't see myself doing that crap though. I prefer to work with my hands and did basic construction jobs before moving on to flipping houses. When the tiny house market kicked into high gear, my business really took off, and she finally saw I could make a decent living doing this. It calmed her down a little."

"Are you rich or something?" Ellie couldn't help but tease him to lighten the heavy mood. Warren didn't give off "rich guy" vibes. His manner of dress was simple. His truck was functional. His tastes in food and drink didn't seem extravagant.

"I do all right, nosey." His lip quirked into a half smile. "Or you changing con directions and coming after me and my money now?"

She flashed her own goofy grin. "It's for reference if I end up going with the spite-marriage plan."

"Oh. I see. I'd better start drafting the prenup now."

"Shut up." For the first time, she noticed a small dimple that accompanied his smile but couldn't focus on it for long, lest she drive them off the road and into a ditch.

And she did *not* want to have to explain that distraction afterward.

Of all the things she thought she'd do today, pretending to be Warren's girlfriend turned out to be the biggest surprise.

"I'm gonna call Gram when we get home and see what she thinks about all this. I know she said she didn't mind being at the nursing home at some point, but this throws a wrench into so many plans."

"Yeah. I really feel bad for her. It seemed like we might have been able to pull off bringing her back to the farm and all. I kind of thought you'd fight your mom more on that." As intense an arguer as he'd proven to be in previous conversations with her, he'd thrown in the towel awfully fast today.

"I was drinking."

"So?" She always argued better when she had a few drinks in her system.

In the cup holder, Ellie's phone lit up with a text. Before Ellie could even contemplate the sender, Warren snatched up the phone.

"Who's Averie?" he asked.

"My sister." She reached for the phone, but he pulled it out of reach. "Give it back!"

"Want me to respond for you? She says, *Guess who I just talked to. winky face.*" He chuckled to himself, the lingering power of his lunch beers making the words sound more amusing than usual. "Who'd she talk to? I'll ask."

This time, Ellie succeeded in snatching the phone. "No. We're not responding to that."

Because it didn't matter. Every possible person her sister might have talked to would no doubt make Ellie feel worse about things, and she had enough to deal with here in this alternate life at the moment.

"Why not?" He stretched the seatbelt across his chest and shifted to better see her.

"Because I don't care who she talked to. I don't want to know." The phone buzzed again in Ellie's lap, but she kept her eyes forward.

"Oh, it's Gram this time." Warren pointed to her screen.

Ellie fumbled as she put the phone on speaker and placed it back in the center console. "Marilyn? Hey. I'm putting you on speaker. Warren and I are driving—"

"Are you almost home?" Marilyn's voice held an edge Ellie had never heard before.

Warren noticed it too, a crease settling on his brow. "No, we're about ten minutes out of Choteau. Are you okay?"

"They moved Belle. Took her out of the rehab unit to the assisted living building. They said it's insurance related, but I don't—" Marilyn's voice broke, and so did Ellie's heart.

Warren picked up the phone as if he could physically draw his grandmother in closer. He and Ellie exchanged a look that proved they were on the same page.

Ellie checked for oncoming traffic and spun the truck in a wide semicircle. "We're on our way."

The nursing home halls were quieter than they'd ever been. Not even the rowdy neighbor blared his rap music now. But the silence coming from room 34 was the most deafening of all.

"After you left, we were talking about how much trouble I was gonna be in, and in they came to gather her things. Said her son gave his okay over the phone, like he knew what was best. The horse's ass had never even come to visit her."

Warren patted his grandmother's hand and forced his most reassuring smile. "We'll make sure you still see each other, Gram. You said you wanted her out at the farm to—"

"That was a dream, Warren. I shouldn't have gotten my hopes up." She pulled her blanket over her lap and wadded the trim in her fists. "I shouldn't have gotten my hopes up about a lot of things. I'm sorry you had to come all the way back here. I didn't know who else to call."

"We don't mind at all." Ellie could barely stand the defeat in Marilyn's eyes. The day had begun with laughter and anticipation. So many things had gone wrong so quickly.

Marilyn shook her head. "I'm sorry for a lot of things, kids—for messing up your visits, for giving you so much to do, making you clean up my messes with management here." She tried to force a smile but failed. "I'm mainly sorry for what you had to witness this morning with Savannah and for making you play along with my lies. You shouldn't have to cover for me."

"It's fine, Gram. Really. Mom still doesn't know about the Airbnb, and Ellie played the part of ridiculous girlfriend really well. She hadn't even had time to rehearse." Warren spoke to his grandmother as if Ellie didn't sit directly beside him. His only care in the world surrounded putting a Band-Aid on his grandmother's spirit. "We're going to fix everything."

Marilyn sucked in a labored breath and took Warren's hand in hers. "There's no fixing things this time. I wanted to think I could, but I think it's time to let go. It's getting harder to take care of everything. Sometimes, I forget what needs done, or the lifting is too much. It's hard to admit that when you're my age."

"We can get help for you out there for when Ellie and I aren't around. Someone can care for the animals and check in on you." Warren cleared his throat, unable to continue with the plan.

"The girls would never have it. That's another expense, more people to manage from a distance." Marilyn reached for a tissue, but only wadded it up in her hand. "Janey called after you left. She said she's already spoken with a couple different homes in Spokane and thinks she's found the best option for me. They're serious this time, Warren."

Ellie tried to process everything this meant for Marilyn. A month gave the woman barely enough time to pack, let alone wrap up matters with her farm. Moving to Spokane meant saying goodbye to all of her animals, including Hilda. But who would take them in her absence?

Soon, Ellie would be back in Ohio, leaving Marilyn and the animals to their fate. "Can't they wait a little longer until you're ready?"

Marilyn sighed. "They don't think I'm being realistic. And maybe they're right about that too."

Each word cut through Ellie like a knife.

Marilyn gave Warren's hand a squeeze. "There's always a silver lining: I'll get to see more of you if we both live in the same town."

Warren smiled. "That's a pretty good silver lining."

He stared at his grandmother for a long while; he appeared to be thinking hard. "What about John?"

Marilyn bowed her head then and took her hand from Warren's. "That's the other thing I wanted to apologize for. I think I sent you on a wild goose chase."

"What do you mean?" he asked.

She turned to Ellie then and reached beside her chair to pull out a small envelope. "It's no wonder you could never locate my secret envelope. It was in my pocketbook the whole time."

Marilyn began dumping the contents of the envelope into her lap, and all air left the room.

Each small sheet of paper had been clipped from newspapers,

others printed and cut to size. Warren picked a few clippings to read, and Ellie peered over his shoulder. All three were the same—obituaries. And all three showcased the same name—John Clay.

"Do…" Warren shook his head. "One of these is your John?"

"Oh, Marilyn." Ellie couldn't bring herself to say anything else.

Marilyn reached forward and took the papers back from her grandson. She examined each one again for a moment. "A few of these are his relatives, but many of the others came up when I searched for him on the internet. There were so many. Some don't give enough information for me to know if it's him." A tear trickled down Marilyn's cheek. "The more I searched for him, the more I found with his name. I had to force myself to stop looking—couldn't bear the thought of one of these really being for him."

"But if none of these are definitively him, he could still be out there." Ellie wasn't sure her heart could take much more of this conversation.

Marilyn needed a win. They *all* did.

"I think it's time I let him go. I've been carrying him with me in vain for so long, and it's getting too heavy now. It was a fool's hope." She tucked each obituary back into the envelope with tender care. "It will be a fresh start for me in many ways when I go to Spokane."

A nurse entered and began stripping Belle's bed of its sheets and blankets, while the trio sat in silence on the opposite side of the room.

Everything going on back home seemed so small now compared to what Marilyn faced.

Ellie's phone buzzed in her pocket. Without giving it any thought, she swiped the screen and read the message.

And then she read the message again.

And again.

And then she checked the sender, as if none of what she'd read had made enough sense to be true.

Sean: Ellie, I don't know if you still have my number and I'm
not sure if it's OK that I'm texting you after everything, but
I talked to your sister today. She said you're going to start
working for her soon and plan to move into your grandma's
old house to fix it up. She said you might need some help
with it, and I just wanted you to know I'm always here if
you need me. I hope you'll consider. (And please tell your
parents thank you for the nice birthday card.)–Sean

THERE WERE BAD DAYS. And then there was *this* day.

Ellie wished she could go back in time and start it all over again or crawl into bed and pretend not to exist for a while.

Thankfully, Warren had sobered up enough to drive them home because, for the entire trip, she blinked away hot tears that clouded her vision. She kept her gaze toward the window to keep Warren from noticing. Marilyn had dumped enough heavy info on the two of them already during their long afternoon spent trying to comfort her in Belle's absence that he didn't appear to mind the quiet drive.

Her phone buzzed in her hand. Each vibration triggered another wave of anger.

> Averie: SO SORRY! You HAVE seemed sad since you broke up with Sean. I know I'm not making that up!!!

> Ellie: Breakups are sad, Averie! But I'm not sad because we're done, and now he wants to help me fix up Grandma's house like nothing ever happened between us.

Her fingers wrapped so tightly around the phone, she couldn't even bring herself to hit Send. There was still an argument to be had with her parents for sending a birthday card post-breakup. But that was not a conversation Ellie had the energy for now.

Warren turned down the lane, and the setting sun blazed

through the front windshield. Before them, Hilda sprang to life and ran to meet them halfway. The poor dog didn't know what to do with having the whole place to herself for an entire day.

"I'll get everyone inside the barn if you can take care of setting food out." Fatigue shrouded Warren's voice. They might as well have been away for weeks with all that had happened to them since they left for the nursing home that morning.

Food sounded so good right now, but the animals had to come first. Ellie nodded her agreement and hopped down from the truck to get started on chores. Her phone weighed heavily in her pocket now. She had other texts to read besides Averie's. Her mother had probably heard about the girls fighting. Blake probably wanted to know why she hadn't responded or invited him out to the farm in the past few days. She'd used over 75 percent of her data.

That kind of thing.

Tori's response to Ellie's summary of the day was the only one she cared about, but that meant wading through the others to read it.

Ellie moved like a zombie through each feeding, finishing with Hilda on the front porch of the main house. She patted the dog's soft head as she ate. "Good girl, Hilda. It's going to be all right."

Who would take this goofy bulldog when Marilyn moved to Spokane? Hilda belonged on this farm, ran it like a four-legged supervisor. If she didn't have her chickens to boss around, cars to chase up and down the drive, and sheep to herd into a frenzy, what would become of her?

Hilda's ears pricked up, and she turned toward the driveway. Her nubby tail wagged when headlights illuminated the porch.

Great. All they needed was another visitor at this hour.

But the moment the vehicle veered to an angle and parked, Ellie sighed like a thousand pounds had lifted from her shoulders. From the passenger side, Tori hopped out, a pizza box in her hands and a warm smile on her face.

"I thought I'd beat you guys here and have to fight Hilda off so she didn't eat this." Tori appeared relaxed in her leggings and over-sized tank top. Her hair had been twisted into a messy bun, and she wore slide sandals instead of the usual hard-toed boots Ellie had seen her in before.

"You brought dinner?" The tears threatened to come all over again.

The window in the backseat of Tori's SUV rolled down and two small girls poked their heads out, their wild brown curls falling into their faces as they looked around and waved to Hilda, who ran to greet them. From the driver's seat, a man in a baseball cap waved hello.

"I told the fam we were taking a little drive tonight," Tori said. "I'm so sorry to hear Marilyn might be leaving us. Things won't be the same around here without her."

Ellie nodded and sniffled back the emotions.

"I can't tell you how badly I needed this pizza." Even the smell brought some comfort. The darn thing could be covered in ancho-vies and ghost peppers, and Ellie would enjoy every single bite.

Tori smiled. "We can talk more tomorrow after you've gotten some rest. I know it's a lot to digest, especially since you just met all these people. We rural folk can get a little intense and suck you right in. Sorry about that."

"Don't be." In the past two weeks, Ellie had felt more a part of something than she had in many years. "I like it."

Better yet? She'd somehow picked up a new friend in the process. One who came with pizza, which was the best kind there was.

"Good."

Tori's daughters giggled and squealed as Hilda leapt up to lick their fingers. They were beautiful, both of them. Ellie longed to in-troduce herself, walk them through the farm and introduce them to every animal, and laugh with them as they watched Hilda chase her Bilexin ball all over the bean field.

But she was still leaving in about a week. The thought of one more goodbye to someone she had come to care about kept her in place.

"Your daughters look just like you," Ellie practically whispered.

Tori beamed. "They're dying to meet the city woman who came to the country and ruled over the farm like a queen. I told them they'll have to wait until they're not in their pajamas."

Those few little words worked like magic on Ellie's tired heart.

She'd never been the queen of anything. More like the court jester.

"Dr. Hill, I think you might be my favorite medical professional in the history of medical professionals." The smell of melted cheese and tomato sauce wafted through the ventilation slits in the box. The scent would remind Ellie of this moment for the rest of time.

"It's all part of the Hippocratic oath or something like that." She giggled to herself. "But seriously, I like having you in town. Maybe it's because you're bringing a level of entertainment I haven't seen in ages, or maybe it's because female friendships are so hard to come by and I like your style. Either way, I'm glad our paths crossed." The joyful cheers in the background turned sour, as Tori's daughters began arguing over whose turn it was to reach down to Hilda. "I'd better go. It's bedtime, and it's about to get ugly. Text me tomorrow."

Ellie waved and offered her sincere appreciation once more. As they drove off to tackle their family's evening routine, Ellie patted her leg for Hilda to follow, and the pair headed inside to hunt down some paper plates.

The screen door springs squeaked as Warren came in from the barn.

"Oh, hey. Was someone just here?" He kicked off his boots and rounded the corner, the welcome committee wagging her tail in greeting. "Is that pizza?"

"Tori dropped off dinner for us. I think it's extra cheese from the looks of it."

"She did? Why?" Warren grabbed a couple drinks from the fridge.

Ellie shrugged. "I told her it was a stressful day, and she wanted to help."

"Huh. That's really nice. Like, *super* nice." He nodded for her to grab the pizza and follow him to the living room and then melted onto the couch. "I don't know why sitting in a nursing home all day is so exhausting. It's not like we did anything."

"Definitely something to be said for emotional fatigue." Grease coated Ellie's fingers when she pulled apart two cheese-melded pieces of pizza. Her stomach begged her to abandon all small talk and stuff her face.

Warren tore off a piece of crust to appease Hilda, who trembled with delight at his knee. "I really thought this day would go differently."

The plan had been to prepare the house for Marilyn's return once they returned from a routine visit. Now, everything had a big question mark beside it.

Ellie's problems had felt so big. She, too, was being uprooted from her home. Yet, it was hardly comparable to Marilyn's situation. Ellie was only leaving an apartment, not a lifetime of work and memories.

"What happens if they move her to Spokane?" A week ago, she'd never have guessed she'd sit side by side with Warren on this couch, sharing dinner and speaking so amicably. She just wished the topic wasn't such a gut punch.

He tossed another bit of crust to Hilda. "Well, she's right that it'll be easier for me to visit, so we'd have that. Unfortunately, I'd bet money that the closer proximity doesn't bring more visits from Mom and Janey. And the farm will sell very quickly, I'm sure of it, but it'll come with its own drama."

"And the animals?"

Warren shook his head. He didn't want to answer that question any more than Ellie actually wanted to ask it. They both knew they'd end up scattered around. Marilyn might never know their fate.

"If Mom had stayed in Spokane, we could have pushed this

off for a while and gotten Gram back here to live where she wants, because she does want to be here. She might have said she's okay with moving, but I know it's not true."

Ellie had to agree. Marilyn had taken a beating today, and it'd definitely affected her on an emotional level.

Warren reached for another slice of pizza on the end table. "I guess we can be glad it was Mom and not Janey who came down here. I'm sure it's hard to imagine, but Janey is way more high-strung. She would have thrown Gram on a plane the moment she got here and dropped a FOR SALE sign out the window as they flew over the house."

Oof. Considering how "close" he was with his own mother, his relationship with his aunt must be a doozy. "She sounds like fun."

"So fun. I was thinking about it on the drive back, and I think we should keep on with our original plan. There's no way Mom will stick around long enough to actually pack Gram up and get her re-established at a Spokane home. She probably just came to put that idea in Gram's and *my* head—most likely hoping I'll see her point and start getting it ready to sell."

"But Marilyn said Janey has already talked to other homes. Doesn't that mean the ball is rolling?" One day, Ellie would be forced to make these kinds of decisions about her parents with her own sister. She doubted Averie would give her thoughts any more merit than she did now.

Warren yawned and reached for his beer. "I'm hoping that once Mom leaves, Janey will calm down too. She's the younger of the two, but hates being second. If Mom does one thing, Janey has to do it bigger. Once Mom gets back to work, Janey will refocus on her own thing. It's…pretty jacked up from a psychology perspective."

Ellie smiled. In that respect, maybe she and Averie weren't on track to be like Savannah and Janey. Averie was first in every area of success, and Ellie could be cool with coming in second.

"So, ramp building is back on?" Ellie asked.

"That's the plan. Mom will stay distracted with Gram or find some other diversion in Great Falls that will keep her away from the farm. I'm sure you couldn't tell by looking at her, but she's not a big fan of the country lifestyle." He rolled his eyes.

"I'll help. I am Team Marilyn all the way." She took another big bite of the cheesy goodness and soaked in the fleeting sense of relief Warren's new plan brought. She hoped he was right about this.

"Deal. Even if things go terribly wrong, we might be able to get her back here for a few days to set her affairs in the order of her choosing." His expression soured. "Sucks either way."

"It does." Her phone vibrated in her pocket, reminding her of all that existed outside of this moment and how much she didn't want to deal with any of it.

Warren must have heard the buzz. "So, who had you all worked up on your way home? I've never seen anyone text with that level of intensity."

She groaned. "You're not the only one experiencing familial disharmony."

"Familial disharmony? What the hell does that mean?" He tossed his paper plate like a Frisbee onto the empty recliner and laughed.

"That's a nice way of saying my family is driving me crazy." Must be something in the air these days. "My sister, Averie, is this wildly successful individual who my parents have decided is the ideal child. I, however, haven't met their expectations, and have spent the last few years of my life batting away their suggestions like I'm playing badminton. They've gotten worse recently."

"Why?" Warren shifted in his seat to better see her in the dim lamplight.

"Why what?" she repeated.

"Why have they gotten worse recently?" Previous interrogations regarding her life, and Sean, had been just that—interrogations. This time, Warren held a note of genuine curiosity in his voice.

While discussing her ex with Warren didn't rank high on her wish list, confessions bubbled inside her, as if she *wanted* to tell him everything. Because right now, she did.

"A few weeks before I came out here, I broke up with my boyfriend Sean." The words tasted bitter on her tongue. "He's an optometrist with a nice paycheck, excellent manners, and a pretty face. All that. We were together for six years." She bowed her head. "I broke up with him because I wasn't happy. Our list of commonalities got shorter and shorter as time went on, and everything was just *okay*. No passion. No fire. Nothing. And let's be real. It didn't help that my family kept making me feel like being prominent Sean's little wife would make up for all my shortcomings, you know?"

Stupid words. Stupid reality.

"I see. And you were texting…"

"My sister, Averie." Saying her name stirred the anger all over again. "She must have told him I've been miserable without him and that I was going to be her new employee and work on my grandmother's house. He texted me while we were at the nursing home to offer his help and promised he'd always be there if I needed him."

She growled and crumpled her empty paper plate in her lap. Hilda lunged for a stray crumb that toppled to the floor.

"And are you miserable without him?" The can crackled in Warren's fist.

"I'm not." The speed with which she responded when asked these questions always made her guilt worsen. "Maybe I should be, since he was always good to me. But I just didn't feel that spark and spent so much time wanting out of it. Sorry to dump that all on you. I'm sure you're super glad you asked."

"So, *he's* still got it bad then, huh?" Warren didn't wait for an answer. "Six years is a long time."

Everything in her told her to shut her mouth now. If she said anything else, it'd reveal how terrible a person she truly was. "We only made it that long because I wasn't brave enough to stand up for myself sooner. I knew the relationship wouldn't work out, but I was too scared to end it."

Warren sat quietly, rotating his empty beer can in his hand as he stared hard at the floor.

The words kept coming out of Ellie's mouth. "I'm bad at relationships. Pretty much all of them in every capacity. With men, with my family. All my other friends got married and wanted to do couple-y things with us, and I declined enough that everyone stopped asking me to hang out." She reached for her beer—one more thing in her life she accepted regardless of the fact she didn't like it and hadn't the guts to tell Warren and make him feel bad for giving it to her. "I'm going to shut up now. I know your opinion of me was already teetering without me drop-kicking it over the edge."

Warren leaned over like he meant to deliver a secret. "Do you want to know how my engagement ended?"

Ellie startled, nearly spilling her drink when he came out of the blue with such a question. "Your engagement?"

"Yeah." He shifted to sit up straighter now. "I believe my mother referred to her as the cute little schoolteacher I intended to marry."

Oh, Ellie remembered. "If you'd like to equally embarrass yourself the way I have, please share. If you're going to tell me you were absolute perfection, and she left you at the altar or something, then you can just shove it."

She stuck her tongue out, then took a drink.

"Well, I *am* absolute perfection. We might as well call it a night."

"Oh, hush." She laughed.

His parenthetical dimples got deeper the more amused with himself he became. Screw the exhaustion and emotionally taxing day that had her focusing on things like that.

"Rebekah and I dated for a year before we got engaged. And the engagement lasted about three months before she left me." He didn't portray the sadness of someone suffering a deep loss.

"*She* left *you*," Ellie repeated. "I told you not to tell me *that* kind of story."

"You want to know why?" His smile grew, and Ellie was no longer sure she *did* want to know.

"Why?"

He lifted his empty can. "Because I'm a dick."

Ellie nearly spit her sip of beer. "Well, that makes way more sense than the perfection theory. What did you do, anyway? You seem wholly unapologetic."

"Because I don't have any regrets." He shrugged. "I know it sounds cold, but things were okay when we were dating. Yes, just okay. Better than anything I had before, which were rather short-lived relationships. So I figured something like this is what you want to lock down, right? Then we got to wedding planning, and *okay* fell apart."

Ellie waited for more, but he'd paused to suck down the rest of his drink. "For example?"

"Well, that's about the time when we realized we wanted none of the same things. If what *I* wanted didn't line up with what *she* wanted, she'd cry and call me all kinds of things. She came out with me to the farm once, but she hated it here. Reminded me of how my mom is. Her and Gram even butted heads. I think that was the breaking point for me. I told her it was a dream of mine to own this place, but she freaked. She's a city girl down to her bones, and that's when she said she couldn't do it."

He'd given her a lot to digest, but one part stood out more than the others. "It's your dream to own this place?"

"*That's* your takeaway here?" He grabbed a pillow from behind him and snuggled deeper into the couch.

"Yeah, that's my takeaway. I already knew you were a jackass grandma's boy." She ignored his raised eyebrow and wriggled lower into her seat as well. Below her, Hilda had given up on receiving any more treats and draped herself across Ellie's feet, the snores sending vibrations up her legs. "Have you mentioned this to Marilyn or your mom?"

"No. There's a lot that would have to go into me moving back here. I'd have to transplant my entire business or change careers completely. It'd be a mess, like Mom said." He yawned again and closed his eyes when he continued. "I'm not a farmer. It'd be a lot to figure out, even if I enjoyed it. Plus, that'd mean a pretty hefty investment on my part that would either go directly to Mom and Janey as inheritance or nix their inheritance all together. It'd be so, so very complicated. Like, really, painfully complicated…"

Ellie leaned forward to see him better. His empty can dangled between his legs, barely sticking to his fingers. Soon, his heavy breathing proved he'd drifted off to sleep. For a man who woke up before the sun every morning, he had to be running on empty.

They both were.

– 26 –

WHEN THE TEMPERATURE HAD peaked at 91 degrees, and she'd carried three times her body weight in lumber across the length of the farm in two hours' time, the ice cold beer didn't taste so bad anymore.

After successfully sneaking away while Warren slept on the couch, Ellie had crawled into her own bed and passed out without bothering to check her phone again. If she ignored everyone, they might lose interest and go away. Leaving her phone in the tiny house altogether worked even better.

"I still feel like we're breaking the law or something by doing this," Ellie said. Like any moment, Savannah would show up again and shut down production. It was just amazing that Warren had chosen to call her bluff.

Warren grinned. "Little bit."

"You're the most dedicated grandchild I've ever met." Ellie held the chilled can to her forehead. "This would have been way more fun in the winter."

Building a ramp up to the front of Marilyn's house might not have been the easiest in the snow, but Ellie would have taken that over *this* any day. The added element that they made these changes against Marilyn's daughters' wishes weirdly made it seem even more dangerous and sweaty.

"I've done my share of January construction. Honestly, I don't know what's worse." He reached for another beer, which had to be a coping mechanism and less about hydration. If he kept drinking at this rate, the wheelchair ramp would end up tilted like some new thrill ride. Knowing Marilyn, she'd prefer that.

"Marilyn needs a pool. Go ahead and construct that next, Mr. Contractor." She used her foot to push the board closer to Warren, her strength failing as the afternoon sun melted her flesh. Considering her lack of actual contracting skills, Ellie appointed herself the unofficial mood booster to try and keep things light. They both needed that. The beers helped.

Warren held another board in place and shot the nails through. "I don't do pools. That's a whole other ball game. We'll just have to hose off like real farm kids."

That sounded…interesting.

"What else do you want to tackle today?" Ellie brought him a new nail cartridge when he started shooting blanks.

"Thanks." He switched out the nails and sat back on his feet. "Well, I want to take the bedframe down because it's too tall for her to get into right now. Might need to make a small ramp for that step between the living room and back porch. Bathroom should be fine since it's already a walk-in with a bench. I'll call around about home healthcare nurses or something and sneak a call into Gram to make sure she knows I'm planning a grandma heist."

Ellie laughed. "Love it. It's ornery, so she'll love it too. I hope I'm like her when I grow up."

"Well, you're on the right track." He snickered and ignored her dirty look. "Don't you have work to do or something?"

"Oh, no. I've officially been let go now, so I've got *all day* to spend helping you."

He side-eyed her. "I can't decide which of us is worse off with this information."

"The even better news is that I've gotta learn this construction stuff if I'm going to fix up a house when I get home. So thanks for the private tutoring, Bob the Builder." Even though it'd only been a few days since they became amicable, Ellie was pretty sure fixing up Grandma Val's house would be more fun if Warren was there to bitch and moan about their woes. The merciless teasing was a plus too.

Warren groaned right on cue. "That's exactly what I wanted to do today."

Ellie riffled through the new sheets of sandpaper. "I'll admit, though, this is more entertaining than listening to medical lectures. And if I'm going to work this hard, at least it's to help a friend in need."

Warren tilted his head and flashed a cheesy smile. "Aw. I'm your *friend* now?"

"I was talking about Marilyn." She knelt down on the grass to sand the end of another board the way Warren had shown her—not sure if it was crucial to building a ramp or if Warren had assigned the task to keep her out of his way.

"Rude."

Hilda tore around the bushes with her Bilexin ball and wedged herself between Warren and his task. Warren pried the ball from her jowls and chucked it toward the bean field.

If only dogs could share their endless spunk. Ellie needed a bit more of that spice. "How does she have this much energy when it's—?"

Warren's phone sang the first few lines of the *Golden Girls* theme song, squashing the thought.

"What in the world?" Ellie giggled.

"It's Gram's text tone. Suits her, don't you think? It's like if you put all four Golden Girls in a blender, you'd get Gram." He shifted to read the message in the shade. "She says Mom hasn't shown up yet. Which means she's just hanging out at her hotel, working, most likely. Instead of visiting her family." He let out a long sigh. "That means she's not patronizing Gram, I guess."

"More of that silver lining," Ellie added.

He typed a reply and examined the ramp-in-progress. "I should probably track Mom's phone in case she tries to make a surprise visit out here. Would love to get this done before then so she doesn't catch on to my deliberate disobedience until I've got a better defense."

"I don't envy you being stuck between them."

Warren stretched his tape measure and marked his place on the board. "Sometimes I regret following my family to Spokane. It was definitely the more lucrative choice for me, and it kept everyone off my back for a time, but I think my blood pressure would have been more stable here." His smile broke some of the tension. The *Golden Girls* theme did an even better job. "Well, now that's interesting."

Ellie crawled forward to peer over his shoulder and read the newest text. The blazing sun reflected off the screen and prevented her attempts. "What'd she say?"

"She spent her morning of solitude doing internet searches and is back on track hunting down John. Wants to know how far of a drive it is to Connecticut." He started to type something, but stopped and lowered his phone. "I don't even know how to respond to this."

"Um, it's hella far, Miss Marilyn! I thought she was giving up on that. I mean, it sounded that way yesterday." Unless Marilyn did the same thing they were doing and wanted to give it one last ditch effort before Savannah and Janey put a stop to all their fun. "Connecticut is a leap from that other lead with the horse ranch up north."

He reread the message to himself. "Big time."

Hilda crashed in front of one of the shrubs, panting as the exertion and heat finally caught up to her. Not a care in the world. She also had no idea that her home and everyone she loved could be taken out from under her at any moment. "Warren?"

He looked up from his phone and wiped the sweat from his brow. "Hm?"

"Where would Hilda go if Marilyn moves to Spokane?" She'd

seen a million ASPCA commercials over the years that had broken her heart. Ellie could almost hear the Sarah McLachlan music cueing up as she watched the dog vibrate along with each snore.

"She'd come back with me," he said, like he'd made up his mind. "I can't do much for the others in my downtown apartment, but I can take Hilda."

Ellie smiled for a long moment as she regarded him. In fact, she couldn't stop. "Maybe I could take Sheriff back to Ohio with me."

"I'm sure he'd fly very well in the cargo hold."

"As donkeys do." She bit her lip when she debated adding the next part. "That is, if I can care for him without being too sloppy about it."

His shoulders sank, but his mouth quirked. "I, um, I should apologize for that too."

Her jab hadn't been an attempt at cornering him into an apology, but if he was offering...

Warren pulled his shirt up to wipe the sweat from his face, revealing the toned abs he'd earned from years of manual labor. Was this how he made amends with people? It wasn't a bad way to do business.

Ellie cleared her throat. "Well, go on."

He scooted farther into the shade and, by the way, closer to Ellie. "I'm sorry I called your work sloppy. You were annoying me, as you do, so it was sort of justified." His mouth tightened when he tried to fight away the smile. "But I should back up a little further than that. It was sloppy in there, but it wasn't all your fault."

Warren continued, "It has gotten harder for Gram to care for the animals over the years. I noticed last winter she was having a harder time than usual getting through the chores. She wouldn't admit that, of course, and I sure as hell wasn't going to bring it up. So, I kept watch. While things weren't ideal, the animals' needs were being met, and they were happy. She loves them, and they love her. So, when you came along, you probably just did what you saw done. It makes sense."

"Well, I know better now at least."

"You've been doing a great job for being thrown in headfirst. I should have told you that instead."

The humid air grew impossible to breathe as she stared up at him. She tried to thank him, but nothing came out. Her lips moved, she was pretty sure of that.

"Anyway." Warren cleared his throat and sat upright. "Since I'm gone for long periods of time and can't check in on her or the animals that often, I actually have an agreement with Tori to come out here and assess things from time to time. So far, so good."

"Wait. You and Tori have actually been working together to help Marilyn all this time?" The mention of Tori's name was like a wonderful blast of cool air under the hot sun. "I thought you didn't like each other."

"We pick on each other. She's right—growing up in a small town like this makes everyone feel like a relative. Most of us are sick of each other to that extent." He laughed. "She's one of the few from our class who stuck around and does a whole lot for this area. They're lucky to have her around here, but don't you dare tell her I said that. Wasn't expecting the two of you to get all chummy in such a short time."

Ellie desperately wished she could text Tori this conversation immediately, but she didn't have her phone. "Well, I wasn't expecting to build a ramp, wrestle sheep, or get completely mixed up in another family's epic saga in that time either, but here we are."

"Here we are," he repeated. Another check of his phone revealed he hadn't missed any incoming texts from Marilyn, so he shoved it back into his pocket and moaned. "It's hotter 'n hell out here. I'm gonna spray off and get Hilda a drink."

Hilda leapt from her grassy bed at the mention of her name and rushed to Warren's side like she hadn't been half dead a moment before. Ellie, too, got to her feet faster than she would have expected. The prospect of cold hose mist was enough to drive anyone to action.

Trying to keep up with Warren and simultaneously not trip over Hilda on the walk to the barn proved challenging. She'd likely break her leg and end up at the nursing home too.

She smoothed her frayed ponytail and laughed as Warren shot some water into Hilda's bowl, all while the impatient dog lapped up the water coming straight from the hose. He then aimed the hose high into the air, the icy mist bringing a welcome shiver and an involuntary squeal.

"You want to spray yourself or should I hose you down?" Warren stepped away from the wall and shot the water at her feet.

Ellie jumped back with an even louder shriek. "I can do it myself. I don't trust you at all."

"That's wise." He took another step forward, hose still in hand, finger resting on the trigger.

She put her hand over the nozzle. Like that'd do anything to save her. "I said I'd do it myself, you buttmunch. Don't you dare shoot me."

Warren moved closer still until Ellie had nowhere to go with the barn wall at her back. "You're going to call me names while I'm holding all the power here? That's brave."

Ellie's cheeks hurt from trying not to giggle while simultaneously keeping a threatening face. He waggled his eyebrows and pulled the trigger again. With her hand over the nozzle, water sprayed in every direction.

Ellie screamed and tried to gain control of the handle, but Warren grabbed her wrist to keep her at the front of the hose. Their roaring laughter and Ellie's shouted insults amped up Hilda even more. The dog jumped up on both of them, lapping at the water and trying to force herself in between them.

"Hilda, you are the worst protector." Ellie dipped low and tried to yank the hose out from Warren's grasp, but it only helped him get a better grip on her arm to spin her around into him. Her back met his soaked T-shirt and glued them together.

No matter how she squirmed, she couldn't get out of his grasp. His arm wrapped firmly around her stomach, his warm chest contrasting with the icy water. The combination hardly made her want to break free. But still, she screamed and fought him—even as he drew the hose over their heads and let it rain down over their bodies.

The chill overtook her, soaking her from head to toe now. She barely remembered how hot the sun had burned while they worked on the ramp.

Ellie's sole hope for trying to act like she wanted to escape him involved making a major move here. She spun in his arms until she faced him full on. Reaching up to grab the hose again brought her even tighter against his chest, her face upturned to his. Through the shower raining over them, she saw how big his smile had grown as he stared down at her, his height the only thing keeping the hose from her reach.

He was as wet as she was now, his hair clinging to his forehead, the droplets making his forearm slippery where she tried to grab him.

"You won't win this battle," he murmured. His hand flattened on the small of her back.

She could have shoved her elbow between them and pushed him away. She could have stepped on his foot or twisted around the other direction. Instead, she rose on her tiptoes to reach for the hose again—which drew her face closer to his.

A quiver ran over her skin, but she couldn't blame it on the frigid water anymore. He leaned closer too, and her eyes fluttered shut as she waited for whatever came next.

Where she might have expected a symphony to play in her mind at a time like this, she hadn't expected the *Golden Girls* theme.

Marilyn had the world's worst timing.

– 27 –

WARREN WIPED THE PASTED bangs from his forehead. "We may need to go to town and put out some fires. Gram says she's searching flights. Why did I have to introduce that woman to the internet?"

Goose bumps covered Ellie's skin as water pooled at her feet, mud suctioning her feet to the earth. Wringing out the bottom of her shirt, she tried to act as casually as possible. Had they almost kissed? If Marilyn hadn't texted at that exact moment, everything could have changed for them.

"She's hard to keep up with," Ellie managed.

Like everything else in her life.

"You can say that again." Warren held himself together with so much more confidence, like he often almost-kissed women under a torrential hose shower while a bulldog did some ceremonious dance around them.

His wide smile showed no regret, but it also didn't indicate that he even realized what had just about happened. Maybe Ellie over-thought it. Wouldn't be the first time.

Hilda yipped like she called to an old friend and rocketed off toward the pasture. Ellie followed her direction in time to see Sheriff lumbering across the driveway.

"Oh no." Ellie's shoulders sank. "There goes Sheriff."

Under normal circumstances, his escape would have been an inconvenience. This time, Ellie needed the distraction.

"And there go the goats." Warren clapped his palm to his forehead as he eyed the trail of goats darting through the newest hole in the fence and into the back field. "I'll get them if you get Sheriff. Looks like I've got a lot more work to do out there to keep these escape artists in."

Ellie forced a nervous laugh, then rubbed away the gooseflesh from her arms.

"We can put them back, get ready, and maybe find someplace to eat on the way to Gram's?" His smile wavered when the first hint of nerves became obvious. Had he just sort of asked her on a date?

"That sounds great." Had she just sort of said yes?

Her throbbing heartbeat kept her from standing still any longer. Off she ran to the barn to grab an armful of apples to entice her donkey buddy back to his place in the barn until Warren could fix the pen.

For a creature that lumbered rather than trotted with any kind of speed, Sheriff had made it almost to the end of the long lane by the time Ellie caught up. Hilda reached the target first, offering her assistance by jumping up on the donkey to push him in the right direction.

"Sheriff, we have to get back because I should actually do something with my hair today. I might have a date." She glanced toward the barn but saw no one. "With Warren. I might have a date with Warren. I don't know. I have no idea what the hell just happened back there."

Saying the words out loud seemed so crazy. She kind of wanted to text Tori to run it all by her, but what if she thought it was a bad idea? What would Marilyn think?

Sheriff ate the apple in Ellie's outstretched hand.

"Good boy. Keep coming." She walked backward toward the barn, the promise of more apples leading the donkey onward with ease.

Dating was supposed to be smoother than this, right? It'd been so long since she had a first date, but back then, Sean had simply called her and asked if she wanted to grab dinner. They went to Olive Garden and took a walk. The end. Very simple.

Since arriving in Montana a single woman, her first sort-of date involved wrangling a rooster, and the second came with a garden hose and a runaway donkey. Of course it did. Her life had fallen into absolute bedlam.

The dessert for this upcoming romantic meal would involve talking an eighty-two-year-old woman out of some rash decision to fly across the country and accost a random, unsuspecting fellow from Connecticut. All while laying low in case Savannah popped by again.

By then, maybe she and Warren might not have to *fake*-date anymore...

She had to slow her roll here. There'd been no talk of relationships and dating and *oh goodness*.

Ellie searched her surroundings for Warren but couldn't see him anywhere. The goats and sheep had been corralled, proving he was a much faster animal herder than Ellie.

Hilda gave up on helping and ran off to bark at the world while Ellie fed Sheriff the remaining apples and tried to breathe through her confusion.

She filled the troughs with water *and* electrolytes and wondered if she'd ever again be able to use a hose without setting a small fire in her belly.

It was time to stop stalling and get ready to go.

Hilda's enthusiastic barking grew louder, more intense from somewhere outside the barn. Then voices joined the noise.

Ellie crept toward the doors and peered into the drive. Three people stood together beside a gray sedan. A younger woman wore a pantsuit, which made no sense in the scorching summer weather. She held a folder tucked under her arm. An older woman pushed her sunglasses up to rest on her pixie cut, her white capris demonstrating quite the courage for one visiting a dusty farm.

And the third person...was Blake Robinson.

Smoothing her wet hair back and tugging her shirt to try and keep it from clinging too tightly, Ellie took a deep breath and approached.

"Ellie," Blake greeted. "I didn't think you'd still be around. Why are you all wet?"

"Why wouldn't I be around? My stay doesn't end until next week." The nerves amped up as the two well-dressed women looked her up and down. "Who do you have with you today?"

The words came out like a kindergarten teacher asking a student about a cherished stuffed toy.

The woman with the pixie cut folded her arms, eyes narrowing as she continued to assess Ellie. "So, it's true then."

"Like I said." Blake pointed to the tiny house in the distance. "Marilyn's been renting the little house out to strangers on the internet, and Ellie is one of them."

Ellie took a step back. Blake's tone cut like knives. What was going on here?

"I can't believe this." Pixie Cut's arms fell to her side, fists balling.

Pantsuit giggled to herself and adjusted her folder. "Oh, this is so rich."

"Who are you people?" Ellie hissed so quietly they may not have even heard her.

The screen door slammed at the main house, and Warren appeared at the top of the partially complete ramp.

"Warren." Pixie Cut pointed accusingly at him as he approached. "You knew about this."

"What are you doing here, Janey? And more specifically, why the hell are you here with Robinson?" Warren had changed into dry clothes, but his wet, messy hair still hinted at their afternoon activities. His green eyes grew colder as he regarded the second woman. "And Shannon."

Oh no. Ellie should have grabbed the pitchfork on her way out of the barn.

"Mom's hosting an Airbnb, and I had to hear about it from one of her neighbors?" Janey shouted.

Blake had blown the whistle to Marilyn's daughters?

"Nobody knew until Ellie got here. Gram didn't tell anyone she'd started one, and no one else has been here but Ellie." Warren threw his hands up. The smiling, playful man she'd wrestled with under the hose had vanished, and the cantankerous contractor she met upon first arrival had reappeared, fired up and ready to fight.

Janey took a step forward. The closer proximity made her identity as Savannah's sister much more obvious. "The logistics don't matter. What does matter is that there's been a complete stranger staying out here on the farm while Mom's been in the nursing home?"

Ellie's chest tightened, as she braced herself for another round of character accusations. If she had to prove her innocence one more time, she might just explode.

"It's been handled, Janey. Now, please explain to me why *you* are here with *them*?" he demanded.

"Not that it's any of your business, but I've contracted Shannon to be our realtor as we sell this property. Mr. Robinson is a highly motivated buyer." Janey spoke like a true businesswoman, not a concerned daughter seeking to help her mother in a time of need.

What little composure Warren held before vanished. "Hold up. You're getting way ahead of yourself on that one. You can't contract a realtor before—"

"Mom's moving, Warren. It's a done deal. I already signed the papers with Spring Gardens in eastern Spokane. I'm taking her back with me when I leave tomorrow," Janey said.

"Does *she* know this?"

Ellie had never heard him so angry, not even when they first met and he assumed she'd come to con his favorite human. In that moment, she felt helpless to defend him. All she could do was watch and wait.

"She will. That's our next stop." Janey smirked.

Shannon opened her folder to compare the info on her sheet

with what she saw before her. "I'm going to take a look around, Blakey. You want to come?"

"*Blakey?*" Ellie nearly gagged on the word.

Warren lunged forward until he was face-to-face with Blake. Ellie held her breath, expecting fists to fly, but Warren maintained his stance. "What is your part in this, Robinson? You just couldn't wait any longer to get your hands on this place or what?"

"You're being awfully rude, Warren." He took a step back and winked at Ellie, which made her stomach roil. "Ellie and I discussed Marilyn's condition over coffee. She let me know who to contact to get the property moving, so I made a few phone calls. It's been very informative spending time with her over the past couple weeks, especially the little tidbit about the Airbnb being a secret."

Warren's gaze shifted to Ellie for a quick moment.

"I never told you to call them!" Her face burned hotter than any sunburn she'd experienced. "I told you Marilyn wasn't ready to sell. If I'd had any indication you'd—"

She couldn't even continue. A scream welled inside her lungs she had to choke down. Her fight with Averie, the breakup with Sean, the job loss, the pressure from her family all dulled in comparison to the rage she felt in this moment.

"It's not really your place to tell us what my mother can and can't do, is it?" Janey slapped a hand to Warren's chest then and pushed him away from Blake. "Blake has offered more for this property than Mom could have gotten at auction if we move in the next thirty days." She returned her attention to Ellie. "I guess maybe I should thank you for keeping Blake in the loop because God knows no one else in our family has been told what's going on."

Ellie's fists balled. "I never ever would have—"

"Ellie." Warren held up his hand to stop her.

"I'm serious, Warren. If I'd known—"

"Just stop." He kept his focus on Blake. "You're a snake, you know that?"

Blake shrugged. "I'm a businessman who saw an opportunity."

The way he smiled at Ellie made her want to rip his lips off his dumb face.

"And what part is my mother playing in all this?" Warren could barely speak through his clenched jaw.

Janey shook her head and checked the smart watch on her wrist. "Your mother was being a bit too passive for the situation. So, when I got Blake's call, I took action. Once she sees his proposal, she'll be glad I took over."

"You think so?" Warren asked.

"I know so. As will Mom." She checked her watch again and hummed. "Your mother is on her way out here. I'd better get over to the nursing home."

"Let's go, babe," Blake called after Shannon.

Ellie's blood boiled. He and Shannon were an actual *couple*? How long had that been going on? The entire time he'd pretended to flirt with her and get information about the farm? Oh, she wanted to stuff him with chicken feed and string him up in the pasture.

"You're not going to wait for her and at least tell her what you're doing?" Warren started to reach for his aunt's arm but pulled back.

"Not until I've gotten a few signatures from my mother," she said in a singsong tone.

"Gram won't go for it."

Blake laughed and placed an arm around Shannon's shoulders as he walked her back to the car.

Janey rolled her eyes and took a few steps back. "You might want to start packing up your stuff." Her stare grew more intense as she looked to Ellie. "You too."

She stormed off toward the car to climb into the backseat. Warren muttered a string of swears and pulled his phone from his pocket.

"Warren, I'm so sorry. I had no idea Blake was going to go straight to Janey or that he was dating Shannon. He was acting like—"

"Like what?" He spun on his heels to face her. "You could have mentioned you'd been hanging out with him."

"He brought me coffee one morning and helped me with some animal stuff, that's hardly 'hanging out.'" Her voice threatened to break at any moment.

"It doesn't matter. I can't deal with this." Warren started toward the main house.

Ellie followed. "Warren, I don't want you to think—"

"Drop it, okay?" He stopped so abruptly Ellie nearly crashed into his chest when he turned around. "My mother is on her way out here, and I have to explain to her that my aunt has gone over her head and all but sold this property already. That Gram's got an Airbnb operation going on. That my *girlfriend* isn't actually my girlfriend and is really just some rando from Ohio who's been giving information on my family to the asshole down the road. The same asshole who's been trying to rip this farm out from under us his entire adult life."

What could she possibly say to that? "I'm sorry."

"Yeah, me too." He shoved his hands into his pockets and kept his head low. "There was never any hope for this to work, you know."

"Just a fool's hope," Ellie whispered when she remembered Marilyn's words from the day before.

He nodded and opened his mouth like he meant to add something else, but instead turned and left her standing in the driveway alone.

- 28 -

ELLIE'S COFFEE SHOOK IN her hand as she looked out the window and watched for any sign of Warren.

Or his mother.

Because she'd also arrived in her fancy rental car sometime while Ellie showered. As far as Ellie knew, they hadn't come outside yet for any reason, and she hadn't heard Hilda anywhere either. The dog had taken cover somewhere else, which was smart.

Ellie sank to the chair and let her face fall into her hand. How had it come to this? Why did disaster seem to follow her everywhere she went?

At this point, going home to work herself to death for her family actually seemed easier.

From somewhere outside, muffled voices nearly made her fall out of her seat. She shifted to better see out the window, then nearly fell again. Coming straight at her were Warren and Savannah.

Warren's hands flew at his side as he made some point to his mother, who seemingly could care less. Savannah powered ahead toward the tiny home. Something hadn't gone right in their confessional conversation time. Then again, nothing about that *could* have gone right.

"Oh, no."

Ellie didn't wait for them to get all the way to the door before she opened it and tried not to pass out in reaction to Savannah's blazing eyes and Warren's slumped shoulders.

"You're an Airbnb guest?" Savannah asked before she came to a stop.

Ellie tried to speak, but nothing came out. She cleared her throat. "Yes."

Savannah shifted on her legs and placed both hands on her tiny waist. "Warren is not your *boyfriend*, and you both lied to me. You could have told me the truth, but instead, you let my sister get a hold of this information so she could take over all that I'm trying to do for my family. Am I understanding this correctly?"

Warren slid his hands into his pockets and wouldn't look up.

Ellie couldn't answer either. While that summed it up, the reality wasn't nearly as intentional as Savannah made it sound.

"This is absolutely ridiculous." Savannah spun in a circle, her hands brushing over her slicked hair. "Did she even bother to go through the proper channels for this? It's a huge insurance issue, for one. Mom can't even take care of herself, let alone host complete strangers out here. Maybe Janey was right to take this approach."

"Right to go behind your back and make plans for Gram without consulting anyone?" Warren sounded hoarse. He'd more than likely spent the past hour arguing with this mother.

"My family's always so quick to go behind my back. Your girl-friend? Honestly, you were going to lie about something like that to cover for your grandmother. And you." Her attention turned back to Ellie. "Do you always go involving yourself in other people's private matters?"

"Mom, you—"

"Nope. This would be a first." Ellie's grip tightened on the doorframe.

"I do not understand any of this." Savannah shifted so she could face both Warren and Ellie. "I don't know who's telling the truth and who's lying. This is all going to blow up so badly, Warren, and you're proving to be just as big of a part of the problem as anyone else. You should have put a stop to the Airbnb nonsense the second you arrived. Now, we have this extra *liability*."

Ellie had never been called that before. It weirdly sounded worse than all the other things she'd been called in recent months.

"Everything would have been fine if you and Janey had just stayed in Spokane." Warren pursed his lips like he meant to cut off the rest of his thoughts.

Judging by Savannah's face, no one spoke to her this way. "Excuse me? You want to tell me that I shouldn't have come to see my own mother when she's injured and in a nursing home?"

"It's been two weeks! No one even bothered to call and tell me something had happened to Gram, or I would have been out here right away." Warren's hair had dried in odd directions, and he forced the strands from his face. "Ellie was here when the ambulance took Gram to the hospital. She's the one who took care of things around here in everyone's absence."

"And discussing private matters with Blake Robinson, apparently," Savannah hissed as if Ellie wasn't standing right in front of them. "We don't know her, and she has no business involving herself the way she has."

"I would never do anything to hurt Marilyn." Now Ellie's chest tightened. "Look, I get it. None of you know me, and I don't know you. Talking to Blake was a mistake, but I didn't know that. I care about your mother, this farm, and those animals. So, say whatever you want to say about me, but direct your anger at the right person."

Savannah appeared genuinely appalled. "Wow."

Warren fed off the momentum. "You can still stop Janey. You're the oldest and should have the most say in this. Tell her you're not signing off on this. Go talk some sense into Gram so she doesn't just give up and go along with things she's not comfortable with."

"And what's the alternative, Warren? Let you bring her back here and carry on the way things are now?" Savannah asked. "Because that's not working either. She's eighty-two. We have to start thinking about things long-term. Moving her to a home permanently is the best option. Having her closer to her children *is the best option.*"

"That's not what she wants," Ellie whispered.

"And you know this because you're such good friends with my mother after, what, a couple visits?" Savannah's stare hardened. "Now, if you'll excuse my bluntness, there is no reason for you to still be on this farm. Pack your bags and go home. The Airbnb is closed."

"Mom—"

"No." She held her hand up between them. "The only thing we can do now is be proactive so this transition runs more smoothly and Janey doesn't dump all of Mom's things on the curb and run off with her. First and foremost, someone needs to take these animals, which means I have some calls to make."

Savannah spun on her heel and headed toward the main house.

Warren's eyes shone with defeat when he regarded Ellie. "I'm sorry."

"You have to do something." Ellie wasn't family. Her say in these matters held no weight. Once she got on a plane to go home, that was it. Marilyn's fate was sealed. But Warren would remain, and right now, he was his grandmother's only hope.

"I've tried," he said.

"Not hard enough!" Somehow, a couple weeks in the wilderness of Montana had brought out some internal mama-bear instincts. She never would have guessed that the "cub" she longed to protect would be three times her age.

Ellie's fists clenched, and she started after Savannah. If the woman demanded Ellie go home early, then Ellie would use every last minute here to fight for her friend. Not like she'd ever see Savannah again.

Warren quickly caught up and brushed Ellie's shoulder as he walked beside her. "What do you think you're—?"

"Savannah," Ellie called, which made the angry woman stop in her tracks. People didn't yell at her, and she was going to get it twice in one day. "You can't do this. Marilyn deserves to have her wishes considered in all this. She made it abundantly clear—"

"You stop that right now." The way Savannah stomped forward made Ellie take a step back in case her fists got involved. "I have asked you to leave this property. You have some nerve showing up and acting like you know how to run my family better than I do."

Ellie's limbs shook now. The adrenaline might knock her clean out. "I know I don't, but I can't sit by and—"

"Ellie…" Warren reached to take hold of her arm like he might physically pull her away from this fight.

She shrugged out of his reach. "Warren can take over the farm. All of it. It doesn't have to sell. He loves it out here, and he knows every nook and cranny of this place. He'd take care of it better than anyone else. Animals and all."

"Ellie!" Warren's hands flew to his head.

"I said, '*That is enough.*'" If looks could kill… "You want to run my son's life now too?" She turned her attention to Warren. "You both need to leave. Go home and let me deal with this the *right* way. I don't need you turning against your family any more than you already have."

Warren flinched when Savannah struck a nerve. "Don't you dare accuse me of something like that. You know how much Gram means to me."

Savannah released a long breath. "Yes, I know how much she means to you, which is why I think you're basing these ideas on emotions and not logic. You're letting some pretty face distract you from reality. I can handle it without you."

This time, it was Warren who stormed off, leaving the two women in his wake.

Savannah growled and followed him, but not before hissing over her shoulder, "Have a nice flight."

WARREN DIDN'T SAY GOODBYE.

It'd taken him all of thirty minutes to exit the main house with his bags, gather up his tools, and leave. He didn't even bother glancing toward the tiny home.

Ellie spent the remainder of the night searching for an affordable flight home, weighing the options between using the rest of her credit card travel points on a ridiculously expensive airplane ride or lying low in a cheap hotel room in Great Falls until her regularly scheduled departure in a few days. Neither option appealed to her.

The last of the wine didn't go down smoothly. She couldn't take any of her remaining food and drink with her, so she might as well salvage what she could.

Every few seconds, she'd check her phone, hoping for something—*anything*. She didn't really know what.

Should she call her family and let them know what was going on? She didn't want another lecture—and she really didn't want to explain the rest of what had happened since Marilyn's daughters had arrived and set the world on fire.

Should she call Tori? Every time she imagined pouring out the details, she wanted to cry. Not like it mattered—she'd already cried enough since she got back to the tiny house.

She couldn't call Warren. Her heart toppled into her stomach.

Ellie dropped her head into her arms. The entire week had been filled with squashed dreams and dashed hopes.

How could she go back to Columbus now and live out her days while pretending the past two weeks hadn't happened? She had so much to do. So much to play catch-up with. It was all so draining.

Ellie checked out the window for the umpteenth time as if she hadn't been the only person on the property since Savannah vanished shortly after Warren. She half expected law enforcement to show up and properly evict her. But no one came. She just sat alone, watching her phone clock count away the minutes. Well, Hilda slept at her feet too, so she wasn't completely alone.

Alone enough.

And the only person she thought might understand such a deep loneliness was only a thirty-minute drive away. Ellie couldn't possibly leave Montana without seeing Marilyn. They might as well be miserable together one last time.

Nothing had ever taken so much time as the trip from the farm to Choteau's nursing home. Ellie sat in the parking lot for a long moment, surveying each car that came and went to ensure none of Marilyn's family visited at the same time.

With the coast clear, Ellie drew in a painful breath and walked through the sliding doors.

Goodbyes sucked.

They were so much worse when things ended poorly. And this wasn't a goodbye that came with a "hello" down the road. It was unlike any goodbye Ellie'd ever had to say before.

She rounded the corner toward room 34 for the last time. Inside, Marilyn stared out the window into the parking lot. She didn't even notice Ellie enter.

"Marilyn?" Ellie folded her hands in front of her. She should have brought something—a parting gift or apology flowers. Showing up empty-handed after everything that had happened didn't feel right.

The older woman turned in her chair, gray-blue eyes wet with tears. "Ellie. You're still here."

"For now. I'll go to Great Falls tomorrow and figure things out from there." She sat on Marilyn's bed, and the two joined hands as if they'd done this a million times and hadn't been strangers a couple short weeks ago.

"So they really kicked you out?" Marilyn shook her head. "I'm so sorry."

Ellie gave Marilyn's hand a squeeze. "No, *I'm* sorry. I'm sorry we couldn't find John. I'm sorry you have to sell the farm under such crappy circumstances. I'm sorry everyone's fighting, and we have to say goodbye." Ellie sniffled again as she stared at their joined hands. "I'm really going to miss you."

Marilyn plucked a couple of tissues from the holder and passed one to Ellie, keeping the other for herself. "I'm really going to miss you too. It's been a joy having you in my family, even if just for a short time. I had hoped, at the end of your stay, that I'd offer you a place in my home whenever you could come out, but I'm no longer able to do that."

It was like losing a grandparent all over again. "Are you going to be okay?"

Marilyn smiled, and it was that wonderful, ornery smile Ellie loved so much. "Of course, I will. I always am in the end. But what about you?"

"I'll be all right too." Her problems dulled in comparison to Marilyn's. "I've got a house and a job waiting for me back home. They may not be my top choice—or even close, really—but they'll do until I figure out what I really want."

"Atta girl. The world is your oyster. I have no doubt you'll turn things around in a jiffy after witnessing the way you've handled all I've thrown at you the past couple weeks."

"I appreciate that." If Ellie could play the part of farmhand and wrangle goats, chickens, and, well, Marilyn, she should be able to handle being a nanny for a little while. "But I hate leaving you here to deal with everything by yourself, especially now that Warren's gone."

"Oh, Warren. He didn't answer his phone when I called." She pressed a hand to her cheek. "I can't apologize enough for my family. God knows what you must think of us."

"I don't think any less of you, Marilyn." Ellie couldn't say the same for the rest of the Perry/Oliver/Whatever-Janey's-Last-Name-Was group. "But why wouldn't Warren answer his phone for you?"

"He's afraid he's let me down." She rolled her tissue over in her lap. "When you first got here, and he thought you were some wild woman come to rob me for all I got, I had to calm him down. We talked on the phone for a long time that afternoon. I told him everything about wanting to find John, even though I had hoped to keep that to myself until I had actually found him. But despite my grandson being a stubborn mule, it didn't take much to get him on my side. It never does."

"You sure mean a lot to him," Ellie said.

"He means a lot to me. But I wish he wouldn't take these things so personally. He probably thinks he let you down too." Marilyn ran her thumb across Ellie's knuckles. "He must not have wanted to let you down either."

"Me? Why would he—"

"Warren is a go-getter. He's a self-made contractor and a damn good one at that. Nothing stands in his way when he has a goal. But if it does, he retreats. He couldn't get me out of here. Couldn't fulfill my wishes. Couldn't get you." Marilyn withdrew her hand to readjust her leg on the footrest.

Ellie sat up straighter on the bed. "Come again?"

"Oh, come now. Belle and I saw the way he looked at you." That sly smile returned, and she reached forward to tap Ellie on the knee.

"If you weren't so into ninnies, you could have had a real catch with Warren, Ellie."

Ellie choked on her spit. "What?"

"Child, if I'd had any inclination that the neighbor you kept referencing was one of the Robinsons, I might have clapped you upside the head. Could you not see the devil in that boy's eyes?" A wink accompanied her ornery grin.

"I guess I didn't look closely enough." What a disaster. The whole trip had been wild from start to finish. "I am so sorry about that part too."

"Did you kiss him?" Her eyebrow quirked.

Of all the interrogations she'd gotten over the past few weeks, this one might just take the cake. "No way."

"Oh, thank God. I was going to make you wash your mouth out with soap."

How did she do it? How did Marilyn sit on the brink of her entire life being uprooted, her belongings and pets displaced, and her wishes tossed into the trash, and yet manage to giggle the way she did?

This was the persona Ellie needed to channel in her life. When you get lemons, make some badass lemonade.

"Marilyn, you amaze me. I'm really glad I got to meet you." If she could, she'd pack the older woman up and take her back to Columbus. That'd bring some life and laughter back to Grandma Val's house, especially if they grabbed Belle on the way. "I hope I can come see you in Spokane one day."

"Oh, honey, I'm not going to Spokane."

The words were so matter-of-fact, Ellie had to repeat them in her head to make sure she heard right. It sounded very much like a done deal, according to her daughters.

"You aren't?" Ellie asked.

"I bought myself some time. Janey wanted me to fly with her

tomorrow evening, but I promised her if she gave me one week to make a plan for my animals and arrangements for my belongings, I'd go willingly. I even agreed to let my wretched great niece be the realtor with a hefty percent of the profits if they compromised with me on this." She beamed, like the idea was the best one she'd ever had. "I don't intend to do any of that. I'm checking myself out of this place. Easier to fight on your home turf."

"Can you do that?" Ellie didn't know how things worked, but it wasn't like the nursing home could hold Marilyn against her will. The woman was still of sound mind. Well, *possibly*. "Won't that cause a whole lot more problems in your family?"

"Oh my, yes. This strategy would go a whole lot better if I had Belle to help me sort out the details, but I'll get to her one way or another." Her eyes glazed over in thought, her fingers tapping together in her lap like a cartoon villain's.

Ellie waited for what seemed like forever for Marilyn to continue and then finally said, "And what exactly is your plan?"

"I was hoping you'd ask." She slapped her good leg and pointed at her company. Ellie chuckled at the grand presentation. Seriously, leaving this wonderful woman would be nearly impossible.

Marilyn continued, "You know Belle's son is a fancy lawyer— drives a nice car and wears some spiffy suits. All that. I'm going to talk to him about transferring all decision-making power to Warren. He won't force me out before it's time, and the girls will be absolved of my 'burden' for the time being while I find an actual suitable caretaker for the farm and my animals."

"Marilyn, do you really think the girls will just roll over and accept that?" Granted, it was a more solid plan than she'd expected, but there were still a great many speed bumps in the path. "And will *Warren* agree to it?"

"I've actually debated it for a while. It's a moral dilemma; it really is. My girls should be in charge since they're my next of kin. But they've done nothing but fight their entire lives, and it's ruining this family. Warren will almost certainly hate the idea, as it will cause increased drama for a good long while, but I trust him to make the right choices for me. He just needs to buck up and deal with it."

The prospect brought the first glimpse of hope since she sat in the grass with Warren building a ramp in defiance of his mother. Since he held her close under the cold hose's spray.

"You seem so optimistic. So, why were you crying when I came in?" she asked.

"Mostly guilt and the possible consequences if I fail. I miss Belle. Haven't had that much fun in ages, and I want to talk everything over with her. She's real good at scheming. Been thinking of John too—what life would have been like if things were different, and if I'd be in this mess had we stayed together." Marilyn reached forward and took Ellie's hand once more. "And knowing that you are leaving, and I won't get to enjoy any more of these visits."

Ellie's eyes misted again, but her smile overpowered the tears. "You have no idea how much I'll miss this too."

This didn't *have* to be a one-time friendship. She and Marilyn would stay in contact, and it helped to know that. Ellie would return to Ohio having met several new friends and role models. While this hadn't been the vacation she'd hoped for, it might have been exactly what she needed to move forward.

Marilyn finally released Ellie and clapped her hands together, which shook them both from their tenderness. "Now, I need help convincing Warren to do his part in this, and I've chosen you for the part."

"Excuse me?" Ellie's voice squeaked. "You jumped trains rather quickly there."

"I want you to go and fetch Warren, Ellie. Simple as that. What step are you missing here?" Marilyn shifted her weight in her chair, tilting her head to catch Ellie's eye. "Calling is so impersonal, and if he's going to be a little shit and not answer his phone anyway, you have to go in person. He needs proper convincing, and you're just the person to do it."

"Marilyn." Words didn't come to her for a moment. Ellie should have known she wouldn't be able to escape being part of Marilyn's strategy and getting sucked right back into the scheming. "I'm leaving in the morning. Warren would be all the way back in Spokane by now. He's not going to listen to me if I try to—"

"Oh, pishposh. I already bought you a plane ticket to Washington. Tori's going to drop you off at the airport. Barry's going to take care of the animals. And Warren is going to fall madly in love with you. It's really this simple." She waved her off as if she couldn't believe Ellie didn't get it. "Flight leaves tomorrow. If you don't go, I'm out a bunch of money, and you're going to feel awfully bad about it."

"Marilyn!"

"Ellie." All joking had left her voice now. "When you first stepped in that door, you were a timid little flower who got a whole new lifestyle dumped on her. Over the last two weeks, you've become an advocate, a fierce helper, and a loyal friend to me. I am so damn proud to know you."

Ellie couldn't move. She could hardly even think. "Wow."

"Yeah, wow. Did you go and schedule an earlier flight out of here?" Marilyn asked.

"I—uh. No, not yet. I—"

"Perfect!" Marilyn reached for her pocketbook, slammed it down on her side table, and dug out a printed ticket. "Can you believe how easy it is to get flights these days? Connor helped me print it out, by the way. Oh, child, if I were only sixty-five years younger."

Ellie took the page and reviewed the details, barely able to process the actuality of it all. "You really want me to do this."

Marilyn leaned in. "Ellie, honey, your scheduled trip doesn't end for a few more days. Now, vacations are supposed to be about adventure, romance, and excitement. So, go do those things."

Good heavens. Marilyn had somehow made every bone in Ellie's body turn to Jell-O. She couldn't even think straight now. Her tongue wouldn't form words. She had nothing. Absolutely nothing.

"If you're willing to help an old woman one last time…" Marilyn lowered the leg rest like she was ready to hit the ground running. "I would be forever grateful."

– 30 –

"WHO DOES THIS? NOT normal people." Ellie's knuckles turned white as she clutched the SUV's grab-handle. "I think this is the part where you talk sense into me and tell me to stay out of it because it's none of my business."

Tori put the car in park and clapped her hands together. "Are you kidding me? This is the most thrilling thing that's happened around here since they started decorating the town with dinosaurs."

"This is considerably less charming than the dinosaurs." But who could say no to Marilyn? Well, her daughters could, obviously. No one *nice* could say no to her.

Ellie looked over the crumpled to-do list Marilyn had given her upon first arrival. Two weeks ago, it had seemed like so much. If only Ellie had known what would end up on her list as time went on.

They pulled into the hardware store parking lot, and Ellie checked the backseat to make sure none of the eggs had spilled. Grand romantic gestures or not, certain farm tasks still had to be done, and Ellie didn't want anyone coming back to the farm to a bunch of rotten eggs.

Tori turned off the SUV and smacked her palms to the steering wheel. "All right, sister. All that separates you from this mission is an egg delivery and farm-care rundown, the purchase of some delicious plane snacks, and a long drive to the airport."

"And Blake Robinson." Ellie felt the blood rush from her cheeks.

"Blake? What?" Tori shifted in her seat to find Blake's truck parked a few spaces away. "Oh, how precious."

Climbing out of the car, Ellie tried to channel her anxiety into raw power. "I've got a few things I'd like to say to him."

Confrontation was not something she did. Ever. But Blake was the worst.

"Yesss. I've got your back. You let 'im have it. If things get violent, I've got some tranquilizers in the trunk."

For a seemingly sweet, small-town girl, Tori could be downright scary. Thank goodness they were on the same team.

"Maybe stick with being the getaway driver for now. How much time do we have?" Ellie asked.

"Plane leaves in three hours, and it's a one-hour drive to Great Falls."

Great. If things got too messy with Blake, she had an excuse to hightail it out of there. "You really are the best for doing this, Tori. I know this is taking up a huge chunk of your day."

"Like I said: it's been fun having you around. I adore Marilyn and genuinely want what's best for her. And if I get to watch you take down Blake Robinson along the way, it'll be such a huge bonus." She bit her lip to suppress a squeal before continuing. "The cow insemination can wait a few hours. Cow insemination, Ellie. You can see why this wasn't a hard choice for me."

Ellie laughed, which broke up some of the tension in her chest. With Tori's words for fuel, Ellie hopped out of the car and marched into the hardware store, Tori right behind her.

"Oh, Ellie, hello!" Barry dropped the seed packets he was restocking in a pile for later. "Good to see you too, Doc."

"Hey, Barry," Ellie greeted, trying so hard to focus on him and not on the fact that her enemy lurked somewhere in the store. "Marilyn said you were going to pop in on the animals so I wanted to—"

Blake stepped out from the paint aisle. "Shouldn't you be on a plane by now?"

Seeing him in person spawned a war in her brain. On one hand, his intimidating stare made her want to run and leave Montana forever. On the other, she really wanted to smack him right in his pretty, awful face.

"Listen here, Captain Fartsicle." Okay, so not off to a great start. "What you did to Marilyn was wrong, and you can't go around treating people that way. You're tearing a family apart when they need each other the most, and I am so mad at you for coming out to the farm and trying to befriend me and taking everything I said back to Janey. You…"

A strong enough insult didn't exist, and she'd already proven her subpar ability to make one up on the spot.

"What? What are you going to call me?" Blake maintained his posture, a gross smirk played on his lips, eyes alight with amusement. And Ellie could see the devil in them now. Marilyn was right.

"I think you're a scumbag. A scumbag who isn't going to win this battle because I'm going to stop you." She rested her hand on her hip, and then immediately changed her mind about such a sassy pose.

"Whoa, there." Barry hurried to place himself between them. "I don't think we need to fight about this. Let's get some popcorn and calm down a little."

Blake ignored the suggestion. "The wheels are already in motion. Janey and Shannon should be arriving at the nursing home right now to settle the logistics before their flight. I'll be joining them to place my bid, which Marilyn would be stupid to refuse. I'll buy the farm, Marilyn will go live in Spokane, and you will go home where you belong."

A rustling and crunch behind her let Ellie know that Tori had taken Barry up on the popcorn offering.

"They're meeting right now?" Ellie waited for his condescending nod. "Good. Feel free to let them know they'll be met with a mutiny."

This is why she didn't get into fights. She couldn't do it without ridiculous insults and pirate speak. And Tori was no help, whooping her delight between bites.

"Are you part of this 'mutiny,' Hill? Two nonfamily members who have absolutely no say in anything that's about to go down?" He scoffed and reached into his pocket for his truck keys.

"Oh, no. I'm only here to watch her take you down." Tori beamed. If anyone had been keeping score, surely Blake was in the lead, but Tori hadn't noticed or cared. "You might not want to warm up your checkbook just yet, because this girl's got a plan."

Well, Marilyn had the plan. Ellie was the messenger—a very nervous messenger who couldn't help but set little fires all along her path that may or may not help the situation.

"Has everyone seen our sale on power drills?" Barry interjected in an attempt to reroute the conversation.

"Oh, Barry, we have eggs out in my car for you. Don't let me forget to give those to you before we leave." Tori tossed a piece of popcorn up and caught it in her mouth.

His smile grew wide. "How nice. Thank you. The wife was saying last night we should make omelets, and—"

"Yeah, hey." Blake's voice cut through as he spoke to someone on his phone. He maintained a cold stare directed to Ellie. "You know your little Airbnb guest is still in town, right?" He waited for an answer that Ellie couldn't hear. "She's convinced she's got a plan to take the whole family down."

"Not the whole family. Just the nasty ones," Ellie corrected.

Blake pulled the phone from his face. "Janey would like you to know she will press charges if you don't leave immediately."

Ellie imagined Janey calling the police and telling them the stranger on their mother's farm really did end up being a psychopath determined to destroy them all. She'd end up having to change her name and move out of the country.

Not like she didn't already have to start her life all over again. Doing it in a tropical location could make it more interesting.

"'Kay. Well, you can tell her I've got a great lawyer." She really hoped Belle's son truly was a great lawyer, one willing to take on super bizarre cases on a small budget. "And I'm also protected under the renter bylaws, so let's dance."

Oh my gosh, she needed to shut up.

"Let's all calm down a little. I'm sure we can come to some rational agreement." Barry tried to approach Blake, but he brushed right past him, the phone still pressed to his ear.

"Yes, we're at the hardware now," he said.

The rest of the world—Tori and Barry—went on with business as usual.

"Hey, Ellie." Tori tapped her on the shoulder and held out an assortment of bagged candies from a rack near the register. "I'm going to go ahead and get you some of these burnt peanuts and blue shark gummies. That sound good?"

Barry hurried to the counter. "Excellent choice for traveling."

"Yeah, that's fine. Thank you." Ellie then returned her attention to Blake, who shook his head at the ridiculous interactions in front of him.

"No, I'm on my way. I'll"—Blake's face morphed into something Ellie couldn't read—"Are you sure? She's not in the building anywhere?"

Blake started toward the front door.

"Who's not in the building?" she asked as she ran in front of him and blocked the exit.

"I'll be right there." Blake hung up and stuffed the phone back into his pocket. His confident smirk had vanished. "Did you take her out of there?"

"Oooh!" Tori hurried alongside Ellie, popcorn in one hand and plastic bag of goodies in the other.

Blake reached for the door handle, pinning Ellie in place. "Move."

"Take who?" She wouldn't budge if he didn't talk.

"Marilyn. They said she left the rehab unit, but nobody knows where she is. What did you do?"

The door hit her butt when Blake yanked it forward, but she stood her ground.

Had Marilyn really checked herself out? Part of her worried about her friend and if she was all right. The other part knew that if she backed down now, it could ruin what Marilyn worked toward.

"That's for me to know and you to find out." Ellie almost immediately regretted the words. Instead of implied mystery, now she sounded like a kidnapper.

Tori must have realized the same thing because she took Ellie's arm and pulled her from the doorway. "She didn't do anything to Marilyn. Marilyn has made her own choices."

"Do you know where she is?" Ellie mumbled over her shoulder.

"Not a clue, but you have to sound less criminal if you want to keep this up." Tori pulled her deeper into the store. "We don't need TSA locking you up before you catch your flight."

This would have been more helpful if Marilyn had made another specific list with a chain of events so Ellie knew what was going on.

Blake shot out the door and hurried to his truck.

"Is Marilyn okay?" Barry appeared beside them and readjusted the pencil behind his ear.

Ellie watched Blake fly out of the parking lot, off to his meeting already gone awry. "I'll try to call her."

Tori emptied the last of the popcorn into her palm. "It's Marilyn. She's tougher than the three of us combined."

"That's very true," Barry agreed. "I'll go grab those eggs from you, so we don't forget. Do you have the animal instructions?"

Ellie fumbled through her purse and handed him another of Marilyn's handwritten notes regarding animal care. As Barry switched gears to gather eggs from Tori's SUV, Ellie snatched up her phone and scrolled through the messages and missed phone calls. While her family had been busy asking questions and trying to reach her, there were no calls from Marilyn.

No calls from Warren.

After this adventure ended, she'd really have to sit down with her parents and sister and calm all the storms. She wasn't ready to do that yet. Not until she had answers herself.

"Walk with me. You've got a flight to catch." Tori led Ellie to the car while the phone rang over and over again.

It wasn't until the third try as they turned out of town that someone answered.

Hushed whispers and giggles met her ear. Marilyn wasn't alone. "Ellie, are you in Spokane?"

"No, I haven't even gotten to the airport yet. Where are you? Blake said—"

"The hell are you doing with Blake? I thought I told you to get better taste in men."

Whatever had happened to her, her spunk hadn't been affected. A giddy cackle filled the silence, giving away Marilyn's accomplice.

"Least she's saving Connor for the rest of us. God, I miss that boy," came Belle's voice.

Beside her, Tori giggled, hearing everything the loud women said without needing the speaker.

"Are you in Belle's room?" Ellie asked.

"I don't know if I should tell you our exact location, lest you give us away." Okay, Marilyn enjoyed this mission madness entirely too much.

"Marilyn, now would be a really wonky time for you to decide not to trust me after all we've done over the past two weeks."

"Touché." Marilyn cleared her throat and announced with great pride, "Yep, Belle's room. We're having tea while we wait for you to fetch Warren and keeping busy with my leads on John. Still thinking either Missoula here in Montana or he's selling tires in Connecticut. I'll keep you posted. No one knows I'm here because I hid in the shower when the nurses did their roundabouts. Tried hailing a Goober on my trek across that damn parking lot to Belle's building, but it's not like in the movies at all. Can't for the life of me figure out how you did that, Ellie. No matter. This plan works just as well. And don't you dare say a word to anyone about my whereabouts. You are sworn to secrecy."

Tori pressed her hand to her heart and shook with the giggles. "Did she mean Uber? Oh my goodness I love her so much."

"That Tori? Tori, you make sure she gets to the airport pronto. We're going to take them all down." Marilyn laughed, while Belle cheered in the background.

"Marilyn, I have so many questions…" There was no way this latest Marilyn scheme would work like she thought it would. "You can't stay hidden in the assisted living unit for long."

Marilyn scoffed. "I like a good challenge. Besides, what are they going to do if they catch me? It's not like they can arrest me for simply being tired of everybody's shit."

Tori snorted and covered her face with her hand.

The image of the two older women clinking teacups on Belle's sofa, taking peeks out of the blinds, and Marilyn rolling her wheelchair behind a shower curtain filled Ellie's head. They were like children. If Ellie was the designated adult in this, they were all in big trouble.

"Your family—and probably the entire nursing home staff—are going to be so mad at you," Ellie said.

"Don't care." Marilyn's enormous smile was obvious.

Marilyn had found herself at a crossroads in life. She, too, had choices, and she'd taken one hell of a leap by going into hiding with her new best friend. She knew exactly what she wanted, to hell with the trouble it caused others.

That was Ellie's dream—to be so confident in her decisions and path in life. To take risks and stop living a mundane existence.

And she had to start now.

– 31 –

ELLIE HAD AWOKEN WELL before the sun came up on the other side of the blackout curtains. She stared into the darkness, listening to the air-conditioner click on and off and debating if she ought to numb her brain with HGTV or order room service. Not that either option would provide the distraction she needed right now.

Having landed in Spokane much later than she'd expected, courtesy of a thunderstorm and a layover at SeaTac, Ellie opted to finally use those travel points to get a discounted hotel room. She could have gone straight to Warren's apartment, but her nerves wouldn't allow it. Not that they had gotten any better after a fitful night's rest.

Why was she doing this again?

Ellie's feet wriggled under the crisp hotel sheets, her restlessness causing the entire bed to shake. If she had neighbors on the other side of the wall, they might suspect something much more exciting went on in room 431 than a single woman having a mild panic attack.

Flinging the covers back, Ellie sat up on the edge of the bed. She'd already showered, gotten dressed, and put on a thin layer of makeup after first waking. Her hair tied on top of her head, all she needed was shoes and a strong cup of coffee.

Ellie's phone lit up, letting her know a car would arrive for her soon. Her heart palpitated at an alarming rate. This was it. Within the hour, she'd see Warren. Within the hour, she'd read his face and find out what he thought of her taking this reckless trip. Within the hour, she might know Marilyn was right in regards to how he felt about her.

Because she was pretty sure how she felt about him.

Her hand pressed to her stomach to forcefully quell the nausea. She slipped on her flip-flops and gathered her bags—she'd brought everything with her because she didn't know what else to do with it all. If things went poorly, she'd either have to eat the cost of a new flight back to Ohio from Washington or figure out a way to get to Great Falls and catch her previously scheduled flight in a few days. And what a disastrous—and expensive—mess that would all be. If things went well, she still wouldn't be welcome on the farm while Marilyn's daughters were in town.

It was fine. Everything was fine. Not at all a dumpster fire.

A quick ride in the elevator and stop at the front desk to check out brought her out onto the sidewalk of downtown Spokane where the buildings rose around her like a maze—not too unlike Columbus. But different somehow. If this had been a normal trip, she'd have wanted to sightsee or walk around the block to take in the new atmosphere, but she had work to do. And until she got this surprise visit over with, she wouldn't be able to breathe properly, which was becoming a problem.

Per her instructions, the driver stopped at the nearest Starbucks drive-thru so she could grab the largest caramel cappuccino they made—two, actually, so she didn't arrive at Warren's empty-handed. Ellie prayed the caffeine worked in opposition to her shaking nerves instead of making them worse. Running on very little sleep didn't bode well for a day of confessions, reunions, and scheming.

She still didn't even know what she was going to say to Warren.

The car pulled up to a large apartment complex, much fancier than the one she lived in back in Ohio. But so far, everything in Spokane was fancier than what she was used to. Now, Ellie found herself standing on a sidewalk without a functioning brain cell to make sense of anything, her large bags slung over her shoulder, drink carrier in hand.

This was the address Marilyn had given her. As long as Warren hadn't already returned to work and left for a job site this early, she might still catch him.

Through the rotating door she went, greeting the doorman with a nod and lift of one of the large cappuccinos. They didn't have a doorman at her complex.

His upscale manners and extremely impressive grammar only intensified her nerves. Which then propelled her into the elevator. The more uncomfortable she became, the more she wanted to share that discomfort with Warren. A new, strange feeling. She truly *wanted* to be with someone else and not retreat back to the hotel and clam up in her solo shell.

Ellie pushed the button to the eighth floor.

That bastard had better be home.

A golden-brown carpet met her when the elevator doors opened and stretched down the hallway. Suddenly, she was Dorothy following the yellow brick road. She wasn't in Kansas anymore—er, Montana—and she couldn't decide if she should click her heels together and go straight home or push on toward the man behind the curtain—er, the handsome contractor behind door 817.

Her mind did the dumbest things when she was stressed. Seriously.

She stared at the door number and dropped her bags to her feet. The way she clutched the drink carrier made the cardboard crumple, compromising the safety of the drinks.

She had to get a grip.

Her hand shook when she double checked the address and knocked so lightly it'd have been a miracle if anyone could hear it.

But someone must have heard because, on the other side of the door, footsteps moved across the room. The hallway grew darker, and Ellie leaned against the doorframe in case she passed out.

After six years in a committed relationship, she'd totally forgotten how to do this.

The door opened, and her grip on the cup holder wavered.

A stunned and slightly unkempt Warren stood before her. The blond stubble on his chin glistened in the hall light. He wore an old T-shirt and gym shorts—probably what he'd worn to bed. And his eyes. They shone with a surprise the usually stoic man hadn't expressed before.

This was the time she needed to say something. She swallowed hard and tried to stop standing there, staring at him like a creepy mannequin.

"I brought you coffee," she said.

Not a hello or an explanation of why she'd come. Because that's about as poised and put together as she could possibly be on a couple hours of sleep. Or ever, really.

"All right…" His head tilted as he examined her. "But that answers almost none of my questions."

Warren's lips slowly curled into a smile, which nearly made Ellie melt into the yellow brick carpet.

"I'm here on behalf of your grandmother who, in your absence, has since come up with another scheme." Ellie plucked a cup from the carrier and extended it for Warren to take.

"Of course she has." Warren took the cup, his fingers brushing over Ellie's in a way that sent electricity across her skin.

"And I may have escalated the situation," she added.

"Of course you did." He stepped aside and ushered her into his minimally decorated bachelor pad. Ellie took a quick glimpse around the place, so unlike the tiny home he'd put together in Montana. She preferred that place immeasurably. This apartment put off a cold, isolated quality similar to that of a morgue—without the dead bodies. It made for a great place to hide away from the world and drown oneself in sterility and the street noise below.

Ellie had stepped far enough inside that Warren could close the door. He still stood behind her, near enough she could feel his warmth and smell the lingering scent of his dude soap.

"I can't believe you're here." His voice came out as not much more than a whisper.

Ellie forced confidence into her voice. "Well, you didn't say goodbye, so…"

"Ah." He placed the coffee on the table beside the door and circled around to face her. "About that."

"I know you're angry." Her fingernails dug into the cardboard carrier again now that he stared into her eyes again.

"Not at you." He swallowed hard, a crease forming on his brow as he stared. "I know I should haven't left, but I couldn't bring myself to come back with Janey and Mom about to go to war. I felt kind of helpless, you know?" The corner of his mouth quirked. "I also kind of figured you'd be on a plane to Ohio by this time."

Ellie shrugged. Gravity seemed to pull her forward, and it took everything in her to keep still. "I got on a different plane."

Warren took a slow step forward too. "To bring me coffee."

"And confess my sins." Being in front of him now made all the anxiety evaporate. The three hundred and fifty miles that separated her from Choteau cleared her head. It almost made her forget that Marilyn was an escapee and Ellie might be wanted for elderly-napping.

Warren laughed and ran his fingers through his hair, which only made it stand up more. "I hate to think what you and Gram concocted without me there to reel you back in. I guess that also explains why you're here, since I haven't been answering my phone."

"Well, that explains *some* of why I'm here."

This was happening.

She was going to do this. Pass or fail. Hit or miss. Dear God.

She forced her head high when he looked at her again. "I also came because I want you to know how sorry I am about the Blake thing. I want you to know that I really respect the relationship you have with your grandmother, and it was an honor to witness that kind of love over the past couple weeks. I came because this isn't over yet, and we need you." Her mouth went dry. "I also came because, despite what a jackass you can be, I think I'm kind of starting to fall for you." Had she remembered to take a breath? "And also, you forgot Hilda, so I'm going to need you to come back and get her."

Warren straightened, eyes wide. "You're falling for me?"

"And you forgot Hilda, I said. Don't pick and choose, Warren." It was so very warm in that apartment even with the air-conditioning cranked up.

The idiot needed to make a move before Ellie exploded. But Warren only inched a little closer, his parenthetical dimples diving deep to taunt Ellie with everything they had. He enjoyed this kind of torture. The sicko.

She'd had quite enough of that.

Ellie reached forward and snatched hold of Warren's T-shirt near the collar, drawing him to her. Before she had a chance to fully process what she'd done, Warren's lips met hers, and everything outside of that moment vanished.

Her grip on his shirt tightened, especially when she nearly tripped over her bag at their feet. In her other hand, she held the coffee tray over the end table and prayed she placed it on an actual surface. If not, oh well. She needed her hands free right now.

Warren's fingers brushed her cheeks and trailed to her chin, her neck, shoulders…

Her eyes pressed shut so tightly, and she relished the sensation of his warm body against hers, his tight back muscles under her fingertips, and his soft, hungry lips.

The piercing howl of a police siren broke them apart. Her heart totally stopped beating for a hot second there, sure the cops had come to drag her off to prison for abducting some nursing home residents, among other "crimes" as determined by Marilyn's children. But the sound came from inside the apartment, somewhere across the room.

Warren tapped his fingers to his forehead, his other hand still resting on Ellie's hip to ensure she didn't get too far. "And that would be my mother."

"Your mom's ringtone is a siren?" She forced air into her lungs.

"Can you think of a better heads-up that she wants to talk?" Warren clearly had no intention of picking up. "I wonder what she wants now."

Ellie pulled back enough that Warren's hand finally slipped away, filling her with immediate regret. As much as she wanted to lock the door, throw their phones out the window, and forget *everything*, she was on a very time-sensitive mission.

"I can answer that." She reached for Warren's abandoned coffee and pushed it back into his hands. "You're going to need this. Sorry it's not vodka."

"Okay..." He nodded for her to follow him to the couch—which was good, because he definitely should sit for this.

Ellie joined him there, trying to memorize this moment where he looked at her with kind eyes in case her next words sent him spiraling back to a time when he thought her a criminal. "I'm going to say this quickly, and I need you to know that I'm not the orchestrator of any of this. I'm only the runner—and accomplice, let's be honest."

"Oh, this doesn't reek of disaster at all." He forced a laugh.

She had to spit it out fast. "So, Marilyn has no intention of selling the farm and moving to Spokane. She told your aunt a lie to get her off her back for a bit and wants to put you legally in charge of everything she has so you can override any decisions the girls make. She sent me here to bring you back to sign the papers and whatnot. Sounds like she's narrowed things down to two leads on locating John. And, um, your mom, aunt, Shannon, and Blake were supposed to have a meeting at the nursing home this morning to get the ball rolling on selling the farm, but—"

Warren's evolving expression toward panic made it even harder to continue.

Ellie whimpered. "But when they got to the nursing home, Marilyn wasn't there."

"Not there?" He stood, a spurt of coffee shooting out of the lid. "Where did she—"

"She's in Belle's room over in assisted living. Or, at least, she was when I talked to her yesterday before I got on the plane. They're in hiding." Every time she laid it out, it sounded crazier and crazier. "Yes, Marilyn checked herself out of the rehab unit, wheeled her way across the parking lot, and hid out in Belle's shower so the staff didn't find her there. That happened. I tried calling her again last night, but it went straight to voicemail. I have no idea if anyone has found them there or not, or what the status is now."

So, so ridiculous.

The room went silent. Even the hum from the air-conditioner had quieted as if waiting for answers.

"Wow," Warren finally said. "That's a lot."

"It's so much." With so much more to come.

"I see why I needed the vodka now." He crossed the room to check his phone. "Mom texted 'ANSWER YOUR DAMN PHONE' in all caps several times but hasn't said anything else. That was actually the seventh call I've ignored from her *today*. I guess I should have answered my *damn phone*."

"Are you going to come back with me, or shall we change our names and run away?" The latter option sure was appealing.

He returned to the couch and crashed against the cushions. "I really don't know who to bet on here. My grandmother is an unstoppable force, and her daughters are an unmovable object." He groaned and stood again. His inability to hold still didn't do much for Ellie's nerves. "She really wants me to take over everything?"

"Apparently she's been in cahoots with Belle's fancy lawyer son or, at least, plans to be. I don't know. Everything is becoming a blur." Ellie hadn't had a good night's sleep since arriving at Perry Farm.

She'd also never had so much excitement in her otherwise predictable and disappointing life.

"Cahoots, huh?" he repeated.

"The worst kind."

He sank down beside her again. His fingers coiled around hers, and he stared at their joined hands like they held all the answers. "I'm going to have a lot of fires to put out, aren't I?"

"So many." She tried to offer reassurance with a squeeze of his hand that fit so flawlessly around hers, but the reality of everything awaiting them in Choteau loomed too heavy.

"We can't go back to kissing and pretend they don't exist?" Warren said.

Yes! Yes! Yes!

"I'm afraid not." Her brain betrayed her heart.

He released a heavy sigh and stood once more, this time pulling Ellie up with him. "Then let's go fight my family, I guess."

– 32 –

Hilda barked her enthusiastic greeting when they pulled up to the farm just before midnight. Everything was dark, almost eerie at such an hour. The poor bulldog would have had to sleep in her doghouse with no one at home to bring her inside.

Between bathroom breaks and a stop for supper, their journey took eight hours instead of the six projected by Google Maps. Nothing beat driving across new territory, soft music playing on the radio, and talking about the silliest things as if a war didn't wage at their destination.

"I should go take care of the animals." Warren groaned.

"Marilyn had Barry come to care for them while we were gone. She had the goats picked up too." Ellie hadn't noticed how much noisier the farm was with the goats around. Now that they were gone, everything was quiet.

"Thank you, Gram," he said to the sky. "I don't know about you, but I could go for some Tylenol and a solid eight hours. Let's go, Hilda."

He waved for the dog to follow him to the door, but she took off in the opposite direction. Ellie called after her to no avail. The family drama must have messed her up too.

Warren unlocked the front door, Ellie close behind. He flipped on the kitchen lights and dropped his bag, stopping so suddenly Ellie crashed into his back.

"Ow, sorr—"

Her apology caught in her throat when she realized why he'd

frozen. There, sitting at the table with her computer and a cup of tea was Savannah.

"Welcome back," she said. "Thanks for answering my phone calls…"

"What are you doing here? Why aren't you at your hotel?" He stammered his words, surprise and exhaustion colliding to jumble his thoughts.

"Ellie." Savannah greeted coldly.

Oh, how she wished she could use Warren as a human shield and stay hidden. But they'd come back to be responsible about things, to get the Perry/Oliver/Whatever-Janey's-Last-Name-Was family on a less horrible track.

"Hey," she answered.

"So, why are you *here*?" Warren placed a hand on the countertop to steady himself. They'd had no time to prepare. This was a next-level sneak attack.

Savannah closed her laptop and drew her teacup into her palms. She wore a short-sleeve, plum-colored pajama set—a pretty expensive set if Ellie had to guess. Weirdly, the more casual attire did nothing to lessen the intimidation factor. The woman still scared the hell out of her.

"Well, I was on my way from the hotel to have a meeting with everyone at the nursing home when I received a call that my mother had left the nursing home and stole their wheelchair, followed by Janey informing me that Mom was nowhere to be found. Do you know what it's like to get a call that your mother is missing?" Savannah asked.

"No." Warren might have only *wished* he'd gotten a call like that after the last few days.

"It's terrifying." She scooted her chair from the table and approached.

Ellie felt the cold doorframe dig into her spine when she pressed against it. "Did you find out where she went?"

They still had no idea whether Marilyn's hideout had been

discovered. Ellie just hoped she and Belle hadn't done anything rash—like driving to Connecticut.

"I'm told you knew where she was the whole time," Savannah answered.

Warren's gaze met Ellie's, the string of swears crossing both their minds was obvious without having to express them.

"I did." There was no use lying about it. Marilyn had chosen to confide in someone she hardly knew rather than her own kin. Ellie couldn't help that.

"And who told *you* that?" Warren asked.

"Mom." Savannah gestured behind her. "She's asleep in her room. I went and picked her up from the assisted living facility. I worried the unfinished ramp might prove a problem with getting her inside, but the woman is driven by sheer willpower and unparalleled stubbornness."

Truer words were never spoken.

Though the way Savannah spoke made Marilyn sound like a wayward teenager, not an eighty-two-year-old nursing home escapee. Still, Marilyn would face equal or greater punishment no matter her age—definitely grounding and possibly losing her internet privileges.

"And?" Warren likely had as many questions as Ellie did. That one seemed to cover them all.

"Have a seat." Savannah's cold stare met Ellie. "Both of you."

The hope of a warm bed would have to wait. The war had come to their doorstep.

Warren and Ellie did as she asked, moving slowly and cautiously to the dining room table. Savannah poured herself another cup of tea without offering to do the same for anyone else. That was okay though. Ellie doubted she could properly swallow under interrogation.

"Warren, while I'm beyond angry about you ghosting me, I do want to apologize."

His palms flattened on the table. "What?"

Neither of them could have heard her correctly.

Savannah examined the intricate flower pattern adorning the teacup in her hand, no doubt one of Marilyn's antiques. "I saw a side of my sister yesterday that I've never seen before. She didn't care where Mom had gone, she only cared that it might affect the timeline of the farm's sale. Her intentions weren't to have Mom closer to us in Spokane. She wanted the control. It was like looking in a mirror for a moment, and I didn't like what I saw. So, I went and got Mom."

Ellie nearly slipped from her chair. "How did you end up finding her?"

Savannah kept her body turned toward her son, eyes averted. "I remembered she'd spoken of her friend Belle in the other building, so I went over there to ask if Belle had any information and found my mother trying to wheel herself into the bathroom."

If only she could have seen Marilyn's face when they realized Savannah had tracked them down and stood at the door.

"My mother was hiding from us, Warren. My *eighty-two-year-old mother* went to bizarre lengths to get away from her own children." Savannah massaged her temples. "I brought her back here to the farm, and we spent the afternoon and most of today talking and trying to understand where the other was coming from. I can't say we're totally in agreement yet, but it wasn't wholly unproductive."

Warren sat back in his seat and ran both hands through his hair. He definitely hadn't expected any of these words to come out of his mother's mouth. Neither had Ellie.

"And what about Janey?" Warren asked.

"I told her to get on her plane and let me handle this." Savannah's exhaustion appeared to grow with each word. "While I still think Mom is crazy for not taking Blake Robinson's offer, we've decided to circle back and address that issue when things have calmed down."

Ellie wanted to squeal. One of their biggest enemies had switched sides. They weren't alone in this fight anymore, even if Savannah still refused to look her in the eye.

"Did Gram say anything else?" The way he leaned forward so hesitantly made Ellie think of John. Marilyn would have to be really brave to bring that up.

Savannah shrugged. "Just that she really wants her friend Belle to join her out here. She definitely isn't willing to listen to reason. The two of them without a caregiver would never work—or maybe I should say *supervisor*. It would seem none of the employees at the home were surprised by my mother's antics. In fact, they seemed quite relieved when I told them I'd be bringing Mom home instead of leaving her there."

Ellie bit back a laugh.

Savannah continued, "Why? Was there something else I should know about?"

Warren shook his head and forced his most innocent expression.

Marilyn must not have dropped the John bomb, and she certainly had kept her secret that she planned to give all power to Warren. This conversation would have gone in a totally different direction if that had happened.

"Like I said, I know your grandmother means a lot to you, and she was devastated that your visit got cut short. I was calling to ask you to come back, but Mom told me you might already be on your way." Her gaze finally flickered to Ellie, but she received no other acknowledgment for being the Warren-fetcher.

"I appreciate that." Warren folded his hands and leaned on the table.

"Now, if you'll excuse me, I need to sleep. I hadn't planned to stay past Wednesday and am far behind on my work now. I'm heading back to Spokane early in the morning, so I won't see you again before I leave." She stood and patted her son on the shoulders. "If the Robinsons come around or Janey tries to make any decisions without me, please let me know. For now, try to keep Mom out of trouble."

Warren placed a hand on hers. "I'll do my best."

Savannah headed upstairs without another word or look toward Ellie. If she hadn't been giving them a positive report, this interaction might have been even more awkward than yelling at each other in the driveway.

"I can't believe that just happened," Warren said.

"Did your mom come over to our side?" Ellie still tried to process the entire conversation. So much had happened in the twenty-four hours she spent in Spokane collecting Warren. If nothing else, Marilyn had gotten home, where she wanted to be. Surely she slept better in her own bed, somewhat in harmony with one of her children.

Ellie almost wanted to run in and wake her up to get the full scoop. As tired as she was herself, it might be hard to settle in for the night after a day like this. Things were falling into place. Savannah had stopped shouting. Marilyn came home. Ellie got to stay in Montana a little bit longer.

Oh, and she'd kissed Warren.

That really had happened too.

Warren smiled across the table. "Sounds like we're playing defense now. Figuring out logistics. Keeping Gram from jumping headfirst into some wild new agenda. You gonna stick around, City Girl?"

The joyful moment deflated when Ellie realized one of the next steps in this involved going back home as scheduled.

There was still a ton to deal with, as much as she wanted to ignore it. "For a few days, anyway."

Saying the words out loud made her heart ache. Yes, they'd kissed. No, they hadn't defined the relationship. Maybe it was a fling. Those happened on vacations. They'd both admitted to being bad at relationships. Two people like that would fail before her plane even touched down in Ohio.

His smile had faded. "Then we'll try to make the most of it."

– 33 –

THE BRIGHT SUN PIERCING through the skylight woke Ellie up early as always. She tried to go back to sleep, but the previous day played through her head over and over.

Her days were numbered on this farm; she might as well drink it in.

Ellie pulled on her heart health T-shirt and jean shorts, tied her hair into a low bun, and started for the barn. Since Warren hadn't mentioned what this day might hold, Ellie decided to carry on as usual, let him sleep in if he could, and spend some time with the animals.

Upon entering the barn, Sheriff brayed and bumped against the fence to get as close to her as possible. Ellie would miss him most of all. She tapped her forehead to his and scratched his chin.

"I've loved taking care of you, ya big lug. I might have to get a farm of my own and raise donkeys one day," she said.

Bo and Peep collided, *baaing* their sheep rage and trotting to opposite ends of their pen.

"Think I'll pass on getting sheep." Ellie noted the extra space in the barn now that the goats had returned to their actual owner. "Definitely not goats."

"You pouring out your soul to the donkey again?" Warren stood in the doorway with Hilda at his feet begging for the Bilexin ball in his hand.

"I'm too poor for therapy." This time, she didn't mind at all that he'd snuck up on her. In fact, she preferred it. "Didn't want to wake you if you were still sleeping."

Sheriff nudged her, drawing her attention back to him.

A moment later, Warren's hands found her waist, his arms wrapping around her middle.

Ellie closed her eyes and let herself feel his warmth, the way he held her like she might melt away if he let go. And she might, because her insides had turned to mush.

"It wasn't the most restful, I'll be honest. Gram's still sleeping though." He laughed. "I imagine the past couple of days really took it out of her. Once she's up, we'll have to make breakfast and get her side of the story. I'm sure it varies significantly from Mom's and is undoubtedly a more colorful tale."

Ellie couldn't wait.

Warren's hand followed Ellie's waist as she turned to face him. He had a longing in his eyes that made Ellie want to push him into the hay bales and pretend the barn wasn't full of smelly spectators.

He cupped her cheek and leaned in, but a long snout pushed between them. Sheriff snorted to demonstrate his irritation over having to share affection.

The giggles set in deep when the needy donkey rubbed against her and took her from Warren's arms.

Warren clapped a hand to his post. "I see how it's going to be. I guess we'd better feed them first and then maybe try that again?"

Ellie shrugged. She definitely wanted to try that again. Maybe somewhere *else*.

They cared for the barn animals while Hilda wrestled with herself in the corner. These were the daily moments Ellie would miss so much. It'd seemed like a ton of work when she first arrived, but it'd proved to be the most rewarding thing she'd done in her adult life.

Hilda shot to her feet and ran to the barn door when something piqued her curiosity. Her head quirked and she trotted off.

"Gram must be up," Warren said and finished filling the water troughs.

Ellie started toward the back gate to let the animals out into the pen, but couldn't remember if anyone had fixed the newest escape hole in the fencing. That'd put a damper on their relaxing day for sure.

"Hey, Warren, do you know if—"

Now *he* stood at the barn door, staring out with a tilted head, hands in his pockets. Ellie came alongside him and peered out in time to see an unfamiliar truck coming up the lane, a large animal trailer in tow.

He shook his head as he tried to solve the mystery. "I don't think that's Barry's truck. I left a message with him that we were back, anyway…"

The ever-faithful greeter, Hilda barked as she ran alongside the vehicle.

Who else would stop by the farm with a large trailer on a Sunday? Those things didn't exactly look like the kind of accessory one would hook up for a casual drive.

Savannah had made it sound like so many things had been re-solved, but she'd neglected to mention one aspect of the farm drama.

"Warren, has anyone mentioned calling off the people coming to get the animals?" Ellie couldn't keep the panic from rising in her voice. If Janey or Savannah had already been successful in tracking down someone to take them—and if money was involved at all—this would be a real mess.

Instead of driving out to the barn, the truck came to a stop in front of the house, and the driver hopped out.

"That's not any of Gram's neighbors," Warren said. "I've never seen him around here before…"

Hilda jumped at the man, who grinned down at her as he used a steady hand to calm her. She obviously liked him. But then again, she liked almost everybody. Not Blake or Marilyn's daughters though, she now realized. The dog might be a clutz, but she was a good judge of character.

When he began approaching the house, Warren took off to intercept. Hilda's zigzagging across his path slowed the man's progress, giving Warren and Ellie plenty of time to get to him before he reached the door.

The man startled when he caught a glimpse of the couple approaching, too focused on not tripping over Hilda to notice them before.

A much older gentleman, he wore a faded pair of jeans and a blue-striped button-up shirt. A gray flatcap hat covered his head, white hairs peeking out around the brim. His kind eyes highlighted by his round glasses eased Ellie somewhat—not the eyes of an evil-doer or animal snatcher.

"Morning," Warren greeted in a friendly, yet skeptical, tone. "How can I help you?"

The man examined the house again, then studied Warren intensely. "Good morning. I'm, uh, looking for a Marilyn Perry. I'm delivering a horse."

Ellie's jaw nearly fell clean from her face and into the dirt below. "A horse?" Warren squeaked.

"Yes, she purchased one through our website." He removed his hat and placed it over his heart ceremoniously. "Is she at home?"

Warren held out his hands as if he could push Pause on the entire scene unfolding before him. "She ordered a horse online? Are you serious? How in the world did—"

Ellie grabbed Warren's forearm a whole lot tighter than she meant to. Bits and pieces of the past week slowly came together like a puzzle. Marilyn had mentioned purchasing animals online in the past—and browsing available horses on a very *particular* website.

A website for a horse ranch in eastern Montana where her long-lost love might just work if he didn't sell tires in Connecticut.

"What is your name?" Ellie gripped tighter on Warren to keep from falling over.

Warren's gaze shifted between Ellie and their guest.

The man took another slow step forward and extended his hand. "My name is John Clay. I'm with Heckler Ranch in Missoula."

"Holy balls," Ellie whispered and drew her hands to her mouth.

Like a zombie, Warren reached forward to shake the man's hand, though his eyes had gone wide. "As in *John* Clay who was in love with my grandmother sixty years ago? *That* John Clay?"

John's lips quirked. He looked Warren over again as if seeing him for the very first time. "You're Marilyn's grandson. I see it now in the eyes. Is she at home?"

"Yeah, she's—" Warren ran his fingers through his hair and chuckled like he still couldn't believe this. "She might be asleep. It's been a wild few days, and she's recovering from a broken kneecap on top of that."

"Oh, I'm so sorry to hear that." John returned his cap to his head and reached down to pet Hilda, who still jumped and pawed at him with excitement. "You wouldn't be to blame for that, would you?" he asked her.

"She absolutely is." Ellie's hands had settled over her heart as she watched the dear man before her. Marilyn had spoken so highly of him, and here he was: a gentleman with an affinity for animals, an eye for sharp farm attire, and a smile that made the entire day brighter.

Warren draped an arm around Ellie's shoulder and tugged her closer, an unspoken celebration taking place between them.

"I can't believe Gram bought a horse from you," Warren said. "Does *she* know she did?"

Ellie laughed. "She said she found a John Clay who worked at a ranch and sold beautiful horses, but she didn't mention actually purchasing one."

Whatever decisions the family came to in regards to Marilyn's future, someone needed to monitor her browser history a little better to keep her from accidentally buying a zoo.

"She was searching for *me*?" John slid his hands into his pockets and kept his gaze turned to the dirt path.

Ellie nodded. "I hope she doesn't mind me saying, but she wanted to show you the farm after all these years, said it was a special place for you."

My goodness. The adorableness of it all was too much to handle.

"It's a very special place." John glanced around him and smiled. "In all honesty, I don't normally make the deliveries myself, let alone on a Sunday morning, but when I saw her name, I wanted to come see for myself."

"Gram will appreciate that, though I'm pretty sure this isn't the way she'd planned for it to happen." Warren laughed and scratched his head.

At some point, one of them needed to actually go and get Marilyn, but the disbelief was paralyzing.

John grew thoughtful and bobbed his head to an inaudible tune. "I tried to call first. Unfortunately, she used the phone number for the local radio station for the online paperwork."

"That's Marilyn for you." Ellie pushed away the shock once and for all. "I'm so sorry. We're kind of in slow motion here today. How about we put the horse in the barn for now, and you can join us for a late breakfast?"

"I don't want to be a burden," John said.

Warren snapped back to reality too. "Not a burden at all. This is—yeah, we'd love to have you. I'll help you in the barn, and Ellie can go in and let Gram know you're here."

Prepare her, more like. This would be a very big surprise to wake up to.

John took a few steps backward and examined the farm again. "She needs her rest…"

The nerves and reservations were evident in his blue eyes.

"John." Ellie wanted to melt at the display taking place before her—like an adolescent preparing to ask his crush to the big dance, not a grown man about to see an eighty-two-year-old woman he loved long ago. "Please join us."

"I—I haven't seen Marilyn since April 10th, 1959." He turned his face to the sky. "But I'm so ready to see her again."

"I SWEAR TO ALL that is good and holy that I'm about to hurl."
Marilyn stared at her reflection in the bathroom mirror. The old
fluorescent lighting did nothing for either of their complexions. "I
can't do it."

Ellie combed the back of Marilyn's hair where it had gone flat from
lying on the pillow. With a little water, the silver mane fell into place
around Marilyn's shoulders. "You aren't going to hurl. It'll be fine, and
we'll be with you if you if you need us. Besides, he drove all this way
to see you, and he brought you a horse. Most men just bring flowers."

"Flowers would have been easier on the pocketbook." She
smacked her cheeks for some color and messed with the position of
her mismatched earrings. "I wanted to see him so badly, but now that
he's out there, I don't think I can do it. I'm so nervous, I could spit."

"Don't do that either." Ellie helped her older friend sit back in
her wheelchair before she took another tumble and injured something else. "He really seems so sweet, Marilyn."

Marilyn reached behind her to pat Ellie's hand. "He always was.
But so much has changed. Look at me. I'm not the young, spry thing
he remembers from all those years ago. I'm old and can't walk. When
I imagined seeing him again, I imagined us as we were. Not as I *am*."

"Oh, stop it. I think you're a total babe, and so will he. He's aged
too, you know." Ellie paused in the doorway. "Are you ready now?
Warren was going to get the horse set up and then start on some
breakfast. We can leave you two to talk in the sunroom and—"

"No, don't you dare leave me." Marilyn's free foot stomped against the floor.

"Okay. We'll stay. Good grief." Ellie pushed again, and Marilyn lifted her foot.

With each step Ellie took through the house, Marilyn twiddled her fingers more intensely in her lap. Even her uninjured leg bounced in the wheelchair stirrup. If they made it all the way to the sunroom without Marilyn experiencing a heart attack, it'd be a miracle.

As they approached their destination, Ellie's stomach bottomed out too. All the buildup of this week came to this very moment. The past collided with the present and could create something beautiful or wreck hearts all over again.

Marilyn stilled when they rounded the corner. Whatever Warren and John discussed halted when the women entered. John laid his hat on the table beside his coffee cup and cinnamon roll and rose from his seat.

Marilyn had clearly forgotten all about appearing old or having an injured leg that kept her from walking. And John obviously didn't see wrinkles or gray hair from the way his face lit. Instead, the two of them traveled back in time to two young kids who remembered *everything*.

"It's really you," Marilyn whispered.

Ellie pushed her to the table, where John sank into his chair to meet Marilyn at eye level. He scooted forward, his hand stretching across the tabletop toward her. Warren stood and made his way over to join Ellie at the door.

"I brought you a horse." John laughed and pushed his hat out of reach. "You look lovely, Mare. You haven't changed at all."

Ellie pressed her face into Warren's shoulder, trying not to shriek at the absolutely adorable event. Warren's hand wrapped around hers and gave it a squeeze.

"You haven't either," Marilyn said. "I'm sorry I bought a horse from you. That part was an accident. But I'm not sorry you came. I didn't know where you'd end up—be it the John I found selling horses or the tire salesman across the country. Someone may show up here with tires…"

He grinned. "Heckler Ranch was my uncle's. My brother Greg and I took over the business a few years after we moved from Choteau. Don't suppose I know enough about tires to sell 'em."

Even though he chuckled again, Marilyn bowed her head.

"I'm so sorry, John. I'm so sorry about everything. I've wanted to tell you every day for sixty-four years. Every corner of this farm makes me think of you and the plans we made, and then for me to live here with Sam, I—"

Her trembling fingers covered her face.

Suddenly, it felt like Ellie and Warren had intruded on a private conversation. To leave now, though, might disrupt the moment. Ellie squeezed tighter on Warren's hand.

John scooted closer and took hold of the armrest on Marilyn's chair. Sixty-four years didn't separate them anymore. It had all been erased. "It's my fault, Mare. I didn't stand up and fight for us. I hate to think you've carried this with you all these years. I never would have wanted that."

"But I married into the family who took your home from you," Marilyn cried. "Living here without you never felt right. Now, I'm an old woman, and my family thinks the farm is too much for me to handle. I've done my best with it, but they're not wrong. They're trying to talk me into selling it to the neighbor boy down the road, but he's a loathsome ninny who could use a swift kick to the rear." She took a deep breath and reached for his hand. "You should take the farm back."

Warren stiffened beside Ellie, his expression one of absolute panic. Savannah had asked him to keep Marilyn out of trouble. This certainly qualified as *big* trouble.

Ellie bit hard on her finger and waited for Warren to intervene. But he didn't.

John chuckled. "Oh, Mare. You can't do that. You've built a beautiful life here, and I don't want guilt to taint that." He placed his free hand on her knee, which made her finally look up at him. "You can't give me your home as reparations that you don't owe. I'm sorry if you ever felt that need."

"John," she whispered. "I'm such a fool."

"We're both fools," he answered. "That's why we made such a match."

Marilyn laughed and reached for a napkin to wipe away her tears.

Warren's grip on Ellie's hand had softened, but he still leaned forward like he could fall at any moment. This interaction had gone both exactly how they'd hoped and not at all as they'd expected. It was a roller coaster like every other aspect of this vacation.

"I'm glad we got a chance to do this." John nodded over her shoulder toward Warren and Ellie standing like statues behind them. "You have raised a wonderful family."

With a deep sigh, Marilyn turned to observe the pair and caught sight of their joined hands. She wiped away the lingering tears on her cheeks and nodded to Ellie. "I told you. Didn't I tell you?"

"Yes, Marilyn." Ellie rolled her eyes and ignored Warren's inquisitive look.

Marilyn waved her hand between the young couple. "We're going to talk more about this later."

"This?" John chortled and tried to follow Marilyn's train of thought. "Are they not normally together?"

"It's a recent development." Marilyn pinched her cheeks to pull herself back together. "My roommate and I have been cheering for them since they met a couple weeks back."

John slapped the tabletop. "Well, it seems as if I've come at an exciting time. Please join us, kids. I feel bad that you're standing."

"And I feel bad we've been eavesdropping." Sort of. She wouldn't have wanted to miss this for anything.

"Well, it's not like we had secrets," Marilyn said matter-of-factly.

Warren took his seat close to his grandmother. "Yeah, except maybe the part where you were going to give the farm away…"

Marilyn covered her mouth. "Oops?"

"It's all a moot point, because I wouldn't take it from her anyway." John grew more serious when he addressed Marilyn again. "This is your home, and a spritely woman like yourself should enjoy it for as long as you can. I'm sure you can come up with a better alternative than selling it to your neighbor boy when the time comes."

Ellie wanted to cheer. This was exactly the resolution she'd hoped to witness before leaving Montana.

"Well, I do have a backup plan." She took a deep breath. "I met with a lawyer this week and had him draw up some papers for me in case."

"Gram, this isn't the whole power of attorney thing is—"

"No, I didn't do that." She reached across the table and punched her grandson in the arm. "But I did have my will changed to give you the farm and everything on it—even Hilda."

Under the table, Warren's large hand squeezed Ellie's knee. She'd hardly even noticed he'd put it there through the surprise of Marilyn's confession.

"You what?" he asked.

"It's all yours, Warren. And if you don't want it, then tough shit." Marilyn beamed.

Ellie's eyes watered, but she couldn't tell if it was from pure joy or amusement. Warren had only mentioned his desire to take over the farm briefly, but the delight on his face spoke of a much deeper longing. While his mother may not approve of this significant career shift, certainly it was a decision everyone could come to appreciate.

Warren shook his head. "I don't know what to say, Gram."

"You say thank you, because you were taught manners." Marilyn leaned in closer to him and winked. "Especially since I'm throwing in a new horse to sweeten the deal."

– 35 –

WHILE JOHN PUSHED MARILYN around the farm in her wheelchair, reminiscing about days past, Warren and Ellie went their own ways to clean up and take care of a few personal matters. Warren planned to call his mother and inform her that he would be taking over the farm; Ellie had to deal with the barrage of texts and missed phone calls she'd been ignoring for the past few days.

With Marilyn savoring the return of a lost love and the joy of having the farm transferred to the proper hands, it was time for Ellie to confront her own giants.

Downing her iced coffee for strength, she sank into the chair and turned on her phone. The chimes began one after the other, each notification setting her nerves further on edge. Her texts all had a common theme:

Why aren't you answering?

Are you alive? Where are you?

Ellie?! What is going on with you?

It didn't matter how much time she had to prepare for this conversation. She'd never have the right words. The truth of the matter was that she'd run away from her life, and now it was time to pull herself together.

She downed the last sip of her coffee, trembling finger hovering over the Call button that would connect her to her immediate family.

At this hour in Ohio, everyone might be settling down for dinner. She'd interrupt their meal, make them extra angry with her confessions, then never be able to have a normal conversation with them ever again.

Urgh.

Ellie couldn't take it anymore.

She hit the button and froze.

Her mother's distraught face appeared on screen first. "Ellie! Are you all right? What is going on out there?"

"I'm really sorry about that." Each word revealed her mental strain, but there was no turning back now. "Averie is supposed to join us for this call, so I'll—"

Averie's face popped up in a box beside her mother. "What's wrong?"

"Everything is fine." She'd never assembled everyone over FaceTime before. A warning text might have been good here.

"Then talk, Ellie, because we've been worried sick." Her mother scooted over in the frame so Ellie's father could join. He said nothing, just watched his daughter with great anticipation.

Averie appeared much less concerned for Ellie's well-being and more annoyed that she'd been summoned to this family meeting led by a quarrelsome sister.

"I know. I wanted to talk to all three of you at the same time. One, to apologize for not responding to everyone's texts and calls, but also because I need to clarify some things." Ellie sucked in a deep breath. It was somehow easier to stand up to Warren's intimidating mother than it was to have this conversation with her own family.

Her mother sighed. "What sort of things do you need to clarify? We have spent the last few days trying to decide if we needed to come check on you, so whatever excuse you've got had better be good."

Averie's screen wavered as she moved about preparing dinner while glancing at her phone every so often. She wouldn't commit to the conversation until she got a full apology for the way Ellie spoke to her over texts earlier. That's how it usually went—Averie giving an unsolicited opinion, Ellie getting mad, Averie feeling offended, Ellie apologizing. Repeat.

It had to stop.

Ellie's fist wrapped tighter around her empty coffee can. "I don't really have an excuse, Mom, if I'm being honest. I've been really busy here helping Marilyn around the farm, trying to work, and meeting a bunch of new people." Even though half of those people ended up being on an opposing team. "I know you think I shouldn't have taken this trip because I can't afford it. But I needed a break from the way things have been going and that included a break from my phone for the last few days."

"At the expense of your worried family? We've been concerned over your actions for a while, but this week has made it worse," her father chimed in. While Ellie hadn't spoken directly with him since she arrived in Montana, his feelings on these matters were evident. "You break up with the guy we all thought you'd marry after all these years and then stop communicating with us while you're hundreds of miles away. What are we supposed to think?"

Ellie placed the phone on the table in front of her to give her trembling fingers a break. "This isn't some early midlife crisis, and I need you all to know that. I've been so frustrated lately. I mean, I know you were all about Sean. He's a good man—perfect, really—but no matter how hard I tried, I couldn't envision sharing my life with him. I've felt that way for a long time and kept hoping the feeling would pass and some sparks would ignite. I knew everyone would be so mad at me if I broke up with him, so I kept putting it off. Then it just slipped out and ended weird."

"It slipped out?" Disbelief colored her mother's face.

Averie rolled her eyes, which provided fuel for Ellie to keep going.

"Yes, it slipped out. When we ended, I hadn't planned to do it that night. We were watching a movie, he asked if I had a dream wedding in mind like the main character, and I told him I wanted out. And I couldn't really give him a decent reason either, which probably made it so much worse." Well, that was way more information than she'd planned to share regarding the breakup.

"Oh, Ellie."

There. That expression. The one they made every time Ellie chose a path they didn't agree with or revealed her ridiculous nature. It cut deep every time. They didn't think her capable of much, and maybe they'd been right about that in the past. But they weren't now.

Ellie nodded to no one but herself. "I didn't only take care of the farm animals this week in Marilyn's absence. In addition to visiting her at the nursing home, I've been helping her grandson Warren prepare the farm for her to come back home. I helped stave off her daughters who wanted her to sell the farm to this jerk guy down the road and then I flew to Spokane to get Warren when everything blew up in our faces." She had Averie's full attention now. "I made friends with a veterinarian named Tori who helped me care for an injured donkey. I've wrestled sheep and chased goats. I got to be part of Marilyn reuniting with her first love from sixty-some years ago."

"Wait. Go back." Averie finally decided to join the conversation. "You went to Spokane?"

"I did. Marilyn's daughter came and chewed Warren out, told him to go home, and that's where he lives. She told me to fly home too, but instead, Marilyn sent me to Spokane to convince Warren to come back." It sounded so ridiculous now, but it also made her smile. This trip truly had been filled with adventure and romance. Just what a vacation should be. Marilyn was right.

Ellie's father had moved even closer to the screen. "I'm not under standing any of this."

"I know it sounds crazy," Ellie said. "Some really beautiful things happened this week, and I'm doing a horrendous job of telling it. I just needed you to know what I've been up to."

Ellie stopped talking abruptly with the realization that she didn't need to justify her time away.

"You've been gone for less than three weeks, Ellie. How in the world are you this involved in someone else's family?" Her mom mumbled something to her dad that Ellie couldn't quite make out. It most likely wasn't flattering. "I don't know what to think about any of this."

"Me either," Averie chimed in. "I'm still trying to figure out why you were freaking out on me over text message when I was trying to *help* you."

Ellie took a long look at her sister. Were they doomed to be like Janey and Savannah, always butting heads and competing for first place?

"I know everyone is trying to help me get back on my feet right now, and I appreciate that. I do. You're my family." She took a breath and kept going. "I kind of feel like everyone is trying to fix me these days. Like I'm being compared to Averie's success and falling epically short. I'll never measure up to that. I'm in a tough spot right now, yes, but it's not because I'm going through some crisis. I can and will get back on track. It may not be what everyone wants for me, but it'll be what makes me happy."

On one hand, she wished she could shut up and take whatever lecture her parents had prepared for her. On the other, the dam that held back all these confessions and realizations had broken, and she knew she'd never feel better unless she let them all out.

All except one. She didn't know how she'd be able to finish all of this off by expressing her new feelings for Warren. How, after six years with someone else, she felt more for this guy she'd known for a couple short weeks than she ever had for Sean. Deep down in her gut, it terrified her to think this was a fling, a case of close proximity playing tricks on her.

"I'm sorry you felt that way," her mother finally said after a long silence.

"We wish you would have come to us sooner," her father added.

That may have been true, but Ellie had never had the strength to confront any of them before. Even now, her courage wavered as exhaustion took over. Everything felt so heavy, and she grew tired of carrying it around.

She glanced toward the main house. Warren might still be presenting his case to his mother. Marilyn might be showing John her prized zinnias in the garden. Hilda was probably chasing a chicken.

The tears threatened to choke her.

"What's wrong?" Her mom bent toward the screen like she might reach through and take hold of her daughter.

Ellie shook her head.

"Well, I'm sorry I pushed the nanny gig on you, but your job loss was kind of great timing with me needing help. No offense." Averie pursed her lips.

Not quite the apology Ellie had hoped for.

"Averie…" her mother chided.

"What about talking to Sean?" Ellie asked. That one still seemed much, much worse.

The pause continued for an eternity as everyone waited for Averie to continue. Finally, she huffed. "No, I don't think I am sorry for that part. I absolutely don't get what your problem was with him. Was he too nice? Too sweet, handsome, what? I don't get it, Ellie. He loved you more than anything—which, quite frankly, is exactly the kind of man I want my little sister to be with. He was going to propose, for Pete's sake! And then you dumped him out of nowhere and for some unknown reason, as you claim."

"He what?" Ellie nearly fell from her chair.

Her father cleared his throat and stepped up to the plate. "Sean stopped by the office to ask my permission to marry you about a week before you ended things. I gave him my blessing, Ellie. We already considered him a part of our family."

"So, yeah," Averie continued. "I can't bring myself to apologize for that at this time. Especially when you're spending all this time with some other guy you just met like Sean never existed."

"Averie, that's enough."

Ellie wanted to say the words, but she hadn't expected them to come from her mom first.

"Ellie might be baffling us all right now with her rash decisions and unusual antics, but she's never been coldhearted." Her mother smiled. "We need to trust that she made the right decision for her."

No response came out of Ellie's mouth. On one hand, she wanted to thank her mother for standing up for her. On the other, the compliment still seemed slightly backhanded. Her brain was in no position to sort through it all right now. So, instead, Ellie opted for the high road and smiled through the lingering tears.

Her mother continued, "We're going to have to—"

Averie's face disappeared when she exited the conversation. There was no case any of them could present that would repair that relationship today.

"She'll come around," Ellie's father said.

"I hope so." This wasn't the big family resolution Ellie had hoped to find through this conversation, but she'd opened the door to a change in their dynamic, if nothing else.

Her mother sighed. "What I started to say was that we can discuss this more in depth when you're home and we've all had a chance to think through some things."

"That works for me." Ellie attempted to relax her tense shoulders.

"Try to enjoy what's left of your trip." Her father reached forward to fidget with the phone screen. "And we'll see you soon."

The call ended.

Ellie sank back in her chair and watched the farm from her window. Time fell away like sand through her fingers. The mountainous backdrop and rolling farmland would disappear and be replaced by traffic noise and the business of her brand new, *temporary* lifestyle.

Soon, this place would be nothing but a dream.

– 36 –

JUST LIKE ON THAT first full day together, Warren met her on the tiny house steps with a plate of buttered toast and a travel mug of coffee.

"You're adorable." Never had a simple breakfast warmed Ellie's heart so much.

Or broken it.

"Gotta make sure Perry Farm gets those top ratings." He forced a smile, but his words lacked enthusiasm.

The past two days had flown by in a frenzy of ramp building, animal feeding, laughter, and talking late into the night until half the party had fallen asleep on Marilyn's sofas. And somehow, there'd also been time for stolen kisses and long walks through the countryside.

Her flight left in a few hours to deliver her back to reality. Alone.

"You're going to have to step up your hosting game from now on, you know. I don't think Marilyn and Belle will take it easy on you." Ellie slowed her walk toward the house, wanting to cherish every moment she could get alone with Warren.

He laughed. "Uh, yeah. Belle has been here for approximately one hour and has already requested I install a complaint box."

"That doesn't surprise me at all." The thought of Marilyn and Belle keeping Warren running all day would entertain her for the rest of her existence. She hated to miss it.

"They've already started talk of John moving in too. I'm one bran muffin away from running my own assisted living facility." Warren slowed their pace even more as they got closer and closer to the house.

Along the drive sat both John's and Tori's vehicles, ready for the brunch send-off of the century. Ellie had insisted they not go to too much trouble; Marilyn insisted they did.

"You're the new Connor in food services." She nudged him as they reached the bottom of the ramp.

"Lucky me."

Ellie paused, her feet refusing to take another step. She'd wanted nothing other than to be with these people lately, but now, seeing them only to say goodbye filled her with such dread.

And Warren.

They needed to talk about what might happen next, but he never brought it up. Ellie couldn't force herself to bring it up either. What if this really was just a weeklong thing?

Long-distance relationships were hard enough when separated by a few hours. But across the country? While her job allowed her plenty of flexibility for communication, Warren would never even hear his phone over his power tools and the needs of his resident grandmothers. He'd already be stretched thin enough between managing his workers in Spokane and caring for the farm.

She had to let him go.

Her heart grew heavier when she climbed the ramp. She reached for the doorknob, but Warren's hand intercepted hers. He leaned against the doorframe and took a deep breath. For a second, she thought he might take this last moment before they joined the party to kiss her. His nervous energy made her think otherwise.

"What are you—?"

"Listen." He checked their surroundings and spoke in a low voice to avoid being overheard. "I know it'll be hard to believe, but Gram and Belle went a little overboard preparing for this—confetti everywhere, that sort of thing. I don't really know what all 'festivities' you're about to face, but I want you to know that I'm only partly responsible for certain events. And if you're not sure which part, it's probably the part without glitter."

Ellie chuckled as she imagined the beautiful mess on the other side of the door. "I'll keep that in mind."

With that, he opened the door and ushered her inside.

"Surprise!" a chorus of voices yelled.

Marilyn sat in her wheelchair with John standing behind her. Belle beamed from her seat at the table, purple and pink confetti dotting her aquatic blue curls. Tori hid behind her hand, laughing so hard she had to cross her legs.

"You can't say 'surprise' for a party she knew about." Warren dusted some confetti from his shoulder.

"But we wanted to," Belle said. "We don't tell you how to run your surprise parties."

Oh, these people. These beautiful, odd people.

Shredded pieces of construction paper really were everywhere. They'd even created chain-link streamers Ellie hadn't seen done since elementary school. Cupcakes and punch filled the center table—much more than six people needed. But the best part were the signs they'd made.

We'll miss you! Goodbye! You're a treasure! We love you!

"You guys..." Ellie swallowed back the emotion. "This is the greatest surprise-party-I-already-knew-about I've ever been to."

"Good thing we're having the party here and not at the nursing home." Marilyn reached into her breast pocket. "Or we wouldn't have been able to use our kazoos."

The room filled with the sound of nonsensical humming when the three elderly goofballs took to their next phase of fanfare. Tori, however, couldn't pull herself together enough to play the one in her hand.

Ellie waited until they finished their "song," which went on longer than it should have. "That was really lovely. Thank you. I'm glad you got to move in just in time for this, Belle."

"Me too, darlin'. I wasn't going to miss your going-away party, and I badgered my son until he agreed to get me out here *today*. I've got lots to unpack, but that can wait until later," she said.

Ellie wanted to offer her help, but she wouldn't be around for that this time. "It's so great that your boys agreed to this plan, though. I know Marilyn will be happier now."

"Well, it took some convincing, but since we've agreed to have a nurse come out to look after us, and we'll have John and Warren to help us manage the day to day, they had no choice but to agree—especially since it's the cheaper option." She giggled and pointed at Warren. "And let me add that I'm real glad to see you finally locked down this chunk-a-hunk."

"Ooo-kay. That's not the weirdest thing I've ever been called or anything." Warren tousled his hair and shook off the strange compliment. "This'll be fun…"

"Tori, you want to pop out here on occasion and check on Warren for me?" Ellie laughed.

"You got it." She plucked two cupcakes from the table and passed one to Ellie. "You sure you have to go? That could be us in fifty years, but we won't know unless we try." She gestured toward Marilyn and Belle, who had gotten into a confetti-throwing fight. John blew his kazoo like a ref whistling during a sporting match.

Ellie pulled Tori into a side hug and tried so hard not to fall apart. "But which of us would have the blue hair?"

"Who says we have to choose?" Something caught Tori's eye over Ellie's shoulder and she forced a stoic look. "Oh, turn around. Marilyn is ready for phase two, er, three. I dunno. I lost track of the phases."

This must have been what Warren talked about before they came in. Judging by the way he scratched at his stubble, she was right.

"I'd like to make a speech," Marilyn announced and held her plastic cup out in front of her. "Eleanor Reed, you've been a real godsend to me over the past few weeks. I don't know what I would have done without you. My donkey would have run off, my treasures would be missing, and my cheese would have spoiled. Thanks to your help, my prodigal grandson has returned to take over my estate, and love has filled my home like never before. A toast to you, my dear, one of the kindest and best travelers to ever cross the Wild West."

John reached forward to shake Ellie's hand. "It truly has been a pleasure, miss."

Marilyn shifted in her seat and narrowed her eyes at John—an odd way to look at someone she cared so much about, particularly during a tender moment like this.

"Oh!" John retracted his hand and straightened up. As if speaking a rehearsed line, he proclaimed, "If only you could stay longer!"

With those words, a loud clap sounded. Ellie spun to see Belle holding a spoon in one hand and a blue plastic bedpan in the other.

"Sorry. They don't make these metal anymore, but it's the best gong we got." She lowered the bedpan to her side and grinned. "Stole it from the old folks' home."

Warren groaned. "Pretty sure this is the part I warned you about."

"And you're only partly responsible?" Ellie could hardly keep from giggling now. "The bedpan heist part?"

Somehow, Ellie had wandered into a practiced going-away party where everybody played a role—or sound effect. She loved every second.

"Eh, not that part," Warren said.

"Well, now, our timing's off. We're going to sound ridiculous at this point," Marilyn whined.

John patted her leg to console her. "We'll try it again, Mare. We worked too hard to fail now." With that, John shot forward and raised a finger to the sky, boldly repeating, "If only you could stay longer!"

The fake gong "rang" again from Belle's chair, and she howled with delight. Tori stuffed the rest of her cupcake into her mouth in order to toss a handful of confetti she'd gathered from the table.

Marilyn rolled her chair forward and activated her jazz hands. "Ellie, I come to you today, not with a goodbye, but with a proposition."

"A proposition?" Ellie pointed to the handmade banners. "Not a goodbye? Because that one specifically says *goodbye*."

"It's a ruse, kid. Work with me here." Marilyn used her uninjured leg to shove a chair out from the table. "Sit."

Ellie did as she was told and tried to ignore Tori's laughter and Warren's protest that his grandmother needed to calm down a bit, which she waved away.

Marilyn continued, "This isn't really a going-away party, Ellie dear. It's more of an intervention to *keep* you from going."

The room had quieted down now, everyone's faces confirming Marilyn's claim.

"I would love to stay, but I—"

"I'm not done with my sales pitch, so you just listen." Marilyn patted Ellie's knee like she'd done so many times before. "Like Belle said, she's only allowed to be here if we take on a nurse's aide, and to be frank, we both need the help. Warren will be back and forth to Spokane with his business, and our dear Tori has all the critters in Montana to deal with. So, I want to offer you the job."

It was all so much to take in at once. "Marilyn, I'm not a licensed nurse by any means. The most official medical title I hold is certification for transcribing and a few Bs on an incomplete college transcript from, like, a decade ago."

"Well, *nurse* is a liberal term. We just need someone to help out, more like a personal assistant than anything else. The trust is willing to pay you handsomely for your work. You'll be welcome to stay in the tiny house, or the trust will build you a new one." Marilyn gave Warren a thumbs-up.

Ellie turned to him then. "Are you 'the trust'?"

"I am." He drew a chair from the table and pulled it close enough to sit next to her.

"Is that the small part you played in this?" she asked.

He nodded "It's going to take a very special person to work with these two hooligans on a daily basis, and they're both very fond of you. You know the farm. You know them. So, this seemed like the best solution if we could possibly talk you into it. And to be quite honest, Ellie Reed, I don't particularly want you to leave either."

She opened her mouth to respond, but nothing came out.

"Neither do I," Tori added. "But you knew that already."

Warren inched closer, as if it might keep the others from hearing. "Things are about to get really crazy out here—crazier, I should say. And I know we haven't talked about what happens next for us, but I'd kind of like to see where this goes. It'd be a lot easier to do without thousands of miles between us, you know?"

"Ditto," Tori chimed in again.

"Would you stop?" Warren issued a threatening look over his shoulder.

This couldn't be real.

Belle cleared her throat loudly until Ellie finally looked up at her. "I'm going to recap this info for you, sweetie, because you're clearly needing some help. If you stay, you get to hang out with us old people all day, get coffee with this gal over here, and canoodle with this tall drink of water."

Warren's cheeks flushed, and he held a hand up between his face and where Belle sat across the room. "Seriously, don't leave me alone with them."

Laughter consumed the tender moment. Staying had never really crossed Ellie's mind. Not seriously, anyway. She'd have needed a job and a place to live, but Marilyn had a plan for that. One that would actually be *perfect*.

With only a few weeks left on her apartment lease in Ohio, she could go home, pack her things, spend some time helping with

Grandma Val's house, and even make peace with Averie by helping with the kids for a bit.

Just the thought lifted a thousand pounds from her shoulders.

Marilyn scooted even closer, pinning Ellie to the table with her wheelchair. "What do you say? I'm getting sweaty with anticipation."

"Same," Belle said.

Ellie glanced around the room at each face awaiting her answer. She'd grown to care about this ragtag group so quickly. How could she pass up the opportunity to keep the adventure going?

"If that's what 'the trust' wants." Her gaze flickered up to meet Warren's.

He smiled. "Oh, 'the trust' definitely wants."

Epilogue

THE COOL AUTUMN BREEZE rustled the hem of Ellie's gown and enhanced the aroma of the burgundy, coral, and pink rose bouquet in her hands.

Warren looked so handsome standing at the altar in his gray suit pants, suspenders, and bow tie paired with the wine-colored button-up shirt. He'd slicked his hair Gatsby-style, a brilliant smile playing on his lips that was for her and her alone. There had never been a more gorgeous wedding in all of history. Ellie was certain of that.

"By the power vested in me by the state of Montana, I now pronounce you husband and wife." Reverend Kaehr closed his binder and nodded to the couple before him. "You may kiss your bride."

Ellie sighed as she watched John cradle Marilyn's cheeks in his calloused hands, whisper something tender only she could hear, and kiss her. The small crowd gathered at the outdoor ceremony erupted in cheers, a few whoops and hollers coming from the front row where Belle sat unsupervised.

Hilda, the untamable ring bearer, ran through the aisles, thrilled that all these people had come to the farm just to play with her.

A string quartet launched into a Frank Sinatra number, and John took Marilyn's arm to escort her down the aisle. She'd insisted on doing this without her walker, much to her physical therapist's dismay. Nobody could tell that woman what to do. Ellie had learned that in the past couple months of playing "nurse." She couldn't imagine a more difficult patient—or loving a job more than she did this one.

After accepting the invitation to move to the farm full time, Ellie had returned to Ohio to settle things and pack up her apartment. As expected, her parents had some concerns over the rash decision to move, but after joining Ellie for move-in day, they immediately came to understand why Ellie loved it so much. And Marilyn was a big hit with them, offering to play host any time they wanted to visit.

John had moved in prior to Ellie's arrival, having jumped on the chance to finally retire and enjoy every minute with his first love and her best friend—a package deal. Caring for Marilyn, Belle, and John kept Ellie on her toes in the best of ways. Even with this new exciting social life, Ellie still found time for girls' nights and coffee runs with Tori. She even learned to ride Captain Twinkle Snout—Marilyn's mail-order horse.

"Fancy meeting you here." Warren extended his arm to lead Ellie toward the reception setup, as Marilyn had instructed him to do as the best man.

"You're looking good, kid. You got a tool belt hidden under those suspenders?"

He smirked. "Wouldn't you like to know."

Birdseed rained overhead as they passed through the audience. Everyone had only been given a handful of seed and run out after John and Marilyn passed through, but Belle had clearly taken more than her share of the party favors.

"Did they give her a robot arm in therapy?" Warren chuckled. "She should not be able to throw that hard."

Ellie ducked when another handful came flying at them. She'd have her work cut out getting all the birdseed out of her bra later.

"Hey." Tori appeared at Ellie's side, a squirming toddler on her hip. "I just wanted to tell you that you look super gorgeous in that dress. Also, I'm pretty sure Sheriff is on the front porch..."

"Oh, crap." Ellie stretched to see the wayward donkey standing merrily by the ramp. "How'd he do that without us seeing him?"

"The guy's a pro." Warren began loosening his tie. "I'll go get him."

"Oh, no. I'll get him," Tori said. "You schmooze. Ruby is dying to pet him." The little girl squirmed harder in her mother's arms, trying to get down.

Ellie grabbed Ruby's hand to gain her attention. "Ruby, you be good for Mommy, and we'll get cupcakes and take a ride on Captain Twinkle Snout when you're done, okay?"

She nodded vigorously, calming in her mother's arms as they left to corral a donkey.

"I think I'd rather deal with Sheriff than play greeter," Warren mumbled.

"Ah, the duties of the best man and maid of honor." She patted his back and smiled at another elderly guest rising from her seat to join the party.

Across the way, Marilyn and John huddled together at the cake table, tapping frosting to one another's noses, lost in their own world. No one in their right mind would disturb a couple delighting in their recent vows after all these years of waiting.

"Uh, oh." Warren gave a slight wave to someone across the way. "Reverend Kaehr is summoning me. If it's a fishing story, I'm going to be a while. You all right here by yourself?"

Ellie nodded to reassure him she could handle the oncoming guests—alone. After all, she knew *most* of them now. There were the Fergusons, kindly neighbors who took over the Perry Farm fields when Marilyn told the Robinsons to take a hike. A few representatives of the nursing home had come—including Connor from food services. Then there was Tori's family, John's sons, Hardware Store Barry, Babs, and Reverend Kaehr's wife.

Oh, and Warren's mother.

Savannah portrayed every bit the classy businesswoman in her chocolate-brown long-sleeve dress, accented with shiny gold jewelry. She sauntered down the aisle, but instead of veering off like other guests to hunt down the snacks, she kept her sights set on the maid of honor. Ellie almost wished she could go back to when Savannah avoided eye contact with her altogether, because this was much more terrifying.

"Hello, Ellie." Savannah extended her hand, nails shimmering from a recent manicure.

Ellie tried not to make it too obvious when she searched the crowd for Warren and mentally sent him an SOS.

"I'm glad you could make it." Ellie caught a glimpse of Warren *all the way* over by the cake table, still caught up in one of the reverend's tales. She was on her own here. "I like your dress."

Savannah breathed a laugh, possibly the first one Ellie had ever heard come out of her. "Thank you. Yours is lovely too." She took a step closer, and Ellie tried not to jump backward. "I was hoping to have a word with you, and this is as good a time as any. So here it goes: I'm very sorry for the way we met this summer. I believe we got off on the wrong foot."

That was an epic understatement. "I think we did."

"Between Mom's injury, the news of her starting an Airbnb, and my sister's regrettable actions, I struggled to process everything in a kindly manner. I'm sure Mom told you all about Janey not coming today as a form of protest." Savannah's bracelets jingled when she readjusted her hand on her hip.

Janey refused to acknowledge that Warren would assume responsibility for the farm. They needed to give her a little more time to come around and stop pouting. Marilyn had faith she would eventually, and Ellie really wanted to believe that.

Savannah glanced in Warren's direction. "You obviously mean a lot to my mother, and I really do appreciate how you're caring for her. You were absolutely right about everything you said that day in the farmyard. So, if you'll accept my apology, maybe we can start this over again."

"I would like that very much." Ellie thought the wedding day couldn't have gotten any better, but she was wrong. She lunged forward and wrapped Savannah in a hug, startling the poor woman into a rather loud gasp.

"Oh. Okay," was all Savannah said. She patted Ellie's back twice before letting her arms fall limp at her sides.

Ellie straightened again and smoothed down her gown to have something to do with her hands. "Sorry."

"It's fine." Savannah couldn't even make eye contact now. They still had a long way to go in this relationship, but it was a start. "I'm going to go wish the newlyweds well. Excuse me."

The band launched into Marilyn's favorite Al Green song as Belle commanded the partygoers to start "shaking their booties."

"I came as soon as I could." Warren appeared at Ellie's side, offering a plastic champagne flute full of bubbly. "I couldn't tell if you attacked my mother or if she attacked you."

Ellie's grin grew too wide to take a sip. "We hugged. Well, *I* hugged *her*. The most awkward hug of my life. Your mom and I are going to start over and try to be friends."

"Wow. Hopefully that means she's accepted that we're really dating and not faking it anymore."

"That was a fun ploy, but I prefer the real deal." She pressed into him, savoring that familiar sensation of butterflies taking flight in her stomach that hadn't gone anywhere after three months' time.

Warren only got to come out to the farm every few weekends since summer ended, but he and Ellie always made the most of their time together. Another couple of weeks and he would have things arranged in a way that allowed him to make the permanent move. Ellie and Marilyn had already started the countdown.

"I guess it paid off hiring some weirdo hipster from Ohio to care for my grandmother," Warren teased.

"You bet your sweet bippy, it did." Marilyn wrapped her arms around Ellie's waist from behind. John clapped a hand to Warren's shoulder, and the two men exchanged a chummy hello. They'd grown so close since meeting. Ellie loved watching them interact around the farm and take on new projects together. In fact, her favorite pastime involved drinking lemonade on the porch with Marilyn and heckling the menfolk from afar. Marilyn was very good at it.

"Congratulations, you two kids. Such a beautiful wedding," Ellie said.

Marilyn rested her chin on Ellie's shoulder as she observed the partygoers enjoying their evening and trying to protect their cupcakes from a rather determined Hilda. "I couldn't agree more. I'm honored to have you stand beside me today."

"It's been my great pleasure." Ellie placed a gentle kiss on the older woman's head. "You're my best friend, Ms. Marilyn."

"And you're mine, Ellie dear." She giggled and gave Ellie another squeeze. "But don't say that in front of Belle, or we're dead meat."

"Wouldn't dream of it."

Warren raised his champagne flute. "I'd like to propose a toast. To being brave and taking risks. To fresh starts and bright futures. To the wild shenanigans sure to come in our future on this farm and the zany newlywed couple leading the charge."

"Hear! Hear!" John exclaimed.

Ellie clinked her glass to Warren's. "I'll drink to that."

She still didn't know what all the future held for her in this new family, but there was no place she'd rather be than right there, squashed in a group huddle, drinking cheap champagne, and knowing that at any moment, a bulldog could take them out like a set of bowling pins.

It was worth the risk.

"Great speech, Warren. You're a gentleman and a scholar." Marilyn tossed her empty glass over her shoulder and clapped her hands together. "Now, let's dance."

It's always a good idea to expect the unexpected...

Read on for a quick look at

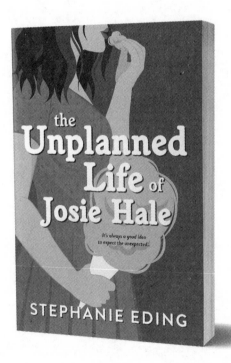

Now Available from Sourcebooks Casablanca

- 1 -

Deep-Fried Emotional Support

ONLY A FEW MORE days until the county fair closed for another season, and Josie hadn't gotten her fried food fix yet. She could run into anybody there. Literally anybody: her grandmother, an ex-boyfriend, that one girl from the smoothie shop who already judged her for not sticking around to save her marriage...

The car engine shut off, and Josie breathed in the aroma of cow manure through the open car windows. She probably should have sought therapy at a time like this, but instead she opted for a corn dog.

She didn't want just any ole corn dog either. It had to come from the county fair, made in an overheated food truck, and deep-fried to a crisp. Twice. A funnel cake or elephant ear would suffice for dessert. After all, she was eating for two now. She was absolutely, unquestionably, dollar-store-test-certified pregnant as of an hour ago.

Despite the late August sun burning with the fury of hell, Josie trudged through the fairgrounds, tugging her jean shorts down between her sweaty thighs whenever the need arose.

She should be in her bed crying right now, making a plan. Surely, that's what the evening held in store for her: punching her pillow, doing some internet research, and crying some more. But cravings took precedence over common sense at the moment.

After she shoved a few corn dogs down her throat, she'd feel better. Her parents would be home from work soon, and she'd break the news to them. Not like she could hide a baby for long when she lived with them.

And Grant, the baby's father, deserved to know how their failed attempt to mend their marriage had resulted in new life.

That was some sucky irony right there. As if she hadn't longed to erase that drunken night a thousand times already. Josie bit hard on her knuckle and walked across the grassy excuse for a parking lot.

At the Lions Club booth, she examined the fair's layout and simultaneously scoped out her surroundings for anyone she knew. Fairs always brought the locals together. The idea of having an impromptu reunion with everyone in her hometown almost made her forget about lunch.

Almost.

After she got the corn dog, she'd be able to think more clearly. Deep-fried food made everything better. It was science.

Josie hit the dusty midway, and the golden mix of sand and earth powdered her sweaty legs. An earsplitting ring sounded when some guy hit the Skee-Ball jackpot. Distant carousel flutes sang their usual haunting ditty that always made her check over her shoulder to ensure no murderous clowns stalked about.

No bloody clowns, but the carnies definitely heckled harder than she remembered from high school. In their boredom, they pleaded for her to come and play.

Not today, Satan.

The setup had changed somewhat from the last time she'd visited. It seemed cruel to hide the food vendors from a preggo lady, but Clarkson, Illinois's biggest attractions remained a Pizza Hut and a half-dead mall. They couldn't afford anything close to a mega-fair for people to get lost in.

Josie rounded a corner and found rival schools set up with their food stands, attempting to earn money for their respective band programs. It was like gang territory for small-town folk. But even a turf war with flying baritones couldn't keep Josephine Hale from her goal.

She took longer strides up to the food stand, retrieved a few dollars from her pocket, and searched the menu. "Can I get a corn dog?"

"Ketchup?" The raspy-voiced vendor either smoked five packs of cigarettes a day or had taken a shot of boiling fryer grease at some point in his career.

"Yes, please." Josie leaned against the counter. Sort of. It came up to her shoulders, so more like she tucked herself underneath it. If she knew anybody at the fair, maybe they wouldn't look *below* the food truck. Even if they did, her position should give off enough don't-talk-to-me-vibes to keep them away.

After gathering her napkins and catching sight of the vinegar squirt bottle, she tapped on the glass window to add fries to the order. She'd nearly forgotten that most important of side dishes, and holy mother, did she need it.

She ground the heel of her flip-flop into the dirt and forced her focus onto the horse racetrack behind the food truck line. The midway began filling up quicker than Josie wanted now that school had let out. She willed the raspy man to fry a little faster. The longer she stood with nothing to do but wait on her food, the more she recognized faces: a teller from her bank, some guy that ran for office and had his mug plastered all over people's yard signs, her eighth-grade science teacher.

"Josie Claybrook?" A smooth, husky voice rose behind her.

Oh, no.

She clutched the countertop until her fingers threatened to snap off. The muscles in her shoulders seized, and her face contorted into what had to be all kinds of attractive. Nothing good came from a surprise guest who referred to her by her maiden name. She could not mentally deal with a blast from the past right now.

Her flip-flops squeaked under her feet as she made the agonizing pivot toward her company. With a deep breath, she lifted her head.

"It *is* you!" The last person she expected to see rushed forward to pull her into his arms.

It had been twelve years since she'd nearly suffocated in that bear hug. Twelve years since she went away to college with promises to keep in touch. Their late-night instant messaging sustained them for a few months, but even that died because adult life killed all things good and wonderful.

"Kevin?" Josie coughed into his chest when he squeezed her again. She sucked in her stomach as much as physically possible, trying not to make the pregnancy announcement that already felt like a neon exclamation point over her head.

Kevin smelled exactly the way she remembered, triggering a montage of flashbacks: cruising in circles around town, climbing onto the roof to listen to music, toilet-papering their enemies' houses on Saturday nights. He'd been her best friend once. The first guy she danced with at a school function. The one who'd call her at midnight just because he couldn't wait to tell her about a movie he watched. One of the few people who ever knew her deepest, darkest crush.

"You look great." He released her to reveal the same goofball smile he'd given her during sixth-period chemistry when the teacher made them select project partners. "I totally didn't expect to run into you today."

"Likewise. I mean, wow. It's been forever. How have you been?" She immediately regretted the question. When asked, people reciprocate.

The corn-dog man interrupted the exchange like an apron-wearing hero. Josie grabbed the goods and stepped to the side for the next person in line: Kevin, apparently.

"Can I get two dogs?" He held up two fingers, then turned to Josie, clearly not about to let her get away so easily.

He hadn't changed much since high school. He'd cut his sandy curls shorter, though he still had to shake them out of his face. His shoulders had broadened. He stood a full foot and a half taller than her but had now gained a bit of muscle definition to go with it. Turning thirty suited him so much more than it did her.

"You're smaller than I remember," Kevin teased as if they hadn't spent more than a decade away from each other. He used to love setting his lunch tray on top of her head in the cafeteria or squishing her up against the bus window to use her as a pillow on field trips.

"Maybe your head just got bigger." Josie eased her posture and popped a fry into her mouth. Not *too* much had changed. Their friendship had always been an easy one.

"That's my little JoJo. Just as I left you." When he reached out for a high five, Josie balanced her food in one arm to oblige, but he didn't let go of her hand right away. "Dude, wait until Ben sees you."

Josie's entire body tensed, the edges of her lips trembling from her forced smile. Did he mean Ben Romero?

The sun turned up the heat a hundred degrees.

No. Not that Ben.

Anyone but him.

People like Ben were exactly why she shouldn't have gone to the fair over a stupid craving. Her world already threatened to hurl her into outer space at any moment, yet she *had* to risk her last thread of dignity by chasing down a corn dog.

Josie searched the heavens as she prayed for a freak storm that would send everyone dashing for cover. If she could escape in time, it'd be like none of this had ever happened.

Except she was still pregnant. Rain couldn't wash that away.

"Ben," Kevin called off toward one of the band pavilions.

Josie examined the sky, but no storm brewed. Not a single clap of thunder or bolt of lightning offered to save her from coming face-to-face with Benjamin Anthony Dominic Romero.

That deepest, darkest crush from high school and, conveniently, Kevin's best friend.

She bit her lip and pinched her eyes shut.

"Josie? No way." A hand cupped her shoulder, gently turning her to the side to face him.

No other choice. She met his gaze.

"Hey, Ben." Josie leaned into his side hug. At sixteen, she'd have given her left boob for this guy to smile at her, let alone pull her into his arms. He just had to do it now, when she looked like she'd crawled out of a dumpster, rather than in high school when she wore clothes that fit and shaved her armpits regularly.

"What are you doing here?" Ben took a bite of his pulled pork sandwich, dark eyes wide and as intoxicating as ever. "Thought you moved away."

She had to get a grip.

"I'm home now. Just wanted a corn dog." Because that explained everything. "I mean, I moved home this summer and came here for lunch today. I think corn dogs are the only reason anyone comes to the fair, right?"

"Not this traitor." Kevin gestured to his friend and rolled his eyes. "He eats pork from the enemy."

Ben's sandwich must have come from their high school rival's band booth. A decade ago, he wouldn't have dared set foot in enemy territory, lest his fellow football teammates ridicule him mercilessly.

"Come on, girl." Kevin slipped an arm around her and guided her along the midway. "Let's grab elephant ears and catch up."

How could she ever shake these guys if they knew her every deep-fried weakness? She didn't have the strength.

"Great." Her heart jumped so fast she'd likely cough it up if she didn't force it back down with some food. She clutched the paper container holding her lunch. Second lunch, if she wanted to be honest with herself.

"Gotta hear about all that's happened since graduation," Kevin added.

Josie ripped the corn dog from the bag and bit it so hard she nearly broke the wooden stick. Next time her life fell apart, she'd remember to just cry about it instead.

- 2 -

The Corn Dog Pact

KEVIN CHOSE THE CLARKSON High School band pavilion as the venue for their little reunion. The tattered shelter provided adequate seating with picnic tables, shade from the scorching sun, and an audience to enjoy the awkward reconnection taking place between three old friends. The only thing that could make it truly perfect was if one of the birds in the rafters dropped a bomb on Josie's head and added a hint more embarrassment to her situation.

"Drinks on me, like old times." Kevin scrunched until his long legs fit under the picnic table, and he placed a tray of frosty root beers at its center.

Thank God he'd returned when he did. She and Ben may have choked on their silence if the glue that held them together all those years ago hadn't come back. While the three of them often spent Friday nights together in high school, Kevin could hardly take a bathroom break without Josie and Ben becoming the two most uncomfortable creatures on earth, staring at the TV in silence or trying to make conversation over essay due dates. Kind of like the last few months of her marriage, actually. Only not in the same dreamy teenage way one avoids making eye contact with a crush. More like the silence-is-better-than-fighting way people use to attempt to save themselves from divorce court. Lot of good that did.

"Old times? When have you ever bought drinks?" Ben side-eyed his friend and took a big bite of his sandwich.

Josie held up her corn dog like a pointing finger. "Well, there was that one time at the football game when he refilled my water bottle at the drinking fountain."

"See? Generous." Kevin shifted again, and his knees knocked on the underside of the table. "So, JoJo. What's been going on with you? Why you keep holding your stomach? You sick or pregnant or something?"

A piece of french fry caught in Josie's throat. She swallowed hard to push it down, reaching for her root beer for help.

Ben groaned and whacked his friend upside the head. At least Ben understood the basic rules for *not* asking women taboo questions. Kevin, however, threw his hands in the air as if completely confused by the unwarranted violence.

Josie twiddled her thumbs in her lap, trying to gather her thoughts enough to address this beautiful nightmare before her. "Um, what's been going on with me? Well, I graduated from UIC, got married, rented an apartment in Chicago, worked at Lincoln Regional High School as a history teacher for four years… And, yes, it turns out that I am, in fact, with child."

Saying it out loud felt like a lie. Like she played a role in someone else's life.

If her math was correct, and she'd never been particularly good at that subject, she was about three months along. If her last birth-control shot hadn't eliminated her periods, she might have gotten a heads-up sooner. Not like she could count on her shorts getting tighter as a legitimate indicator, considering how much she'd eaten lately.

Three months pregnant. Holy shit. It was like she had no baby in there at all, and then boom! One appears and it's the size of a plum. A whole flipping plum coming out of nowhere.

Which sounded weirdly delicious right now. Did the ag building still have those produce stands?

"That's awesome." Kevin extended his fist, ripe for the bumping. His need for hand-to-hand validation hadn't changed over the years.

Josie's shoulders drooped, and she stared at his closed hand, unable to return his enthusiasm. This was her Kevin. He'd hugged her when she hadn't made the track team. He had walked her home after late-night football games to make sure no one abducted her. He had seen her cry many times when relationships fell apart, when Ben hadn't asked her to prom, or when she and her BFF, Ella, had fought over something stupid...

She sucked in a deep breath and stared at the contents atop the picnic table. "I'm also in the process of getting divorced, which led to leaving my teaching job, moving out of Chicago, working part time at a smoothie shop, and living in my parents' spare bedroom. So that's great too."

Neither Kevin nor Ben spoke or indicated they'd even heard her. She should have sugar-coated it somehow instead of dropping a cringe-worthy bomb. Now everything would be awkward.

Er. Awkward-*er.*

Acknowledgments

Matt, what a weird and amazing life we have together. Thank you for prioritizing my dreams through the chaos. Ross, Lizzie, and Annie, getting to be your mom is the best gig in the world. Sharing my publishing joys with you is more incredible than I could have ever imagined. I love you all.

I have the most supportive and wonderful family and friends a girl could ask for. Thank you all for cheering me on, helping with the kids, and being the greatest fan club of all time.

Katie Salvo, you are the agent of my dreams and a cherished friend. Thank you for walking alongside me on this journey. I couldn't do this without you.

To my editor, Deb Werksman, thank you for helping me grow as a writer and for seeing the potential in my messes. I'm so appreciative of everyone at Sourcebooks for working so hard to give my stories a home.

Many years ago, I stumbled into the greatest critique group of all time. I'm forever thankful for your friendship and wisdom— Chace Verity, Kate Sheeran Swed, Leigh Landry, Isa Medina, and Alex Samuely.

You're all truly amazing. Thank you.

About the Author

Stephanie Eding specializes in humorous women's fiction about the struggles of adulthood in the twenty-first century. She works as a freelance editor, cleans when stressed, and hates cooking but loves to eat. Away from her desk, she's a wife, mother, expert napper, and leader of a cat horde. You can find Stephanie on Twitter @EdingStephanie, on Instagram @stephanieeding, and at facebook.com/saeding.